D0716234

'An excitingly and brilliantly realised, poetically written tale of
magic, subterfuge and intrigue. Not to mention clocks'
SFFWORLD.COM

'Witcover conjures an enlightenment-punk vision of England,
before taking detours to the Alps, subterranean London and the
utterly fantastic. ****'
SFX magazine

'Witcover's prose is playful yet persuasive . . . unrestrained
by the conventions of any one genre . . . segueing seamlessly
from wonder, whimsy and conspiracy to intrigue, espionage
and action . . . thrilling'
TOR.COM

'Vividly evokes an authentically dangerous, dirty and smelly 18th
century London Henry Fielding would recognize . . . *The Emperor of
All Things* is a real page-turner which had me gripped'
HISTORICAL NOVELS REVIEW

'A unique, imaginative, twister of a book, which is
wondrously inventive'
BOOKGEEK.COM

www.transworldbooks.co.uk

www.transworldireland.ie

Born in Zurich, **Paul Witcover** is a writer and critic. With Elizabeth Hand, he created the cult comic book series, *Anima*, and he is the author of the novels *Waking Beauty*, *Tumbling After*, *Asylum* and the acclaimed historical fantasy *The Emperor of All Things*. He has also served as the curator of the *New York Review of Science Fiction*. He lives in New York City.

Also by Paul Witcover

WAKING BEAUTY
TUMBLING AFTER
DRACULA: ASYLUM
EVERLAND AND OTHER STORIES

The Productions of Time
THE EMPEROR OF ALL THINGS

THE
WATCHMAN
OF ETERNITY

Book 2 of
The Productions of Time

PAUL WITCOVER

BANTAM BOOKS

LONDON • TORONTO • SYDNEY • AUCKLAND • JOHANNESBURG

TRANSWORLD PUBLISHERS
61–63 Uxbridge Road, London W5 5SA
www.transworldbooks.co.uk

Transworld is part of the Penguin Random House group of companies
whose addresses can be found at global.penguinrandomhouse.com

Penguin
Random House
UK

First published in Great Britain in 2015 by Bantam Press
an imprint of Transworld Publishers
Bantam edition published 2016

A CIP catalogue record for this book
is available from the British Library.

ISBN
9780857501608

Typeset in Dante by Falcon Oast Graphic Art Ltd.
Printed and bound by Clays Ltd, Bungay, Suffolk.

Penguin Random House is committed to a sustainable
future for our business, our readers and our planet. This book is made from Forest
Stewardship Council® certified paper.

To Cynthia,

My tick and my tock

1

The Crossing

THE LUGGER LURCHED AND GROANED. AYLESFORD FOLLOWED SUIT, ROLLING to the side to spew into the bucket that had been the trustworthy receptacle of his sickness until now. But the bucket, too, had lurched aside, and the depleted contents of his stomach spattered in a thin gruel over the wooden slats of the floor. The lantern swinging madly from the low ceiling flung its meagre light across the cabin in a haphazard manner that made him feel as if the vessel had already come apart, shaken to pieces by the squall that had struck midway across the Channel.

The glass of the single porthole threw back shards of light but admitted none from without. All was darkness there. The sounds of wind and wave, like a constant battlefield roar, drowned out everything save the creaking yet somehow defiant protests of the *Pierre*'s tortured frame and Aylesford's groans and whimpers, which he could not silence, though they filled him with shame, as if he had been reduced to the state of a child, or, worse, a mere animal. And like an animal, he longed to strike at what tormented him. He would have torn the throat out of the storm if he could. Give him an enemy, and Aylesford was not slow to strike – as a gaggle of London lordlings might attest, were they still alive to do so, and many more besides, all cut down without mercy: whether from behind, in skulking fashion, as he'd dispatched Daniel Quare that same night in the bed of a blowsy barmaid whose name he'd forgotten upon hearing it, or

1

face to face across blades, made no matter. But lacking a target of flesh and blood, he could only suffer. He rolled back, squeezing his eyes shut as though blindness were a refuge, and wiped his mouth with the damp sleeve of his coat. The cot bucked beneath him like a drifting gig at the mercy of the storm.

He wished he'd never set foot aboard this ship, with its unlucky name. He'd been told it had been christened after Captain Bagot's eldest son, but the instant he'd heard the name he'd crossed himself, for *pierre* meant 'stone' as well, and now the smugglers' craft seemed certain to sink like one. Only the French would tempt fate so frivolously, as if good fortune were their birthright and the elements themselves must bow to their every whim. They were a different breed of human, he sometimes thought, a fairy-touched race whose follies were inseparable from their glories. He both admired and resented them, always conscious of how completely his suppliant nation relied upon the support of a people by nature capricious and not to be trusted, save in one thing only: their implacable hatred of England.

He'd lived among the French for years, part of the court surrounding the Bonnie Prince, yet they had never accepted him, though he spoke French with scarcely an accent by now. Neither had his own people fully accepted him, for he had come late – by their measure – to the cause, dispatched across the water by his foster father when already a young man. But he had won some measure of respect since then, thanks to his talents with a sword, and his eagerness to put those talents to use on behalf of king and country as a courier and, not to put too fine a point on it, or rather to do precisely that, an assassin. In that capacity, he had killed for the Bonnie Prince but also, in the name of harmony and mutual self-interest, for King Louis himself – as if each thrust of his blade were a needle stitching Scotland and France together.

Yet though blood and sentiment alike might bind two countries for a time in a commonality of interests, only a fool would put faith in an edifice erected upon such unstable ground. And Aylesford was no fool. French policy was determined not in the council chambers but in the boudoirs of Versailles, where the whore Pompadour pulled the strings – and prick – of her puppet king. There the gravest decisions, upon which the fate of the Jacobite cause must rise or fall, were made on the basis of petty resentments and airy enthusiasms taken up and cast aside like the most ephemeral of fashions. There was much to be said for hatred, Aylesford reflected. But in the end, it only got you so far. It might crown a king, but it could not steer a kingdom. Or, for that matter, float a stone, he thought as the ship plummeted, eliciting a fresh surge of nausea.

The cabin door banged open with a report like a gunshot, and the voice of his travelling companion boomed out as Aylesford bent over the bucket that had by some miracle slid back to its former place. 'What, still mewlin' and pukin' are yer? It won't do, me lad. It won't do at all.'

'Go tae the devil, Starkey,' he growled without raising his head.

'Like enough I'll end up a pensioner o' that gentleman,' replied the tall, pallid, whippet-thin man in a Cockney accent so thick it had struck Aylesford at first as another language entirely. He slammed the door behind him. 'But that don't mean I'm eager ter make 'is acquaintance. Let 'im seek me out. I'll shake 'is 'and when the time comes, but till then I shall spit in 'is eye.'

'What are ye on about now?' Looking up through a tangle of matted coppery hair, he watched Starkey fumble at the bolts of the door before shooting them loudly home.

'I'm about savin' yer miserable 'ide, that's what. And me own.' Starkey turned from the door, one hand on the pommel of the rapier belted at his side. His glittering eyes darted like those of a trapped rat over the close confines of the cabin. His pale, pinched face, with its long, narrow nose and receding, dark-stubbled chin, down which water streamed and dripped, made him look all the more ratlike, as did the stoop of his shoulders, as if he had bumped his head upon so many low ceilings that he went about in constant apprehension of a fresh collision. His clothes were drenched. His greatcoat hung from his spare frame in a sodden, colourless mass, and the tricorn he had jammed onto his head upon leaving the cabin some time ago was gone, no doubt swept overboard; his long brown hair, which had been pulled back in a tight queue, now suggested a bedraggled snarl of seaweed tossed up by the tides. Indeed, so pale was he, from a life-time spent underground, that he looked half drowned, as though he had followed his hat into the sea before somehow managing to claw his way back aboard the *Pierre*.

'What news from Bagot?' Aylesford inquired, for Starkey had left the cabin in search of the captain, despite that gentleman having ordered them to remain below.

'Gone,' said Starkey simply as he rushed to the travelling chest that contained his belongings, unbattened it with a few kicks of his boot heel, and began to drag it across the floor, evidently with the intention of using it to block the door. 'Give us a 'and, Aylesford.'

But Aylesford made no move to assist, though he did, with prodigious effort, prop himself on one elbow. 'Gone? What d'ye mean gone?'

Starkey shot him an exasperated glance, hunched over the chest like a resurrection man interrupted in his business. 'I mean no longer aboard this vessel. I mean clasped ter the bosom o' Davy Jones. Full fathom five our captain lies. Is that not clear? Gone overboard is my meanin'. Drownded like a cat. And we are like ter join 'im.'

As he spoke, he resumed tugging the chest across the floor, positioning it in front of the door. He then flung the lid open and rummaged inside.

Aylesford was too wrapped up in his own sufferings to immediately make sense of this information. *So Bagot is gone*, he thought, wishing that Starkey would leave him in peace or at least move about in a less unpleasantly energetic manner. *What o' it? What is that tae do with me?* But at last a glimmer of understanding penetrated his sickly self-absorption. 'Who then is in command?'

'No one,' said Starkey, surfacing from the interior of the chest with a mahogany case that Aylesford knew from prior acquaintance held a pistol and accessories. This, more than Starkey's words, had the effect of focusing his attention.

'Why are ye arming yourself?'

'I suggest yer do likewise,' Starkey said. He closed the flat top of the chest and laid the pistol case upon it, holding it steady with one hand while, with the other, he flicked open the metal clasp and raised the lid. All the while, his widespread legs balanced him almost insouciantly against the yawing of the ship. It did not seem fair to Aylesford that he, a veteran of numerous Channel crossings, should suffer the torments and indignities of the damned each time he ventured upon the wet part of the world while Starkey, who, if his own testimony were to be credited, had never before set foot aboard a seagoing vessel, had taken to it like a duck to water.

'What has happened?' he demanded. 'Is it the English? Are we boarded?'

'Mutiny,' Starkey answered, practically spitting the word, his lips drawn back in a snarl that also had something of a grin about it. 'It were no wave what 'eaved Bagot overboard, poor sod, but the 'ands o' 'is own traitorous crew.'

Aylesford sat up at that, swinging his feet – still wearing their boots – down to the hard floor. He stood, only to find himself propelled, as said floor abruptly tilted like a wagon going over a cliff, into Starkey, who dropped the pistol he was in the process of loading. It struck the top of the chest and bounced to the floor, skidding off into shadows.

'Damn yer for a clumsy oaf!' he cried, and shoved Aylesford away.

This impetus, added to that imparted by the movement of the ship, which at the same instant swung back like a pendulum, sent Aylesford stumbling and sliding across the cabin into his own battened-down travelling chest. He collapsed heavily upon it, his insides slithering about like a basket of eels pulled from the Thames, and fought his rising gorge.

What came to his aid then, as it had so often before, was rage. White-hot fury took possession of him. The storm was forgotten. His sickness was forgotten. All was forgotten but the burning need to repay the wrong that had been done him. When he stood again, he did so with the grace of a seasoned sailor. No hint of unsteadiness marred his stance. Neither did his arm tremble . . . nor the blade now extended at the end of it, a rapier which a moment ago had hung from a hook in the wall, safely tucked into its scabbard. He had no memory of pulling it.

'Oaf, am I? Ye'll want to rephrase that,' he suggested in an icy tone, his brogue thickening as it always did at such moments.

Starkey, who had retrieved his fallen pistol and resumed his preparations, rolled his eyes, an expression of annoyance flitting across his sharp features. He made no move to draw his own blade. 'Rephrase it? Oh, aye, I'll rephrase it. Did I say oaf? Bloody lunatic is more like it! 'As that infernal pride o' yers not caused us trouble enough? Will yer run me through and face the mutineers down wif naught but a pigsticker against the lot o' 'em?'

Before Aylesford could reply, a clamour of angry voices arose from outside the cabin. Starkey stepped aside with alacrity as the knob rattled uselessly. This was followed by a heavy thump, as of a stout shoulder slamming into the door.

'Ouvrez la porte!' cried a voice. And another: 'Let us in!'

'Not by the 'air o' me chinny-chin-chin,' replied Starkey, accompanying these words with a wink in Aylesford's direction. With elbow crooked, he held his primed and loaded pistol at shoulder height, the barrel pointed upward, his stance that of a duellist awaiting the command to fire.

A chorus of curses and threats in French and English erupted, along with renewed efforts to batter down the door, as ineffective as the first. Then came the heavy thud of an axe.

This noise did not diminish Aylesford's rage but did serve to redirect it. 'The damned disloyal devils,' he swore. 'I'll see 'em in hell.' As if only now becoming aware of the sword he was holding, he tossed it onto the cot and opened his travelling chest. What was stowed there would be more useful now than any blade. 'Why did they murder Bagot?' he asked, shouting to be heard above the din.

'A difference o' opinion,' Starkey answered, 'in the matter o' the storm. The captain wished ter ride it out and see the mission through. The crew 'ad other ideas. Said the blow were unnatural like. A curse brought down upon the ship on account o' some evil she carried. I reckon yer can guess what that might be.'

Starkey's words were punctuated by axe blows and the sounds of splintering wood, not all of the latter coming from the door. The intensity of the storm had increased. The winds shrieked like a brace of banshees, and the *Pierre* surged and wallowed and heeled in a drunken dance, threatening at every instant, or so it seemed, to founder, but always righting herself somehow, tripping gracelessly along the razor's edge of disaster. The flame of the lantern likewise guttered but stubbornly held, though the lantern itself appeared to be swinging not merely with the movements of the ship but actively against them, invested with a frantic impetus of its own, like a prisoner clapped in irons who suddenly perceives, in the dank gloom of the hold, that the restraints to which he had submitted as an unavoidable indignity of transport now bid fair to become the ornaments of his tomb. What was not nailed down or otherwise fixed in place had come loose and gathered into a motley mass, a mob of objects that seemed afflicted with indecisive panic, rushing back and forth across the floor, first one way, then another, always moving yet getting nowhere. Starkey's trunk had joined the general ebb and flow, ponderous as a pachyderm. The very shadows seemed to have been torn loose from what cast them. Despite his sea legs, Starkey was now in some distress and clung fiercely, with his free hand, to the lines affixed to the cabin wall. But to Aylesford this chaos was no more than the outward manifestation of his rage. He was the eye at the centre of the storm, a calm, still point that radiated pure destruction. He was in his element now.

'Didn't I warn yer?' Starkey continued peevishly. 'Didn't I tell yer ter keep it 'id away? But no. Yer came swaggerin' on board, boastin' o' what were supposed ter be a secret known only ter the two o' us. 'Ow yer carryin' a weapon what will change the course o' the war and restore the rightful king ter England. That weren't so bad o' itself. What's another big mouth more or less in the world? But yer 'ad ter take offence. At what? God only knows! Not five minutes after we're aboard, yer challenge the captain ter a duel!'

'No man may call me a liar without answerin' for it.'

''E never said nuffink o' the sort!' exploded Starkey.

'He didnae need to,' Aylesford answered, digging deeper into the open chest. Where was the damn thing? 'I could see it in his eyes.'

'Could yer now? I saw no such fing. It were dark as 'ades on deck. Yer must 'ave a owl's eyes.'

'I heard it in his voice.'

'An' the ears as well! Why, 'tis a wonder yer need a ship at all. Could yer not just flap yer wings and fly ter Frog Land?'

This sally was ignored by Aylesford, whose whole attention was focused on the interior of the chest. A riot of clothes and objects flew up from inside as he rummaged about.

' "Welcome aboard the *Pierre*, gentlemen," was the captain's words as best I recall 'em,' Starkey went on. ' "I anticipate no difficulties with the crossin'," said 'e. Then invited us ter make ourselves at ease below decks, where 'e would come speak wif us as 'is duties permitted. Oh, aye, what man wif a shred o' 'ealthy self-regard could not but take offence at such a rank insult?'

By now, the shouts from outside the door had quieted, but the axe continued to fall. Indeed, it seemed a second axe had been added, and the blows came in quick succession, like a drum beating the crew to quarters. An ominous crack had appeared in the door, lengthening and widening with each blow.

'I dinnae expect ye tae understand,' Aylesford said loftily, looking up from the chest.

' 'Course not! What could a lowly Morecockneyan like meself know about such things as 'onour? That's the birthright o' those what cling like ticks ter the topside o' the world. So yer challenge Bagot, bold as yer please. And when 'e larfs, thinkin' yer 'avin' 'im on – as what sane man wouldn't – yer strike him!'

'He was a blackguard and a coward.'

' 'E were captain o' this ship, which makes 'im like unto a king. Why, 'e would've been within 'is rights ter 'ave yer killed on the spot! Instead o' which, 'e apolergizes fer any offence 'e may 'ave given, like a gentleman.'

'Like a coward,' sneered Aylesford. 'How dare he take such an attitude with me, as though he were my better!'

'And as if that weren't bad enough,' Starkey ploughed on, 'yer pull out the 'unter. In full view o' 'alf the crew, yer stand there on the deck like some demented conjurer wif that 'orrible watch in yer 'and, one gruesome relic in the grip o' another, all aglow with witchy fire. Aye, there were a sight calculated ter win the devotion o' sailors!'

Aylesford laughed heartily. He had quite recovered his good humour, for he had found the object of his search at last. 'If I live tae be a hundred, I'll never forget the look on Bagot's face! He knew who he was dealing with then, I'll warrant!'

'I don't doubt it. But now yer see the result o' yer brash display. Bagot thrown ter the fishes and the crew eager ter send us after 'im.'

'Bah. I dinnae fear that rabble. Let 'em come. I shall greet 'em as they deserve.'

'Too much sun, that's what I fink,' mused Starkey. 'It's boiled yer brains, made yer mad as March 'ares. All o' yer topsiders.'

The conversation was interrupted by a resounding crack. This was the door splitting down the middle as the busy axes accomplished their task. Before that sound had faded, Starkey's pistol blazed – and misfired. He dropped it with an oath even as the first mutineers appeared in the doorway: three men, with more crowding behind them. Their pale, glistening faces wore expressions of grim determination, but their eyes shone glassily with fear. Some wore knit caps and tarred straw hats, while others were bareheaded like Starkey, with strands of wet hair plastered to cheeks and foreheads. The leader carried a pistol, while others were armed with daggers, belaying pins, and the hatchets used against the door. They squeezed in through the gap, shoving the sundered halves of the door aside, then, their object attained, hesitated, glancing about nervously, like children who have forced their way in among the grown-ups at a party, carried away by some infectious enthusiasm of the playroom, and now, having outrun that impetus, which has proved insubstantial as a dream, are suddenly rendered timid and shy.

'Come tae add tae your crimes, ye damned despicable dogs?' demanded Aylesford. 'Ye'll not find me an easy victim!' And he pulled a burlap sack out of the trunk.

Rather than cowing the intruders, this had the effect of stiffening their spines. The sailor with the pistol, a short, round-faced, pockmarked man wearing a Monmouth cap, whom Aylesford recognized as the first mate – though he could not put a name to that cratered face – said, in French-accented English, "And it over and live. I will not ask again.'

At this, Starkey drew his rapier. 'Take it and die.'

The man shrugged, pointed his pistol at Aylesford, and pulled the trigger . . . with no better effect than Starkey's earlier attempt; indeed, a worse one, as not so much as a spark was struck. With a curse, he threw the pistol at Aylesford, who dodged it easily. Then, as Aylesford opened the sack with one hand while cradling it in the crook of his other arm – somehow balancing himself like an acrobat all the while – the moon-faced man reached behind his back and drew a long and wicked-looking dagger.

'*Allons-y!*' he cried. But rather than rushing forward, the clump of mutineers gathered itself still more tightly together, as if each individual was prepared to act, but only as part of something larger than himself, and that compound creature could not be willed or commanded into being by any of them alone but must arise in its own time and by the exercise of its own coalescent will.

Time stretched thin. The air of the cabin trembled like a sheet of glass with the flickering of light and shadow. Ship and storm seemed to hesitate, caught for an instant in an equipoise of opposing forces.

Then the *Pierre* gave a groan such as she had not yet produced. The note of defiance that Aylesford had heard earlier, or that he'd convinced himself he was hearing, was gone. This was a cry of pain and despair, as if the wood were alive and suffering not only from the lash of the storm but from an awareness of the fate bearing down on it and an understanding that this fate could not be avoided. The sailors flinched, seeming not so much to hear the sound, or lamentation, rather, as to feel it in their bones. Some, at the back, turned and ran, dropping what they carried. But the men at the front, the moon-faced first mate and three others, rushed towards Aylesford.

He flung the sack into their faces. One man went down, but whether that was due to the sack or to the slick and cluttered floor, Aylesford did not know. In any case, that man fell heavily, knocking his head against the edge of Starkey's chest, and did not rise; the sack, meanwhile, wound up striking the lamp that hung from the low ceiling. The cabin was plunged into darkness.

But not for long. An icy blue light clung to Aylesford's clenched fist and what he held there. It perched like a tamed yet still malevolent will-o'-the-wisp.

'*Diable!*' gasped the first mate, who had stopped short, dagger upraised as though to ward off a blow. The ghastly light further ravaged his features, giving him a leprous look. He squinted against it as if half blinded. But it was not brightness that made the light painful to endure; it had the effect of bruising whatever it touched, so that everyone and everything in the cabin seemed not just illuminated but also infected by it, rendered as sick and unwholesome as what shone upon them.

'Is this what ye're after?' demanded Aylesford with a sneer. 'Come on – take it!'

In his hand, brandished like a club, was another hand, which he held by the stub of its wrist. It had the look of having been sawn cleanly from the arm of a life-sized statue. The stark lines of bones and veins and tendons stood out in the sharp glow shed by the object caged in its pale, frozen fingers: a pocket watch of the type known to horologists as a hunter. Flat, somewhat ovoid in shape, with a featureless lid closed over the face, this watch seemed part of the hand that held it, as if the two had been carved from a single piece of marble. Or bone.

'God save us,' cried one of the sailors.

'The Lord 'elps them what 'elps themselves.' Taking advantage of the fright that had paralysed the mutineers, Starkey dispatched one and then another with ugly punches of his blade that took each man in the side. That left two remaining: the man who had fallen to the floor, and still lay there, unconscious or dead (now joined by his two fellows who would not rise again), and the first mate.

This last, seeing that the odds had shifted, turned and fled the cabin, pursued by Aylesford's mocking laughter. Starkey pursued him as well, and would have taken him in the back had his feet not become tangled in the sprawl of bodies on the floor, which he now joined with an oath.

Aylesford's laughter choked off abruptly, but not due to the predicament of Starkey, who was engaged at close quarters in a life-or-death struggle with the last of the mutineers, who, as it developed,

11

had only been feigning unconsciousness. This man was armed with a dagger such as common seamen carry, the tip blunted but the edges keen as razors. Starkey had dropped his rapier and now clung desperately to the man's wrists. The two adversaries were locked in a savage striving punctuated with grunts and curses, kicking and snarling at each other as the *Pierre* threw them this way and that in her own, less equal, striving. The corpses of the men Starkey had killed, exacting revenge from beyond the grave, battered and bludgeoned him, their arms swinging like flails, their heads like clubs, though at least they did not discriminate, lashing out with the same dumb ferocity at their former comrade, as if imbued with hatred for everything alive.

'Aylesford!' Starkey gasped out. 'A little 'elp, fer God's sake!'

But Aylesford was in no position to offer assistance. In fact, he required it. For what he clutched by the wrist was no longer a dead thing, hard and cold and stiff as the plaster cast of a partial limb. Lifeless no longer, it twisted and flexed in his grasp with a force and a will that filled him with fresh nausea. Yet he could not drop it. His fingers were fixed to the suddenly soft and warm skin as though the severed hand had fused itself to him and they now constituted a single flesh.

Only once in all the times he had held this dreadful trophy of his long and long-fruitless search had it been warm to the touch, and that had been when he'd first picked it up from the ground after his sword had cleaved it from the arm of Daniel Quare, that meddlesome, devilishly hard-to-kill agent of the Worshipful Company of Clockmakers, who, Aylesford fervently hoped and fully expected, was as dead now as this fragment of him had seemed to be.

He hadn't dared to touch it then, not flesh to flesh. It had been drenched in blood, the fingers locked as they still were about the hunter that Aylesford's masters in Paris had sent him to London to acquire, this weapon that had the power, or so he had been assured, and did most readily believe, of winning the war for France and restoring the line of the Stuarts to the English throne. The Worshipful Company, on the other hand, whose secret remit went far beyond the mere manufacture and regulation of timepieces, would use its power to preserve and extend the reign of the Hanover upstarts.

There, deep beneath the streets of London, in the gloomy sub-terranean realm of the Morecockneyans, the watch had glowed in the dead grip of the severed hand like a fiery ruby set in a devil's sceptre. Washed in its bloody light, Aylesford had known himself to be in the presence of something more dangerous than he could understand. He'd removed his cloak and thrown it over the severed hand, muffling but not entirely hiding the light, then quickly raised the package in trembling fingers and dropped it into a burlap sack provided by Starkey. He'd held it in his hand, bundled in the wool of his cloak, for mere seconds. But even so, he'd felt the warmth of it, like a loaf of bread pulled fresh from the oven. A powerful pulse had passed through the thick fabric, as of a beating heart, and, more unsettling still, he'd sensed the regard of a cold and watchful intelligence, as if the hunter were aware of him. Indeed, in the space of those seconds he'd felt himself weighed and judged, as God might judge the souls of the dead. And though his heart had quailed at the penetration of that eyeless gaze, he'd also felt a thrill of something prideful, for he'd sensed that the hunter – whatever it might truly be – was not entirely displeased at what it had made of him. And might yet make of him.

He and Starkey had left the underground realm of the More-cockneyans almost immediately, after a brief audience with the King Beneath the Ground, as their young monarch styled himself, who had invested Starkey with the authority of an ambassador and pro-vided him with letters for Charles Edward Stuart and the French king. So it hadn't been until some hours later, above ground again – 'topside', as Starkey called it – that an opportunity to examine the amputation more closely had presented itself to Aylesford.

He was alone in a private sitting room at the Red Lion, a Holborn inn secretly owned by the Morecockneyans, one of many such establishments scattered throughout the city that permitted easy, dis-creet intercourse between London and its self-effacing subterranean sister, and kept the coffers and larders of the King Beneath the Ground flush besides. Starkey was gone, readying the carriage that would take them south to Hastings: a day's journey along winding, tortuous roads that could easily protract itself due to any one of the innumerable contingencies of travel, from bad weather to bad luck to bad men. Later this night or early the next morning – if all went according to schedule – they would be rowed out to meet the ship that would smuggle them across the Channel. That ship, or so Starkey had assured, would be waiting for their signal, as a man had already been dispatched to Hastings with news of their coming.

Dawn was just beginning to break outside the second-storey casement window, casting a pale and enervated light over a cobbled courtyard bestrewn with damp straw. Starkey and men unknown to Aylesford came in and out of view at unpredictable intervals below, their figures blurry in the latticed panes. A scruffy little black dog amused itself by tormenting a pair of bedraggled hens, harrying them about the courtyard with an air more of mischief than malice. The chickens responded to its sallies with every appearance of affronted dignity, and Aylesford imagined them as spinsters picking up their skirts and dashing about in clucking consternation at the interest of a man. Sometimes those were the juiciest hens of all.

He had not slept a wink, and there did not seem much prospect of sleep in his immediate future, with a bouncing, bumping carriage for a bed – not until they reached Hastings, in any case, and perhaps not until he was safely aboard ship. Yet he was not tired. On the contrary, he was filled with feverish energy.

After fortifying himself with a meal of cold roast beef, bread, cheese, and small beer, Aylesford had turned his attention to the sack, which lay on the floor to one side of the table where he'd broken his fast. He leaned down in his chair and pulled it closer, the dead weight sending an instinctive shudder through his frame. His intention was to prise the hunter from the frozen grip of Quare's hand. He would retain the former and throw the latter into the sewer, which was all the burial it deserved, though at the same time he smiled to think of the impression such a memento would make in Paris. Perhaps it would launch a new fashion. Well, he would leave that honour to another.

He did not relish the prospect of having to break the fingers, which he felt certain would be locked in rigor, or of having to wash away the blood and gore, though he had procured a basin of water and

14

towels for the purpose. Even in death, Quare was proving to be a damnable nuisance. But this was the last time the man – or a portion of him, rather – would trouble him.

Yet Aylesford hesitated, the sack unopened at his feet. It was neither squeamishness nor fastidiousness that made him take another swallow of beer but the memory – or not memory, for doubt fostered by the passage of time had undermined his certainty of what had happened back in the cavern beneath the guild hall; say impression, rather – the very strong impression that he'd been subjected to an examination of sorts, as if the hunter were an eye, and the garish light it shed the visible manifestation of a gaze from which, like the workings of a guilty conscience, there could be no hiding. Not that he had ever known those workings himself. His conscience was clear. What he'd done had been done for a great and sacred cause, and as such, even if crimes had been committed, which he did not for an instant concede, he had, as it were, been absolved in advance and in perpetuity. This was war. He had shed blood and would no doubt shed more of it before he was done. He did not flinch from the necessity; indeed, he welcomed it and would wear the stains like badges of honour.

Setting his jaw, Aylesford opened the sack and pulled out the bundle within. This he wasted no time in laying upon the table, elbowing his pewter plate aside. He had expected his cloak to be sodden with blood, but it was dry to the touch and, like his conscience, unmarked by any stain as far as he could see. And no warmer than a wool cloak should be. Gingerly, and with no little anticipation, he drew back the folds of the cloak to expose what lay within.

Quare's hand reposed palm up, still holding the pocket watch in its nerveless grasp. This object had lost its cherry glow and resembled any ordinary, undistinguished timepiece of its kind. The plain, unmarked case, which had the look of oft-handled silver, shone dully in the early morning light. There was no trace of blood. Not so much as a drop or even the faintest stain. It was as if both appendage and watch had been methodically licked clean by a cat. But that was not the strangest thing.

The hand was white and smooth as marble. The stump of the

wrist, where Aylesford's blade had cleaved flesh and bone, was solid, the ragged wound sealed without scar or blemish. He was drawn and repelled in equal measure; the impossibility of what he was seeing stimulated his curiosity even as it raised the hairs at the back of his neck. He picked up the knife he had used on the joint of beef and, after wiping the greasy blade negligently on his sleeve, touched the tip tentatively to the wrist, where he could see a raised ridge of tendon, like a slender root running just below the surface of the ground. He might have been tapping stone. He saw to his amazement that the fine hairs along the wrist had turned translucent as glass, like the tentacles of tiny anemones. Probed by the knife, they proved to be as if carved into the stone, or affixed to it. He could not insert any portion of the blade's edge between the hairs and whatever substance, stone or bone or something else entirely, lay beneath them.

He paused to wash the dryness from his mouth with another swallow of small beer. Then, still leery of touching the hand directly, he took the fork from atop his plate. With that implement in one hand, and the knife in the other, it occurred to him that he must look like a refined cannibal contemplating where best to begin carving. Deftly, as though he had practised the manoeuvre dozens of times, he used fork and knife to flip the hand over.

The back presented a similar spectacle, save that the translucent hairs were present in greater profusion and the veins and tendons more vividly displayed. Curiosity outstripping caution at last, he set down the knife, which he had been holding in his right hand, and ever so gently brushed the tip of his index finger across the pale dorsum. A tingling thrill shot through him, as if some spark had passed from Quare's hand to his. He drew back with a gasp, the fork dropping to clatter on the floor. The minute hairs had seemed to prick mildly at his skin. When he examined his fingertip, he saw that a sort of rash had sprung up . . . a cluster of tiny red dots. Why, the damned thing had stung him like a jellyfish!

Returning his attention to the appendage, he observed a faint blush colouring the hairs. It faded as he watched, until they were translucent again. No, he realized queasily, he had not been stung but *bitten*. His blood sucked into the severed hand. A moment ago he had smiled at the conceit of himself as a cannibal preparing to dine. But the figure had been apropos. Only *he* had been the meal.

The hand had drunk his blood. For what purpose?

And how was such a thing possible?

He had known that the hunter was no ordinary timepiece. His masters had told him that, though they had not been able – or, at any rate, willing – to delve into the specifics of its unique qualities, on which they placed so much importance. He had assumed that what made it so valuable was some abstruse technological innovation that could be put to a more practical use in warfare. His knowledge of horology was superficial, consisting of assorted details and techniques committed to memory in the course of a fortnight's study in Paris under the exacting tutelage of masters from *la Corporation des maîtres horlogers* – the French clockmakers' guild – in order to masquerade as a Scottish journeyman of the Worshipful Company of Clockmakers freshly arrived in London. Of course, any close examination of his supposed skills would have unmasked him immediately as a fraud, but for once the casual English prejudice against his country had worked in his favour: Englishmen found it sufficiently miraculous that a Scotsman might wear a coat and breeches and speak English, however barbarously, to inquire too deeply into any other civilized accomplishments he might lay claim to.

But Aylesford had heard and seen enough in his pursuit of the timepiece, from the strange circumstances of Master Magnus's death to Quare's emergence from the lowest levels of the guild hall with the watch upraised in his hand and shedding a ghastly crimson glow as if in anticipation of the blood about to be spilled, to know that what set the hunter apart had little to do with natural science.

Little? There was nothing natural about it. Mere contact had worked this incomprehensible change upon Quare's flesh and bone. What other changes might it not work in time? Perhaps prolonged contact was not even necessary. A single touch might suffice. Indeed, for all he knew, proximity alone rendered one subject to its baleful influence. He had touched it. Had carried it close to him for hours now. It might already be changing him, working upon him in ways too subtle for his senses to perceive.

It occurred to him that Quare's uncanny resilience had its explanation at last. For on the night of the massacre at the Pig and Rooster, as Quare lay in a drugged stupor in the barmaid's bed, he had stabbed him in the back, the dagger angling precisely down, right through the heart, yet the man had shown himself no worse for the injury. Aylesford had told himself that his thrust must have gone astray in the dark, but now he realized that the watch had been protecting Quare somehow, shielding him from death, though he knew with certainty that Quare had not had it in his possession at the time. No, the watch had been in the hands of Master Magnus that night: the very night, in fact, that the misshapen genius – head of the Most Secret and Exalted Order of Regulators, the Worshipful Company's cadre of spies and special agents, of which Quare had been a member – had perished in his guild hall workshop, the watch clutched in his hand . . . just as it was now clutched in Quare's hand.

Were the two events, Magnus's death and Quare's unlikely, not to say impossible, avoidance of that fate, separated though they had been by distance, linked through some arcane agency? Had the hunter killed one man while interceding to spare another? To ask the questions was to answer them. Though reason might rebel against the conclusion, preferring to take refuge in coincidence, Aylesford would not allow himself that consolation. His own experience argued too forcefully against it. The watch had worked its will upon both men. Upon the world. But by what means, and to what end, he did not know nor could even begin to imagine, save that there was more than a stench of brimstone about it.

And why would the watch, or whatever demonic force or spirit inhabited it, having protected Quare once, lift its protection now and allow Aylesford's sword to sever the hand that held it?

Could it be that the watch had *wanted* him to have it? Again he recalled how, lifting the bloody amputation from the ground, he had felt himself come under scrutiny, as if the watch were an eye that was staring back at him unblinking – or, rather, staring into him, piercing him to the heart with its gaze just as he had pierced Quare's heart with his dagger, but to greater effect. Was that gaze fixed upon him even now?

As these thoughts and questions arose in his mind, Aylesford sat like a man who has received some piece of news too shattering to take in all at once. Then, as if some inner coil had come unsprung, he bolted upright, sending his chair crashing to the floor. He snatched the knife and stood ready to fend off any attack from the object on the table. He was aware of the absurdity of his pose – he could practically hear Starkey's mocking laughter – but he felt himself to be in mortal peril and meant to defend his life as he would against any flesh-and-blood adversary.

The hand, however, lay motionless as ever. It appeared just as it had when he'd first unwrapped it. No hint of colour remained.

Hurriedly, taking care not to inadvertently touch it again, and keeping the knife near by all the while, he wrapped it back in his cloak and returned the package to the sack. Then, keeping the sack in view, he crossed the room and sat in a chair as far away from it as possible.

Sweat ran down his forehead and back. His finger, his whole hand, was tingling. Was the sensation moving up his arm? He couldn't be sure. It might be his fancy at work, or rather his fear. But it might not. His heart felt strange, as if it were not beating but rather clenching and unclenching. As if it were not a heart but a hand. A hand that held an unholy watch.

Aylesford sprang to his feet and began pacing the confines of the room. At that moment, despite his mission, despite his fervent allegiance to the inseparable if not entirely commensurate causes of Scottish independence and Jacobite restoration, for which he had sacrificed so much in his twenty-two years, despite everything he had worked for, hoped for, dreamed of, he would have pitched the sack and its contents into the nearest sewer, as he'd planned to do with Quare's hand once he'd wrested the watch from its dead grasp, if only he could have done so from a safe distance. But he had no thought now of prising the watch free. No, let Quare keep his prize.

I will do my duty, he told himself. *Take the timepiece tae France. But then I will wash my hands o' it. There are things in this world a man should nae meddle with.*

Isn't it a bit late for that? a voice seemed to whisper in reply. *Haven't you already meddled with it?*

And it has meddled with me, he thought grimly. *As it did with Quare before me.*

A mood of fatalism had settled over Aylesford by the time he and Starkey were on their way to Hastings. As the carriage rattled and bounced over the rough roads, Starkey, seated on the bench across from Aylesford, stretched out his legs, pulled his hat low over his face, and proceeded to drowse, for all the world as if he were in a soft – and stationary – bed.

Aylesford envied him his equipoise. He could not have slept here, or anywhere else. Not now. He had tried to get Starkey to take charge of the sack and its contents, but the man had refused, insisting that the relic – his word for the severed hand, as if it had belonged to a saint, not a spy – was Aylesford's responsibility. And so Aylesford, not without misgivings, had brought the sack into the carriage, concluding that his duty, in good conscience, required him to keep the damned thing close . . . but not too close.

The carriage was comfortably appointed. The benches were cushioned and upholstered in maroon leather, and a sprung suspension system reduced the shocks of the road from bone-breaking to merely teeth-rattling. A netted pouch for small items of baggage was affixed to the ceiling above the benches, and there, over Starkey's nodding head, Aylesford had stowed the sack, where he could keep a gimlet eye upon it. If Starkey was at all apprehensive about sitting beneath this Damoclean object, he gave no sign of it.

The interior of the carriage was warm and close, smelling of sweat and old leather, and less savoury stinks emitted at intervals by the snoring Starkey, but Aylesford kept the window shut against unwholesome breezes, for the smells of the horses and the clouds of dust introduced by those breezes would, he knew, constitute a cure worse than the original affliction. The hyacinth-scented handkerchief he pressed to his nose – one of the few French fashions he had adopted in his years there – did not eliminate these odours but provided a degree of distraction from them, as well as armouring him against the ague and other infirmities of the air. Alas, the bucolic charms of the English countryside unscrolling behind the grimy glass of the window proved less distracting, and he found his attention drawn back again and again to the lodestone opposite him.

Aylesford was simultaneously appalled and thrilled to think that he had in his possession a weapon that would win the war for France and restore the Stuart dynasty to Scotland. He did not give a fig for England and considered that all the troubles of his native land could be traced to the overweening ambition of James VI to achieve by peaceful succession what conquest had failed to deliver: the union of the two neighbouring kingdoms into a single entity, ruled by a single sovereign. But though successful at first, that strategy had proved an unmitigated disaster, as England, which James had thought to swallow, had instead, ogre-like, swallowed Scotland, spitting out, like so much gristle and bone, both James's posterity and what little had been left of the Holy Catholic and Apostolic Church after the depredations of Henry Tudor and his wicked daughter, the regicide Elizabeth.

England could go to the devil for all Aylesford cared – indeed, he would gladly help to send it there. He quite understood there could be no free and independent Scotland until England was brought to heel. But that was the extent of his interest. Unlike many of his compatriots – including, unfortunately, the Bonnie Prince himself – Aylesford had no wish to see his sovereign repeat the vainglorious mistakes of his predecessors by taking up a crown that, however glittering, had bent the neck of every Stuart who had worn it like a millstone . . . bent it lower and lower, until it was of a height to rest comfortably on the chopping block.

Still, as a loyal subject, Aylesford knew where his duty lay, and he was determined to perform it, regardless of his personal opinions. The important thing right now was to ensure that England *was* defeated. Without that, there was nothing. And now, thanks to him, victory was at hand – quite literally so.

Even considering the hunter's uncanny nature – which on the whole he preferred *not* to consider – it seemed incredible to Aylesford that this single small object could tip the balance in a war that had already dragged on for more than five years. How, he wondered, would victory come to pass? To what use would the watch be put by his masters? What powers did it possess that sober-minded men like the duc de Choiseul, the French minister orchestrating the present invasion, and Lieutenant-Colonel James Grant, military adviser to the prince – and Aylesford's patron – who had been with him since the prior invasion, that of 1745, when London itself had been so briefly within grasp, should set such store upon it, as though it were the equivalent of five hundred cannon? All Aylesford had seen and experienced of the watch had convinced him that it was an object to be respected and feared. He had no doubt that it could kill a man, and do worse than kill. But how it might defeat an army or humble a nation – much less an empire like England – he could not imagine. It was, in the end, just a small thing, after all. Perhaps it could be the weapon of an assassin – though even a dagger might serve for that purpose, as he well knew – but if so, surely he was bringing it in the wrong direction, away from any useful target.

It was fruitless to speculate, he told himself. The answers would become clear soon enough. When he had left France, five months ago at the height of summer, plans had been under way for a bold invasion of England and Scotland, and he knew those plans must have advanced considerably in his absence. Of course, it was too late in the year to launch an invasion now – to cross the Channel in force during the winter months would be suicidal. But he felt in his heart that the coming year, 1759, would be decisive, a year of miracles, thanks in no small part to what he now carried: a watch that would win a war.

As the bearer of England's bane, Aylesford would at last receive the respect that was his due . . . and that had been denied him for so long. Men who were his inferiors in every way that mattered had looked down upon him his whole life just because he could not say who his parents were. There were many with titles appended to their names and honours heaped upon them who had no better idea of their dams and sires than he did. Yet they presumed to judge him. He well knew that he had not been given this assignment as a mark of favour or even of confidence. The rumours of the watch, which had drawn him to England, first to Lincolnshire and thence to London and the underground realm of the Morecockneyans, had been too tantalizing to ignore yet at the same time too outlandish to wholly countenance. No seasoned agent could be risked in what might well turn out to be a wild-goose chase.

Thus had Grant's eye fallen on him, a hot-tempered young man of some promise, notwithstanding his questionable pedigree, a ward of the Church at home in the company of gentlemen, who had already proved his willingness and his ability to kill in furtherance of the Jacobite cause. He was not unique in these respects; such ambitious young men were attracted to the orbit of the Bonnie Prince like September wasps to honeyed wine, and like wasps were as apt in their drunken inspiration to sting indiscriminately as to drown ignominiously. This made them irritating at court but useful elsewhere. But his value was enhanced not only by his precocious skills with a blade but by his youthful and innocent appearance; who would believe that this blue-eyed lad, with his blaze of red hair and freckled, smooth-cheeked face, on which no trace of a beard had yet sprouted, might be a merciless spy and assassin?

And so he had been dispatched to Paris, where the knowledge of a journeyman watchmaker had been crammed into his cranium over the course of a fortnight, and then bundled across the Channel. Aylesford did not think his masters had expected him to succeed in his quest. Perhaps they had not even expected to see him again. But he had succeeded, and now he would reap the rewards of that success.

He smiled, imagining himself with a title, an estate. A baronetcy, perhaps even a barony. *But why aim so low?* Ambition whispered its honeyed words. *Why not an earldom?* The Earl of Rannaknok. It had a pleasant ring. The name of the small village outside Perth where he had been left as a babe, swaddled on the steps of the old stone church like some fairy changeling, with no name or history in the world of men. He had been found there by the local rector, Father Aylesford, a secret adherent of the Catholic faith and a loyal Jacobite besides, who had baptized and adopted him, christening him Thomas Aylesford, as though he were the man's own flesh and blood. That was, of course, what most of the villagers believed, and young Aylesford had grown up to taunts of bastard and by-blow.

But no natural father would have treated him so unnaturally. For from the age of eight or so, Aylesford had been as much wife as son to the rector when that holy man was in his cups, which was most nights, it seemed, until, at sixteen, he had been sent to France in furtherance of his education and there attached himself to the glittering if somewhat threadbare court that surrounded Charles Edward Stuart in pale imitation of the majesty of Versailles, like a once-gorgeous tapestry faded by too-long exposure to the rays of the sun. Aylesford had seen his adoptive father only once since then. That visit had not, strictly speaking, been within the remit of his mission, but he had considered it in the manner of a personal debt he was honour-bound to repay, and so had detoured north for a time.

Yet what if Starkey were to claim all the credit? Yes, that would be just like the sly Morecockneyan, Aylesford thought. *Let me do all the work and take all the risk, so that he may reap the benefits. The blackguard! Just look at him, sleeping so soundly . . . Or is he asleep? Is he not, rather, feigning sleep, the better tae spy upon me, waitin' for an opportunity tae strike me down in cold blood and take the relic as his own?*

Aylesford's fingers strayed towards the dagger at his side. A quick thrust between the ribs . . .

But that would be messy, in more ways than one. To say nothing of the possibility that Starkey was shamming sleep, watching him from under the brim of his tilted tricorn. Besides, he found himself unable to quite put from his mind the memory of stabbing Quare as he slept, how his victim had woken as the blade pierced him from behind and had writhed against him in the dim moonlight; how the serving wench, awakened by the struggle, had stared at him over Quare's shoulder and given him a lascivious wink, misinterpreting entirely what was going on in her bed, though that error had saved her life, appealing as it had to his sense of humour, and to a baser sense as well, so that he had finished by giving her a piercing of a different sort from what he had originally intended. That had been the beginning, rather than, as he'd had every right to expect, the end of his acquaintance with Quare, and here he was still bound to the man, or a part of him.

No, he would not be so quick now to strike another sleeper, still less in the presence of the watch, which, he was convinced, had somehow warded death from Quare that night, and, for all he knew, though he very much hoped and prayed otherwise, was continuing to keep him alive even now.

The truth was, he needed Starkey. Whatever the Morecockneyan was personally – thief, spy, and worse, no doubt – he was also the ambassador of the King Beneath the Ground, and it would not do to poison relations with that monarch by an intemperate murder. When the time came, his subterranean soldiers would be indispensable, boiling up from London's netherworld in their thousands like an army of enraged ants to sow terror and death among the city's defenders. No, Starkey must live . . . for now.

But that did not mean he had to leave temptation dangling above the man like an apple ripe for the plucking. He tucked the handkerchief back into his sleeve and lurched to his feet, clinging tightly with one hand to a thin wooden bar set into the side of the jouncing carriage. His legs meanwhile sought in vain the reassurance of solid ground, calf and thigh muscles shifting, balancing and rebalancing his weight with every minute jolt and swerve, toes clenching within his boots as if he might, cat-like, extrude claws to anchor himself in place. His stomach rolled unpleasantly, feeling itself quite literally at sea, for the organs of the body have their own memories, independent of the mind, and the horror of his Channel crossings lay like a shipwreck at the bottom of his belly, stirred anew by any and all currents of similar sickly sensation.

Yet Aylesford persevered, reaching with his free hand for the netting affixed to the ceiling above Starkey's nodding head. The damn thing was fastened with knots he could not in his present state unravel, so, with mounting frustration, not thinking clearly, if at all, and possessed by a sudden frantic need, as if his prize were about to be stolen from him, lost for ever, he tore at the netting, ripping it open.

The sack tumbled free before he could grab it. It struck Starkey upon the head, knocking his tricorn to the floor and waking him most rudely. He came spluttering to his feet, in the process bringing the crown of his newly bared head into collision with the bottom of

Aylesford's jaw, with the result that both men cried out in shock, confusion, and pain, and fell back like bruised boxers onto their respective benches. The sack lay between them on the floor.

Aylesford saw it, and wished to claim it, but his body would not obey the promptings of his will. Thus it was Starkey who, gathering his wits, reached first for his hat and then for the sack, placing the former back upon his head and settling the latter on his knees.

'Bloody 'ell, Aylesford,' he said, glaring at him. 'Could yer not wait till we stopped ter change 'orses?'

''Tis the fault o' the damned driver,' he complained . . . or tried to. But what slurred from his lips bore little resemblance to these words, or, indeed, any other.

'Yer bleedin' like a stuck pig,' Starkey informed him, not without satisfaction.

Aylesford realized belatedly that it was so: he had bitten his tongue. Blood was filling his mouth, had already dripped upon his jacket and the carriage floor. Leaning forward, he spat onto the floor, then drew the scented handkerchief from his sleeve and pressed it to his lips to staunch the flow.

'Just 'ad ter check the time, did yer?' Starkey asked tauntingly. ''Ere – take it. The bloody relic do make my skin crawl.' He tossed the sack none too gently to the bench beside Aylesford, where it landed with a heavy thump. Aylesford clutched it to his side like a treasure as Starkey, stretching out his legs again, and pulling his hat down over his eyes once more, continued, 'Now do me a favour and let me sleep in peace, eh? Yer could stand ter do the same. Yer sleeve's lookin' a mite ravelled.'

'What?' he managed to reply, though his tongue seemed to have swollen to twice its normal size, and throbbed painfully besides. 'What about my sleeve?' He eyed the arm of his coat dubiously.

'God 'elp us,' came Starkey's voice from under the hat. 'Do yer not know *Macbef* – a countryman o' yours. "Sleep, what knits up the ravelled sleeve o' care, the death o' each day's life, sore labour's bath, balm o' 'urt minds, great nature's second course, chiefest nourisher in life's feast."'

Aylesford gave a dismissive grunt. He did not much care for

poetry. Nor did he know this Macbeth fellow. Englishmen always assumed that all Scotsmen were acquainted with each other, as if the country that lay to their north were no more populous than a hamlet.

Starkey almost immediately began to snore again.

The carriage bounced onward.

Aylesford's anxiety dissipated now that he had his prize safely in hand. Calm descended, and the sharp discomfort of his bitten tongue faded to a dull pulsation, the pain still there but distant, muffled, he thought, as if by one of those devilish London fogs that drew a thick curtain between the senses and what they perceived, turning the familiar city into a place only half real, or rather wafting it midway between two realities, the old city fraying apart, the new one not yet assembled. He had wandered those sepulchral fogs, shivering yet numb, sights and sounds alike seeming to coalesce out of the mists and sink back into them like the visitations of a waking dream.

That fog was inside him now. Drowsiness stole over him, as welcome as it was unexpected, for he had thought sleep beyond his grasp. Yet he grasped it now, or it grasped him; in any case, Aylesford felt himself drifting off. The weight of the sack reassured with its solidity; its warmth exuded a soothing balm that radiated throughout his body, for he had shifted it to his lap, and he stroked it idly now, as if it were a cat, and heard, or seemed to hear, as much as felt, the soft and gentle rumble of what might have been purring.

Or perhaps he was already asleep. Yes, surely he slept, for he no longer felt the rough road grinding beneath the wheels of the carriage but instead seemed to be reclining upon cushiony swells of smoke. All around him the tops of buildings poked above an eddying grey mass that stretched as far as he could see, a stony archipelago set amidst an ocean of cloud. Over his head the stars shone like sparks flung from a black cat's fur, and the moon was a bright ivory claw poised to disembowel the world. Was this London? Or some other city? He could not say.

The buildings that rose out of the fog were chalk-white or weathered grey, like grave markers or the standing stones one occasionally saw in the countryside, monuments raised by peoples otherwise lost to history, for purposes equally lost – whether tombs or temples or something else entirely, there was no knowing, though superstitious country folk termed them the work of fairies or devils or Druids.

They were blank, utterly without ornament save what wind and rain had carved there, and lacked as well any visible openings, no doors or windows. No way in or out. And they listed at odd angles that disturbed his mind, like the ruins of an alien geometry. *Nay*, he thought, *this is nae London.*

He was moving through this strange city, which was as quiet and still as a cemetery, and possessed as well the abiding sense of watchfulness characteristic of such places, as if there were something here that merely tolerated, and but briefly and suspiciously, the trespass of the living. It was, he felt, a dead city, a necropolis. Or perhaps a city not yet born. Yet he was not afraid, or anyway not in the normal sense of that word; he felt both insignificant and set apart, as if he had been chosen for some important task, a task beyond human strength but which he might nonetheless accomplish with the aid of powers greater than human. It was a curious sensation, to feel at once as lowly as a bug and yet exalted above all other bugs in the eyes of something whose existence was too grand for his perceptions or even his thoughts to encompass.

His passage through the fog quickened, and he realized suddenly that this was no random drifting on idle currents but instead a purposeful progress. He glanced down at the cushions on which he reclined like some pasha's guest and saw without surprise, as if it could not possibly have been otherwise, that they were not cushions at all. They were cats. A river of cats, thick and deep and swiftly coursing. They seemed fashioned of fog themselves, yet separate from it, coalescing out of what lay ahead and deliquescing into what was left behind, so that it was as if he rode upon the crest of a wave that brought itself into being as it rolled forward, its existence inseparable from that movement. The cats raced through the necropolis as though following paths concealed beneath the fog, turning sharply here, more gently there, now ascending, now descending, always in an effortless glide. The patter of so many paws was like steady rain on a thatched roof, and their purring was the wind.

Aylesford felt like a shipwrecked sailor borne towards an unknown shore, an obscure offering of the sea to the land. It did not occur to him that he might drown – or whatever passed for drowning here. He had forgotten that he was asleep and dreaming, but the conviction that he was being preserved for another fate insulated him from apprehension and fear.

At last they left the maze of bone-like slabs and entered what struck him as a kind of central square. The buildings, or whatever they were, tilted haphazardly on all sides, but here was a clearing, like a wide lake in the midst of a city, where the fog pooled, thick as pudding, or so it seemed to him, for the speed of his passage gradually slowed, and he felt an increasing resistance, as if the wave on which he rode had all but exhausted its impetus and was being dragged back by a countervailing force, just as ocean waves stretch moonward even as the jealous earth claws them back.

Ahead loomed another wave, dwarfing his own. It rose out of the mists like a mountain. Aylesford craned his head but could not see the top of it; it seemed to be of the same substance as the night, as if it were a pillar supporting the sky, or the trunk of a tree whose branches were the heavens. At first he thought it was rushing towards him, and he knew that there could be no escaping or surviving that encounter. The knowledge did not leave him fearful or despairing, however. Instead, he felt a strange satisfaction, as if it would be a kind of consummation to expire at the base of that immensity, to prostrate himself there as a willing sacrifice, his blood feeding the roots. But then he realized with a jolt that the towering shape was not moving at all – that his perceptions had been knocked askew by the sheer size of it.

Nor was he moving any longer. The cats that had carried him so far on their fluid backs circled beneath him, rocking him on gentle swells. They began to mew and cry like hungry kittens importuning an aloof and uninterested mother.

And she – or at any rate something – answered, in a voice like an avalanche that shattered everything he was or had thought himself to be. The voice smashed his flesh to pulp and ground his bones to paste. Then built him up again, not gently but with rough urgency

– almost, he might have said, in the blink of an eye, had he a voice to say it, or an eye to blink – as if time were of the essence and the sculptor shaping him anew from the primordial clay of his former being was executing a quick study for a later work to be undertaken in a finer medium, at greater leisure, when the opportunity presented itself.

'Rise to me, Thomas Aylesford,' said the voice – which spoke to him as he thought God himself might speak. It was not a soothing voice, nor was it seductive. It was hard and deep, as free of love and pity as the night or the moon whose ivory sliver gleamed overhead. But it compelled his submission. And more. For he felt again, intensified a thousandfold, the desire to sacrifice himself, to pour himself out like a libation. Only in that way, it seemed, could he express the violent feelings of awe, reverence, and desire that filled him to overflowing.

Aylesford had, a handful of times in his life, experienced the power of love to exalt and inspire. This was the first time he had experienced its power to annihilate. The hopelessness of his feelings, the unbridgeable gulf between them and their object, inflicted an exquisite misery, so that, as he climbed to his feet in obedience to the summons, he wept openly, without shame or restraint. He wept as a cut man bleeds.

To stand would have struck him a moment ago as impossible, absurd, yet now he did so with ease, feeling as though he were balancing on a surface at once rippling and solid, like water that manifested simultaneously the properties of liquid and ice. The ticklish glide of the cats beneath his bare feet goaded him to climb. (Yes, his feet were bare, and his body likewise exposed, though whether it had always been so, and he had only just now noticed, or, on the contrary, his clothing had melted away like fog in the instant of his rising, it did not occur to him to wonder. Nor did it seem strange or, for that matter, shameful that his cock was hard, pointing upward like a compass needle drawn ineluctably north.) He lifted one foot, and the empty space thus created was immediately occupied by a cat that offered its sleek back to him in dignified silence, like a footman proffering a stool, and bore his weight without complaint. He stepped up, and another cat slid smoothly into the place awaiting it.

Up he climbed, up and up a stairway of cats that arched their backs beneath his feet as if his weight were a welcome caress. Below him the pale slabs of the city dwindled to dots all but indistinguishable from the stars. Though he was normally not sure-footed in high places, Aylesford trod this narrow way with confidence, feeling the tug of the voice that had called him, though it had not spoken again. It seemed to him that he was in the grip of its gravity and would not have fallen had he strayed off the path. The voice, or the sovereign will behind it, would have buoyed him up. That and his own desire, which strained ever upward, as though his cock had sprouted wings and might lift him off his feet and carry him through the air, impatient with the slow pace of his mounting. He felt himself trembling on the edge of a release too shattering for flesh and bone to endure . . . yet he ached for that release with everything in him. He had been changed into something new, destroyed and born again by the touch of that voice, baptized afresh in his own tears. Now he climbed as if towards a wedding that would seal his transformation for all time.

At last he reached the top of the mountain, a flat expanse, shrouded in fog, from which rose a circle of twelve stones such as he had wondered at below. These were not as large as those had been, though they were taller than he was, and wider; the space between them was wider, too, like gateways through which a column of men could have marched four or five abreast. They were shaped curiously, as though modelled after the figures of some language or numeric system he did not know. Afloat in the air above them, at their very centre, was a silver orb that shone with a pale, flat, wintry light. It hung there as motionless as the moon; or, no, not motionless, exactly, for as he drew closer he saw ripples passing over its surface, as if it were a drop of dew suspended in a spider's web and trembling to every breeze and footfall, however faint. It was, he knew somehow, alive and alert, and its attention was fixed on him like the regard of an unblinking eye.

He felt ravished by that gaze. It ripped his scanty defences away until his soul stood as naked as his body. There was no part of

31

him, no secret shame or base lust or ignoble act, no fond memory or lofty ambition, no hope or regret or joy, that was not known to the predatory intelligence residing in that orb or eye. It did not judge him. It invaded him. Possessed him. He felt himself to be a part of something immeasurably greater than he was, an entity that contained multitudes yet hungered for more, like a perverse cornucopia that did not share its plenty but instead would swallow everything in the world, and the world itself, before it was appeased. As it had swallowed him.

But it was bliss to be so swallowed. Never had he known such happiness, such sweet fulfilment! Never had he rejoiced, body and soul, in the throes of an earthly embrace as he did in this celestial one. Yet release was denied him. He could not move, could not breathe. It was as if a fist had constricted around him, or the coils of a serpent.

Trembling in that grasp, every nerve afire, he watched as a shadow crept across the silver-blue orb like an eclipse eating the face of the moon. It flowed in a slow, viscous darkening that struck him as akin to the upwelling of blood from a deep wound. A sudden image surfaced in Aylesford's mind, so clear that it might have been engraved upon his eyeballs, of Quare's blood oozing from beneath the pale curve of his shoulder blade, black as bile in the moonlight. And that image led to another: Quare's severed hand lying upon the ground, blood pooling from the stump of the wrist, fingers locked about the hunter in death's stubborn rigor.

It was then, with the force of a revelation arrived at by a chain of association rather than logic, that Aylesford understood he was not dreaming. That the watch had worked a kind of enchantment upon him and pulled him into itself. That the hunter held him now as tightly in its grasp as the fingers of Quare's hand held the hunter.

The orb afloat above the twisted pillars – the watch gripped in the fingers of a hand that was neither alive nor dead by any common measure of those words – appeared engorged with blood. It leaked a light that stained everything crimson.

Even the voice that now returned, crashing down like thunder, seemed awash in blood. 'You have climbed high, Thomas Aylesford,' it said. 'Higher still shall you climb in my service. Do you know me? Answer!'

'Are ye God?' Aylesford had dropped to his knees. His voice sounded small and tremulous in his ears.

'I am your god,' the thunder replied, more softly now, a rolling grumble across the sky. 'And you will be my prophet. For this you have been chosen above all others.'

'Nae *all* others,' he protested like a petulant child. 'Ye chose Quare afore me.'

'Daniel Quare served his purpose, as will you.'

'What purpose?'

'To carry the ark of my covenant like a scythe amid the battlefields of the Earth and reap a rich harvest there.'

'The ark . . . Do ye mean the watch?'

'The hunter, yes.'

'What is it?' he asked, appending the word 'Lord' somewhat tardily as a roil of darker red in the depths of the orb made him suddenly afraid of angering his divine interlocutor.

'Death to all that lives,' the thunder answered. 'And life eternal to what dies. It is my shell, my armour, my self. It is a hammer. A doorway. An egg. An eye. It is all things, Thomas Aylesford, as I am. What was, is, and shall be.'

'But what o' Scotland, Lord?' he could not forbear asking. 'Do ye not mean tae aid us in our fight against England? It is for that purpose as I was dispatched tae find ye and bring ye back tae France.'

'Speak not to me of the petty purposes of mortal men!' the thunder said, and the mountain trembled as if in fear. 'My purpose is all that concerns you now. You say you found me? It is you who were found. You think to bring me? It is you who are brought.'

'But why me, Lord?' he persisted. 'Why not Quare or another?'

'There is a hunger in you like a faint echo of my own. It has carved you out, Thomas Aylesford, made you a fit vessel for my purpose. Serve me well, and great shall be your reward, an eternity spent at the highest pitch of love's groaning ecstasy. Let the merest touch of my love sear itself into your memory now and burn there undimmed through the days to come, lighting your way forward even in the blackest and bleakest hours.'

At that, the sphere bulged and burst like a bubo. A dark torrent of blood gushed forth, cascading over Aylesford's head and body. It was warm and alive, a wet and velvety caress, like the inside of a woman. It stank of generation. He felt embraced by it, stroked and squeezed, and his seed erupted out of him, less an explosion of his need than an expression called forth by a need greater than his own, as if this moment of ecstasy beyond anything he had ever known or imagined was but a drop in an infinite ocean. The force of it knocked him down, swept him away, carried him down the mountainside he had so laboriously climbed.

He woke with a start to sounds of braying laughter.

At first he could not orient himself. Everything seemed strange, unreal. Starkey's mottled face leered at him from across the carriage.

'Ter sleep, perchance ter dream,' Starkey choked out amid gales of laughter. 'Aye, there's the rub! Fer in that sleep o' death, what dreams may come?'

The Morecockneyan laid stress on the last word, pointing to Aylesford's lap, where, indeed, Aylesford had become aware of a cool dampness. Looking down he saw a stain, as if he had pissed himself. But of course it was not that.

'Aye,' repeated Starkey. 'There's the rub!' And was overtaken by mirth again, nearly sliding from his bench to the carriage floor.

Aylesford, meanwhile, flushing with mortification, snatched up the sack containing the hand and the hunter, which had at some point tumbled from his lap to the floor. As he settled it back onto his lap, hiding the stain, he felt its heat, like that of a cat which has basked all morning in a sunbeam.

Starkey rallied himself for another sally. 'Aylesford, yer ol' goat yer, I've 'ad me share o' 'and jobs in me day, many a quick rub an' tug in the shadows topside and below, but it 'as always been me practice in such matters o' the 'eart ter first make certain o' the presence o' a lady at t'other end o' the 'and!'

'Go tae the devil, Starkey.'

'Why, it would seem you 'ave been there before me! Or, rather, been visited by a devil, a succubus such as do 'aunt the dreams o' men betimes. What were she like, eh? Tell us, Aylesford, ol' boy. Were she cloaked as a angel o' light, as the Bible do say? Or did she dress 'erself in a more earthly raiment? Did she come as a nymph o' the forest, dappled o'er in shadow, or were she like a slattern o' the streets, painted and rouged as a corpse all prettified by the undertaker's art?'

'Ye would nae understand,' Aylesford answered with a kind of lofty and dignified anger, clutching the sack close as if for comfort. 'I've been chosen. To be a prophet. God has a mission for me.'

'More like an emission, if yer ask me,' Starkey said with a chuckle.

'Ye'll see,' Aylesford insisted, glowering, filled with righteous conviction. 'The whole world will see.'

'I 'ope not,' said Starkey, tilting the tricorn over his eyes again. 'I seen too bloody much already.'

At the next coaching inn, while the horses were being changed out, Aylesford and Starkey took a quick meal of bread, cheese, sausage slices, and small beer in the common room. They ate in silence, like two travellers thrust together by chance, each occupied with his own thoughts. Three other men breaking their journey and their fast at the inn, who introduced themselves as London-bound merchants – by which Aylesford understood 'smugglers' – attempted to engage them in conversation, but a few words from Starkey discouraged them as thoroughly as if he had set a loaded pistol down upon the table.

'And where might you gentlemen hail from?' This from a pink-faced, rotund man of middle years who had spread a large white handkerchief over his ample bosom as he dismembered a roast chicken with thumbs and forefingers only, his remaining digits widely distended, giving him the look of a finicky crab.

'One from across the water,' said Starkey. 'T'other from beneath the ground.'

In the ensuing silence, Starkey continued with his meal as if blithely ignorant of having cast a pall over the room, but Aylesford grew increasingly uncomfortable with the curious and, if he were not imagining things, fearful glances cast in their direction, which nevertheless seemed invested with a component of cold calculation, as if the three men, each in his own way, were figuring up a calculus of risk and reward involving the two of them, as well as the sack conspicuously placed at Aylesford's feet, which, for all they knew, might contain gold or other riches . . . as it did, though not of a sort they would have rejoiced to find.

His appetite gone, Aylesford picked up his hat, lifted the sack, and left the inn. The carriage was ready, the new horses harnessed, the driver – a lump of a man called Prowls, whose puffy face had the look of a rice pudding, and who had proved thus far as talkative as one – was leaning back on his perch, one leg extended, enjoying a pipe. He touched the brim of his straw hat at the sight of Aylesford but did not otherwise bestir himself. Aylesford nodded and settled onto the carriage step to wait for Starkey.

He was impatient to be gone from this place. Now that he had been awakened to the true value of what he carried, he was tormented by the sense that it was the cynosure of every eye, and that all who saw the sack schemed to take it from him. He cradled it in his arms like a swaddled infant. Aylesford wished to protect what Starkey, with more justice than he knew, had christened 'the relic', to hide it away where only he might gaze upon it in its naked glory. Yet at the same time, he felt a strong urge to display it, to pull it from the sack and brandish it like a club or, no, a cross, to preach to Prowls, the horses, the courtyard, the scraps of grey cloud scudding across the sky like foam blown across a beach, the sky itself, or the birds that flew there, the way Saint Francis had done.

He shivered, remembering his bath of blood and ecstasy. How, he wondered, could he rekindle that self-obliterating, transporting, transcendent joy? Could he coax it forth with a touch, or with whatever honeyed words might spill from his lips as he preached of death and eternal life? The words of the thunder still echoed within him, instructing him in the great task for which he had been chosen: *to carry the ark of my covenant like a scythe amid the battlefields of the Earth and reap a rich harvest there.* He did not think that echo would ever fade. But how was he to accomplish his mission? How to win converts to his cause? He had always been a man of action, not words; any eloquence he possessed lay in his sword, not his tongue. Yet now he had been called to preach and prophesy. *You have climbed high, Thomas Aylesford. Higher still shall you climb in my service.* He strained within himself, seeking some hint of what he must do, some living ember of that sublime vision, or visitation, rather, which he could fan back to blazing. And there it was in his memory, undimmed in recollection yet far off, like a distant but steadfast star by which a storm-tossed mariner might steer his ship safely home. He would put his faith in that star and follow its shine wherever it might lead, whether to Bethlehem or to Bedlam.

At last Starkey emerged from the inn, loudly clearing his throat and spitting to one side as he approached the carriage. Aylesford stood.

'What did ye mean by inviting the speculation of those men?' he asked with some asperity when Starkey was still a way off.

Starkey spat again and grinned. 'I did nothin' o' the sort,' he protested, spreading his hands.

' "One from across the water, the other from beneath the ground,"' Aylesford repeated in a supercilious tone. 'Do ye nae think such enigmatic words might excite rather than discourage attention?'

'I been travellin' back and forth betwixt London and 'astin's fer many a year, Aylesford. I fink I know wot ter say by now.' He strode past Aylesford and rapped his knuckles sharply on the side of the carriage. 'Time ter be off, Prowls.'

'Aye, sir,' said Prowls, though he did not so much as twitch an eyebrow.

Starkey opened the carriage door and gestured for Aylesford to precede him. Aylesford stooped as he entered, cradling the sack in his arms. He settled himself on the bench as Starkey entered behind him and swung the door closed, then took a seat opposite. The carriage jolted into motion. Starkey removed his tricorn and placed it on the bench beside him, then leaned forward.

'Yer a stranger 'ere, Aylesford,' he declared. 'Yer don't speak the lingo. Those men wasn't askin' where we 'ailed from. They wasn't lookin' ter pass the time o' day in idle conversation over a glass o' beer. It weren't by chance that they 'appened ter be there at the inn when we arrived. They was soundin' us out, like. Testin' us, so ter speak. We might be innercent travellers. We might be customs men. Or we might be in the smugglin' business our own selfs. This coast may be part o' England on a map, but it's a sight more complercated on the ground. It's the gangs wot rules 'ere, Aylesford, old son. The 'awkhursts and the 'adleighs and all the rest o' the great smugglin' confraternities. Such men 'ave no more love for King George than you or meself, for 'is laws and taxes do trample upon their ancient freedoms. I told 'em you was no friend o' the king, and thus no enemy o' theirs, and that I be under the seal and pertection o' the King Beneaf the Ground, wifout 'ose friendship the flow o' goods ter London would slow ter a trickle or dry up altogether.'

Aylesford listened to this lecture with mounting annoyance. 'It's the king above the ground I'm worried about,' he grumbled. 'I left behind a gaggle o' dead lordlings in London, if ye recall, on the floor o' the Pig and Rooster. There are those who would pay handsomely for my capture. Nor is the Worshipful Company apt tae be so easily resigned tae the loss o' the hunter – especially since I did for one o' theirs into the bargain. Sure it is that there are regulators looking for me even now – looking for the two o' us.'

'No doubt. But where are they lookin', eh? Not 'ere. We'll be out o' the country and across the water afore they fink ter look outside London. And when next we set foot on these shores, it will be wif an army at our backs.' As he spoke, Starkey pulled a clay pipe from his coat pocket and filled it with tobacco from a pouch similarly produced. Now, sitting back, he kindled the pipe to life and puffed contentedly. 'Besides, if yer so worried about attractin' unwanted attention, why d'yer keep luggin' that sack around? Nobody wot sees it can 'elp wonderin' wot's inside, and the fact that you never let it out o' yer sight could lead a person ter conclude it's worth stealin', whatever it might be.'

'I should like tae see anyone try,' Aylesford said. 'They wouldn't get far.'

'But why tempt fate? Stow it in yer trunk till we reach Frog Land. The fewer wot sees it and wonders, the better.'

'Yes, ye'd like that, wouldn't ye, Starkey?'

'Wot d'yer mean? 'Course I'd like it. I said so, didn't I?'

'I mean ye'd like nothing better than to take it for yourself. I've seen how ye look at it.'

At this, Starkey belched smoky laughter. 'Take it for meself?

'Gorblimey! I'd sooner cut me own 'and off than touch that bloody relic! Why, it's made you daft, it 'as! Just look at yer, clutchin' it like a miser clutchin' a bag o' gold!'

'It's worth far more than gold,' Aylesford said. 'It's the ark o' a new covenant.'

'It's talk like that wot puts notions in people's 'eads.'

'If I could but show ye—'

'I seen enough! More than enough! Did I not see it glowin' all spectral like in Quare's 'and? And did I not see that poor sod's expression after yer cut 'is 'and off? I won't soon forget the look o' blessed relief wot came over them tortured features once 'e were separated from that lodestone. I'll be seein' it in my dreams, I will. Nightmares, more like.'

'Daniel Quare was not worthy tae bear the hunter. He was but an instrument, a delivery boy.'

'And yer not? One minute yer accuse me o' 'avin' designs upon it, the next yer want ter show it ter me like a father showin' off 'is first-born son. Get a grip on yerself, man. 'Ave a smoke. Yer too wound up.'

This choice of words struck Aylesford as so apt that he could not forbear chuckling with satisfaction. Yes, he was wound up. He was a timepiece gripped in God's hand. And really, wasn't that true of all men?

Aye, we are all hunters in our way, he thought, deeply pleased to have realized it. *Our workings are flesh and blood instead o' gears and oil, but we are made to measure out a span o' time. Why, the timepieces we take such pride in are made in our own image, if we but knew it! And as we glance at them to situate ourselves by hour and minute, like ships at sea marking their position with a sextant, so, too, do greater eyes than our own regard us, taking measurements we canna comprehend, for purposes we canna imagine!*

Starkey was regarding him warily, the pipe clenched in the corner of his mouth. 'What's the joke, Aylesford, eh?'

'Ye shall see it soon enough,' Aylesford contented himself with replying. 'The whole world shall see.'

It was evening when they reached Hastings. It was hard for Aylesford to believe that this small fishing village, with its scattering of drab homes and businesses set along narrow, twisting streets that rose from a shingle beach, and which seemed to have been deposited above that beach by a particularly high and loathsome tide some aeons previously, was one of the most notorious smuggling centres in Sussex. But Starkey assured him that such was indeed the case.

'Fisher folk by day, smugglers by night,' he said as the carriage pulled to a stop in the lane before a dilapidated-looking inn whose weathered clapboard sign featured the head of a regally antlered stag that appeared to have been rendered by an artist who had never seen the real thing. 'Just like men, towns and cities 'ave their secret lives, wot go on out o' sight o' the sun, whether underground or under cover o' night.'

'I suppose every man is a bit o' a smuggler when it comes down tae it,' mused Aylesford, still in a reflective state of mind. 'Either that or a spy. We all have secret lives, secret selves.'

'Some more than others,' Starkey observed significantly. 'These be prickly folk, Aylesford. Surspicious like, and wif good reason. Keep yer trap shut tight an' that sack o' yers shut tighter. Don't be waggin' yer tongue nor wavin' the relic about. Yer called yerself a prophet – fair enough. But this ain't the place ter start preachin'. Yer won't win no converts 'ere. Be strung up, more like, and me wif yer.'

'So much for the protection o' the King Beneath the Ground,' sneered Aylesford.

'Not even the King Beneaf the Ground can protect a man from the conserquences o' 'is own stupidity.'

'I know my duty,' Aylesford rejoined stiffly.

'Glad ter 'ear it,' Starkey said.

The inside of the Stag Inn outdid its rundown exterior. The common room was small and low-ceilinged, crammed with nautical bric-a-brac haphazardly arranged in nooks and crannies like salvage from a hundred shipwrecks. Indeed, the room – the inn itself, for that matter – listed to one side as though it were a ship run aground. The air roiled with malodorous smoke from fat tallow candles set upon narrow tables and from the pipes of three ancient topers there assembled, who seemed to be puffing, with no pleasure whatsoever, on seaweed rather than tobacco. This grim-faced trio gazed at Aylesford and Starkey with cold, slate-grey eyes in which there was not a scintilla of welcome. A miserly fire did not so much banish the damp as hold it at arm's length. Nor did the smoke banish the smells of brine and tarry resin oozing from the dark wood of the ceiling, floor, and walls. The atmosphere was in every sense a combustible one, thought Aylesford.

But Starkey evinced no apprehension or hesitation. "Oo died, eh?' he queried the closed faces arrayed against them like a gathering of gargoyles. 'Ain't we all old friends 'ere?'

'Not all,' growled one of the men, whose deeply lined face seemed unused to even the minimal movements of the mouth occasioned by these words.

'Who's your mate, then, eh, Starkers?' asked another, loquacious by comparison.

'Why, this is Mr Aylesford, 'ose comin' were foretold,' said Starkey with easy jocularity. Then, seeing the unchanged expressions that greeted this sally, he added more seriously: 'Did not a messenger from 'is Majesty precede us?'

The men exchanged glances. Cups were raised to lips and lowered as if at some unspoken signal. The third man, the eldest of the group, his face as clenched as a barnacle, leaned to one side and spat thickly into the low-crawling flames of the fire. A fierce sizzling erupted, as quickly subsided. 'Been no messenger here from your king,' he said in a voice like the squeak of a rusty hinge. "Twas our own men brought news o' your comin'.'

'From the inn where we changed 'orses, no doubt,' said Starkey in an aside to Aylesford. Then, addressing their interlocutors again: 'Mr Aylesford and meself are bound for France, gentlemen, on business o' the King Beneaf the Ground and 'is royal brother across the water.'

'Wot, the old sot?' asked the second man who had spoken, to a chorus of laughter from the others . . . or what Aylesford supposed was laughter, a low, phlegmy rumble. 'Boozy Prince Charlie?'

This was too much for Aylesford. 'Ye are speaking o' your rightful king, sir,' he said, baring his teeth in a feral grin. 'Mayhap ye require a lesson in manners.'

The phlegmy rumble went once more around. Once again cups were raised and lowered.

'Mayhap we do,' the barnacle said after another judicious expectoration had been cooked by the flames. 'But it won't be you what delivers it, snippersnapper.'

The sack in his arms prevented Aylesford from drawing his sword with his customary speed, and before he could complete the action, three more men entered the room from the recesses of the inn, swords at the ready. Two were stout fellows of middle years, while the third was a bare-faced youth Aylesford judged to be his own age, if not younger.

'Let's not get 'asty,' said Starkey at this development, stepping in front of Aylesford. 'As yer can tell by 'is speech, Mr Aylesford 'ails from Scotland, so it's no wonder 'e's a mite sensitive on the subject o' the Stuarts.'

'Stuart or Hanover, it don't matter a fig to us,' declared the barnacle. 'We be freeborn Englishmen here and don't bend the knee to any Earthly power. But we knows you well enough, Starkers. If you vouch for this man, we'll take you at your word.'

'I do vouch fer 'im. And what's more, so does 'is Majesty.'

'Fairly spoken. And what of you, Mr Aylesford?'

'Me?' inquired Aylesford.

'An apology would not come amiss.'

He bristled. 'Why, I—'

Starkey's elbow jabbed him in the ribs.

'I meant no offence,' he continued through gritted teeth, wishing them all dead. 'I do crave your pardon.'

'You have it,' the barnacle replied, then inclined his head towards an empty table. 'Sit ye down, sirs. Have a drink and tell us what brings ye here.'

'Wif pleasure,' said Starkey. 'I 'ope yer will permit me ter top off yer glasses.'

'I would not decline,' squeaked the barnacle. 'Boxer, a bottle.' And the youngest of the three men who had entered with swords drawn withdrew into the shadows that had spawned him.

'Aylesford, allow me ter introduce our 'osts,' said Starkey in his former expansive style. 'This ancient an' sagacious relic' – indicating the barnacle with a tilt of his head – 'do go by the cognermen o' Nasty Face. There beside 'im is Stick-in-the-mud. And the third o' these wise men be Ol' Oatmeal.'

Aylesford, not sure how to respond to such outlandish monikers, merely bowed.

At this point, Boxer returned with bottle in hand.

'Boxer yer know already,' continued Starkey, and the lad gave a toothy, guileless smile as he refilled the cups of the three seated men; his hands, Aylesford noticed, were the size of small hams. 'T'other two be Towzer and Butcher Tom.'

Aylesford sketched another bow. 'Thomas Aylesford,' he said.

'What d'ye have in that sack, then, Scottish Tom?' inquired Nasty Face.

'Now, Nasty,' said Starkey before Aylesford could reply, 'yer know what they do say about curiosity and the cat.'

'A cat, is it?' rejoined Nasty Face. 'That what ye got there, Scottish Tom? Not too lively, by the looks o' it.'

'Mayhap 'tis sleepin',' said Stick-in-the-mud.

'Or dead,' opined Old Oatmeal.

'It's a 'and,' said Starkey.

Nasty Face, who had been leaning over to spit once more into the fire, swallowed audibly at this and sat up. 'Come again, Starkers?'

'A severed 'and,' Starkey went on. 'As it 'appens, the 'and o' the last man what asked too many questions about the contents o' that sack.'

A brief silence greeted this declaration before Nasty Face exploded in wheezy laughter, looking as if he might shake himself to pieces. Stick-in-the-mud and Old Oatmeal joined in heartily, while Boxer grinned with amiable idiocy and Towzer and Butcher Tom looked on impassively.

Starkey placed a firm hand on Aylesford's elbow and shepherded him with surprising force to an empty table. He guided him into a chair, then sat beside him. Aylesford kept a tight grip on the sack all the while, his eyes shifting about the room.

''Ow about that drink, Boxer, me lad?' Starkey continued unflappably.

Two tin cups were produced, filled, and passed to Starkey, who handed one to Aylesford. The smell of gin was almost enough to make him gag.

'Ter yer 'ealth, gentlemen,' said Starkey, raising his cup.

Aylesford's hand trembled as he followed suit. The three old men did likewise, echoing Starkey's toast. Then all drank. The liquor burned Aylesford's throat and delivered a mule kick to his heart. A dizzying vapour wafted upward into his brain, moistening his eyes as it drifted past. He felt the urge, after his apology, which he understood as a diplomatic necessity yet felt shamed by, to reassert his independence and manhood. He raised his cup. 'Tae the King Across the Water,' he said challengingly.

Starkey rolled his eyes but raised his cup, as, after the slightest hesitation, did the others.

'The King Across the Water,' came the ragged chorus.

The cups were drained and set upon their respective tables – Starkey drinking with relish and banging his cup down loudly, with a certain finality, while Nasty Face, Stick-in-the-mud, and Old Oatmeal did so with circumspection and delicacy, as if their cups were made of porcelain and not battered tin.

'Now then,' said Nasty Face, his voice scraped raw as a gypsy's fiddle, 'to business. What is it brings ye to Hastings, Starkers?'

'Right now I am more concerned wif what did *not* bring 'is Majesty's messenger 'ere afore us. D'yer fink 'e were waylaid upon the road?'

'Not by us he weren't,' said Nasty Face. 'Not if he were travellin' with the writ o' the King Beneath the Ground upon him. Could be it were some gentlemen o' the road what did not know or care about the arrangements and understandin's what binds us in eternal friendship to His Subterranean Majesty. Could be it were customs men or other agents o' the Crown, for they have been troublesome o' late, due to the boisterous spirits o' our Hawkhurst friends. If it be the latter, then your mission, Starkers, whatever it may be, is in jeopardy – and mayhap your lives as well.'

'The thought 'ad occurred ter me,' Starkey confessed glumly. 'A French lugger lies off the coast, waitin' fer a signal ter draw near.

But if the messenger ain't got through, the signal ain't been given, which means there ain't time enough ter give it and get away – not tonight.' He sighed, drumming the fingers of one hand upon the table top. 'It appears as we must beg the 'ospitality o' the 'ouse fer a day, Nasty.'

'This be a ticklish business right enough,' said Nasty Face. He spat into the fire, then contemplated the result with close attention as his compatriots nodded in slow approbation, making Aylesford wonder if this were not some odd method of divination: expectoromancy.

'Ye can stay a day, but no longer,' Nasty Face proclaimed at last. 'I do not wish to be drawn more deeply into whatever web is bein' spun betwixt the King Beneath the Ground and his brother across the water. The affairs o' kings are beyond the ken o' such small folk as our humble selves. All we ask is to be left alone. Yet in times like these, when war do raise its bloody head, a man must choose, it do seem. Very well – we will stand with those what respects our ancient rights and privileges, and allows us to worship as we will, like the King Beneath the Ground has sworn, and the Bonnie Prince, too. But we be no more than poor fisher folk here, Starkers. If King George do send his lobsters, well, then it be catch-as-catch-can.'

'Fair enough,' said Starkey. 'If yer will supply me wif a lantern, Nasty, I will go and signal now. Yer best stay 'ere, Aylesford – the less anyone sees o' yer mug, the better. I be known 'ereabouts, but yer a stranger and as such a topic o' interest and speculation, apt ter give rise ter rumour and gossip what might reach the wrong ears. If all goes well and the frogs signal back nice and proper like, then we shall go aboard tomorrow night.'

'Scottish Tom will be safe with us, never fear,' said Nasty Face. 'Here, Boxer, take a lantern and conduct Starkers to East Hill to do his business. I trust that will serve?'

'It will,' said Starkey. 'I'll send Prowls in as well, if yer don't mind. 'E's got a long ride back ter London and could use a bit o' refreshment and shut-eye.'

'The Creeper, is it? Send 'im in, send 'im in. I dare say ye could do with a bite yourself, eh, Scottish Tom?'

'I should be most grateful, er, Nasty Face,' Aylesford said sincerely.

'I'll send word for the boys to keep their eyes and ears open for any sign o' your missin' messenger,' Nasty Face added, addressing Starkey. 'Mayhap he'll turn up yet.'

'Aye, mayhap,' said Starkey, but his tone belied it.

After a meal of fish stew and small beer, Aylesford was led upstairs by Boxer to a closet of a room whose whitewashed walls appeared as lumpy as day-old porridge. Grey curtains cut from sailcloth imperfectly hid a window that looked out beyond the rear of the house, where, in daylight, Aylesford judged he would have been able to see the waters of the Channel. Now, in the light of the lamp that Boxer placed upon a wooden table to one side of the window, he saw only his own ghostly reflection distorted in the runny glass. A constant wind whistled by outside, and the curtains gave an occasional desultory flutter, like the wings of a weary albatross hunkered down on some forlorn spit of land.

'Best keep away from the window, sir,' advised Boxer, whose grin had not faltered in the brief time that Aylesford had known him and did not falter now. 'Ye never know when there might be customs men lurkin' about.'

'Why, one would think ye under siege here,' Aylesford said.

'Aye, and so we are, in a manner o' speakin'. But don't ye worry, sir. Granddad be too sharp for the likes o' them.'

'Ye're Nasty Face's grandson?'

'Aye,' he said proudly.

'And what o' your father?'

'Dead, sir. Drownded these seven year.'

'I'm sorry, Boxer.'

'He were a good man, but the sea do take her own.' Boxer lingered, his brown eyes glittering muddily in the lamplight. 'Be it true, sir? Be it really and truly a severed hand ye've got in that there sack like Mr Starkers did say?'

'Would ye like tae see for yourself?' he asked.

Boxer's pale complexion turned ruddy. 'Oh, I couldn't! Er, could I? I ain't never seen no severed hand before!'

'Not worried your own hand'll be forfeit if ye do?'

'That were just one o' Mr Starkers's japes . . . weren't it?'

Aylesford moved to a narrow pallet along one wall and sat there, settling the sack upon his lap. A mood had come over him to gratify Boxer's curiosity, but also to toy with the credulous bumpkin, as if the lad's fear might bolster his own courage. And in truth, the urge to gaze upon the contents of the sack himself had grown too strong to resist. He had felt it tugging at him for hours, as a corked bottle on the mantel might tug at a drunkard's sober resolve. He opened the sack, rummaged inside, then held up its edges in an inviting gesture. 'Come and look, then,' he said.

Boxer shuffled forward warily a few steps, then stopped. He craned his neck over the opening of the sack as though peering over the edge of an abyss. Yet even now his grin remained plastered upon his face. 'Crikey! Look at it! White as a mackie's belly it be! Here, what's that it's holdin'?'

'Can't ye see? Have a closer look.' And he lifted the sack towards Boxer, who drew back sharply.

'That were never alive!' he said, his grin now rather ghastly.

'It was,' Aylesford said. 'And what's more . . . it still is!'

'What d'yer mean, sir?' squeaked Boxer, whose voice had taken on a distinct resemblance to his grandsire's and who had retreated farther, as much as the close confines of the room allowed, and stood now as if poised to flee, his gaze shifting like that of a trapped animal between the sack and the open door.

Aylesford stood and reached into the sack. 'Let me show ye . . .'

'No thankee, sir!' No trace remained of Boxer's smile. 'I'd best be gettin' back downstairs!'

Even before he had finished speaking, he was out the door. Aylesford, who could hear his footsteps clattering down the stairs, fell back upon the pallet, laughing as heartily as he had in some time.

''Ere now. What d'yer mean by frightenin' that poor lad 'alf out o' 'is wits?'

Starkey stood frowning in the doorway, his face flushed.

''Twere all in good fun,' Aylesford said.

'Boxer be but a 'alf-wit ter begin with,' Starkey said, entering the room and shutting the door behind him. 'D'yer want ter leave 'im entirely witless? And I fought we'd agreed yer would not be wavin' that relic about until we was safely across the water.'

'I wasnae—' But he realized that, in fact, he had removed the hand after all and was cradling it in his arms. He hastily stuffed it back into the sack and got to his feet. 'Did ye signal the ship?' he asked to cover his embarrassment.

'Aye,' said Starkey. 'They'll swing in close ter shore tomorrow night. Nasty's boys'll row us out ter meet 'em. Till then, we be confined ter quarters, so ter speak. I do not like 'avin' ter wait like this, but it cannot be 'elped. I wisht I knowed what 'appened ter that blamed messenger!'

Aylesford shrugged. 'Don't worry, Starkey. We'll be fine.'

'That another o' yer prophecies, Scottish Tom?' he asked snidely.

'Scoff if ye like, but God speaks through the hunter. Aye, and acts, too. "Truly the signs o' an apostle were wrought among ye in all patience, in signs, in wonders, and in mighty deeds."'

'So yer an apostle now, is it? Ain't that a bit o' a promotion? What's next, eh? Pope? Or d'yer plan on startin' yer own religion like that Mahomet bloke?' Starkey removed his tricorn and tossed it negligently onto the table, then ran a hand over the tight coif of his brown hair, smoothing down the errant strands. His shadow leapt upon the lumpy white wall. 'Signs and wonders aplenty 'ave I seen, Aylesford, me lad, since we 'ave acquired that bloody relic, and none o' 'em good. Yer behaviour o' late is a cause o' concern, I don't mind sayin'. I seen men in thrall ter women, ter drink, ter all manner o' things, but this be the first time I 'ave seen a man in thrall ter a watch.'

'Bah,' said Aylesford irritably. 'Ye're just jealous that I have been chosen tae bear it. I warn ye, Starkey – the hunter is mine.'

'Is it now? I wonder what they will think about that in Frog Land. 'Ave yer fergot on 'ose be'alf, and fer what purpose, yer was sent ter England in the first place? Yer naught but a delivery boy, Aylesford me lad. That 'unter is destined fer other 'ands than yers.'

Aylesford blinked, taken aback. In fact, this detail had slipped his mind. But he recovered seamlessly. 'I serve the King Across the Water,' he said. 'The rightful king o' Scotland and the defender o' the one true faith. But we are all the servants o' a higher power, are we not, Starkey?'

'Speak fer yerself,' came the answer. 'I serve a lower one.'

'What d'ye mean? Are ye some kind o' devil-worshipper?'

Starkey laughed. He settled himself on the pallet that Aylesford had vacated, back propped against the wall, legs stretched out before him and crossed at the ankles. 'We Morecockneyans 'ave dwelled beneath London since afore the Great Fire. But we was not the first ter call them caverns and chasms 'ome. Our forebears did enter them dark places like trespassers come ter a city o' empty 'ouses. Aye, everywhere they ventured, they found signs o' others what 'ad been there afore 'em, people long vanished into the mists o' time. Or so they thought. But as they delved deeper, they found signs that p'raps them vanished folk were not so vanished after all, but were only 'idin', in the manner o' brownies and suchlike eldritch sprites as the ol' tales do tell of.'

'What, d'ye believe in fairy tales, Starkey?' Aylesford mocked.

''Oo is ter say what be real and what a fairy tale in a world where such things as that 'unter exist? But I do not speak o' pixies or gnomes, Aylesford, only o' flesh-and-blood men – men like yer 'n' I . . . yet more strange in their appearance and their ways than any Red Indian from the New World. The first Morecockneyans found these creatures deep beneath the ground, a 'ole civilersation, if yer want ter use the word, what 'ad lived down there since afore the time o' Caesar – aye, lived without sight o' the sun, wif only the golden light o' the mushrooms ter see by. Some did think them Druids. Others what came afore Druids. The truth be buried too deep ter be unburied now. But in time the two subterranean races met face ter face. We was interlopers, and they wanted us gone. Pitched battles was fought beneath the peaceful and unsuspectin' streets o' London. A 'ole bloody war were fought. At the end o' it, we conquered . . . and, in the way o' such things, was conquered in turn by them as we 'ad subdued. For they became our wives and 'usbands. Our blood mingled, that is ter say . . . and more than just blood. Yer see, they worshipped a god what was older than the Christian god. Older than any god above ground. And in the realm o' the everlastin', Aylesford, what exists first do 'ave precedence over all what comes after. That's 'oo I serve. The first and greatest god, the god from 'oom all other gods do descend, whether they – or their worshippers – knows it or not. And 'e ain't ter be found in 'eaven. No, nor in 'ell, neither, fer that be what yer seem ter be about ter say. 'Is kingdom be altogether otherwhere.'

'Does he have a name, this god o' yours?'

'Aye, but 'tis a name what cannot be profaned by bein' spoke ter 'eathens like yerself.'

'How then d'ye mean to convert me tae your faith?'

Starkey laughed. 'Why, 'e 'as no need o' converts! Yer already serve 'im, Aylesford, if yer but knew it. All men do.'

'A strange sort o' god, whose name cannae be spoken, and who seeks nae converts tae his cause. What sort o' priests does he have, I wonder. What sort o' churches? I should like tae attend one o' your services, Starkey. That must be a curious sight.'

'They ain't open ter the public.'

'But what are they like?'

'I can't say.'

'Not fit for the ears o' a heathen?'

'It ain't that. I ain't seen 'em.'

'What, never seen your own priests or your own churches?'

'Neither one. Yer see, Aylesford, the mysteries o' the faith ain't available ter just anyone. There is levels o' secret knowledge, depths o' revelation, like. A Morecockneyan might live 'is 'ole life and not learn more than what lies at the very surface, in the same way a topsider might spend 'is life in London without never suspectin' the kingdom what lies beneath 'is feet. There be a aristocracy belowground just as above, only it do extend in the opposite direction. Only them what 'ave dwelled beneath the ground for five generations be eligible fer admission inter the full mysteries. I were born below, and my parents afore me, but my grandfather were a topsider, and that do make me but third-generation Morecockneyan.'

'But how, then, have ye learned aught of your faith? How d'ye practise it?'

'There be missionaries sent up from below ter teach the rudiments o' the faith. And chapels o' sorts in which such rituals o' worship as 'ave been deemed suitable by the priests are conducted. Thus each new generation is shepherded deeper inter the mysteries, until they be judged ready ter descend ter the lowest level, the 'oly o' 'olies.'

'I shall keep my own god, I think,' said Aylesford. 'Not the lowest but the most high.'

'Does the Bible not say that 'e 'oo exalts 'imself shall be 'umbled, and 'e 'oo 'umbles 'imself shall be exalted?'

'That refers tae men, not tae God, as ye know right well.'

'A strange sort o' god what feels the need ter exalt 'imself above mere mortals! Why, 'e doth protest too much, methinks. 'E be 'idin' somethin', and no mistake. Aye, there be somethin' shady in 'is past, yer can depend upon it! It's always them with the guiltiest consciences what seeks ter make others feel guilty, and those the most uncertain o' their perches what suspects others o' wishin' ter pull 'em down. My god don't look down from above, Aylesford. 'E looks up from below. 'E is not a ceilin' beyond reach. 'E be the very ground we do walk upon. Aye, 'e be the foundations and pillars o' the Earth, and all else visible and invisible.'

'Ye surprise me, Starkey. I had nae taken ye for a theologian.'

Starkey grunted at this, and a faint blush coloured his cheeks, but he said nothing, as if he regretted having spoken at all.

Aylesford went on. 'Your arguments are tae deep for the likes o' me, I'm afraid. I am but a simple man, in possession o' a simple truth.' He held up the sack. 'Here is my answer, sir. Thus will I refute your arguments, not with words but with actions. I shall win the world tae my cause, and that o' the God that has chosen me and speaks through me: the one true God.'

'And what do 'e say?' asked Starkey with apparent interest, his equanimity evidently restored. 'This god what dwells within a watch? What be 'is gospel, eh?'

'Blood,' said Aylesford. 'Blood and fire.'

A snort from Starkey. 'Yer disappoint me, Scottish Tom. And 'ere I were 'opin' fer somethin' new. Blood and fire, indeed! Why, that be business as usual round 'ere, if yer 'aven't noticed. We be 'eadin' right inter the thick o' it.'

'It will be a lot thicker before I am through,' Aylesford promised.

*

Aylesford awoke the next morning curled about the sack as if it were the sole source of heat in a frozen world. The day passed slowly. He was a virtual prisoner in the tiny room, discouraged from so much as peeking out the window – though he did peek, and saw grey skies over a grey, rocky landscape on which nothing larger than a shrub grew, and beyond that, like some formless void that might birth a new world, or swallow this one, the dull, endlessly rocking surface of the slate-coloured sea. The cries of gulls, the ceaseless whine of the wind, the everyday noises of the town and inn – these were his companions as the hours dragged by. Starkey popped in from time to time, apprising him of any news – of which there was precious little: no sign of the missing messenger, but, on the plus side, no evidence of unusual activity by the local customs men, nor sightings of any strangers. Boxer brought food and drink but showed no further interest in the contents of the sack, nor inclination towards renewed friendly discourse.

Yet Aylesford did not chafe at the delay or the isolation. Indeed, it was the interruptions that annoyed him. He craved privacy as a newly married man might crave to be alone with his bride. And was he not joined now to the hunter by bonds as sacred as those of matrimony? Had he not sworn, in a manner of speaking, to forsake all others? In that moment of ecstasy, when he had experienced a foretaste of the loving eternity that had been promised him, he had understood that his life was no longer his own but belonged to God. He had surrendered to that understanding gladly, giving himself up to it utterly. Indeed, in this union he felt himself more bride than groom, for he had submitted to a power and authority greater than his own. He had been ravished by a will that could not be resisted or denied. Nor did he wish to deny or resist it. On the contrary, he ached to be ravished again.

In the intervals between visits, he studied the relic. Or, to be more precise, worshipped at its altar. Quare's hand, removed from the sack, was unchanged. No hint of decay was present; as before, the flesh was white and hard as marble. He had no compunction about touching it now; indeed, he thrilled to the glide of that cold skin

52

beneath his ardent caress, the pricking of its briary hairs that drew and then drank a faint bloody tribute. The watch, which was less in the grasp of those stony fingers than fused with their substance like a raw silver ingot encased in worthless rock, drew his fingers to it by a power of attraction that seemed to be as much or more a part of its purpose as any measurement of time.

With fumbling urgency he opened the case and beheld the dial of the watch. It was like that of any hunter . . . save for two details. First, the minute and hour hands had been crafted with exquisite precision into the head and tail of a dragon. Second, the twelve symbols arrayed around the perimeter of the enamel face were no numbers or letters that he knew. He found it hard to keep his gaze fixed upon them. The more intently he stared, the more his vision blurred . . . Or, no, it was as if the symbols themselves blurred, wriggling free of his attempts to study them. And yet he was sure he had seen them before. With a start, the answer came to him: were these not the same shapes he had glimpsed in his vision, the strange stones standing atop the mountain, above which had floated that quicksilver orb or eye?

He strained with all his might to focus upon the symbols, not so much to see them as to see past them and into the world of his vision . . . and not so much to see into that world as to be seen by what dwelled there. He stared as fixedly as he could, in fervent wordless prayer, his attention like a fisherman's baited line. But nothing came to nibble at his hook, and he could not keep up the effort for longer than a few seconds at a time before unpleasant things began to happen inside his head, as if his brain were being clawed apart like a ball of knitting unravelled by a clowder of cats. Then his gaze would slide to the inside of the cover, where the initials *JW* were engraved in flowery script, along with the date 1652 – over a hundred years ago. What did those initials stand for? What was the significance of that date? No answers suggested themselves.

The watch had a stem, but it proved to be purely decorative. The timepiece could not be wound. And yet it ran. When he laid his ear against the glass, he heard nothing. Felt no vibration, however faint. And yet it ran. The draconic hands moved. They did not keep an accurate time, as he ascertained by inquiring the hour from Starkey on one of his visits; nor did they move at a steady rate, as he verified by simple experiment, observing how, whenever the relic absorbed his blood like a sponge soaking up water, the hands briefly quickened their circumambulation of the dial as if energized by the influx of his substance, though they slowed again almost immediately, the motive force exhausted. What, he wondered, would be the result if the watch were supplied with more than a few paltry drops of blood? How much blood would it take to keep the timepiece running constantly? And what then? Would the god in the machine come forth into the world at the advent of some appointed hour? *But o' that day and hour knoweth nae man*, he thought. *Nae the angels o' heaven, but my Father only.*

Earlier, in the carriage, it had not been blood alone that had been wrung from him. And in truth it was not blood alone that he yearned to spill now like a libation poured out from his very core. But that desire, like his other prayers, went unanswered. Only the memory of what it had been like to feel the touch of divinity stirred him, not the thing itself, and though that memory had been seared into him, it did not satisfy. How could it? Yet what could he do? There was no way for him to compel God. It was for God to compel him. And hadn't he been given a mission? Hadn't a compulsion been laid upon him? That was his path back to God, one that would lead to Him in this world as surely as the path up the mountainside had led to Him in the world of his vision. He must be the messenger, the prophet.

The reaper.

Aylesford was pacing the narrow dimensions of the room when Starkey came to fetch him just before midnight.

'It's time,' he said, his features given a garish cast by the lamp he held in one hand. He carried his tricorn in his other arm, pressed to his side.

'And about bloody time, too,' Aylesford answered, grabbing his own hat from the pallet and likewise tucking it under his arm. He had fashioned the burlap sack containing the relic into a kind of sling worn about his neck. 'Let's be off. I'm sick o' this place.'

Starkey looked as if he might comment on this modification to

Aylesford's wardrobe, but evidently thought better of it and simply nodded. 'Follow me.'

Nasty Face, Stick-in-the-mud, and Old Oatmeal were waiting in the common room, seated at the same table, in the same attitudes, as Aylesford had last seen them the night before. Boxer stood behind them, wearing a Monmouth cap. There was no one else present.

'Well, good luck to ye, Scottish Tom,' said Nasty Face. 'Ye'll have a dram with us afore ye go.'

It was not a question. Boxer did the honours, splashing a few fingers of gin into five tin cups.

'Thanks fer the 'ospitality, Nasty,' said Starkey, raising his cup.

'Make sure 'is Majesty do hear of it,' Nasty Face said.

'Which d'yer mean? The one beneath the ground or the one across the water?'

'Tell as many kings as ye like, Starkers, so long as King George ain't among 'em.'

'No fear o' that,' Starkey said. 'Yer 'ealth, gentlemen.'

Everyone drank.

'Time for one more, I reckon,' squeaked Nasty Face, redder of cheek and shinier of eye than he had been a moment ago. Boxer again did the honours. When the cups had been refilled, Nasty Face lifted his. 'To fair wind and smooth seas,' he said.

'And dry land,' added Aylesford fervently. He did not relish the prospect of this trip across the Channel.

The cups were drained. Boxer conducted Aylesford and Starkey to a storage room at the back of the inn whose flooring had been partially removed, revealing an opening that descended into darkness. The space exhaled a damp coolness, like the entrance to a crypt.

'This be a tunnel,' confided Boxer, 'what'll take us to East Hill, above the beach.' He lowered himself backward into the opening, descending by means of a ladder. When he reached the bottom, perhaps six feet down, he stretched up his hand and asked Starkey for the lamp, which was duly passed to him.

'Down yer go,' said Starkey, indicating that Aylesford should precede him.

'What about our baggage?' he inquired.

'Gone afore us,' said Starkey.

'It be waitin' at t'other end o' the tunnel,' Boxer added from below. 'Along with some o' our boys to load the skiff and row ye out.'

Aylesford put on his hat, adjusted the sling about his neck, and climbed down the ladder, then stepped aside to make room for Starkey. He stood in a vault whose rough, pale walls, glistening with moisture, appeared to have been gouged out of the chalky stone. The space was larger than he would have guessed, insofar as he could make out its dimensions by the weak light of Boxer's lamp. There were wooden casks, crates, and other items he assumed contained smuggled goods of one sort or another.

Starkey stepped down to the floor with a grunt.

'This way.' Boxer led them to a stack of crates along one wall. The stack pivoted smoothly at his touch, revealing a low-ceilinged but surprisingly wide opening in the rock face. Holding the lamp before him, Boxer bent forward and entered the tunnel.

Starkey again indicated that Aylesford should precede him. Aylesford tucked his hat under his arm, stooped, and followed Boxer, who was moving steadily ahead, a dense shadow limned in the lamp's soft glow. Stout wooden beams, slick with moisture and smelling of tar, shored up the walls and ceiling.

Though the tunnel was wide enough for the three of them to walk abreast – no doubt to facilitate the ingress and egress of contraband – they progressed in single file. The ceiling did not rise, and they were forced to maintain their stooped posture. Aylesford reflected that, over the last few days, since the murders at the Pig and Rooster, and his first failed attempt to kill Daniel Quare, he had spent as much or more time beneath the ground as he had above it. Why, he was becoming a veritable Morecockneyan!

When he'd first entered their subterranean realm through London's sewers, and then, escorted by Starkey, descended deeper still, into a mazy metropolis of tunnels and caverns lit by torches and candles and, lower yet, at levels whose inhabitants had never known the sun, by the shine of the phosphorescent mushrooms cultivated there, an oppressive awareness of all that lay above him had pressed down without respite. He'd been short of breath and constantly sweating, feeling half buried alive. The darkness massed at the limits of his vision had seemed no mere absence of light but a solid and weighty presence that actively sought to crush him and could be kept at bay only by tireless vigilance. Had this continued for the entirety of his stay, no doubt it would have driven him mad. But Starkey had explained that new recruits to the ranks of the Morecockneyans often experienced these terrors and that a remedy existed, should he wish to avail himself of it. He very much did wish it.

The remedy turned out to be a foul fermentation of mushrooms, a faintly glowing liquid that smelled worse than it looked and tasted worse than it smelled. Only desperation gave him the fortitude to swallow it.

For the next hours, he did not think once of the looming weight pressing down from above. He thought of nothing but the agony shredding his insides. He writhed and moaned on the cold stone floor of a bare cell lit by a single candle, to which he'd been brought for the occasion, sure that he'd been poisoned, betrayed by his hosts. This was followed by a bout of vomiting such as he had never experienced and hoped never to experience again. But afterwards, a pleasant lethargy settled over his body. The floor on which he lay might have been a feather bed. He was at peace, and when the candle was suddenly snuffed, he did not cry out or panic but let his mind drift into the dark spaces that had once seemed so desirous of obliterating him. That darkness was no longer malevolent but maternal: Mother Earth cradling him lovingly to her bosom. He had slept, secure in her all-encompassing embrace, and when he had awakened, the fear was gone. Nor had it returned. And now, at this trivial depth, Aylesford felt not the slightest twinge of apprehension, but moved as carelessly under the low ceiling as beneath an open sky.

He did not have a clear idea of distance or time, however, and this, too, reminded him of his days with the Morecockneyans, when the measured certainties of life above ground had melted away, so that he'd often found himself wondering, half seriously, whether he hadn't been there for weeks already, a traveller strayed into a fairy realm.

Ahead of him, Boxer's bent and shadowed form might have belonged to a dwarf, while the glimmer of the lamplight upon the moist walls and beams made them appear to be encrusted with gold and precious jewels. The sounds of their footsteps echoed back from all sides, doubled and redoubled, until it seemed to Aylesford that they were being conducted by spirits come not to haunt but to help ease their passage.

The ground began to slope upward, and a briny breeze, faint as a breath, grew stronger and steadier as they neared the surface. A low, querulous whistle sounded from ahead, and Boxer whistled back sharply. Then Aylesford saw other lights bobbing in the dark. These resolved into five lamps set upon the ground or held in the hands of nameless men gathered in a rough-hewn cave of approximately the same dimensions as the cellar beneath the inn. Aylesford recognized his baggage and Starkey's piled to one side. He thought of Ali Baba and the Forty Thieves, though there were less than half that number of men here, perhaps not even a dozen. They were all armed: some carried muskets, others pistols, and all had cudgels tucked into their belts.

'What kept ye, Boxer?' asked a swarthy individual with a cap like Boxer's pulled low over his forehead. All the men were dressed alike in Monmouth caps and dark clothes.

'Not late, am I?' replied the lad in a defensive tone.

'We're on the cusp o' the tide,' said the man, 'and must make haste if we're not to lose it.' His eyes widened almost comically as he looked past Aylesford and caught sight of Starkey. 'Well, well. If it ain't me old mate Starkers.'

'Footsey,' said Starkey with evident pleasure. 'Good ter see yer. 'Ow's it 'angin', mate?'

The source of this nickname seemed obvious, as the man wore a pair of shoes fit for a giant. 'No complaints,' he answered with a gap-toothed smile. Then, his gaze shifting to Aylesford: 'And you'll be Scottish Tom.'

Aylesford nodded.

'Gentlemen,' said Footsey, 'as I told young Boxer here, we must hurry if we're to catch the tide. There be a skiff down the beach. We will conduct ye there and row ye out to the ship. Now douse your lights, men, and let's be off.'

The lamps were extinguished, plunging the cave into darkness. But though Aylesford was left as good as blind, the others seemed better able to see. At least, he could hear their grunts as they lifted the baggage. He felt someone take his arm.

'This way, Scottish Tom,' said Starkey, who had the eyes of a cat.

Aylesford advanced gingerly, guided by Starkey, keeping one hand raised before him to ward off any collision. But he encountered nothing, and after a series of sharp turns beheld an irregular patch of grey cut from the deeper dark. Against this backdrop he could see figures moving briskly out of the cave.

Once outside, he clapped his tricorn to his head and stood a moment, letting his eyes adjust. Thick clouds covered the sky, hiding the stars and reducing the moon to a waxy smudge. Still, there was light enough to see the rocky outcroppings to either side and, before him, a steep defile leading down to a wide, flat expanse. Beyond that was the broad, undulant blackness of the sea. Somewhere out there a ship was waiting. A wayward wind coursed and whistled among the rocks.

'Looks like ye might be in for a spot o' weather,' said Footsey in a low voice. Aylesford started; he had not realized the man stood so near. 'That's to be expected this time o' year,' he added. 'I hope ye have a strong stomach, Scottish Tom. It's a rough crossing, and no mistake.'

'Canna be helped.' He shrugged, his hand straying to the re-assuring weight of the relic in its sling.

'Is it true what I've heard?' Footsey continued in a low voice. 'That ye have the prick o' James I in that sack?'

Starkey choked back a laugh. 'Yer can't believe everythin' yer 'ear, Footsey.'

'What then?' persisted the other.

'Ye don't want to know,' said Boxer, who had come up behind them, the last to leave the cave, and now moved past without waiting for a reply.

'The lad's got the right o' it,' said Starkey. 'I wish I did not know meself.'

Aylesford grunted, feeling that there was something disrespectful, even blasphemous, in these rude references to what he carried. He set off after Boxer, following a path that zigged and zagged down to the beach. Starkey and Footsey came behind.

He moved with care, afraid of tripping and falling, but reached the beach without mishap. It was covered with small, flat stones that glistened dully in the washed-out, sourceless light and crunched underfoot as the smugglers, spread out loosely now, crossed with the stiff and graceless economy of labourers engaged in rote work. The leading group had already reached the skiff, whose shape was just visible at the limits of Aylesford's vision, looming like a lone boulder or some monstrous fish belched up onto the shore.

The wind was stronger, blowing in from the sea and bearing a misty freight. Aylesford's face was wet, his clothes damp. Everything had a watery aspect to it: the air, the light, even the beach, whose stony carpet shifted beneath Aylesford's boots, sucking at his heels as he lurched and stumbled towards the skiff, his progress frustratingly slow compared to that of the others. Boxer had moved far ahead, as had Footsey, and even Starkey loped by with apparent ease, offering a whispered exhortation to ''urry up!' as he passed. Aylesford bit back an angry retort and redoubled his efforts.

In the course of doing so, his scabbard became entangled between his legs, and before he could grasp what was happening, he had fallen heavily. The breath was knocked out of him, and it was a moment before he was able to push himself up onto all fours. He shook his head, half dazed. His chin throbbed as if he'd been punched in the face.

The others were far ahead now. He groped for his hat and set it back in place, and was beginning to rise when a voice from up ahead and to his left called loudly, 'Stand fast, in the name o' the king!'

Bright lights flared at the same instant, and torches sprang to life, revealing a group of armed redcoats. It seemed to Aylesford that they had materialized out of thin air. Their muskets were pointed towards the smugglers, who immediately dropped to the beach and, without a word, began firing their guns. The soldiers stood their ground, responding to the ragged shots with a practised volley at the command of their leader. The noise was deafening.

Aylesford had no firearm of his own, only his sword, useless in these circumstances. He did not know whether to push ahead or retreat. Neither option seemed promising. Yet neither could he stay put. Though he had fallen far enough behind to be out of the thick of the fire, he could hear the whistle of errant shots coming too close for comfort. The torches had been extinguished after the first volley, and the beach was dark again, save for the flash of each weapon's discharge. He remained kneeling, painfully aware of the stones digging into his knees, mesmerized by these deadly flowerings. The air reeked of gunpowder. Shouted commands mingled with the screams and moans of wounded men.

It was another light that broke the spell. A soft blue glow drew his eyes downward to the sling. Quare's severed hand, or perhaps only the hunter it held, was glowing. It must have been very bright indeed, he thought, to be visible through the densely woven cloth. But visible it was: a stark and shining silhouette. Rain pattered the sling: one drop, then another, and another. Or, no, not rain, he realized. The hand he raised to his chin came back bloody. He had cut himself in his fall.

It occurred to Aylesford belatedly that the light must be visible to the soldiers as well, making him a target, and at this realization he turned away and clambered awkwardly to his feet, trying to shield the glow with his hands. The light spilled past his fingers like water.

He felt an urge now to approach nearer to the battle. A fierce and undeniable hunger. He did not question whether this was his own desire or a compulsion laid upon him by the relic. There was no difference between himself and what he carried. He felt flooded with power and importance, certain that no musket ball could touch him or, if it did, cause him any harm. He was hard as iron. He pulled his hands away from the cloth, no longer concerned with covering up the shine but, instead, eager to bare it entirely. Why, he would remove the severed hand and carry it upraised before him into battle like a standard!

'You've led me a merry chase, Thomas Aylesford.'

He did not know which he became aware of first. The gruff voice or the figure to whom that voice belonged. The figure was suddenly there, in front of him, as if conjured by the blue light. Tall, though not quite as tall as he, slender, dressed cap-a-pie in grey, features hidden by a grey mask. And holding a rapier in its grey-gloved right hand, point angled downward, like an invitation for him to draw his own blade.

He accepted the invitation with a grin, glad to have a target within reach at last. 'Is it the famous Grimalkin I have the honour o' addressin'?'

'I have been called by that name.' The flick of a wrist brought the rapier into line. 'You have something that belongs to me.'

'That's rich,' he said. 'Comin' from a thief.'

'Thief or not, I will have it back.'

Aylesford's grin sharpened as he took his stance. He had noticed that Grimalkin's blade was shorter than his own; indeed, it was shorter than any rapier he had seen, almost as though it were a child's weapon. He did not see what possible advantage this might confer, though he was wary of Grimalkin's reputation as a swordsman and counselled himself to caution. 'Come and take it,' he said. 'If ye can.'

The light from the relic seemed to encase the moment in ice. Aylesford felt as if he and his opponent stood frozen in time, far from the beach and the battle being fought there, the two of them whisked away to some private duelling ground entirely otherwhere.

In truth, he had long wished to test himself against Grimalkin. The masked thief was a living legend. People spoke of him with respect and fear and wonder. His swordplay was said to be without peer. Beneath that grey mask, or so Aylesford had heard at different times, was to be found an exiled Russian prince, a bastard from some kingdom far to the east, a face so hideously scarred that it no longer resembled anything human . . . and in fact was not human at all. His allegiance – if he had any beyond himself – was unknown. His purpose – beyond the acquisition of rare timepieces thought to be proof against theft by any means short of the miraculous – was equally unknown. He was an enigma, a mystery . . . and Aylesford did not like mysteries.

He did not attack but waited for Grimalkin to make the first move.

He was not confident of his footing, though he trusted the speed of his reflexes to make up for any difficulties in that regard. He had crossed swords with only a handful of men whose artistry with a blade surpassed his own, but even among that select group he had never encountered anyone faster than he was, and once a certain level of swordsmanship had been attained, speed made all the difference.

So it was with something like disbelief that he found himself hard-pressed to counter an attack that came at him in a style he had never seen before, with a speed beyond anything he had imagined possible. Grimalkin fought like a dervish, using his legs to kick as well as to manoeuvre. The short rapier that Aylesford had regarded with condescension if not outright scorn proved quite long enough to come within a hairsbreadth of skewering him twice in the first flurried exchange, in which it took every bit of his skill to parry what the other man threw at him. There was no chance for a riposte of his own. He staggered back, trying to put some distance between himself and the demon that faced him.

Grimalkin paused. Above the mask, grey eyes glittered coldly in the blue light. 'You're bleeding, Mr Aylesford.' The voice was measured, calm.

'Not from any touch o' yours,' he replied, already breathing heavily. Grimalkin, he noted, was not winded in the least.

'Not yet,' said Grimalkin. This time the attack was even more outlandish. He tumbled forward like an acrobat, and came up in a spray of stones.

Aylesford, briefly blinded by the unexpected barrage, thrust towards the spot where he judged Grimalkin's trajectory would take him. But he judged wrongly, it seemed, for he encountered nothing. Then felt a whistle of air past his face, and another, followed by a shock to the wrist of his sword arm that caused him to drop his blade.

'Step away, and I will spare your life,' said Grimalkin. 'Which is more than you did for those men in London.'

Aylesford's vision cleared. Grimalkin stood a few steps away, ready to resume his attack. Aylesford's sword lay upon the beach, too far to easily recover, and even if he could have reached it, his right hand was numb from Grimalkin's blow and could not have picked it up, much less wielded it. The sling no longer hung about his neck but lay at his feet. All of this had happened more quickly than Aylesford could understand, as if the intervals of time, however brief, that perforce separated the distinct actions of any duel had been snipped away somehow, and the actions then knit back together seamlessly. Not even in his earliest training bouts had he been so thoroughly bested. Perhaps if he had been able to watch Grimalkin in action against another foe, he might have seen better how to respond to his unorthodox style of fencing.

'I will not ask again,' said Grimalkin.

'Why should ye spare me?' asked Aylesford to buy some time. He clutched his right hand in his left, trying to wring some feeling back into it.

'I would not willingly consign any man to the eternity of torment awaiting all who die in proximity to that cursed watch. Already it has a claim upon you. What is left of your life will be warped by a longing that can never be fulfilled. But that suffering will at least have an end. Now, step back, sir, or you will learn that there are fates worse than death.'

Aylesford felt he would rather die than be parted from the relic and the eternity that had been promised him: an eternity filled not with torment but love. *Help me,* he prayed silently, fervently, to the god within the machine. *Let me not fail here, before our work has even begun. Help me that I may serve ye now and for ever.*

'So be it,' said Grimalkin. But then, even as he began a lunge that Aylesford knew must prove fatal, stopped short. His head came up as if he had heard a sudden, disconcerting sound. A call that could not be denied. Yet Aylesford heard nothing. 'No,' came the thief's voice, sounding very different now than it had a moment ago, pitched to a higher register and filled with angry frustration. 'Not now!'

Aylesford saw his chance and took it, diving for his blade. His right hand was still useless, but he grabbed the hilt of the rapier with his left: he had trained himself to fight with either hand, though not with equal effectiveness; if he had not been able to contest Grimalkin right-handed, he knew that he would fare no better with his left. But he might at least die with a sword in hand. That was something.

He rolled to his feet, hat lost in the tumble, rapier raised to parry an attack that didn't come. Had his adversary slipped behind him? He whipped around, but saw nothing. Grimalkin was gone. And not merely gone: it was as if the man had vanished into thin air. There was only the empty stretch of beach, and the sack containing the relic, whose glow, he noted, seemed brighter than ever. He rushed to it and picked it up, no longer filled with the desire to display it openly but rather wishing only to keep it hidden and safe. He tucked it beneath his coat, where the glow was entirely muffled.

The fight was still going on up the beach. During his encounter with Grimalkin, he had all but forgotten it. He had heard nothing, seen nothing, save for his grey-cloaked adversary. But now that the thief was gone, the sights and sounds of the skirmish came rushing back. The gunfire had grown more ragged, the shouts and screams less frequent. Still, it was plain to Aylesford that the battle had moved to a new phase, though in fact it seemed less a battle now than a brawl, dark figures grappling hand to hand in the night, shadow against shadow.

Footsteps came crunching towards him across the beach. Aylesford took his stance, sword ready. He still did not trust his right hand, but his left should be more than sufficient to deal with any of these men. But then he heard Starkey's voice.

'Put up yer sword – it's me!'

Aylesford dropped his guard as Starkey reached him. Boxer was with him.

'What are yer waitin' fer, a bloomin' invitation?' hissed Starkey, sword in hand. 'We 'ave been betrayed, it seems. But we ain't caught yet. Come quick!'

With that, Starkey took hold of one arm, Boxer the other, and together they hustled him towards the skiff. Aylesford stumbled along between them. He could feel the relic beneath his coat, and though he could not see it, it seemed to him that it was still shining, its blue light penetrating the intervening layers of cloth to reach his skin, then piercing that as well, seeping into his blood, his very bones, until he, too, was shining. Shining like a cold blue star. Could no one see it? He had prayed for help, and his prayers had been answered. He felt drunk with joy and power. The fighting going on around him – for he was in the thick of it now – seemed ridiculous, a war of witless ants.

Rain had begun to fall, and lightning flickered, revealing stark tableaux of men thrusting with swords, swinging pistols and muskets like clubs, grappling upon the beach. The air reeked of gunpowder and blood. Aylesford felt the hunter's hunger as if it were his own. These men were his to take. Their souls were his to claim, their blood his to drink. All he needed to do was remove the relic from its bundle and the harvesting would begin.

But alongside the hunger, he felt the countervailing restraint of an iron will, and he knew that this was neither the time nor the place for such an unveiling, that his moment was yet to come, and that he must wait until he was safely across the Channel, where the vast battlefield of Europe would yield a harvest beyond measure. Laughter bubbled up from his core.

'Hist!' came Boxer's voice. 'Quiet!'

Thunder roared. Or, no, not thunder but a pistol at close range. Boxer screamed shrilly, like a goat, and fell. Starkey, without pausing, smoothly skewered the redcoat who had fired and dragged Aylesford on. Aylesford looked back, saw Boxer sitting on the beach, mouth open in a silent wail, one arm upraised as if in mute appeal to the lightning flash that illuminated him. At the end of that arm was the bloody pulp of what had been a hand. *They will have tae find a new name for him now*, Aylesford thought, and laughed again.

'Are yer mad?' demanded Starkey and without waiting for an answer thrust him bodily into the skiff.

Aylesford fell heavily, striking his chin on one of the wooden benches of the boat. Dazed, bleeding again, he lay between two benches for a moment, his sword knocked loose, clutching the relic to his body more tightly than ever, as if it were not Quare's severed hand but his own. He felt the skiff slide across the loose stones of the beach, then a sudden rocking as the boat entered the water. He heard shouts, splashing, and then felt the boat lurch again as men clambered aboard.

Starkey was among them. 'Row, lads!' he cried. 'Row fer yer bloody lives!'

There were four men in addition to Starkey and Aylesford. They grabbed oars and began to pull for all they were worth. Aylesford, who had by now gathered his wits and his sword, the latter of which he'd returned almost instinctively to its scabbard, took an oar himself and joined in the general labour, the relic tucked between his feet. The skiff shot forward.

'Well, that were a right bollocks,' came the voice of Footsey.

A few shots pursued them, but no one was struck. Aylesford feared there would be a customs ship waiting near by to take them into custody, but they appeared to be alone on the water.

They rowed feverishly for what seemed like hours, with no conversation between them. The eldritch light of the relic ebbed to nothing within the first moments, and thereafter all was dark save for flashes of lightning that showed Aylesford more than he cared to see of mountainous waves, deep troughs, and angry clouds. Surely, he thought, it would have been better to fight the redcoats upon the beach than to sally forth against the elements in this way, with no defence save the thin shell of the skiff and the strong arms of the rowers. But no one seemed inclined to turn back, so he kept his misgivings to himself and tried to match the others stroke for stroke. He feared he was hindering more than helping, for he couldn't fit his rhythm to theirs, and in any case the skiff seemed utterly at the mercy of the waves, tossed about like a cork.

At last Footsey kindled a lantern somehow – it flared briefly, illuminating his dripping face, which looked to have aged ten years in the last half hour, then vanished. An instant later, from across the water, came an answering flash.

'There she be,' said Footsey. 'Just a bit farther, boys.'

Aylesford couldn't suppress a groan. His arms felt weak as a child's, as if he had rowed a dozen miles already, and was being called upon to row a dozen more, all in the midst of a tempest such as the world had never known. Where, he wondered, was his God now? Could he not send his spirit to calm the waves and still the wind, hold back the lightning and thunder and quench the rain? But no – surely this was a test. Surely the God who had stood beside him on land would not abandon him upon the water. He felt suddenly ashamed of his weakness, his lack of faith.

'What's that, Scottish Tom?' said Footsey meanwhile. 'Are we not rowin' fast enough to suit ye?'

'Leave off,' growled Starkey before Aylesford could reply. 'It ain't 'is fault the lobsters got wind o' us.'

'Perhaps not,' granted Footsey grudgingly. 'But I didn't notice him fightin', neither. Is that the way o' it, Scottish Tom? Ye expect us to fight and die for ye, and to row ye to safety into the bargain, while ye lay back like some lily-livered lordling?'

'I fought,' he said.

'Did ye now?' said Footsey. 'Right glad am I to hear it! For it seemed to me that ye stayed well clear o' the fray, and that Boxer and Starkers had to go back and fetch ye.'

'Grimalkin was there,' he said, addressing Starkey now. 'He tried to take the relic, but I—'

Footsey interrupted. 'The Grey Ghost, is it? We have had our share o' run-ins with that gentleman over the years. Ye must be quite the swordsman to have bested him!'

'I didnae best him,' Aylesford admitted. 'He bested me.'

'Spared ye then, did he?' Footsey followed up. 'Took his prize and scarpered?'

'No, he left it,' Aylesford said, and only then understood that Footsey did not believe him. He felt the customary chill of anger steel his nerves. 'Are ye callin' me a liar, sir?'

'Fer God's sake!' cried Starkey as lightning flickered and thunder rolled. 'Will the pair o' yer leave off? D'yer bloomin' idiots mean ter draw swords and 'ave at it 'ere and now?'

'Are ye blind?' questioned Footsey in turn. 'He's the one what betrayed us!'

This accusation elicited mutterings from Footsey's men, who had, until now, been silent.

''E did no such thing,' answered Starkey vehemently. 'I understand what yer feelin', Footsey. But don't make Scottish Tom the scapegoat fer that debacle upon the beach.'

'Who's to blame then, eh?' demanded Footsey, and for the first time, Aylesford heard the anguish in his voice. He remembered the sight of Boxer with his maimed hand. Footsey had lost friends this night.

'Maybe no one,' said Starkey soothingly. 'There is always risk in this line o' work, is there not? But I blame Grimalkin. It were 'e what must've waylaid our missin' messenger and compelled 'im ter spill 'is guts. Aye, it were the Grey Ghost and no mistake. 'E brought in the lobsters as a diversion like, so as ter give 'imself a chance ter confront Scottish Tom face ter face.'

'Are ye sayin' Grimalkin is an agent o' the Crown?' asked Footsey, scepticism evident in his tone.

'Why not?' answered Starkey. 'Why should a thief not also be one o' Pitt's men?'

'Canna we discuss this while rowin'?' Aylesford interjected as the skiff plunged sickeningly. 'We are like tae capsize in this storm!'

Footsey responded with mocking laughter, which the others, save Starkey, were quick to join. 'God bless us, boys, did ye hear that? 'E calls this bit o' weather a storm! Why, this ain't but a gentle breeze, ye landlubber!'

'Laugh all ye like,' said Aylesford hotly, 'but I dinnae think the customs men will have given up so easily. Ye canna say as we are not hunted even now.'

'Landlubber or no, 'e 'as the right o' it,' Starkey said.

Further conversation was cut off by a voice to starboard, faint but audible over the wind and waves, the French accent unmistakable. '*Alors*, ze skiff! Zis is Captain Bagot of ze *Pierre*! I believe you 'ave got some cargo for us, *non*?'

The *Pierre* was a large, three-masted lugger of nearly sixty feet. It loomed out of the night like a leviathan as the skiff was rowed near. Hawsers were thrown down from the deck, made fast, and the skiff pulled in close. This operation was performed by Footsey and his men with quiet, practised efficiency despite the dark and the rain. Nevertheless, the two hulls crashed noisily together with a force that brought Aylesford's heart to his throat. A sort of sling was lowered, into which Aylesford was bundled by Footsey and the others none too gently but with the same blunt efficiency they had exhibited a moment earlier. When he tried to assist them, he was rudely commanded to be still. He sat uncomfortably, cold and wet and miserable, the relic once more tucked beneath his coat. He could feel the enmity emanating from the men around him, and he ached to put them in their place . . . but dared not say or do anything lest they throw him overboard. If not for Starkey's presence, he felt he would have met that fate already.

Meanwhile, a second sling descended, and Starkey was similarly made fast.

A voice called down from above – not Bagot's this time: 'Are ye squared away?'

''Old yer 'orses!' cried Starkey, who then addressed Footsey: 'Why not cross with us, Footsey? If yer go back, the lobsters'll snap yer up. Best wait till the coast is clear.'

'Thanks, mate,' said Footsey. 'I know ye mean well. But I'd rather face a hundred lobsters than sail with Scottish Tom here.' He spat over the side. 'The man's a right Jonah and no mistake.'

''Ere, none o' that kind o' talk!' said Starkey.

'Ye know I'm right,' Footsey persisted. 'Well, I don't blame ye,' he added philosophically and stuck out his hand. 'Good luck to ye, Starkers. Don't reckon I'll clap eyes on ye again.'

Starkey shook his hand vigorously. 'Never say never, Footsey, ol' boy. Good luck to yer. Tell Nasty 'e 'as my thanks and that o' the King Beneaf the Ground. 'Is Majesty will not forget what the men o' 'astin's 'as done this night.'

Footsey grunted. 'I'm sure that'll be a great comfort to Boxer and t'other lads,' he said, then yelled: 'Ahoy the *Pierre*! Haul away!'

Aylesford was jerked aloft. He cried out in surprise, then grunted more in shock than pain as the sling swung hard into the side of the lugger. In another moment, he was being hauled onto the deck like a fish on a line.

Anonymous hands deftly if somewhat roughly disengaged him from the sling and pulled him to his feet. Near by, Starkey was undergoing the same treatment.

'Welcome aboard ze *Pierre*, gentlemen,' came the voice that had first addressed them, that of Captain Bagot, who was visible only as a darker, vaguely man-shaped mass amidst the gloom. 'Do I 'ave ze honour to address Messieurs Aylesford and Starkey?'

'I'm Thomas Aylesford,' he said, stumbling slightly with the rolling of the ship. The rain was falling more heavily now, and the wind had picked up considerably. It moaned through the rigging, a forlorn sound. 'Did ye say *Pierre*?'

'*Oui* – she is name after *mon fils* – my eldest boy. Ze name, she bring good luck, monsieur.'

'We could use a bit o' that,' said Aylesford. 'What o' our baggage, Captain?'

'It is being seen to,' said Bagot, and indeed, Aylesford noticed a commotion at the rail, though he could not make out what precisely was going on there.

Meanwhile, Starkey joined them. 'Glad ter be aboard, Captain,' he said. 'Looks like we're in fer a right blow, eh?'

'Pah,' said Bagot, making that contemptuous puffing noise that Aylesford remembered so well from his time in France – an affectation cultivated by the lower and higher orders alike, so that he had come to think of it as a distinctive expression of the national character. And by no means an attractive one. It had always made him feel as if he were being looked down upon from immeasurable heights of disdain, and the effect was no different now; indeed, after the contemptuous treatment he had received from Footsey and his men, this arrogant and dismissive display – as Aylesford experienced it – put his back up.

'Zis is nothing,' the captain continued smoothly. 'Ze weather, she is typical for zis time of year. Zair is nothing to worry about. Ze *Pierre* 'as make zis crossing in worse weather, I assure you. Make yourselves at ease below, messieurs, and I will join you when my duties permit. I 'ave sealed orders for you, Monsieur Aylesford, from Lieutenant-Colonel Grant.'

'I will take those orders now, sir, if ye please,' said Aylesford.

'I regret I do not 'ave zem at 'and,' said Bagot. 'Zey are in my cabin.'

'That seems a most cavalier way tae treat an important dispatch, sir,' said Aylesford. 'Tae leave it lyin' about where anyone may take it.'

'It is not "lying about where anyone may take it", monsieur,' Bagot rejoined with some asperity. 'It is not in ze galley. It is, as I told you, in my cabin. Zat is to say, in ze captain's cabin, ze most secure place on zis ship.'

'We shall see about that,' said Aylesford. 'I insist ye bring the orders tae me now, sir. Or, rather, conduct me tae your cabin, where I can take possession o' 'em before they fall into the wrong hands – assuming that has not happened already.'

'I do not like your tone of voice, monsieur,' said Bagot, bristling. 'You accuse me of negligence and perhaps worse. Or 'ave I misapprehend? My English, she is, 'ow you say, rustic.'

''Ere now,' interjected Starkey rather breathlessly. 'We're all friends, eh? Friends and allies, sworn ter the same noble cause. Mr Aylesford meant no insult, Captain. 'E's a bit shook-up, yer see. We 'ad a spot o' trouble ashore, I'm afraid. Seems someone tipped off the customs. We 'ad ter fight our way out.'

'Then we 'ad best make 'aste for France *tout de suite*,' said the captain. 'Ze *Pierre*, she is fast. But she is no fighter. If zair are English cutters about, we 'ave no 'ope to beat zem.' He made to turn away, already calling out orders to his crew.

'Hold, sir,' said Aylesford, reaching out to pluck Bagot's sleeve even as he addressed Starkey. 'How do we know it was nae someone aboard this ship that tipped off the customs?'

Bagot wrenched his arm free. 'Do you accuse me, monsieur?'

'What if I do?' said Aylesford. 'Are ye man enough tae give me satisfaction?'

'Gorblimey, not again,' said Starkey despairingly.

Captain Bagot gave an incredulous laugh. 'Zis is *ridicule*! You cannot challenge ze captain of a ship to a duel, monsieur! Not at sea!'

'So you are a coward,' said Aylesford, and quickly struck the captain across the face with the back of his hand. The blow was not a heavy one, for he was off-balance, but even so he felt better for having delivered it.

'I could 'ave you clapped in irons for zat,' said Bagot, rubbing his cheek with one hand and controlling his temper with apparent difficulty. 'But we 'ave not ze time for it. And I see zat you are indeed "shook-up", as Monsieur Starkey 'as say. Zair is no cause for us to fight, monsieur! If I 'ave give offence, I do assure you it is not my intent. I beg of you to go below, and on my 'onour, I will bring you ze orders once we are under way. If you still desire satisfaction zen, monsieur, I will be at your disposal once we are safely docked and ashore. But now my duty is to my ship, my crew, and my passengers – zat is to say, to yourself and Monsieur Starkey.'

'Why, ye smooth-talkin' rascal,' said Aylesford. 'You cannae put me off so easy as that! D'ye not ken who I am?'

'A most rude and importunate person,' answered Bagot without hesitation. 'I will 'ave you off zis deck, monsieur, and below, where you cannot interfere further with ze running of zis ship.' Again, he made to call out an order to his crew.

Again, Aylesford interrupted him. 'I'll not be ordered about by the likes o' ye, ye damned French ferryman! Not while I carry this!' And he produced from beneath his coat the severed hand of Daniel Quare, which he had surreptitiously worked free of its wrappings.

'*Morbleu!*' cried the captain, drawing back.

Aylesford laughed at the abject fear on the man's face. That face, streaming with rain, was lit clearly in the icy blue glow of the relic, seeming almost as if rimed with frost. Steam rose from his open mouth and thick beard. It was obvious now that the source of the glow was the hunter itself, but the nimbus of light clung about the entire appendage like a glove of Saint Elmo's Fire.

'Fer God's sake, Aylesford!' said Starkey.

'Yes, for *His* sake,' Aylesford echoed, holding up the hand like a torch.

'What is it?' demanded Bagot. 'What 'ave you bring aboard my ship?'

'Victory,' said Aylesford. 'That's what I have brought, sir. Behold the weapon that will win the war and restore the Stuart dynasty to the throne! And d'ye imagine that the man who bears such a treasure shall go unrewarded? So perhaps ye understand better now who ye're dealin' with! A prince – aye, and a prophet!'

'A madman, by ze sound of it,' muttered Bagot. 'Monsieur Starkey, you must control zis man, or I will do it.'

Aylesford brandished the hand like a club. 'Ye cannae touch me! I'll smite ye – I'll smite the lot o' ye!'

Movement to one side drew his attention, and he stepped away from a glowering man in a Monmouth cap who held a belaying pin in one fist. As he did so, something hard and heavy struck the back of his head, and he went down as if a spar had fallen on him.

When next Aylesford opened his eyes, he was lying in a tight bed in a tight, poorly lit cabin, as ill as he had ever been in his life. His previous crossings of the Channel had left him prostrate, but never to this degree; the slightest movement triggered a fresh bout of vomiting, and because the storm had broken while he lay dead to the world, he had woken to find himself in constant motion, tossed this way and that by what seemed the frantic efforts of the ship to escape a predator, like a rabbit zigzagging through hedges just inches ahead of a wolf's slavering jaws . . . except in this case, the hedges were also heaving. He was too caught in the coils of his own misery to reflect on what had gone before, though he knew where he was and assumed that one of Bagot's crew had knocked him unconscious with a cowardly blow from behind. Yet even that knowledge was not sufficient to trigger more than the dullest craving for revenge.

Starkey, who was in the cabin when he awoke, had informed him brusquely that the relic had been stowed in his trunk. And then, with a decided lack of sympathy, had departed in order, as he put it, 'ter escape the stink o' yer sickness and apologize again ter the captain'.

It was only later, after Starkey had returned with news of the mutiny, and after the mutineers had battered their way into the cabin, that Aylesford realized his sickness stemmed less from the movements of the ship than from the absence of the relic. His rage at the indignities heaped upon him by impersonal Nature and all-too-personal humanity had spread a soothing oil over the twin tumults in his belly and his mind, armouring him in a familiar cold enmity, as if, like Quare's hand, he were gloved in blue fire. But it was not until he had opened his trunk and dug out the relic, not until he held

74

it again triumphantly in his hand, flesh to flesh, as it were, that he understood the cause of his sickness to be the lack of what he now held, for as soon as it was restored to his grasp, he felt that a hole in his innermost heart had been filled, and for the first time since he had awoken, he was fully himself again, or rather more than himself: a new and better self. Even as he faced the mutineers and mocked them, he vowed silently never to be parted from the relic again.

And then blood was spilled, and everything changed in an instant.

The severed hand, shining with a witchy blue light, came alive in his grasp. He had witnessed the hand and the hunter it held drinking his blood, so the fact that it thirsted for that substance came as no surprise to him. But in the past, the hand had remained as if carved from marble, like an altar upon which a sacrifice was made, a libation poured.

No longer.

He recoiled as the thing twisted in his grasp like a serpent. Yet he could not let go; his fingers seemed fused in place, his flesh one with the flesh of what he held. Quare's hand clutched the hunter as firmly as ever, but its wrist, supple now as Aylesford's own, rotated as if stirring the air. And indeed a wind sprang up from that motion. Aylesford's ears popped, and the temperature plummeted. Steam rose from the blood that covered the floor and leaked from the bodies of the mutineers who had fallen, pierced by Starkey's blade. Steam that shone darkly in the blue light.

Starkey, meanwhile, was grappling with the last of the mutineers left alive, the others having fled the cabin in terror. The Morecockneyan and his adversary rolled back and forth across the floor, part of the general detritus, human and otherwise, deposited there by the violence of the past moments.

'Aylesford!' Starkey gasped. 'A little 'elp, fer God's sake!'

Aylesford did not, could not, reply. The mist had thickened, coagulating into a dense mass, like a thundercloud, and he watched as dark streamers unravelled from that cloud and came snaking towards him in slender ribbons that converged on the hunter, sinking into its centre. He felt then, for an instant, the boundless thirst of the hunter, how it craved not simply blood but life itself, and something more than life, something eternal that existed in the midst of life yet apart from it, like a soul. Yes, that was what the hunter was drinking now: not just the blood but the souls of the men who had fallen here.

As it did, its glow changed from icy blue to cherry red, until the timepiece and the hand that held it both shone like molten iron, so brightly that Aylesford was blinded, as if his eyes had been burned from their sockets, though the relic radiated no heat. Rather, it seemed to suck all the heat from the cabin and from Aylesford himself, who shivered and fell to his knees.

But it was not only cold that convulsed his body. Though blind, in his mind's eye he stood again atop the mountain of his vision, in the presence of the orb that floated above the standing stones there. And as had happened then, so now was he ravaged by the boundless love of the God who had chosen him above all others as His prophet. Here was the reward he had been promised. Here the glimpse of what awaited him beyond this life, in the eternity to come, when he would be joined with his God in a never-ending embrace, the two of them locked in intimate congress, fucking for ever and ever, amen. His climax, when it came, stretched out past all enduring, pulling him as thin as thin could be, and then thinner still, until it seemed that he must already be dead, sucked into the hunter with the rest of them, devoured, digested, transfigured.

Then it was over. He blinked, still on his knees, sight restored. He felt disoriented, as if he had been returned to an existence for which he was no longer suited. He held the relic – again a thing of marble – cradled to his chest, and by its fading light beheld the wreckage of the cabin, lifeless now as a tomb. The ship lurched, timbers creaking, and he toppled to his side, landing on the body of a mutineer. He pushed away from its hard angles, on all fours now – all threes, rather, his left hand still clutching the relic. The body was as pale as the corpse of a drowned man, as if all the blood had been drained from it. The others were of a similar hue . . . save one.

Starkey groaned and stirred. His eyes fluttered open and focused on Aylesford. 'What . . . what 'appened?'

'Are ye hurt?' Aylesford asked in reply. 'Get up, man. We've got tae get out o' here!'

'What 'ave yer done?' Starkey rose on one elbow and looked about him with an expression of mounting horror as, with his free hand, he rubbed the back of his head vigorously.

'Saved our lives,' said Aylesford, hauling himself one-handed to his feet by means of the ropes that girded the cabin walls.

Starkey was suddenly sick, turning aside and spewing the contents of his stomach over the floor. When he had done, he turned back to Aylesford, wiping his mouth with one sleeve. 'That thing were in my 'ead,' he said. 'I could feel it wormin' about in me thoughts, rummagin' through me like I were a curiosity shop.' He spat, then pulled himself to his feet. 'I felt its eye upon me – gorblimey if I do not feel it even now! 'Tis a baleful regard, full o' 'unger and greed like. Look 'ow it shines!'

''Tis a Godly thing,' said Aylesford.

'There be more o' goblin than god ter it,' Starkey replied. 'Better yer should throw it o'er the side!'

'Are ye daft?' cried Aylesford. 'Why, 'tis the key tae winnin' the war! Surely ye can see that! Our enemies will go doon before it like wheat before a scythe!'

'Mayhap they will,' said Starkey judiciously. 'Aye, 'twill be a bloody 'arvest, of that I 'ave no doubt – a 'arvest o' friends and enemies alike. But what price victory, eh? What shall it profit a man, if he shall gain the world, and lose 'is own soul?'

Aylesford laughed. 'Ye're not above quotin' the Bible, I see – though ye worship the devil or somethin' as like tae 'im as makes nae difference. Well, let us see which o' our gods is the stronger, for it will take a miracle tae get us safely off this ship.'

'Yer 'ave the right o' it there,' said Starkey glumly.

Before Aylesford could reply, the *Pierre* struck something hard. Aylesford and Starkey were thrown to the floor as the ship, with a terrible drawn-out grinding and noise of splintering wood, slewed sideways, tilting precipitously as if about to go over. The bodies of the dead sailors and the rest of the items already on the floor, as well as a slew of other objects small and large which had thus far avoided that fate, rained down upon the two men, who were flung about like rag dolls. Then, as if seized by a giant hand, the ship suddenly

77

stopped, though it trembled in every timber and sent up a groan that seemed to issue from a living throat, so full of pain and despair was the sound.

Somehow, Aylesford had kept his grip on the relic, which was shining more brightly now, with a sickly purplish light . . . perhaps due to the fact that he had been struck on the back of the head again and was bleeding anew. Yet he seemed to have escaped greater harm. The same could not be said of Starkey, who was pinned, apparently unconscious, behind his own trunk. Aylesford made his way over to him, crossing by means of a wall that had become, willy-nilly, the floor . . . a floor rapidly filling with ice-cold water pouring in from somewhere.

'Starkey!' he shouted, reaching out with his free hand to shake the man by the shoulder. 'Can ye hear me?'

There was no reply. The ship sagged alarmingly, then seemed to find its balance again, however briefly. There was no time to waste. He had to get out. Yet when it came to it, the notion of abandoning Starkey did not sit well with him. He took hold of the trunk with one hand and managed to pull it aside. Deprived of its support, Starkey slumped over, and though Aylesford saw no blood, it appeared to him that Starkey's left arm was broken; at any rate, its position did not appear natural.

'Starkey!' he shouted again, once more shaking him by the shoulder. 'Wake up, damn ye!'

This time he was rewarded by a groan and sluggish movement. The head lifted; the eyes blinked groggily, trying to focus. He shook harder. 'Can ye walk?'

'Wha—'

'Can ye walk!'

Starkey cried out in pain as he instinctively moved his arm.

'Aye, it's broke, and no mistake,' Aylesford said. 'Come on – I'll help ye!'

Somehow he managed to get Starkey up. Then the two of them, with arms flung about each other's shoulders, and with their other arms clenched to their sides, made their way out of the cave of the cabin and up to the deck.

There they found chaos. The deck was canted at an impossible angle; the *Pierre* seemed to have run aground, though Aylesford could see no sign of land. He could see very little at all, and that only by the light of the relic and flickers of lightning that did not so much illuminate the scene as shatter it into garish fragments that reason couldn't quite fit back together. What he mostly saw was sheets of driving rain that merged into, and indeed were indistinguishable from, the spray of waves that crashed over the deck, or what was left of it. One of the three masts was down, lying athwart the sloping deck like a fallen tree. Another was missing altogether. The third stood upright – 'upright' in this sense meaning perpendicular to a deck that was slanted at perhaps forty degrees, which gave it, to Aylesford, the fanciful appearance of a single gigantic spear planted against the cavalry charge of the storm. It was stripped of its sail but not its rigging, and the long ropes flayed the air like a multitude of whips. The mast was bending back and forth as if trying to work itself free.

The sound was deafening, thought-crushing. It was like being carried along in the midst of an avalanche, or present at the birth of a volcano, or witness to the end of the world. The two men cowered in the futile shelter of the hatch, gazing out uncomprehendingly, clinging to each other like small dumbfounded animals confronted by a cataclysm to which instinct has no answer.

There was no sign of the first mate or the sailors who had fled the cabin. Perhaps they had found places of their own to hunker down. More likely, they had been swept overboard. It seemed to Aylesford that he and Starkey must soon join them.

'Look there!'

Starkey's voice, shouted into his ear, was all but overwhelmed in the general roar.

'There, damn yer!'

Tangled in the rigging of the fallen mast, just above the reach of the waves, was what appeared to be a boat of some kind.

'That be our chance,' shouted Starkey as the *Pierre* shifted again, with fresh sounds of splintering from the hold.

Aylesford cast a look behind him; water was boiling up from below.

'Come on, man!' cried Starkey, who had seen it too, and pulled Aylesford onto the deck. 'We'll drown like rats unless we try!'

They did not manage more than two or three faltering steps before their feet flew out from under them. Aylesford clung to the relic with both hands as he slid down the slick surface of the deck. He had no time for prayer or thought. He registered impacts to his body, but they seemed dull with distance, not really having to do with him. All that mattered was not to lose the relic.

He came to a hard, sudden stop. He lay against something solid, gasping for air and finding precious little of it in the watery world. He spat, coughing. He couldn't feel his body. If not for the blue light emanating from his midsection, he would not have known that he still held the relic. That light revealed that he had fallen against the boat Starkey had shown him. But this was no miracle: the vessel offered no escape, not even much of a refuge from the storm, for it was splintered and holed.

Aylesford knew despair. He felt abandoned. Even Starkey had left him, gone without a trace. Had it all been for nothing? Had he come all this way to die, found the relic only to lose it to the waves? In the Bible, Jesus had calmed the storm and walked upon the water. But that lay beyond his power, and, it seemed, if not the power then at least the inclination of the God who had chosen him.

Why have ye forsaken me?

He did not know if he screamed those words into the teeth of the wind or had only shouted them in the hollow of his heart.

But there came no answer.

Perhaps, he thought, this was a test of faith. Did he or did he not believe in what had been foretold? Did he or did he not trust the promises that had been made to him? Was he or was he not worthy to bear the relic?

Aylesford knew then what he must do, but it was hard. He did not want to die, and death raged all around him. There was no way to avoid it.

Therefore he would embrace it. He would not lie here and wait for some errant wave to seize him, or for the ship to shatter beneath him. He put his head back, gathering his strength and nerve, no longer feeling the force of the rain and sea spray pummelling his face. He looked up through that onslaught and seemed to see, in a lightning stutter that clawed the veil of the storm to shreds, two serpentine shapes contending in the sky. The violence of their fight had spawned the storm and drove it now. They were big as writhing thunderheads, bigger than his mind could grasp, too large even for the sky that was their battleground. The thunder was their bodies in collision; the lightning, sparks struck from their flinty scales; their copious bloodletting was the rain; and the lashing winds had themselves been lashed into being by the quicksilver coilings and uncoilings that propelled them through the air. They fought on, oblivious to the chaos they caused, as if the world were no more than a speck of dust to them, and he less than that.

Yet Aylesford sensed that the relic in his arms was not a matter of indifference to these airborne leviathans. No, nor were they a matter of indifference to what he held. It knew them. Hated them. Yes, and feared them, too . . . though he did not understand how that could be. How could God fear anything?

But they were gone now, or anyway he could no longer see them. The hole in the sky had healed itself, if it had even been there at all, and the light of the relic had gone out like a taper extinguished in the storm. He hesitated no longer but flung himself from his nest of flinders. Greedy waves snatched him away.

2

Persuasion

'DO YOU KNOW,' SAID THE LARGER OF THE TWO MEN AS HE LUMBERED DOWN the candlelit stone corridor, leaning upon a walking stick and wheezing for breath after every few words, so that his speech seemed made up of sentences that began and ended arbitrarily, 'until the recent . . . unpleasantness, these rooms had not been . . . used for their original purposes in . . . over a century. Now, in little more . . . than a month, they have seen those purposes . . . restored. First as cells for miscreants. Then as torture . . . chambers. To think I once looked upon them . . . as quaint relics of a barbarous age! Alas, they . . . have proved as needful as ever in our own.'

The speaker was very large indeed, both in height and girth, and appeared even larger by virtue of his powdered wig and heavy great-coat, which had the effect of puffing him up, rather in the manner of a cockatoo. This was Sir Thaddeus Wolfe, Grandmaster of the Worshipful Company of Clockmakers, commonly known to the apprentices, journeymen, and masters of his guild as the Old Wolf.

'Please, Sir Thaddeus,' cut in the smaller man, who was indeed very much smaller, yet at the same time could not be said to be small in an absolute sense, but only when measured against the larger man, whose twin, in every other respect, he might almost have been, so alike were they in their general proportions and style of dress, right down to the walking stick, 'do not use that word, I beg you. It is redolent of the Dark Ages. This is, after all, the eighteenth century.

We are civilized men, are we not? Men of science. Horologists. Englishmen. We do not torture. We persuade. I prefer the term "persuasion chamber".'

'Call it what you like, Malrubius,' wheezed Sir Thaddeus. He made a dismissive gesture with one massive hand, every finger of which sported a glittering ring. 'I care not – so long as you produce results.'

'And I have produced them,' said Malrubius with a sympathetic wheeze of his own. 'As you shall hear soon enough.'

To this assurance the Old Wolf said nothing, merely gestured again as if shooing away a fly.

In only one glaring respect, other than size, was the smaller man to be distinguished from the larger, and that was the condition of his face. Sir Thaddeus's face was as round as the full moon and quite as fat, though generally much redder, as it was now, flushed from his exertions and fairly glowing behind a sheen of sweat. But Malrubius's face – though it, too, was flushed at present – did not resemble the moon at all, or, if so, only in one of her lesser phases. It lacked a pleasant symmetry. It was fleshy but not round, rather like a potato, with lumps and pits – the scars of smallpox. There was, too, evidence of a more recent calamity. Dark bruises cratered his eyes. His nose was inflamed and badly swollen – a smaller potato sprouted from a larger – and his lips were puffy and scabbed. He had the look of a man who had suffered a severe beating.

The two continued on wordlessly, passing heavy wooden doors on both sides of the corridor. None of these doors offered a hint of what lay behind them. The only sounds were the scuff of footsteps, the click of canes, the jingling of a set of keys hooked to Malrubius's belt, and a soft, steady wheezing, as of two bulldogs drowsing before a fire. At last Malrubius halted at a particular door. He unhooked the keys and began to sort through them in the light of a thick candle burning in a sconce beside the door.

The Old Wolf grunted and gestured impatiently with his stick.

The proper key at last procured and employed, Malrubius swung the door inwards. A foul stench rolled out of the dark.

Cursing under his breath, Sir Thaddeus pulled a handkerchief from the sleeve of his greatcoat and pressed it to his mouth and nose. Malrubius merely frowned, seemingly untroubled by the smell. Or perhaps the state of his nose protected him from the worst of it.

No sound came from the darkness behind the door.

'Fetch a light, fetch a light,' Sir Thaddeus directed, his words somewhat muffled behind the handkerchief.

Malrubius lifted the candle from its sconce and, holding it before him warily, as if uncertain of what he might find, passed through the door. The Old Wolf followed on his heels.

The room – or rather cell – they entered was bare of furnishings save a single wooden stool, a small table, a covered bucket, and a simple cot. And the stench of rotting flesh, which was like a physical object itself. There were candles in iron sconces on the walls, and these Malrubius methodically lit while Sir Thaddeus shuffled nearer to the cot, where, face-up upon a filthy ticking, lay a young man in a ragged shirt and torn breeches that were filthier still. Whether he was alive or dead was not immediately apparent. Mindful of fleas, the Old Wolf kept a prudent distance.

The prisoner was shackled to the wall by one ankle. His lank hair stuck to his pale, skeletal face, which was streaked with grime and glistened as if with fever. His right arm trailed off the side of the cot, one big hand – like a model for Michelangelo's sculpted hands – lying open on the floor as though beseeching alms; his left arm was crossed over his chest and ended in a nest of blood-and-pus-soaked bandages. It was from there, the Old Wolf judged, that the stench arose. Gangrene.

He reached out with his stick and poked the young man in the leg. When this elicited no response, he repeated the action more vehemently. This time the prisoner moaned, his leg stirring slightly, and Sir Thaddeus gave a satisfied nod. Alive, then.

'A poor enough specimen,' he said, turning to Malrubius, who, having lit all the candles in the cell, now stood beside the small table, where he had set the remaining candle alongside a corked bottle and a variety of metal implements that did not have the look of anything useful to a horologist. They seemed rather more in the surgeon's line. These were Malrubius's instruments of persuasion.

'One works with what one is given,' said Malrubius somewhat apologetically. 'The other members of the Hastings gang escaped the ambush. They are still being hunted down. I must say, the customs men are frightfully inefficient! Either that, or they have been bought off. Still, we did manage to bag this lad – Boxer, they call him. He saw everything. And he has been most eager to talk.'

'After some persuasion, I see.' Sir Thaddeus nodded towards the bandages.

'Please,' said Malrubius in an aggrieved tone. 'Do you think I am as crude as that? No, he came to us this way. Injured in the fighting.'

'Has he been seen by a physician?'

'He is beyond help. The men who captured him had wounded of their own and were not inclined to waste their resources on traitors. Indeed, by rights the fellow should be dead already. I have been at some pains to keep him alive this long.'

Sir Thaddeus absorbed this information. 'I suppose you'd better wake him before he is altogether beyond waking.'

Advancing towards the cot, Malrubius reached into his coat and pulled out a small vial. This he uncorked and held – at arm's length, and with every sign of wishing that length a longer one – under the prisoner's nose.

Boxer started violently, gasping for breath. He half rose, then sank back with a groan. His eyelids fluttered.

'Get him some water,' said the Old Wolf.

Malrubius returned to the table, picked up the bottle, and waddled back to the cot. Pulling out the cork, he tipped the bottle abstemiously over the chapped and bleeding lips of the prisoner. Boxer swallowed convulsively at the dribble of water, most of which ran down his chin.

Malrubius pulled the bottle away. 'Awake, are we, Boxer? Do you remember me?'

A weak nod.

'Do you remember what we talked about? What you told me?'

Another nod.

Malrubius inclined his head towards Sir Thaddeus. 'I want you to tell this gentleman what you told me and answer any questions he may put to you, honestly and to the best of your ability. Can you do that?'

Again a nod.

'Why, he cannot speak!' the Old Wolf exclaimed, shooting Malrubius an angry glance. 'You should have brought me sooner, Malrubius.'

'I can speak,' said a reedy voice that seemed to have come from a very long way off.

'Then do so,' commanded Sir Thaddeus. 'At once!'

'Go on, Boxer,' encouraged Malrubius. 'Tell Sir Thaddeus what you know about the murderer Thomas Aylesford.'

'Scottish Tom? Aye, I know 'im.' A swollen tongue licked at cracked lips.

'More water, Malrubius,' the Old Wolf said. 'Keep his lips moist.'

Malrubius bent dutifully, almost solicitously, over the prone form.

'Now, lad,' said the Old Wolf. 'Tell me what you know of Aylesford. Leave nothing out.'

''Twere the hand, sir,' he said with a moan. 'That horrible hand!'

'Hand? What the devil is he on about, Malrubius?'

'I seen it,' said Boxer before Malrubius could reply. 'I seen it all aglow, shinin' with the devil's own fire! It took me hand, it did! Cursed me – cursed us all!'

'Easy, lad,' said Sir Thaddeus as Boxer subsided into weak sobs.

'Tell Sir Thaddeus what was in that hand,' prompted Malrubius.

''Twere a watch, sir,' said Boxer, his voice shakier than ever.

'The hunter,' said Malrubius in a tone of triumph.

'Yes, yes, I know,' said the Old Wolf irritably. 'Where did you see this watch, Boxer?'

'On the beach, sir. When the customs attacked us. Someone must o' tipped 'em off.'

'Indeed, someone did,' said Malrubius. 'I only learned of it after the fact, Sir Thaddeus, but in time enough to dispatch a regulator to Hastings. He met the customs men on their way back to London and negotiated for the release of Boxer into his custody.'

'Negotiated, eh?' said the Old Wolf and chuckled. 'No, don't tell me any more than that. I neither need nor wish to know. It seems

Mr Pitt is not including us in his counsels. Well, two can play at that game, eh, Malrubius?'

'My thought exactly,' said Malrubius with a smile rendered hideous by his injuries. 'Now, Boxer, in the confusion of the attack, Aylesford got away, did he not?'

'Aye, clean away. He were rowed out to sea. A ship were waitin' offshore to take him to France.'

'This is very important, Boxer,' said Sir Thaddeus. 'Was there anyone with Aylesford?'

'Aye.'

The Old Wolf bared his teeth. 'Who was it? Did you hear a name? Daniel Quare, perhaps?'

'Don't know no Quare, sir. The man with Scottish Tom were called Starkers.'

'Starkers? Who in the blazes is that? Malrubius, who is this Starkers?'

'I don't know, Sir Thaddeus.'

'Another accomplice of Quare's, no doubt. Quare must have passed Aylesford the hunter, and then Aylesford and this Starkers fellow carried it to their masters across the Channel. Damn the infernal luck – to have it slip through our fingers this way! What of our agents in France? Have they reported anything?'

'No, Sir Thaddeus,' said Malrubius.

'So the trail has gone cold.'

'Not quite,' said Malrubius. 'Boxer, tell Sir Thaddeus what else you saw.'

'Scottish Tom were laggin' behind,' said Boxer, who had begun to shiver now, his teeth chattering, 'and I were goin' back to f-fetch him. That's when I seen him. A man dressed all in grey. He were f-fightin' Scottish Tom. Had him beat, he did. On the ground and at his m-mercy.'

'Grimalkin,' said the Old Wolf, his blue eyes widening above the handkerchief that was still pressed to his mouth and nose. 'And then what happened, Boxer?'

'D-disappeared, sir.'

'What, ran off, you mean?'

'Nay – v-vanished into thin air . . . like a g-ghost! It's God's truth, sir, I swear it!'

'I believe you, lad,' said Sir Thaddeus. 'And then what?'

'Me and Starkers p-picked up Scottish Tom and d-dragged him to the boat. I were shot then, sir. D-don't know what happened after that. D-don't remember much o' anythin' till I got here and f-found meself in the care o' this gentleman. He promised to f-fetch a doctor if I told him what I knowed, and I have t-told him, and you, too, sir, and now I'd like that d-doctor, if ye please. I c-can't feel me hand no more, nor me arm, nor much o' anythin' 'cept the c-cold.'

This speech evidently exhausted Boxer. He sagged back into the cot, his eyes closed, his breath coming short and fast, his body racked with shudders he seemed helpless to control. A patter of liquid testified to the release of his bladder.

'I am sorry for you, lad,' said the Old Wolf, stepping back to avoid the spreading pool. 'Fell in with a crowd of traitors – and look how low it's brought you.'

Boxer made no reply. He appeared to have lost consciousness.

'Shall I fetch a physician?' asked Malrubius.

'To what end? Did you not assure me the case is hopeless?'

'I did promise him,' said Malrubius.

'That is your affair,' said the Old Wolf with a shrug. 'I would as soon see him hanged as not, as an example to others. Yes, give him to Pitt. That is all the physician he merits.'

'Will not Mr Pitt wonder how we came to be in possession of a prisoner that his men reported to have escaped on the road to London?'

'Let him wonder. Let him draw what conclusions he likes. Perhaps it will teach him not to be so stingy with his intelligence next time.'

The Old Wolf turned and made his way out of the cell, Malrubius following close behind. 'Meanwhile,' he continued, removing his handkerchief once he was safely in the corridor, the door shut and locked behind him, 'I shall renew my petition to His Majesty for permission to question Lord Wichcote. His part in Quare's cabal is a curious one.'

This elicited a snort from Malrubius. 'Wichcote is an effete and decadent parasite, a dilettante who dabbles in clocks he cannot understand and squanders his fortune even faster than the king his cousin! We'll learn nothing from him.'

'I don't agree. There is more to that man than meets the eye. Much more. Why should someone with every advantage of birth and more wealth than Croesus jeopardize all by conspiring with the enemies of king and country? What is the connection between him and Grimalkin – for there must be one, else why would he have disguised himself and his friends as that infamous fellow when they so rashly attempted to steal the hunter?'

'Rash,' agreed Malrubius, 'but successful.'

'Indeed,' said the Old Wolf sourly as he retraced his steps up the corridor. 'Had I known how dangerous the hunter could be, I never would have used it as bait for a trap. But who could have known?'

'It killed Master Magnus. Was that not indication enough?'

'Indication of what? We did not know the watch was responsible for Magnus's death, only that he was holding it in his hand when his corpse was found. I was so relieved to see my old enemy removed from the board at last that I did not question the circumstances of his death as closely as I should have done. I knew the hunter was at the heart of it somehow, but I assumed he had been killed *because* of the thing – not *by* it. Besides, I had no time to investigate further. I had to move quickly to secure control of the regulators and purge the Order of those elements loyal to Magnus.'

'I dare to say I was of some use in that business, Sir Thaddeus.'

'Yes, yes – I have already placed the day-to-day operations of the Most Secret Order in your hands, Malrubius. Do you wish some other reward?'

'I merely wish you had taken me into your confidence that night and allowed me to be present when you sprang your trap.'

'Do you imagine you would have made a difference? No, sir. You were lucky to be elsewhere. Had you been with me, you would have died. Everyone else in that room was slaughtered – drained of blood. I alone survived . . . and I am at a loss to explain how. Quare had it in his power to kill me as he did the others, yet he did not. He spared me. Why?'

Malrubius shrugged. 'Who can say?'

'It was the hunter,' said the Old Wolf firmly. 'I am convinced of it. The hunter stayed his hand.'

'You speak as if it were alive, Sir Thaddeus.'

'If you had seen what I saw that night, Malrubius, you would not dismiss the possibility. Quare and the rest were in my power. Disarmed. Helpless. And then, in the blink of an eye, everything changed. The tables turned. Seeking to compel Quare's cooperation, I cut off one of his fingers . . . and damned if the hunter did not drink the man's blood! It was glowing, sir – shining like an evil star. That was the last I knew, until I awoke and found my guards dead as doornails. I was alone, facing Lord Wichcote, the traitor Gerald Pickens, and Daniel Quare, all of them dressed alike as that damned thief, the hunter shining like a fallen star in Quare's maimed hand. In another moment, I should have been dead and the hunter gone, carried to France. I did not hesitate. I fired my pistol point-blank at the blackguard. Aye, and struck him, too. A fatal wound, I am sure of it. Yet he did not die. No, 'twas Pickens who perished, for no sooner had he hastened to his fallen comrade's side than Quare slit his throat as pretty as you please. And once again the hunter feasted.'

'There is no honour among thieves, as they say,' observed Malrubius.

'There you are wrong, sir. For Lord Wichcote could have escaped at that moment but did not. He engaged me sword to sword, allowing Quare to get away.'

Malrubius frowned at this information. 'But did you not tell me – and indeed, Mr Pitt as well – that Lord Wichcote and Quare had escaped together?'

'I did, but it was not the truth. I did not think you or anyone else would believe the truth. I did not believe it myself! But something young Boxer said has put me in a different mind. Do you recall? He said that he saw Grimalkin vanish into thin air as he and Aylesford fought upon the beach at Hastings.'

'Bah.' Malrubius waved a pudgy hand as though brushing a cobweb away. 'The lad was raving.'

'Perhaps. Yet I am inclined to believe him.'

'May I ask why?'

'Because that is precisely how Lord Wichcote left my chambers. Vanished into thin air! It was the last thing I saw, and I am not likely to forget it ever. I had just run him through with my blade – even as I felt his dagger enter my side: a dagger poisoned with a sleeping draught, as it turned out. But even as I succumbed, I saw him, or rather didn't see him, for in one moment he was there, before me, and in the next he was not.'

'Impossible.'

'I would have said so myself had I not seen it with my own eyes. There is much I had thought impossible that appears to be quite otherwise. These are strange times, Malrubius. But just assume that what I have told you is true. What would that imply?'

Malrubius was silent for a moment. Then: 'Are you suggesting it was Lord Wichcote, in the guise of Grimalkin, upon the beach at Hastings?'

'In fact, I am suggesting that Lord Wichcote and Grimalkin are one and the same.'

'A peer of the realm lower himself to the level of a common thief?' scoffed Malrubius. 'It hardly seems likely.'

'There is nothing in the least common about Grimalkin,' Sir Thaddeus said. 'Think for a moment of what it would mean if – never mind how, exactly – our regulators could vanish in the blink of an eye from one location and reappear in another as it appears Lord Wichcote can do.'

'Why, we could end the war at a stroke! We might even . . .' Malrubius's voice trailed off, but his bruised lips turned upward in a broken smile. 'There is nothing we could not do!'

'We must learn Lord Wichcote's secrets,' Sir Thaddeus said. 'We must make them our own.'

3

Of Mice and Men

HE HAD GONE BY A NUMBER OF NAMES OVER THE YEARS. IN HIS WIDE-RANGING youthful travels he had been Michael Gray, a journeyman of the Worshipful Company of Clockmakers, the venerable London guild whose royal patent granted it absolute authority over the mechanisms designed to measure time, if not over time itself. Later, he had been Longinus, a servant at the guild hall of that august institution, and, in that capacity, a spy for Master Theophilus Magnus, now deceased but formerly the head of the Most Secret and Exalted Order of Regulators, a fellowship of confidential agents operating semi-autonomously within the Worshipful Company. Unknown to all, he had been Grimalkin, the notorious grey-masked thief with a penchant for timepieces and the unnerving – some might say unnatural – ability to enter any room, no matter how well secured, and exit it again undetected, bearing away his prize . . . though he was quite capable of fighting his way in or out if necessary, as it sometimes was, despite the best-laid plans. And all the while, beneath those masks both literal and figurative, he had been Josiah Wichcote, 3rd Earl of Gowrie (or, as he preferred, using his courtesy title: Lord Wichcote), cousin to His Majesty King George II.

This man of many names, wearing an opulently embroidered green silk dressing gown, lay propped on plump pillows of red silk on a daybed upholstered in matching red silk as richly embroidered as the dressing gown. The daybed was situated in the antechamber of his bedchamber, a room that might have been mistaken for a bed-chamber itself by anyone new to the house, so grand was its size, so sumptuous its furnishings. But what really distinguished the room from similar rooms in other great houses (though not from other rooms in this great house) was the number and variety of clocks to be found there. They stood on tables, on shelves, and on the mantel above the fireplace, in which a low fire crackled. Some hung from the walls; others stood upon the floor in long and elaborately ornamented wooden cases. This seeming superfluity of clocks was rendered more eccentric still by the fact that no two of the timepieces were in agree-ment. The hands of each displayed a different time. Perhaps less obvious at first, but more remarkable when noticed and reflected upon, the sounds of the hidden mechanisms that drove and regu-lated the orbits of the various hands about the various dials were not synchronized. In fact, the closer one listened, the more it seemed that there was no harmony at all to the noises that issued from the clocks, no soothing orchestration of tick and tock such as one might find, for example, in the fine shop of a London clockmaker in good standing with his guild; but instead an unruly jumble of mutterings that meshed only briefly and, as it were, by accident, like the self-absorbed whispers of a crowd of polite madmen who might chance on occasion to utter the same word. This man of many names did not appear to give the mild cacophony the slightest notice, as if entirely used to it.

A sash window, behind heavy curtains of crimson damask that had been tied back, looked out over a well-appointed garden whose sunlit greenery was shot through with swathes of colour that testified to both the flamboyant final excesses of a summer slow to fade and the irresistible onset of autumn's garish pageantry. The garden's precisely laid out gravel pathways, its placid ponds, its fountains, sculpted hills, and statuary, and the no less thoughtfully arranged plantings, wonderfully blended art and nature to provide a source of pleasant reflection or a goad to philosophical rumination. From that window one could gaze out at the garden and its high enclosing walls – which had been built in such a way as to, by a trick of perspective, make the extent of the garden appear much grander than it was or could possibly be – and imagine oneself far indeed from the hustle and bustle of London, rather than, as was the case, lying as near to its beating heart as a jewelled pendant dangling from the slender neck of a fashionable woman lies to hers. As near . . . and as far.

The daybed had been arranged to provide Lord Wichcote with an unobstructed view out the window. His face was unpowdered, its sallow colour and sharply etched lines indicative of age and infirmity. His eyes, however, were alert, alight with intelligence and lively curiosity. Old he might be, and suffering the enervating effects of some illness whose nature was not immediately apparent, but the mind looking out at the world through those eyes was anything but feeble.

Rather than admiring his garden, however, Lord Wichcote was staring fixedly at the foot of the daybed, where a small grey mouse returned his attention with equal avidity. The bold creature twitched its whiskers and ran a slender paw behind one pink ear while its apple-seed eyes seemed to soak up the sight of the man.

'Will you not approach any nearer, little one?' asked his lordship in a soft, inviting voice. 'I mean you no harm.'

The mouse continued its quiet study of the man.

'How I wish you could speak,' Lord Wichcote said. 'I have so many questions . . . and your mistress is in no state to answer them.'

Indeed, the young woman to whom he referred was lying unconscious in one of his guest rooms. He had last spoken with her but briefly, and that more than a week ago, when she had appeared in his attic workshop like some mirror image of himself – for she, too, had been dressed in the grey garb of Grimalkin – and made the astonishing claim, before falling in the dead faint from which she had yet to awaken, that she was his daughter: a daughter whose existence, until that instant, he had not known of or even suspected. Nor did he yet believe it. But he did not disbelieve it, either.

For one thing, as he had discovered when, after her collapse, he had gone to her assistance (to the extent he was able, gravely injured himself, hence his presence on the daybed, and the bandages beneath the dressing gown), the young woman wore a necklace upon which hung a golden wedding band. It was a necklace and a ring that he recognized at once, though he had last seen them more than forty years ago, on the swanlike neck of Corinna, the daughter of Herr Doppler, burgomeister of Märchen, the isolated Alpine village where his life had changed for ever, and not just because he had fallen head over heels in love with that fascinating and obstinate maiden, who had turned out to be so much more, so much *other*, than she seemed.

His snowbound stay in Märchen had been measured in months only, the blink of an eye in anguished retrospect but at the time a blissful eternity in which their love had shyly announced itself, taken root, and blossomed. Time enough to steal glances and kisses and more, behind the back and indeed under the very nose of Herr Doppler. Time enough to plan for a future that would never be. That never could have been, as he'd learned too late, in those last frantic moments when his world had been turned upside down and everything he thought he understood about Märchen, about Corinna, even about himself, had been shattered.

Nothing had remained in the dazed aftermath of that shattering but his love for her. And perhaps this child, this young woman who so resembled her. She could not be older than twenty, he thought, and perhaps not even as old as that . . . and he had been absent from the village for twice as long. But time, as he well knew, did not run to the same tame measure in that place, that *Otherwhere*, as he had learned to call it; there it was no placidly flowing stream but something altogether wilder and more whimsical, which even the carefully composed cacophony of clocks in this room could only hint at. He had experienced its vagaries for himself, entering the town's clock tower hand in hand with Corinna in the midst of the harshest winter he had ever known only to emerge mere moments later into a ripening spring, Corinna gone, Märchen gone, both for ever after beyond his reach – for he had never stopped trying to find his way back. Nothing had remained of his sojourn there but the pocket watch Corinna had stolen from her father and given to him for safekeeping, the same watch whose later theft, little more than a week ago – from the attic of this very house, by this same young woman now claiming to be his daughter – had upended his life for the second time.

None of that was proof that she really was his daughter, of course. She might have claimed anything in order to secure his help, badly wounded as she was – even worse than himself, as it turned out, for while he bore only the deep puncture wound of a rapier (whose point, according to his physician, had missed his heart by less than a cat's whisker), she appeared to have been mauled by a wild beast. So, much as Lord Wichcote found himself yearning to accept the woman's claim as the truth, and in so doing establish a connection to Corinna, perhaps even a way back to her (though he knew very well that he could not go back to her in any real sense, that she was as far above him as a god might be, her true form not just unknown to him but in all likelihood unknowable), he reasoned that, on the whole, more evidence was required, for these were perilous times, with the future of England at stake, and the theft of the pocket watch had already placed a powerful weapon into the hands of enemies across the Channel and beyond.

There was another piece of evidence that testified, if mutely, in the young woman's favour, and this Lord Wichcote found more difficult to explain away than he did the necklace and ring, which, after all, could have been stolen from Corinna or counterfeited in order to fool him. That evidence stood or rather perched before him.

The mouse.

On that first night in the attic, when his doppelgänger had brazenly stolen the watch, and then again on the second night, days later, when the imposter had returned, a mouse very much like this one – for all mice resembled each other, just as, he supposed, all Grimalkins did – had been her companion, carried in the folds of her grey cloak. It had peeked out at him from there with the same unnerving gaze it fastened on him now (unnerving because those ink-spot eyes would not look away, as if feeding on the sight of him), then scampered off into the shadows when she fell. That mouse had called to mind the extraordinary mechanical mouse that Corinna had made in Märchen, a cunningly crafted clockwork creature that had seemed as alive as the other automatons there: the tiny, waspish fire-breathing dragon that nested within the cuckoo clock of Inge Hubner; the grander, one-eyed dragon that coiled about the base of the clock tower at the centre of the town; the mechanical men and women he'd watched marching across the proscenium of that tower in a silent parade that had included, at the end, like some bumbling bumpkin afraid of being left behind, his own spitting image.

Märchen, as Corinna had later told him, was situated between the real world, in which an unbridgeable gap divided flesh-and-blood from mechanical, and what he supposed must be termed the *realer* world, the Otherwhere, a realm without shape or substance that nevertheless had given birth to everything that existed, animate and inanimate, real and imaginary: time and death and love, sun and moon and stars, gods and men and even mice. Märchen, by virtue of its in-between nature, was characterized by a promiscuous mingling of otherwise separate categories. Boundaries dissolved; things flowed into each other; dreams infiltrated the waking world, and the waking world shaded into dream. Thus it had been a place of wonder and terror to him, those two emotions fused into something new like so many hybrid things there: the prosthesis that had replaced his maimed lower leg, for instance, a limb carved of some pale wood or metal he did not know, with an interior of gears and chains and levers – veins and tendons, too – that had been grafted seamlessly to his stump by Dr Immelman and ever since had served him as well as, and in many respects better than, the amputated original. So, too, the mouse that Corinna had made to pass the time and to provide herself with a friend. She'd named it Henrietta, a thing of wood and metal and paint that she'd kept close to her person, like a girl with a favourite dolly. Only this was no mere doll, but a lively imperson- ation of a mouse that, at a distance, had been indistinguishable from the real thing, a tame pet that had scampered up and down her arms and taken refuge in the folds of her clothing and the blonde ringlets of her hair. Charmed and intrigued, he'd asked to examine it, and it was not until she'd lifted it from her dress and placed it in his hand that he'd realized it was a construct. It was heavier than a mouse and lacked the softness and warmth he'd expected, which was not to say that it was cold: no, it had heat, but not a living heat. It was more like a stone warmed by the sun. Cupped in his hand, it regarded him with fathomless black eyes, wire whiskers twitching. Its tiny claws pricked his palm. He could feel the regular ticking of its inner workings.

'Why, it is an automaton!' he'd exclaimed with a delighted laugh. 'But who made it? Surely this must be another of Herr Wachter's miracles!' Jozef Wachter being the wizardly clockman who'd led him a merry chase across half the earth until finally drawing him to Märchen and its perverse clock tower, known to the locals as Wachter's Folly, whose secrets he would have sold his soul to learn. Alas, what he'd learned was that Wachter was long gone from the town, most probably dead, and the workings of the timepieces he'd left behind forbidden to his investigation. Yet here, perhaps, was a forgotten or overlooked example of Wachter's craft.

It was not to be. For Corinna, blushing, had confessed that she and not Wachter had made the mouse. That had been the first proof of her talents as a clockmaker. Unschooled though she was, this lonely young woman, whose keen, questioning intellect had made her something of an outcast in the town, had a genius for the intricate mechanical arts that rivalled and perhaps even surpassed that of his friend and mentor, the master clockmaker and inventor Theophilus Magnus of the Worshipful Company, whose unorthodox mind was the most fertile he knew.

Yet when she'd opened the mouse for him – she would not let him perform the task himself, as though afraid he might inadvertently hurt or harm her creature – he'd seen an impressive clockwork design impressively executed, but nothing that accounted for the uncanny counterfeit of life. Indeed, once opened, the workings laid bare, it was as if a spell had been lifted, a glamour stripped away, and the automaton was exposed as a clever assemblage of bits and pieces such as any skilful craftsman might put together.

'But what is the secret?' he'd asked her. 'What is it that imparts the semblance of life?'

'Why, can you not guess?' she'd answered coyly, and then, before he could reply, leaned boldly in to kiss him for the first time. With that kiss, a new and more potent glamour had taken hold of him. And held him still.

Which was why his heart, despite the cavilling of his sceptical mind, and with no more proof than these memories, unfaded by time, had already accepted that the young woman was, in fact, Corinna's daughter. His daughter. Love, after all, has no need of facts; it can thrive in their absence and may even be killed by a superfluity of them. What love requires most of all is hope, and this Lord Wichcote had in plenitude, having stored it up in the granary of his heart for over forty years.

Now it was as if this mouse had nibbled its way into that store-house, and all the accumulated hope had come pouring out. His heart ached with it – though his mind coldly remonstrated that the ache had more to do with the blade of Sir Thaddeus Wolfe, Grandmaster of the Worshipful Company, which had so nearly put an end to him in the guild hall, where he'd gone with Daniel Quare to steal the hunter back . . . only to witness that malign relic of the Otherwhere, or what it contained, take possession of poor Quare and make of him its cat's-paw. Where he was now, and what he was doing with that watch – or, rather, what the watch was doing with him – Lord Wichcote would have given much to learn. Perhaps the young woman in his guest room had the answer to that question, too, if he could but wake her. But the secret of that lay beyond his physician and beyond him as well. Certainly a hopeful father's hopeful kiss had not sufficed.

After he had crawled to her across the attic floor only to find her unresponsive to his touch and to his voice, he had felt himself in danger of joining her in oblivion. He had called for help, but his voice had been no more than a ragged whisper, too low to carry beyond the confines of the room. He had pulled her head into his lap and gazed down at her bruised but beautiful face with such a thorny tangle of emotions as no words can express, searching her features for echoes of Corinna's eyes and nose and mouth, which he had so often studied from precisely this angle, and, it seemed to him, finding those echoes, so much so that, feeling himself losing hold of consciousness, he had pressed his lips to her forehead, tasting the salt of sweat and the chill, or so he feared, of death.

*

When next he'd opened his eyes, he'd been lying propped on pillows in his own four-poster. The watery shimmer of candlelight suffusing the air told him that it was night. He could hear the rustle of someone moving about close by but could not see them. Apparently his call for help had been heard. But what of his mysterious visitor? Did she yet live? He tried to move, but doing so caused such pain to shoot through his breast that it was as if he'd been stabbed a second time. He groaned in agony and fell back.

A black tide rolled in, receded, and he found himself gazing up through teary eyes at the face of his housekeeper, Mrs Bartholomew. That pockmarked, moonish face had never seemed so welcome or so dear, though her mouth was pinched in disapproval, and her blue eyes, beneath her starched white cap, seemed to express more annoyance than concern. As soon as he saw that, Lord Wichcote knew that he was going to be all right. Had he beheld tears welling in those eyes, or a quivering in those lips, he would have given himself up for a goner in the instant.

'What foolishness,' she said as she deftly laid a damp, blessedly cool cloth across his forehead. 'To be gallivanting about the city again after all these years, and you no longer a young man. For shame, your lordship. For shame.'

'We are neither of us as young as we once were, Mrs Bartholomew,' he managed to say, his voice little more than a wheezy whisper. Certainly she was not. She had seemed old to him when he had succeeded to the title some fifty years ago, though he supposed she must have been in her thirties at the time, a widow even then. She had been his father's housekeeper, as much a part of Wichcote House as its enduring architecture, and he had inherited her just as he had the house and title. There had never been any keeping of secrets from her sharp eyes and suspicious mind: she had tumbled to his grey-garbed alter ego almost from the first, and had proved, over the years, a useful if not entirely willing accomplice on those nights when, as this one, he'd come home somewhat the worse for wear. 'And yet,' he added, 'we remain what we always were, do we not?'

'Arrant nonsense.' Mrs Bartholomew snorted and shook her head, her hands meanwhile smoothing his bedclothes and then tucking them back around him with all the tenderness of Bia binding Prometheus to his stone. 'Why, you're off your head. Like as not this fever will do what that sword, by the grace of God, did not!'

He had not realized he was feverish, but now he felt the truth of her words. He licked his dry lips, at which Mrs Bartholomew, after turning briefly aside, raised a glass of water to his mouth and urged him to sip from it. He gulped instead, and when his coughing fit had subsided, and the pain thus engendered had retreated to its hot, pulsing core, he inquired hoarsely: 'The girl. What of her?'

Mrs Bartholomew's frown deepened. 'She lives but has not awakened. Who is she, and why was she dressed as that wild rogue?' To Lord Wichcote's knowledge, Mrs Bartholomew had never uttered the name Grimalkin, as though it were beyond the bounds of polite discourse. She resorted instead to a stable of euphemisms, of which 'wild rogue' was the most common. Or had been, in those days when he had donned the grey and, as she put it, gallivanted about the city on a regular basis, which he had not for almost ten years . . . until the events of three nights ago had caused him to bring that masked gentleman out of retirement.

'I do not know who she is,' he said. 'I should like very much to question her on that subject and others.'

'Others indeed,' said Mrs Bartholomew, raising her eyebrows in a way that signalled, if possible, an even deeper disapproval: of him, of the girl, of the world itself – who could say?

'Why, what do you mean, Mrs B?' he asked. He had called her by that name when he had first met her, to her plain annoyance. At the time, being a scapegrace recalled to London by the unexpected death of his father, to whom he had not spoken in years, he had quite enjoyed provoking her; nowadays, older and wiser, or so he liked to imagine, he seldom employed that form of address, and only as a term of rough endearment, though she gave no sign of enjoying it any more than she ever had.

She certainly did not now, her eyes flashing, though her voice was unruffled as ever. 'As to that, I think it best the doctor have his say. He will want to examine you again in any case.' She moved out of his view in a rustle of skirts, presumably to summon his personal physician, Dr Rinaldi.

He shut his eyes, overwhelmed with weariness, and must have slept, for when he opened them again the room was filled with daylight, and Dr Rinaldi was bending over him, with Mrs Bartholomew hovering in close attendance behind.

'So you are awake,' said the good doctor with satisfaction, as though he took full credit for that circumstance. He leaned back, seeming to balance on his ample round ball of a belly, which strained against the seams of his silk waistcoat, and gave a satisfied smile, exposing the beautiful white teeth, strong and even, in which he took such pride. 'You are lucky to be alive, your lordship. An inch to the right and that blade would have skewered your heart.' He flicked a plump wrist as though turning a key in a lock. 'A serious wound in any case,' he went on. 'A fatal wound, I dare say, nine times out of ten. Such hurts upset the delicate balance of the humours and cause the system to tip into dyscrasia. Hence your fever, which Rinaldi has battled while you lay in the embrace of Morpheus – blessedly so. I have, with some difficulty, through a course of bleedings and cuppings, restored balance. Few physicians, I make so bold as to assert, would have attempted it. Fewer still would have succeeded. But you, my lord, have Rinaldi at your side, and where other physicians hesitate, Rinaldi pushes forward. Others may doubt: Rinaldi *knows*. The result? Your fever is vanquished, putrefaction – a danger not to be underestimated – avoided. In short, my lord, Rinaldi has wrestled with Death on your behalf and won a victory. I have pulled you back from the brink and planted your feet, as it were, once more upon solid ground.' He inclined his head modestly, as if he would much rather have kept silent on these matters but was compelled by a profound respect for honesty and truth to acknowledge his own brilliance.

Lord Wichcote was not ungrateful or unappreciative of Dr Rinaldi's talents – he had employed the services of the man for more than twenty years, after all – but at present he had more pressing concerns than stroking the boundless egotism of his personal physician, who, apart from Mrs Bartholomew, was the only member of his household staff to know that he and Grimalkin were one and the same. 'How long have I been lying here, dead to the world?'

'Why, it is a full two days since we last spoke, your lordship,' Mrs Bartholomew answered.

'Two days!' He made as if to rise, but found that he had no more strength than a baby. Yet unlike his last attempt, there was no pain now; he felt hollow, emptied out. In truth, it was something of a relief. 'What of the girl, Rinaldi?'

'There is no change, my lord. Corinna yet sleeps.'

'Corinna! Why do you call her by that name?'

'Why, you yourself did so,' Rinaldi asserted with another preening smile, spreading his hands as though offering a benediction. 'It was the only word that passed your lips as I plied my healing arts. Over and over you repeated it, as if it were a prayer.'

'Her name is not Corinna,' Lord Wichcote said.

'I beg your pardon,' said Rinaldi. 'I had assumed—'

'I do not know the young woman's name,' Lord Wichcote interrupted. 'Indeed, I know nothing about her. What is the matter with her, Rinaldi? Can you not wake her? It is most urgent that I question her.'

'As to that, my lord, there are limits to what even Rinaldi may accomplish. The body often knows better than we do what it requires. In many cases, time is the most salubrious of treatments. The wise physician knows when to intervene and when to step back and observe. If the humoral balance is upset, it strives to correct itself. Many times it will do so unaided . . . or with the aid of the Almighty, whom even Rinaldi must acknowledge as his master.'

'In other words,' Lord Wichcote said dryly, 'you have no more idea than I do what is wrong with her.'

'I beg to differ, your lordship,' Rinaldi asserted. 'The truth is, I have examined this young woman, and I have found her to be most . . . unusual.' He glanced towards Mrs Bartholomew, whose face had inexplicably flushed crimson.

'Why, what do you mean, "unusual"?' Lord Wichcote demanded. 'Unusual in what respect?'

Mrs Bartholomew reddened further. 'She is' – her voice dropped to a whisper – 'a morphodite.'

'A what?'

'Hermaphrodite,' Dr Rinaldi corrected, flashing his toothsome smile. 'It means—'

'I know what it means,' Lord Wichcote said. 'But how . . . ? That is . . .' He found himself at a loss for words.

Not so Rinaldi. 'The young woman was sorely wounded. She appeared to have been mauled by a wild beast. That much was plain from the most cursory examination. Your lordship was my primary concern, of course, but after I had seen to you, and left you sleeping soundly, I returned to my other patient. Incredibly, in the brief time I had been away, her wounds had healed to such a degree that, had I been but newly consulted, I would have stated with confidence that weeks and not mere hours had gone by since those injuries had been sustained. With the able assistance of Mrs Bartholomew, I removed the young woman's clothing – I do not inquire into how she happened to be dressed in the costume of your lordship's, ah, illustrious alter ego – and discovered, to my amazement, and Mrs Bartholomew's distress—'

'I was like to have died, sir!' the housekeeper put in, wringing the folds of her gown. ''Tis not proper for a young girl, I mean boy . . . Oh, which is it?'

'I had, of course, heard of such cases in my studies,' continued Rinaldi unflappably, 'but had never thought to encounter one in the flesh. These sports of nature are more to be pitied than feared, Mrs Bartholomew.'

'Why, I do pity the poor thing, whatever it may be. Still, there is something indecent about it. Something improper. "Man and woman created He them", Doctor, as the scripture does say. It is a judgement of the Almighty, or the devil's work . . .'

'Here now,' said Lord Wichcote, finding his voice at last. 'You know very well that such superstitions have no place in Wichcote House, Mrs Bartholomew. Reason rules beneath this roof, and always shall.'

'Beg pardon, your lordship,' she said, without seeming in any way to do so.

'Your lordship is quite correct,' said Rinaldi, beaming approvingly. 'Just as the states of sickness and health are not polar opposites but rather lie along a spectrum, one shading imperceptibly into the other according to the humoral ebb and flow, so too is there more variation, shall we say, in the organs—'

'Dr Rinaldi!' objected Mrs Bartholomew.

The good doctor inclined his head gravely, as medical men are wont to do when availing themselves of that licence granted to their profession to speak even in mixed company of the most shocking and unpleasant matters. 'Suffice it to say that when it comes to human anatomy, my lord, normality is more of an abstract ideal than the layman is apt to credit. We who seek to follow however imperfectly in the footsteps of Galen and Asclepius should not judge what we do not understand: we should rather seek to understand it through observation and experiment. Or so it has always seemed to Rinaldi.'

'And what, pray, has Rinaldi observed?' Lord Wichcote inquired tartly.

'Since the time of Galen, we have known that the woman is the mirror image of the man,' Rinaldi said as Mrs Bartholomew busied herself at tasks on the far side of the room. 'They come together to make a whole, and only out of that whole can a new life be engendered, from the commingled seeds of each, fused in the heat of coitus and implanted in the womb. Our mysterious young patient represents an incomplete fusion, it seems to me. That is, she – or he, if you prefer – possesses in all respects the external character-istics appropriate to each sex, though to any casual observer, judging only by face and figure, our patient would appear to be an attractive young female.'

'Extraordinary,' said Lord Wichcote. 'And do you suppose that this condition may be in any way related to the speed with which her wounds have healed?'

'A most perspicacious question, my lord,' said Rinaldi, with the air of a tutor praising an apt pupil. 'I do suppose it. In fact, I con-sider it likely that the two are related in some manner. Whether that relationship is one of cause and effect, and, if so, which may be the cause and which the effect, or whether they are both effects of some hidden cause, Rinaldi does not yet hazard an opinion. To press a physical examination any further at this point would be medically unsound and morally dubious. We must wait for the patient to awaken, and as to that, I am afraid, I can make no prediction, other than to assert with some confidence that she will awaken of her own accord, when the time is right.'

'Is she then out of danger?'

'Are any of us, ever?' the doctor rejoined with an affable shrug of his round shoulders.

'I must see her.'

'As to that, my lord, you are in no condition to leave this bed. And unless your wound proves as preternaturally quick to heal as hers have, you shall not be fit to do so for some time yet. Nor would I advise having the girl brought here. I do not think it wise to move her.'

It was later that morning, after Mrs Bartholomew and Dr Rinaldi had left the room, as Lord Wichcote lay pondering the implications of what had been revealed to him – he felt, somewhat to his surprise, no trace of aversion towards the girl, as he could not help thinking of her despite everything; indeed, he felt that this new and astonishing information only added to the likelihood that she was his daughter, for how could his union with Corinna, the union of a man and something that had the look of a woman but was in fact entirely other, a being as far beyond him as a goddess might be, result in any normal issue? – it was as he lay musing on these and other, related questions that the mouse had paid its first visit. Or, at any rate, the first visit of which he was aware.

Assailed by the prickly sense of being observed, he had glanced about him nervously, for he had not heard anyone enter the room, and he knew very well that, beyond the high walls of Wichcote House, gears were grimly grinding, and it was by no means impossible that Sir Thaddeus would dispatch a team of regulators to capture or kill him, or, for that matter, prevail upon Pitt to exert sufficient pressure on the king to compel his royal cousin to remove the protection that had shielded him for so long. Indeed, he considered Wichcote House to be no more than a temporary sanctuary; sooner or later, either by stealth or openly, by royal command, it would be violated. Too much was at stake to imagine otherwise. But there was nothing he could do about that now, helpless as he was. Though not entirely helpless, for a variety of weapons lay concealed about and within the bed. Whoever came against him would not find him as easy a mark as he might seem.

But his searching gaze found no intruder beyond a small mouse that had raised itself up on its hind legs to regard him with inscrutable interest from the foot of the bed. Lord Wichcote had no fear of mice, yet neither did he have any particular fondness for them.

'Hsst!' he said, gesturing with his hand to frighten the rodent away. 'Get you gone!'

The mouse ignored him. And it was only then that he'd remembered Corinna's mouse, recalled the mouse that had accompanied the false Grimalkin on her two visits, and began to wonder, and then to suspect, and finally to be convinced that the two mice were one and the same, and that Corinna's mouse – whose name, Henrietta, surfaced unexpectedly out of his memory – had been passed on to her daughter, and that the creature knew him, remembered him somehow, in whatever part of its mechanism in whatever manner made a record of such things. Henrietta had come to him now for a reason, he felt sure. She stared at him out of more than dumb curiosity. But his own curiosity remained unsatisfied, for the mouse did not respond to him in any way, and there was nothing in its silent and still regard that offered a hint as to its purpose.

Over the next few days, Henrietta appeared suddenly and vanished quickly, never seen by eyes other than his own. But he came to expect her visits and drew a strange comfort from them, as if Corinna were gazing at him through the tiny black eyes of the pet she had fashioned and in some manner unknown to him brought to life – or something indistinguishable from life. At least once a day and usually more often he would feel the prickle of its gaze and look up to find it studying him as intently as ever, as if he were a riddle the creature was driven to unravel. He spoke to it, not expecting an answer, really just talking to himself, or to Corinna perhaps, watching him somehow from wherever she was now, here or Otherwhere. His heart was full of all that they had shared so long ago, all they had lost, and at times he smiled, while at other times tears ran down his gaunt and whiskery old-man's cheeks. How could it be that so much time had passed? What was time that it could mean so much, yet so little? The answer to that riddle was not to be found in any of his clocks, nor even in all of them put together. Would he ever see her again, in this world or another? And what of the girl, their daughter? Could he, for so long a lonely bachelor, be a father to the child he had engendered without ever knowing it? Could that child forgive him, welcome him, love him? He would forgo all such blessings, however devoutly wished, if only she would wake.

But she did not wake.

Each day, when Rinaldi came to examine him and change his dressings, the doctor reported no alteration in the girl's condition save for the accelerated rate of healing he had already observed, which by now had rendered her wounds all but undetectable even to his trained eye. Not so much as a scar would remain to mark her mauling. Each day the mouse took up its solitary vigil at the foot of his bed, as if waiting for some sign from him that he did not know how to make. And each day he felt himself growing stronger as his condition improved, his wound healing with what seemed to the doctor and Mrs Bartholomew unusual rapidity – though to him the pace seemed excruciatingly, dangerously slow . . . for his agents and men of business about the city reported to him meanwhile that indeed, as he had both expected and feared, Sir Thaddeus had made appeal to Mr Pitt, who in turn had appealed to His Majesty, whose heretofore stout and unquestioning loyalty to his scapegrace cousin was beginning, or so it was whispered in the Court of St James, to waver.

The entirety of the monarch's reign had been marked, at least in his own mind, by the steady erosion of royal prerogatives, and this deplorable trend had given rise to the most stubborn resistance on the part of the king when any question of further encroachment arose, as it invariably did in matters pertaining to his own family, even as far-flung a branch as Lord Wichcote's. Thus had the jealous self-interest of the king served as an impenetrable shield behind which his lord-ship had cultivated a reputation for eccentricity that was itself a kind of shield. But now, under the pressure of a war that was going badly, and with the apparent loss of a weapon that, as little understood as it was, yet promised victory to whoever possessed it, His Majesty had seemingly begun to worry more about retaining his crown than about defending the ancient privileges that went along with it; indeed, if what Lord Wichcote was hearing was correct, and he had no cause to doubt it, his cousin had come around to the position – entirely reasonable – that it might be not only wise but necessary to sacrifice some of the latter in order to retain his grip on the former. After all, privileges, once given up, may be clawed back, but a kingdom, once lost, is more difficult to recover, as history demonstrated again and again, most recently in the case of the Bonnie Prince, who in 1745 had attempted to restore the House of Stuart, only to be flung ignominiously back to France, tail between his legs . . . from whence he barked even now, and might yet bite, too. Already Lord Wichcote had received diplomatically phrased inquiries from his royal cousin as to his health, along with wishes – that did not quite rise to the level of commands – that he present himself at court or, failing that, open his doors to a ministerial deputation, that he might reply to questions that had been raised about his knowledge of certain recent events at the guild hall of the Worshipful Company of Clockmakers. No, time was not on Lord Wichcote's side, and well did he know it.

Such were the concerns weighing on his mind as he lay abed and regarded the mouse called Henrietta. Eight days had passed since Sir Thaddeus, a blundering behemoth when it came to the arts of the blade, had taken advantage of a moment's distraction to run him through, a humiliation he ached to avenge. Eight days in which he had lain immobilized and all but helpless while his enemies in London and farther afield plotted and acted against him and against England . . . and Daniel Quare, no longer his own man, followed the orders of whatever it was, dwelling within the hunter, that had possessed him, an entity about which his lordship knew only one thing for certain: it had a thirst for blood.

It was intolerable. Yesterday, Dr Rinaldi had at last allowed him to be moved, albeit only from his bedchamber to his dressing chamber just outside, where a daybed had been prepared for him and arranged so that he might look out upon the beauty and tranquillity of the gardens. The view had brought no comfort, however, serving only to remind him, as he watched the deepening colour that marked the changing of seasons, how his own season was changing, his long golden summer giving way at last to a colder, more constricted clime. Without noticing it, he had become old. Life had passed him by, and though he would rise from his sickbed, he felt that it constituted an unexpected and unwelcome signpost along his life's road, a mile marker indicating an end that was much nearer than he had supposed. Small wonder he preferred to regard the mouse, the sight of which roused memories of a happier time, when he had been in the full flower of youth and had been pierced to the heart by the exquisite glance of a beautiful girl. He had not been in love before that glance; since that glance, he had not been out of it. Perhaps that was why so little time seemed to have passed, despite the testimony of his grey hair, creaking limbs, and the loss of speed that had permitted the Old Wolf to skewer him. The muscle of the heart weakens with the years, its beating stutters and slows, and finally stops altogether, yet, like a garden in a fairy story, it may nurture something eternal, or so Lord Wichcote believed.

'Is that the secret of your mistress's sleep?' he asked the mouse. 'Does she await the kiss of a handsome prince? Alas, there is only this old frog. But he would give much to wake her, if it lay within his power to do so!'

Henrietta cocked her head suddenly; then, more quickly still, vanished like a puff of grey smoke dispersed in a gust of wind. At that same instant, or as near to it as made no difference, the door to the room burst open. Dr Rinaldi strode in, his gleaming white teeth, as it were, preceding him, lighting his way.

'You must come at once, your lordship,' the doctor said breathlessly. 'She is awake and asking for you!'

'At once' was quicker to utter than to practise, and this was especially true in Lord Wichcote's case, for he could not yet walk unaided, and

Dr Rinaldi insisted that he not walk at all. His lordship was lifted deferentially from the daybed by a pair of footmen who seemed to take pleasure in ignoring his commands for haste. They deposited him into a cushioned invalid's chair as though his bones were made of porcelain, then wasted more time in arranging his legs in a manner that met with the doctor's grudging approval, his own comfort be damned. As if this were not maddening enough, a blanket was then laid across his lap, and another draped over his shoulders, so that he felt as if he were being weighed down by the very qualities of age and infirmity he was so impatient to throw off.

'For God's sake, Rinaldi! I am not so decrepit as all that!'

'Decrepit, no. Fragile, yes. You are not out of danger, my lord. Rinaldi knows his business!'

'How is she, Doctor? Tell me that, at least.'

'Why, she is like you, my lord: fractious, wilful, and entirely too apt to disregard the advice of her physician.'

'Take care, Rinaldi. You are not the only physician in London.'

'Indeed not. Your lordship is free to avail himself of the services of any quacksalver he likes – God knows there is no shortage of them here. Now, if you are quite ready?'

'I have been ready these ten minutes or more!'

Rinaldi bowed stiffly and gestured to the two footmen, one of whom hurried to open the door while the other, stationing himself behind the invalid's chair, began to push.

It was in this humiliating fashion that Lord Wichcote travelled the heretofore inconceivable distance separating him from the young person who had come to him in the guise of Grimalkin just over a week ago.

'Why,' exclaimed his lordship with a start, 'do you mean to tell me she has been here all along? So near? You might have mentioned that fact, Rinaldi!'

For, once through the door, the chair had been pushed across the hallway to the door just opposite.

'For a man in your condition, there is no near,' Rinaldi responded. 'There is only far. I did not wish to tempt your lordship to a dangerous exertion.' The doctor rapped once at the door before opening it wide and striding through.

'My dear,' he exclaimed in a jovial voice, 'Rinaldi has returned. I bring your host, Lord Wichcote.'

Wichcote, in his impatience, would have risen from the chair, but he found all strength fled from his limbs; he could only gesture with an old man's petulance for the footman to speed his entrance. Rinaldi, meanwhile, blocked his view like the moon eclipsing the sun. Then, as if with a showman's instinct – perhaps not so foreign after all to those in the medical profession – the doctor stepped aside.

Of the room itself, Lord Wichcote took scant notice. He had eyes only for the girl who lay dressed in a white shift and propped on pillows in a daybed the twin of the one he had left behind. One glance, and all doubt vanished from his mind.

He had last seen her in shadows, her bruised features streaked with blood. Now her face was unmarked, lit by the fulsome daylight streaming through the windows but also as if by an inner glow. Blonde tresses trailed from beneath a white bonnet to fall about her shoulders in shining waves. The necklace and ring glittered about her neck. She was the very image of Corinna as he remembered her.

And yet, she was not. Her face was narrower about the chin, and her cheekbones were neither as high nor as starkly chiselled as Corinna's had been. Her eyes regarded him with an intensity that matched his own stare. They were not Corinna's vivid springtime green but instead an earthy brown . . . the very colour, unless he deceived himself, of the eyes that regarded him each morning in his looking glass.

There was, it seemed to him, a hint of the masculine in the cast of her features – a manifestation, no doubt, of what Rinaldi had delicately termed 'an incomplete fusion'. But all that was mere anatomy. What struck him more than any physical similarities or differences was the fact that she possessed Corinna's otherworldly aura; it was as if she partook of a higher order of reality than what surrounded her, and, by contrast, made those surroundings seem like flat imitations – stage props, as it were, in some drama that, without

112

her presence, he would have taken for life itself. Perhaps, without the indelible impression left by his time in Märchen, he would not have been able to articulate what it was about her that set her apart or, rather, above. But he had not forgotten, nor ever could forget, how, in his months there, he had so often felt out of place, as if he were a marionette lifted off the stage and raised to the hidden heights of the puppetmasters . . . though without becoming one of them in the process. He had remained a clumsy creature of wood and rough-painted features, like the doppelgänger automaton that had emerged from the interior of Wachter's Folly, and which he had impulsively followed, at the cost of his right foot.

That was what he felt now, at the sight of this young woman whose appearance tugged so poignantly at his heartstrings . . . except it was nothing like being raised; rather, it was as if a puppetmaster had stepped down to join the marionettes onstage. She had brought something of the Otherwhere with her. Wichcote felt a tingling sensation in his prosthesis, the wonder-working appendage that Dr Immelman had fashioned to replace his amputated limb, and which had served, like the seven-league boots of the fairy tale, to give him access to the Otherwhere, or to the forking pathways that led through the Otherwhere – though he had never been able to find a path leading back to Märchen. But it had made his career as Grimalkin possible, giving him the ability to lift his foot from one piece of ground and put it down again on another that might be not just seven leagues distant but seven times seven.

If worse came to worst, that was how he meant to escape the Old Wolf and Mr Pitt, though a journey through the Otherwhere, however brief, carried dangers of its own. Not the least of them was Corinna's father, the man he had known as Herr Doppler, burgomeister of Märchen, who, as Corinna had told him (if he understood aright), had raised himself above all the others of his kind and was now engaged in a war for control of the Otherwhere, a war that had spilled over into this world, and its wars, with the theft of the hunter. That pocket watch, like all the timepieces of Märchen, but more than any of them, even the monumental tower clock through which 'Michael Gray' had entered and then exited the town, was more than it appeared to be, much, much more, just as Doppler and all his kind were more than they appeared to be. Corinna had entrusted him with the stolen watch, into which, it seemed, her father had poured some potent measure of his magic – enough that, without it, he was significantly diminished, though by no means powerless. He would look for it, she had told him in the last moments they were together – moments seared into his memory, never to be forgotten.

'Do not attempt to open it,' she had warned him. 'Do not seek to learn its secrets.'

'But what is it?' he had asked.

'Infinity bounded in a nutshell. My father will seek it ceaselessly, but as long as it sleeps, locked in matter, he cannot find it. Without it, he cannot win his war. Keep it secret, Michael. One day I – or, it may be, another – will come to claim it. But be on your guard, for my father has agents mortal and otherwise, and they will fool you if they can, or take it by force if they must.'

'But if it isn't you who comes to claim it, how will I know it is not some emissary of your father's?'

Those had been the last words he had spoken to her. She had never answered. And, in fact, as he now knew, it had not been Corinna who had come at last to claim the hunter but instead the young woman reclining before him: his daughter.

But why had she not identified herself? Why had she come disguised as Grimalkin and stolen the watch from him rather than simply asking for it? So much would have been different! If she had not stolen the watch, Daniel Quare could not have stolen it from her in turn, and if Quare had not stolen it, and returned with it to the guild hall of the Worshipful Company, Master Magnus could not have examined it, and if he had not done so, he could not have accidentally cut himself, and if he had not cut himself, his blood could not have spilled upon the hunter, and if his blood had not spilled upon the hunter, the hunter could not have awakened, and if the hunter had not awakened, with its insatiable thirst for blood, Master Magnus would still be alive, and poor Quare would not be at large somewhere in or beneath the city, in thrall to whatever bit of Doppler dwelled within the hunter he carried, a fragment actively seeking to be reunited with its master. So much death and despair, and the prospect of worse to come, all because this young woman, his daughter, had not come to him openly but instead hidden her identity behind the mask of his own alter ego. If that had been a message to him, a declaration of sorts, he had been too dense to decipher it.

All these thoughts flashed through Wichcote's mind as Mrs Bartholomew, seated beside the girl, rose to her feet. Glimpsing his expression, as it were, in the mirror of his housekeeper's face, Lord Wichcote assumed an easy smile of the sort he had learned at court – another of his many masks.

'So, you have awakened at last, like the Sleeping Beauty from her enchantment,' he drawled as the invalid's chair bore him closer to the daybed.

'Oh, but you are not well,' said the girl, evidently distressed by the sight of him in his absurd conveyance.

He waved a dismissive hand. 'A temporary inconvenience. I am on the mend – or so the good doctor assures me. But look at you! Why, 'tis a miracle, surely!'

'I have always been quick to heal,' she said, a flush of colour rising to her cheeks. 'It is a legacy from my mother.'

'I would hear more of her,' Wichcote said. 'And of you.'

Dr Rinaldi cleared his throat. 'Let me remind your lordship that our young patient is but newly awakened, and, appearances to the contrary, not fully recovered.'

'I am quite well,' the girl asserted. 'I do not mind answering your questions. And I have questions of my own.'

'Yes, we have much to discuss, I think,' said Lord Wichcote. At last the torturous progress of the chair brought him near enough to the daybed that he could have reached out and taken one of the slender hands resting atop the blanket that covered the girl from the waist down. But he restrained himself from doing so. Those hands were delicate, feminine, the fingers long and elegantly tapering. The hands of a harpsichordist. Or, he thought, remembering her mother, a clockmaker. The last time he had seen those hands, they had been stained with blood. And one of them, the right, had been holding a rapier *en garde*. He recalled vividly how quickly she had dispatched his men that first night in the attic workshop. Three men dead in as many minutes. Why, she had drawn his blood that night as well! It shook him deeply to contemplate how near he had come to death at his daughter's hand. And to realize how pointless and unnecessary had been the deaths of those loyal men. Their families would be seen to, of course, but the waste and stupidity of it angered him. That was what came of secrets. He was done with them.

'Dr Rinaldi,' he said, 'I thank you for your efforts on behalf of our guest. But I would be alone with her now.'

'That is most—'

'I do not wish to argue, sir,' Wichcote interrupted sharply, accompanying his words with a glance sharper still. 'Leave us, if you please. I assure you, I shall do nothing to unduly tax your patient. Mrs Bartholomew, perhaps you would be so good as to fetch some tea.'

'At once, your lordship,' she said. 'And some broth. The lass needs nourishment.'

'Most thoughtful,' said Wichcote in a clipped, impatient tone.

'Don't let his lordship frighten you,' Mrs Bartholomew said to the girl. 'He can be full of bluster, but he has a good heart.'

'I am not frightened,' stated the girl.

'Frightened indeed!' exclaimed Wichcote in exasperation. 'Would that some in this house had the sense to be afraid! A little fear might have a salutary effect.'

'*Oderint dum metuant*, eh?' put in Rinaldi. 'That was Caligula's motto, you know.'

'Let them hate, so long as they fear,' the girl translated, to Wichcote's surprise.

And Rinaldi's delight. 'Why, we have a scholar in our midst! Where did you learn your Latin, child?'

'*Ab avo*,' she said with a little grimace of distaste. 'From my grandfather. It was his motto, too.'

'Enough!' said Lord Wichcote. 'If Caligula was burdened with a household like this one, I begin to understand that gentleman better, I think. No wonder the poor man went mad. But he could at least see

116

his tormentors properly repaid. Alas, I may not kill but only dismiss those servants who displease me.'

'Your lordship will have his little japes,' said Rinaldi.

'Out,' said Wichcote, pointing towards the door. 'All of you. Now.'

Rinaldi bowed and withdrew, an unctuous smile pasted upon his cherubic face. He was followed by Mrs Bartholomew and the two footmen. When the door had closed behind the last of them, Lord Wichcote sighed and turned back to his guest. For a moment, the two regarded each other in silence. The only sound was the unsynchronized ticking of the myriad clocks scattered about the room.

'There have been too many secrets between us, madam,' he said at last. 'See where they have led. Let us make a pact, you and I, to speak plainly and honestly to each other. Do you agree?'

'With all my heart,' she said.

He nodded, pleased. 'A mutual acquaintance, Daniel Quare, once told me of a conversation he had with you on a London rooftop. Some sort of guessing game, I take it, or contest of wits, with three questions being allowed . . . after which any further inquiries would incur a frightful penalty of some kind. I should like to know in advance whether our conversation is to be conducted on the same lines.'

She laughed and clapped her hands like a delighted child. 'Ask whatever you like. You need fear no forfeit. I swear it.'

'Do you recall what you told me in the attic, before you lost consciousness?'

'Of course. That I was Corinna's daughter . . . and yours.'

'Is it true?'

'Can you doubt it?' she asked in turn. 'Can you not see my mother's face in my own?' Her hand went to her slender throat and plucked the golden ring dangling on its chain, held it out to him. 'Do you not recognize this ring?'

'I can and I do,' said Wichcote. 'Where is she, then? Why has she not come to me, or contacted me in all these years?'

'She is no more,' said the girl, letting the ring drop from her fingers.

117

Those four blunt words dealt him a more grievous blow than Sir Thaddeus had managed. He heard himself give an anguished moan, the kind of sound a dumb animal might make when afflicted with a hurt beyond its ability to comprehend.

'Shall I ring for the doctor?' asked the girl, concern in her voice.

Lord Wichcote raised a forestalling hand, but it was a moment before he could speak. 'No. No thank you, child. Your words have struck deep. I loved her, you see, so very, very much.' He dried his cheeks with the sleeve of his dressing gown – the silk catching on his rough whiskers, for he had not been shaved today – and forced his sorrow down. This was not the time to grieve. 'How . . . how did you lose her?' He could not bring himself to utter the grim and final word, though he winced to employ such a banal euphemism.

'In childbirth,' the girl answered matter-of-factly. 'My mother departed this world when I came into it. I never knew her. She left me three things: this necklace and its ring, which had once belonged to her own mother; a cunning little mouse she had made with her own two hands; and a name.'

'The ring I know very well,' he said, a faint smile coming to his face despite everything. 'The mouse as well; indeed, Henrietta has been a constant visitor at my bedside these last days. But I do not know the name. Will you not tell me?'

'Like you, Father, I have gone by a number of names,' the girl said, and the note of pride in her voice struck him as entirely charming, like the innocent and unrestrained egotism of a small child, so that his smile widened and his heart swelled painfully to hear it; indeed, he felt as if his heart were stretching into a new shape to accommodate all he had lost, all he had gained. Never had he known such a mix of joy and sorrow. The two fused into a love that was new to him. Corinna was dead . . . yet she lived on in this girl. His girl. Stranger and daughter both. He swore that he would be a proper father to her. For her mother's sake . . . and his own. How strange it was! Just days ago Daniel Quare had asked Lord Wichcote if he were his father – and Wichcote had responded that he would have been proud to claim that title . . . never dreaming that he was, in fact, a father already and had met his daughter all unknowing.

'To some, I am Grimalkin,' the girl went on blithely. 'I pray you forgive me for stealing your *nom de guerre*.'

'A thief must expect to be stolen from,' he returned. 'But I do not begrudge the theft. I give the name to you freely, child. I shall give you more still. Much more. I shall acknowledge you as my daughter. You shall be my heir.'

'You are most generous,' she said with a smile at once tender and condescending, as if she, like her mother, were heir to more than he could offer – more than he could imagine.

'And the name?' he prompted.

'To your young friend Daniel Quare, I was Tiamat,' she said. 'Though in truth that name, too, belongs to another. It is my grand-mother's name.'

'Was it she who raised you?'

'Alas, no. I did not meet her until I was grown. I was raised by two men. My grandfather, whom you know.'

He grimaced. 'Herr Doppler. Corinna fled from him. It would not please her, I think, to know that he had a hand in your upbringing.'

'Do not be so certain. She loved her father, though she rebelled against him. And he loved her, despite her betrayal, or what he saw as betrayal.'

'You mean the theft of the hunter.'

'That, and your escape from Märchen. For you were a part of my grandfather's plans, too. He needed you.'

'So your mother assured me. But she never said why – only that I was meant to marry her. I confess I do not understand why Doppler – a creature of the Otherwhere – should wish to marry his daughter to a mere mortal.'

'There is much you do not understand about the Otherwhere and its denizens, Father.'

'Then you must educate me,' he said. 'But first: your name. And that of the other man who raised you. The questions pile up unanswered. Despite your assurances, daughter, I feel that you are nevertheless playing a game with me.'

'Am I?' A blush rose to her cheeks. 'Perhaps I am. But do not be angry! There is power in names, even here. And I do so enjoy games, as do all my kind.'

'Your kind . . . Your mother once told me that Doppler was a risen angel. I have heard of fallen angels – but risen? I confess I was not sure of her meaning.'

'My grandfather raised himself above the rest. At first, all followed him. But later some rebelled, led by my grandmother.'

'Raised how? And why did they rebel?'

'So many questions! It is well for you that we are not playing by the ordinary rules that bind my kind.'

'There it is again – your kind. What kind? What are you?'

'We have many names, Father! Among ourselves, we are the Risen. It is as good a name as any, I suppose.'

'But you are my daughter. You are half human. Perhaps that is why . . .' Now it was his turn to blush. He broke off, words deserting him.

She laughed lightly, something like mischief glittering in her eyes. 'No doubt Dr Rinaldi has informed you of my . . . physical peculiarities.'

He found himself unable to meet her frank yet teasing gaze. The topic of conversation seemed suddenly too intimate, beyond the bounds of propriety for an older man and a young girl . . . to say nothing of a father and daughter. Parenthood was proving to be more unsettling than he had expected. Or, rather, unsettling in different ways from what he had expected. He looked to the window, through which another section of the garden was visible. There, at least, all was ordered and familiar. 'He termed it an incomplete fusion of the male and female seeds.'

'I assure you, I am anything but incomplete,' said the girl. 'Nor am I so unusual. I may bear a child as any woman – and father one as any man. Or so I have been told and do believe, though I have not done either as yet.'

'Glad am I to hear it! So you are a true hermaphrodite, then.'

'Yes, though my appearance is that of a female, for I was raised so, and indeed do think of myself that way. But you surprise me, Father.'

'Do I? In what way?'

'You do not seem disturbed to learn of my, shall we say, dual nature. You seem to take things very much in your stride.'

He smiled at this, albeit grimly. 'That is more aptly put than you can know,' he said. 'Perhaps I take it in my stride because I am myself an in-between kind of thing. During my visit to Märchen, where I met your mother, I suffered an accident that resulted in the loss of my foot. Dr Immelman, the physician there, attached a prosthesis in every way remarkable. Better, in fact, than the flesh-and-bone foot it replaced.'

'Dear Dr Immelman!' she said. 'I love him more than ever for that!'

'Why, do you know him, then?'

'For half the year, when I was with my grandfather, I lived in Märchen.'

'And what about the other half? Where did you live then? And with whom?'

'With my father – or, rather, with the man I thought of as my father, until I learned the truth about who and what I am. His name is—'

She broke off at a knock upon the door, which was opened by a footman standing outside. Mrs Bartholomew swept in, bearing a tray. 'Tea, your lordship,' she said. 'And beef broth for the lady.'

Lord Wichcote frowned in annoyance. 'Yes, yes. Set it down and go, Mrs Bartholomew. My daughter and I do not wish to be disturbed.'

Only years of service prevented Mrs Bartholomew from dropping the tray. Still, it was a close-run thing. She stood stock-still, lips pursed, regarding him with an expression he had seen frequently over the years: a mix of surprise and disapproval, with a dash of disappointment thrown in for good measure. 'Did you say daughter, my lord?'

'My daughter and heir,' he answered, regretting how his tongue had run away with him. 'But do please keep it to yourself for now. I mean to address the household soon upon the subject, and before I do, I shall confide certain details to you, never fear.'

'Very good, my lord,' she said, and then made a curtsy to the girl. 'My lady.'

'That sounds so stuffy, Mrs Bartholomew,' came the answer, delivered with a pout. 'As if I were a wife and not a daughter. You may call me Miss Wichcote. Yes, I quite like that.'

'Very good, Miss Wichcote.' And she proceeded to set down the tray on a table beside the daybed. There was a steaming pot of tea in the shape of a dromedary, two china cups with painted bucolic scenes that were set upon similarly decorated saucers, silver spoons, a bowl of sugar, a small vessel of milk, and a bowl of tea-coloured broth, also steaming, with a spoon placed alongside.

The herbal scent of the tea mixed with the meaty aroma of beef, and Lord Wichcote suddenly realized that he was starving. But he did not wish to give Mrs Bartholomew cause to interrupt them again and so resigned himself to suffering the pangs of hunger a while longer. 'Don't trouble yourself, Mrs Bartholomew,' he said as she made to pour the tea. 'I can manage, I assure you. I will call for you when you are needed. Until then, please make certain that there are no further interruptions.'

'Very good, my lord,' she said, and, straightening, gave the girl another curtsy. 'Miss Wichcote.'

'Dear Mrs Bartholomew,' said the girl. 'I am sure we shall be great friends!'

'I will be satisfied to serve you in a satisfactory manner,' said Mrs Bartholomew. 'As I hope and trust I have served his lordship these many years.'

'Yes, yes, Mrs B,' said Wichcote irritably. 'Now be off with you, there's a good woman! And you, sir,' he added, suddenly noticing the footman hovering just beyond the door's threshold. 'You will say nothing of what you have heard, is that understood?'

'Perfectly, my lord,' said the man. He pulled the door smoothly closed as soon as Mrs Bartholomew had passed through it.

'Poor Mrs Bartholomew,' said the girl with a laugh. 'She doesn't quite know what to make of me, I'm afraid.'

'I scarcely know myself,' said Lord Wichcote, busying himself with pouring the tea.

His daughter, meanwhile, lifted the bowl of broth in both hands and raised it to her lips. She drank greedily, and when she lowered the bowl, it was empty. She licked her lips with evident satisfaction.

'You have much to learn of table etiquette,' said Lord Wichcote, aghast at this display of manners, or rather the lack of them.

'We are not at table,' the girl pointed out, not unreasonably. 'But I am sorry,' she added in a contrite tone, with a shrug of her shoulders that indicated the opposite. 'It is hard to remember to care for such things. However, I will try my best for your sake, Father. I wish to make you proud of me.'

'Yes, well, you might make a start of it by answering my questions, dear girl. You were about to tell me the name of the other man who raised you – the man you believed to be your father.'

'Why, I do believe you are jealous of him!' she said. Then, before he could respond: 'A little sugar, if you please. And a drop of milk.'

He fulfilled these requests in silence, wondering if indeed he was jealous and deciding that in fact he did resent this unknown gentleman who had usurped his place and, presumably, some measure of the affections that were rightfully his. 'I would hear more of him,' he said and passed the cup and saucer to her.

She took them in confident hands and then, holding the saucer in one hand, raised the cup delicately to her lips with the other, pinky extended, and sipped with equal delicacy. Then she replaced the cup upon the saucer and set the saucer down upon the tray without spilling a drop. 'There! You see, I can do it properly after all.'

'Questioning you is like trying to corner a cat, daughter,' he said in consternation.

'Why, you have guessed it!' she cried, clapping her hands.

'I beg your pardon?'

'My name. It is Cat – that is, Catherine. Or Katarina, if you prefer. That is what my grandfather called me.'

'I shall call you Cat, then, for you first came to me in the guise of Grimalkin.'

'It is the name my father used – forgive me, but I cannot help thinking of him that way. He loved me. Loves me, I should say. For he is alive and well. You shall meet him, Father! The two of you shall be friends.'

'That is doubtful,' said Wichcote, frowning. 'I do not think I can be friends with the man who raised my Cat as his own. That is a theft I am not likely to forgive. What is his name? I insist upon knowing it!'

'Alas, I must decline to give it to you at present. I see that you mean him no good. For your own sake, and his, I will keep that secret a while longer. But do not hate him, Father! Do not blame him. My mother left me in his care.'

'Did she love him, then?' he forced himself to ask, almost meekly.

'As herself. What is more, she trusted him to keep me safe. And she did not wish to lead my grandfather to you, and, through you, to the hunter. Do not forget, Father – more is at stake than your feelings! Than any of our feelings. We are at war. That war has spilled across the Otherwhere and into this world. Now the fates of both worlds hang in the balance.'

'I shall never forget the last time I saw your dear mother,' he said. 'The two of us were fleeing down the labyrinthine corridors that traverse the Otherwhere as, behind us, your grandfather's angry bellow split the air like a hundred cannon firing at once! Corinna pressed the hunter into my hand and pushed me through a door that led back to this world. I was never able to find her or Märchen again, though I soon discovered I could walk those corridors at will, thanks to Dr Immelman's prosthesis.'

'You are the only mortal who may do so,' she said proudly. 'The prosthesis has changed you, Father, as you say. Made you an in-between thing – more than human . . . though less than Risen.'

'But I am not the only one,' he protested. 'Daniel Quare has the power, too, as I learned to my surprise. No doubt it is the influence of the hunter. It has taken him, I regret to say. Enslaved him. I do not know what has become of him, but I fear the worst. When last I saw him, the thing had fused itself to his hand and drunk the blood of every man in the room save for myself and Sir Thaddeus Wolfe – the man who very nearly killed me.'

'Those touched by the Otherwhere are not so easy to kill,' she said. 'But as for Daniel Quare, I have seen him more recently than you, I think. Indeed, it was in rescuing him that I suffered the injuries that came so near to killing me.'

'Rescuing him – from the hunter, you mean?'

'From the Morecockneyans. They held him in a vile dungeon. He was gravely injured when I reached him, racked with fever. The hunter had been taken from him – along with the hand that had held it.'

'Where is he now? And what of the hunter? Do the Morecockneyans have it?'

'Worse, I'm afraid. The hunter is in the possession of Thomas Aylesford.'

'Aylesford!'

'He was in league with the Morecockneyans. And he is bound for France.'

'How do you know this?'

'I faced him, Father. Stood as near to him on an English shore as I am to you now. I would have killed him then, taken the hunter, but it was not to be.'

'Was it he who wounded you so badly?'

'No, though the hunter is a potent weapon that even the Risen must fear. It was one of the Risen who hurt me – Hesta One-Eye.'

'I recall her from Märchen. The one-eyed dog.'

'And dragon. The Risen may take many forms, you see. We are not bound to flesh and blood as mortals are. Even I, with my share of mortal blood, may appear otherwise than you see me. As I faced Aylesford, Daniel Quare cried out for help from his cell, and I was compelled to rush to his aid.'

'Compelled how?'

'By a pledge given to him by one I have sworn to obey. The Risen are creatures of will and desire, and only our will and desire may constrain us. But this they do absolutely. And so I was bound to answer the summons without excuse or delay, though it meant I had to let Aylesford escape with his prize. I rescued Quare, as I said, and brought him into the Otherwhere. But Hesta was waiting for us. She is ancient and powerful, one of the first Risen to follow my grandfather. I am not her match. I was barely able to escape her.'

'And what of Quare?'

'I do not know his fate,' she said. 'I do not think he is dead, for we are bound by blood, he and I – a connection forged in the crucible of the hunter on that night when he took it from me. Indeed, it was our blood, his and mine, spilled and mingled in the moment he surprised me upon the rooftop, that awakened the hunter. I would feel it if he were dead. Yet I cannot sense him. It is as if he has vanished entirely. I do not understand it.'

Lord Wichcote sipped his tea, then set the cup down with a grimace. The brew had grown tepid. 'What is the hunter, Cat? Why is it so important to Doppler, and indeed to everyone else? What gives it its monstrous power, its thirst for blood? Corinna told me none of these things, and I cannot help but think how much bloodshed and suffering might have been avoided had she spoken to me plainly all those years ago. Or, indeed, if you had spoken plainly in the attic on that fateful night. Three of my men died needlessly by your blade, and I came within a whisker of following them.'

'For that, I am deeply sorry, Father. I had only just learned of the hunter's location, but I did not yet realize who you were. When I think of those poor men, and of my sword's edge pressed to your throat . . .' She shook her head and looked away, in evident distress.

'Never mind,' said Lord Wichcote. 'Tell me of the hunter.'

'It is not easy to speak of such things in a manner that mortals can understand.'

'Please try.'

She nodded and took a breath. 'I wish that things had gone differently between us, Father. But no one, not even my grandfather, can alter the past. *Tempus Imperator Rerum*, as the motto of the Worshipful Company has it: time truly is the emperor of all things. Yet it was not always thus. For though time, like all things, emerged from the Otherwhere, it did not emerge of itself. Time is foreign to that realm, and to those who arose spontaneously from it – the Risen.'

'Where, then, did it come from?'

'From Doppler – my grandfather. He conceived of it and brought it forth by the operation of his sovereign will and desire. This he did in order to rise above the rest, to have a means of controlling them. For the others did not understand the danger of time. To them, it was a novelty. To know a before and an after, a yesterday and a tomorrow, a beginning and an end, delighted them. They were like children who stumble upon a bottle of gin and proceed to drink themselves silly, little dreaming that they are poisoning themselves. My grandfather brought this universe into being both as a repository for time and as a garden in which he might grow and harvest this most potent fruit.'

Wichcote shook his head sceptically. 'Are you asking me to believe that Doppler is God? Because I have met him. Spoken with him. He did not strike me as divine.'

'You saw him as he wished to be seen, not as he truly is. Indeed, no mortal could bear to see him or any of the Risen as they truly are. But God? There is no God, Father. At least not known to me. Perhaps if you parted the veil of the Otherwhere, He would be waiting on the other side. But that no one – not even my grandfather – can do. Earth he may have created, but not heaven, though he imagines himself to rule there. He is not God. He is a risen angel – a demiurge drunk on his own ambition, jealous of his power and authority, ever greedy for more. But now he is something else, too. He is afraid. For his creation has escaped his control.'

'Do you mean the hunter?'

'Not just the hunter. Everything in this universe, from a stone to a plant to a person to a star, has been fashioned for one purpose only: the production of time. Birth, growth, age, decay, senescence, death: such are the flavours of time the Risen have learned to savour – for they cannot know time directly but only through that which already contains it. But with that first, innocent taste of time, a dreadful dependency was created. Now the Risen are like drunkards who hide an ever-gnawing need behind the cultivated mask of the connoisseur. Even my grandfather has been caught by the snare he set for others! For that is the great irony of time. Once conceived of, it cannot be destroyed, cannot be contained, cannot be forgotten. It is a fire that spreads everywhere, a plague without a cure – or, rather, only a single cure.'

'But what has this to do with the hunter?' protested Wichcote, who, in fact, had not found anything plain at all in his daughter's manner of speaking but felt shy of confessing it outright, as if to do so would diminish him in her eyes.

'Everything,' she said. 'You see, the hunter is that cure.'

'I'm afraid I don't see,' he said, defeated.

'Those addicted to the taste of time come to require it simply to survive,' she said. 'That is, the Risen are no longer strictly speaking immortal. Like the Greek gods of legend, who must habitually replenish their immortality with draughts of ambrosia, the nectar of the gods, so, too, must the Risen replenish theirs through the things of this world – human beings above all, for humans contain time in its most potent essence: the knowledge of one's own inescapable mortality. This dependence, or rather the awareness of it, sparked the great war among the Risen. It was my grandmother who first rebelled against the tyranny of time – which is to say, against the tyranny of my grandfather. Others followed, until the Risen had split into two camps. One, led by Doppler, dedicated to preserving his monopoly, in which individual Risen, based on loyalty or service to him, were rewarded or punished with greater or lesser amounts of time, and the other, led by Tiamat, determined to smash that unnatural hierarchy and tear down the walls that regulated access to time, so that it might be available freely and equally to all of the Risen. In that war, the hunter is the ultimate weapon, a kind of time bomb, if you will. It began as the eye of a dragon – Hesta's eye, which she sacrificed willingly. This organ Doppler impregnated with a portion of his own essence similarly sacrificed. Such is the manner in which the pure Risen reproduce. My mother, Corinna, was born in this way – from pieces of Doppler and Tiamat fused into something new by the operation of their will and desire. The hunter is an egg of sorts, you see. But Doppler did not quicken this egg, as he had others. Instead, he took it to his workshop, and there, with the aid of Dr Immelman – a mortal like yourself, Father, a master of the temporal and mechanical arts as well as the medical, whom my grandfather had recruited – set the egg at the heart of a timepiece like no other. This device has but one purpose: to consume time and store it up until it is released all at once in an explosion of incalculable creative and destructive force – an explosion designed to destroy this universe and bring a new one into being, one with all its flaws removed, in which my grandfather and my grandfather alone would possess supreme power. It was this that he held over the other Risen as both threat and promise. Those who followed him would be reborn in the new universe, while those who did not would be expunged from it, as if they had never existed. Whether he truly meant to use the hunter in this way, I do not know. But all of that changed when Corinna stole it from him. For whoever had the hunter, with its living heart powered by my grandfather's will and desire – which, once expressed, even he cannot gainsay – would have the means to unmake and remake the universe as they saw fit. That is why Doppler and Tiamat both would do anything to possess it. But what no one foresaw was that Daniel Quare and I would cross paths upon that London rooftop and shed each other's blood, and that our spilled blood, commingled, would fall upon the hunter and quicken it. Awaken it. Yet that is precisely what occurred. Was it chance? Fate? I do not know.'

'And what will hatch out of this egg?'

'That is the question, is it not? My grandfather planned to infuse the egg with his own essence and guide its ripening from within, dying in this universe only to be reborn, phoenix-like, with the hatching of the next: a universe made in his own image. Tiamat, had she possessed it, would have done the same, for all her brave talk of wanting to see it destroyed. Instead, a new and hybrid consciousness came into being within the hunter – part Risen, the offspring of Doppler and Hesta One-Eye, but also shaped by the lives, human and otherwise, it has since tasted or consumed, storing them up as it stores the time that is inseparable from them. Part of me is there, and part of Quare, too. Your friend Master Magnus. And many, many others. Yet it is more than the sum of these parts. It is its own creature, subject to no will and desire save its own. What it desires above all, what it works towards with every ounce of its formidable will, is to be born. And unlike my grandfather, it has no interest in destroying this universe to create a better one. It means, rather, to rule it.'

'Then the egg must not hatch,' said Wichcote. 'We must destroy it.'

'Yes,' said Cat. 'Except it cannot be destroyed by any power on Earth.'

'What, then, of the Otherwhere?'

'You have hit on it, Father,' said Cat approvingly. 'Tiamat believes that if the hunter were to be thrown directly into the Otherwhere, it would be absorbed back into the primordial chaos from whence it came. Yet it might also be that the plague of time would thereby infect the Otherwhere. What the result of that would be, no one knows. But the risk is surely worth taking. What other choice is there?'

'Can Tiamat be trusted?'

'None of the Risen can be trusted. They can only be bound.'

'Bound how?'

'By the exercise of their will and desire, or the will and desire of another Risen to whom they have already bound themselves. All the Risen are bound to each other in chains of mutual obligation. There is a hierarchy, with those at the bottom owing allegiance to those at the top, who have a reciprocal duty to those beneath them. At the very top is my grandfather, lord of all and vassal of none. Just below him is Tiamat, his wife and mortal enemy.'

'But is not the wife subordinate to the husband?'

'Perhaps that is true here, Father – though from what I have seen, I do not think so. But among the Risen the wife may outrank the husband. Indeed, a wife may have many husbands, and a husband many wives, over the course of their endless lives. More than that, they . . .' She paused and shook her head, frowning. 'Never mind for now. Suffice it to say that no, Tiamat is not subordinate to Doppler. She is not precisely his equal, for he was the first born of all the Risen, and his will and desire are the strongest . . . but in order to win her favour, Doppler bound himself to her in certain ways, and those bindings remain in effect and always shall, despite the enmity that exists between them. The obligations thus incurred are far-reaching on both sides. That is how Tiamat was able to rebel against him, and how she protects her followers from his direct retribution. It is also why my father – my other father, that is – gave me up to my grand-father for six months out of every year, and why my grandfather, all his power notwithstanding, returned me to him at the end of that time, however begrudgingly.'

'It is a strange society, that of the Risen,' mused Wichcote. 'There is something primitive, almost medieval, about it. The English system, imperfect though it may be, has at least the benefit of being a government of free men acting in concert to restrain absolute power and direct it for the benefit of all.'

'All, Father? You are a peer of this realm, with a seat in the House of Lords and a personal fortune of immense size. Forgive me, but your perspective is somewhat skewed by your rank and, indeed, gender, both of which carry an array of privileges so ubiquitous as to render them effectively invisible – to you. But not to me. In appearance, at least, I am a woman, yet I have passed as a man, albeit beneath a mask, in the guise of a thief. Well do I know that your precious parliament is far from the altruistic institution you describe. Rather than a force for freedom, it is a bulwark of rank and privilege.'

'It is indeed the worst form of government imaginable,' Lord Wichcote agreed. 'With the exception of all the others. But this is not the time to discuss politics, I think. We must decide on a plan to retrieve the hunter. As to that, it would seem a trip to France is in order.'

'Yes, we must seek Aylesford there,' Cat agreed. 'He should not be hard to find – we need only follow the trail of corpses. Why, hello, Henrietta!'

For the little mouse had appeared at the foot of the daybed. It did not spare a glance for Wichcote but ran up the blanket and climbed Cat's white shift to perch upon her shoulder, just below her ear, where, against her pale throat, and amidst the shimmering golden fall of her hair, it seemed to confide a secret.

Once again Lord Wichcote marvelled at the lifelike quality of Corinna's handiwork. It was hard to believe – though he knew it to be true – that the mouse was a mechanical construct, a clockwork automaton. But nothing in its outward appearance, save its evident tameness, hinted at anything unusual.

Cat, meanwhile, had cocked her head as if listening intently to whispers Wichcote could not hear, though he strained to do so. The sight of this beautiful young woman receiving the confidences of a clockwork mouse stirred him strangely. He felt as if he had been vouchsafed a glimpse into the living heart of a fairy tale. Years seemed to fall away – not just from him but from the world. He held his breath, afraid of shattering the tableau. Then, in the blink of an eye, Henrietta disappeared. The mouse vanished so swiftly that he did not see where it had gone. Nor did he have time to ask, for, in the next second, the door burst open.

He turned and saw Mrs Bartholomew come rushing in. This time she was quite alone.

'I told you not to interrupt us again, Mrs Bartholomew!' he snapped before she could speak.

'Beg pardon, your lordship,' the housekeeper said, red-faced and flustered. 'But I thought you should know there's men gathering outside.'

'Men? What do you mean? What sort of men?'

'Soldiers, your lordship.'

'Damnation!' he exclaimed. 'How many?'

'Fifteen or twenty at least. Maybe more. There is a fat little man among them who seems to fancy himself their leader, though he wears no uniform. He struts up and down the walk like a preening peacock, but the effect is somewhat comical, as both his eyes are blackened and his nose appears to be broken.'

'That popinjay would be Master Malrubius, the lapdog of Sir Thaddeus Wolfe of the Worshipful Company of Clockmakers,' said Lord Wichcote, wincing visibly. He remembered very well how poor Gerald Pickens – dead now, another victim of the hunter – had viciously avenged himself upon Malrubius when they had chanced to come upon him in the guild hall on their way to the Old Wolf's den. He had rendered Malrubius unconscious with a dart, but then Pickens, whom he and Quare had liberated from a dungeon cell scant moments before, had beaten the helpless man savagely before he could intervene – a needless waste of time and energy, though understandable enough, for Pickens had received worse treatment at Malrubius's hands. Now, no doubt, Malrubius blamed Lord Wichcote for his injuries, and he was not a forgiving man.

'Ridiculous he may be,' Wichcote went on, 'but even a lapdog may bite, never doubt it. If he is here, it can only mean that the guild itself seeks my arrest, and that my lily-livered cousin has withdrawn his protection at last. Well, it was only a matter of time.' Sighing, he turned back to his daughter. 'Our enemies are closing in, my dear. I suggest we take ourselves . . . otherwhere.'

'Most wise, Father,' she said.

'Otherwhere?' echoed Mrs Bartholomew, looking from one of them to the other as if they had both gone mad. 'What does that mean?'

'Best you don't know, Mrs B.'

'This is all the fault of that rogue, I'll be bound,' she said with clear disapproval.

'Not precisely his fault, no,' said Wichcote. 'But he is mixed up in it, I confess.'

'I thought as much,' she said. 'I always said that rogue would lead you astray one day,' she added with satisfaction, as though he and 'that rogue' were not one and the same. 'And now Miss Wichcote has been drawn in to whatever bit of ill-conceived tomfoolery has brought these soldiers to our door – your own daughter, sir!'

'His lordship had nothing to do with that, Mrs Bartholomew,' Cat said. 'I am here of my own will and desire.'

'Why, 'tis plain you're his lordship's daughter, Miss Wichcote. You're quite as stubborn!' She looked in consternation to Lord Wichcote. 'But where will you go? The house is surrounded, and it is only a matter of time before an officer presents himself at the door. You are both bedridden. Helpless.'

'Calm yourself, my dear woman,' said Lord Wichcote. 'We are neither of us as helpless as we appear. My daughter and I will be gone for a while – how long, exactly, I cannot say. I leave Wichcote House in your capable hands. Please—'

A loud and violent hammering interrupted him. The noise caused Mrs Bartholomew to flinch and look fearfully over her shoulder, though the source of the disturbance was plainly downstairs.

'The jackals are at the door,' said Wichcote dryly. 'You'd best leave us, Mrs B.'

'Be careful, your lordship,' said the old woman.

'Why, I am always careful,' he replied. 'How else do you think I have lived so long?'

She rolled her eyes at this, dipped a curtsy to Cat, and hurriedly departed.

133

Wichcote addressed his daughter. 'Can you walk, my dear?'

'I can, and more,' was her answer. 'But what of you, Father?'

'Let us see.' Taking hold of the armrests of the invalid's chair, Lord Wichcote gingerly pushed himself erect. The blanket that had covered his knees fell to the floor at his slippered feet. On the basis of earlier attempts, he had expected weakness and pain, but now, to his surprise, he rose to his feet and stood with scarcely a twinge of discomfort, though his legs were shaky, and he did not think he could walk any great distance, or, if it came to it, run at all. But he would not need to run. A single step would suffice: the step that would take them both across the threshold of the Otherwhere. He adjusted his dressing gown. 'Well, this is better than I had hoped. It seems you are not the only one in this family blessed with a hardy constitution, my dear.'

'It is as I told you,' she replied. 'You have been touched by the Otherwhere and are no longer merely mortal. You are part Risen, and as such, like some hero of old, quick to heal from wounds that would kill or incapacitate a lesser man.'

'Perhaps those heroes of old were also part Risen,' he mused, tottering about the room and methodically stopping the timepieces housed there. Meanwhile, the noises from below grew louder. It seemed some resistance was being offered to the entrance of Malrubius and the soldiers. But Lord Wichcote did not give any outward sign, by word or action, that this concerned him, or, for that matter, that he had noticed it at all. 'Arthur, Lancelot, Boadicea, Achilles, even Christ himself,' he continued. 'It would explain much.'

'Mortals are quite capable of heroism on their own, Father,' said Cat with a fond smile. 'They, too, are children of the Otherwhere, albeit, so to speak, once removed. Do not think to find the Risen behind every myth and legend.'

'Come then, daughter,' he said, having finished with the final timepiece, a pocket watch he had pulled from, and now returned to, a side pocket in his dressing gown. He held out his hand to Cat as though inviting her to join him in a minuet. 'Let us away.'

A blush rose to her cheeks as she laid her hand in his, as though she had grown suddenly shy in his presence. She stood in a single graceful

134

movement, and now it was his turn to blush, for somehow, quite independently of his will, he felt himself stirred at her touch in ways a father should not be stirred by his daughter. He thought suddenly of how, in Märchen, his manhood had risen independently of his desire, and how, most often to his horror, his seed had been wrung from him without his consent, as if he were no more than a cow being milked.

'Such is the tribute demanded by higher from lower, Father,' Cat said softly now, as if she knew his thoughts, and he understood to his further mortification that what he had taken for shyness was in fact pity. She herself felt no shame. 'Surely you experienced it in Märchen?'

'I did,' he said, unable to meet her gaze, both for his own shame and her pity, which he felt diminished by. 'But I did not think to experience it again here, and certainly not with you, daughter. It is most unwelcome.' He turned to hide the evidence of his desire.

'Among the Risen, there is no morality as mortals conceive it, and what you term incest is the norm, for all the Risen are brothers and sisters, sons and daughters, and there are no boundaries that cannot be crossed by will and desire. As for you, Father, though you are no longer purely mortal, thanks to the work of Dr Immelman, you are still time-bound, and in the presence of the Risen, even of a half-Risen like me, you cannot help but react as you were made to do; no more than a clock, once wound, can do aught but wind down. So do not feel ashamed. I can dampen the effect to a degree but cannot eliminate it entirely.'

'I understand,' he said, forcing himself to meet her eyes. 'Let us say no more about it.' He recalled that Corinna had spoken to him in just such a tone, and had looked at him, too, with just such an expression, from across a gulf that, however much he desired it, he could not cross. Now he perceived viscerally, in his body, and not just with his intellect, that his daughter, too, was beyond and above him, however much he might love her. As had been the case with her mother, it did not make him love her any less. Indeed, he seemed to feel the cut of it more keenly than ever.

'Go on, Father,' she said now. 'Lead the way, and I will follow.'

'I shall take us far from here,' he told her. 'To Hawthornden, my castle in Scotland, where we shall be safe, for a while at least.'

'We had best make haste,' she said, for it was plain from the sounds below that what resistance had been offered was now overcome. The soldiers had entered the house. Lord Wichcote could hear the distinctive voice of Master Malrubius, a loud braying that had led the apprentices and journeymen of the Worshipful Company to dub him the Old Mule, a mocking play on the Old Wolf, their rather more respectful nickname for Sir Thaddeus Wolfe.

'Indeed,' Wichcote said. And with that, stepped into the Otherwhere.

Or tried to. But neither he nor Cat left the room.

Lord Wichcote stumbled as though his foot had caught upon a snag in the rug; without his daughter's hand to steady him, he would have fallen. He gazed about in puzzlement and consternation. 'I do not understand. That has never happened before. It has always been a simple exercise of willpower to enter the Otherwhere.'

'Best allow me,' said Cat. And this time it was she who opened the way.

With no more success than his lordship had enjoyed.

She sank back onto the daybed. 'The Otherwhere is sealed off,' she said in a disbelieving tone. 'My grandfather must have closed it, as he has often threatened. But I never dreamed he would truly do so! Not even Tiamat believed it.'

'What does it mean?' asked Wichcote.

'Many things,' she said grimly. 'None of them good. The most immediately relevant of which is that we are trapped here, Father.'

'Do not be so quick to despair,' he said, feeling something of his old insouciance return. 'Grimalkin is never without his bolt holes.' He hurried as best he could to one wall. There he pressed a hidden switch, and a section of the panelling swung open, revealing a small, square chamber. Inside, below a wall sconce that held an unlit candle, a narrow table was set. A bell pull dangled in one corner. A wooden railing ran about the circumference of the room at waist height.

'Behold our salvation,' Wichcote said. 'This is a stair-master, the invention of my late friend and colleague Master Theophilus Magnus.

These chambers are marvels of modern engineering, Cat! They provide a swift and secret means of transport within the guild hall. Only Magnus, the Old Wolf, and I know of their existence, and of course only I know of the ones installed here at Wichcote House. Well' – and here he tipped his daughter a wink – 'myself and "that rogue", as Mrs Bartholomew refers to my grey-clad alter ego. But as you, too, have worn the mask of Grimalkin, it is only fitting that you share in this secret as well.'

'But how does it move?' asked Cat, who had risen from the daybed and crossed the room to stand beside her father, peering curiously – and cautiously – into the stair-master as if into the depths of Ali-Baba's cave. 'How do you direct it?'

'Why, by will and desire,' he said with a laugh and entered the chamber, pulling her gently but firmly along. He opened a drawer in the table, removed a tinderbox, which he used to light the candle, and then shut the door – just in time, for he could hear the sounds of tramping feet on the stairs without. 'Hold the railing, Cat,' he said and tugged the bell pull.

There was a sensation of sideways movement, followed by a swift ascent. Lord Wichcote was by now an old hand at this mode of transport and looked with sly interest to see the effect upon his daughter. On the rare occasions when he brought a passenger along for a ride – as he had with Daniel Quare – he enjoyed observing the shock and even outright terror the unexpected movements of the stair-master never failed to elicit. But Cat's features registered only delight.

'Why, it is something akin to travel through the Otherwhere, is it not? The human mind is ever questing beyond the constraints of time and the physical world, seeking to rise in emulation of its creator, and in so doing produces wonders that even my grandfather could never have dreamed of.'

'Perhaps one day we shall join the Risen of our own accord,' said Wichcote. 'Pulling ourselves up by our own bootstraps, as it were, to storm the gates of heaven.'

'Who can say?' answered Cat with a smile.

The stair-master slowed and stopped.

'We have arrived,' said Wichcote, and pulled the door open.

'Arrived where?'

'Come and see.'

Plucking the candle from the wall sconce, he led her out of the stair-master, then used the flame to light another taper upon one wall of the otherwise dark space, and then another, finally setting the candle into an empty sconce.

The room thus illuminated was scarcely larger than the space they had left behind. But it was not so empty. One wall was covered with an assortment of weapons ranging from rapiers to blow pipes to crossbows to pistols. Another was taken up by a single large chifforobe. This Lord Wichcote opened to reveal, hanging in neat rows, what must have been a dozen sets of cloaks, leggings, shirts and cowls, all the same flinty shade of grey. The third wall held an array of footwear, from slippers to boots. These, too, were grey. A narrow door was set opposite the one through which they had entered.

Cat clapped her hands like a child on Christmas morning. 'So this is Grimalkin's lair! How wonderful!'

'One of them,' he said. 'Here we may dress ourselves in somewhat more useful fashion than presently, and arm ourselves as well for whatever lies ahead.'

'But what then? How shall we escape the house? Even armed, we cannot fight our way out.'

'You shall see,' said Wichcote. 'I shall step outside, into the attic, while you dress.'

'You need not go on my account,' she said. 'I am not troubled by maidenly modesty.'

'But I am,' he replied. 'And I have certain arrangements to make. I will be back shortly, never fear.'

With that, he turned to leave, pausing at the narrow door – which, on its other side, masqueraded as the casing of a tall clock – to put his eye to a peephole. What he saw did not please him: his workshop had been invaded by a trio of soldiers. They were fanning out even now to give the place a thorough going-over. It was only a matter of time before they discovered this bolt hole. He had planned to utilize another of Master Magnus's inventions – the Personal Flotation Device – to loft himself and his daughter into the heavens and thus escape Wichcote House by means of the air. But now it was apparent that the air was as closed to them as the ground and, indeed, the Otherwhere. That left but one escape route . . . a route fraught with peril, for it lay below the ground, through the subterranean realm of the Morecockneyans, whose new king, successor to his old friend King Jeremiah, did not hold Grimalkin in the same high regard his predecessor had. When last he'd entered that dark domain, in the company of Daniel Quare, he'd received a prickly welcome from Starkey and Cornelius, two roving ambassadors and jovial ruffians he'd known for years. The pair had been most eager to conduct him and Quare – both of whom had been dressed as Grimalkin – to their king, and he'd been forced to dissuade them from that course of action at swordpoint. Nor had that been his worst offence, for he had compelled their services as guides, and then, in payment, left them bound, gagged, and unconscious. No doubt Starkey and Cornelius, to say nothing of the new king, had felt these insults keenly and would be eager to avenge them. But there was no help for it. He would have to go back. With a bit of luck – admittedly in short supply thus far – they should be able to avoid detection; he did not mean to remain underground for long, just time enough to travel a healthy distance from Wichcote House. He had bolt holes scattered all over the city, and if he could but reach one, he would command resources sufficient to effect a more thorough escape, after which he and Cat could follow Aylesford – and the hunter – to France. With a sigh, he turned back to inform his daughter that they must return to the stair-master and descend into the bowels of Wichcote House.

He caught his breath at the sight that greeted him. While his back was turned, Cat had disrobed as instructed and was now dressing herself in the grey garb of Grimalkin. She was half turned away, a pair of leggings in her hands. The shift was pooled at her feet, leaving her naked save for the white cap upon her head. Her skin was as white as the candles burning on the walls, and, like them, radiant. The delicate bones of her ribcage stood out like a tiger's stripes, and he could see her breasts, small and high on a narrow chest that might otherwise have belonged to a boy. The stark flare of a bony hip ripened into the lean swell of a muscled haunch and long, willowy legs. All this he glimpsed in an instant. She was already in the act of turning to him, a questioning look upon her face. He did not, could not, look away.

Nested in golden hair so fine as to seem translucent, there in the tufted triangle between her legs he saw what Dr Rinaldi's report should have prepared him for but somehow hadn't, at least not for the shock of its physicality, the sheer impossible, undeniable fact of it. Still less was he prepared for the physicality of his reaction: beneath his silk dressing gown he stood at once to attention, as if like had called to like, and he felt a flood of desire such as he had not experienced since his last night in Märchen, when Corinna and Inge Hubner, the proprietress of the Hearth and Home, had unveiled or rather unmasked themselves to him and fought over him.

As on that night, his desire was not a pleasant thing, not a surrender to something wanted and welcomed but rather a response wrenched out of him all unwilling, and as such a thing of horror – multiplied in this case by his awareness that this was, after all, his daughter, blood of his blood, flesh of his flesh, and the response of his body to the sight of her a betrayal of everything he had believed himself to be. A strangled moan escaped him, and he would have fallen but for the implacable force or energy that had him in its merciless grip. His body was trembling like a glass vessel on the verge of shattering. There was no stopping it, though he strained against it with all his will. He knew that, once shattered, there would be no piecing himself back together. He would be broken for ever.

It was then, as the last wisps of self-control slipped through his grasp, that Cat came to his rescue. The light that shone from her brightened suddenly, blinding him. Drowned in that brilliant flood, he lost all sense of himself, of who and where he was. There was only the radiant oblivion of the light, and he was not so much within that light as part of it, suffusing it just as it suffused him. They were one and the same.

When he returned to his senses, or rather they to him, he was back in the stair-master. Cat stood beside him, dressed cap-a-pie in Grimalkin's grey – save for the mask, which hung like a loose scarf about her neck. The light that had blazed from her was extinguished, and the wavering glow of the candle that had been returned to its sconce in the wall seemed not merely dimmer by comparison but of an entirely different – and lesser – order of existence altogether.

His desire had been similarly extinguished, snuffed out. He had a sense of awakening abruptly in the midst of ongoing action, as if his body had gone right along moving and speaking without him, like the crudely carved automaton of himself he'd seen in Märchen. He had no memory of what it might have done or said during that time, yet he, too, was now wearing the costume of his alter ego, and this was not startling or in any way unexpected: it seemed ordinary, unexceptional, as if it were in the very nature of things that he should be so dressed at this moment, in this place. He felt that everything was just as it should be – or rather that things could be in no other way. Only later would he wonder at the gap of time and memory, seeking in vain to remember. But for now he questioned nothing, swept along by the rush of events he'd rejoined, as it were, in mid-stream. He felt he should not question; that questions might lead to answers he had no wish to hear or capacity to bear; that this lacuna was a gift, a mercy his daughter had bestowed upon him, one he would be wise to accept.

'Take hold, Cat,' he said, experiencing an odd stutter of conscious-ness as he slipped – or so it seemed – back into his body. 'Our descent will be a swift one, I fear.' From outside the stair-master he heard the sounds of hammering as soldiers sought entrance to the bolt hole. He tugged the bell pull sharply, and the stair-master plunged downward.

As they descended, he told her of their destination: the entrance beneath his house to the network of underground passages and caverns that constituted the anterooms, as it were, of London's secret sister city, a vast, dark metropolis as old and storied as its surface sibling.

'I am no stranger to that realm,' she said. 'It is one of those places where the walls between this world and the Otherwhere are at their thinnest and most permeable. Indeed, there is a portal there, buried as deep as any of the works of men, that may yet remain open, though my grandfather has closed all others. This one is beyond even his power, I think, for he is bound by ancient compact to leave it open.

If we can get there, we can use it to enter the Otherwhere and from there travel to France in the blink of an eye.'

'You did not see fit to mention this earlier?'

'In truth, I did not think of it until now. So much has happened in the time since I awoke – I've been rather knocked off my stride, I'm afraid.'

'I meant no criticism, dear Cat,' he said. 'I am limping along myself.'

'We shall limp along together,' she answered with a fond smile. 'But the path will not be an easy one. The Morecockneyans may affect the trappings of Londoners, but underneath that civilized veneer they have not changed in many thousands of years. They retain the faith of their forefathers, you see – a faith already ancient when the legions of Caesar first set foot on these shores. And it is no bloodless faith, Father. What's more, I made use of the portal in my rescue of Daniel Quare, and I do not doubt that its guardians will be better prepared now for any trespass.'

'I'm afraid the Morecockneyans have no reason to welcome me back with open arms, either,' he confessed. And then, as the stair-master jolted to a stop: 'We are here.'

Lord Wichcote lifted the candle from its sconce, opened the door, and led his daughter into a room that appeared exactly like the bolt hole they had left behind. Here they armed themselves, as they had not done above – each taking a sword and a long dagger. Wichcote selected other implements for himself as well: a small crossbow and quiver of bolts, a blow pipe and tiny, feathered darts, a pistol, and certain carefully chosen vials that he slipped with practised ease into grey pouches at his belt. He then turned to his daughter, who was regarding him with bemusement.

'Is there aught I have forgotten?' he asked.

'You do not like to leave anything to chance, do you, Father?' she said teasingly.

He shrugged. 'Since chance cannot be avoided, I try to anticipate it as best I can, though it usually manages to surprise me in any case.'

'For today, at least, I hope forewarned is forearmed.'

'With you at my side, dear Cat, we are quite literally four-armed, and it is in those arms that I place my hopes and, indeed, my faith, for I have seen you fight, and I do not think there is a man in England who is your equal with a blade.'

'Or without one,' she riposted quickly. 'Nor woman, either, if it comes to that. Do not forget that I am as much Corinna's child as your own.'

He found himself blushing at the recollection of what he had seen in the attic. 'I have not forgotten, nor ever will forget,' he assured her. 'And now, my dear, if you are ready, it is time we left Wichcote House behind.'

They returned to the stair-master, which resumed its downward course. This time they travelled in silence, Wichcote wondering if he would ever see his London home again or know the pleasures of introducing his daughter to society. Really, what interest could a merely mortal life hold for such as she? In truth, though Cat might have a share of human blood, she was not by that token human: she was something quite other, as he now knew better than he had known previously or, for that matter, had wished to know. She was, like her late mother, a creature of the Otherwhere, as far above him and all his kind as he was above the apes in the Tower Menagerie. He looked at her face, already so dear to him, impressed for ever into his heart. What was she thinking behind that beautiful but inscrutable façade? She did not speak, but instead gazed at the wall of the stair-master as though it were a glass in which she saw things he was blind to.

This time, when the stair-master drew to a halt, and Lord Wichcote opened the door, no room lay beyond but instead a narrow passage – a fissure cut into solid stone – that extended into darkness. The air was cold, infused with a scent both mineral and mouldering.

'I hope you are not distressed by close spaces,' he said as he took the candle from its sconce. 'The way grows wider before too long.'

'It shall narrow again before we are done,' Cat replied. 'The portal we seek lies at the lowest levels of this place. It is a holy site and as such heavily defended. It is forbidden even to most Morecockneyans, let alone interlopers from the surface.'

'Yet you managed to make your way there once, with Daniel Quare.'

'Yes, though, as I said, I expect it will be better guarded now. Besides, the last time I passed through that portal, Hesta One-Eye was waiting on the other side. That was no coincidence. She knew I was coming.'

'It would seem the Morecockneyans are in communication with Doppler,' said Wichcote.

'Yes, they are his allies, it appears, doing his bidding here on Earth. I have turned against my grandfather, and he would dearly love to get me back. I am a prize he values above all others save the hunter itself.'

'And what of Daniel Quare? Where does he fit in?'

'Once Quare lost the hunter, he had no value to my grandfather save as bait to lure me here. They let me free him, and then herded me towards the portal, where Hesta was waiting. She was meant to capture me and bring me to my grandfather, or so I surmise. But the attack did not go as foreseen. Poor Quare was lost, and I escaped, as you know.'

'And now I have brought you back into the lion's den.'

'The dragon does not fear the lion,' she said. 'It is not you but circumstances that have brought us here. Whether blind fate or machination lies behind them matters not. We can only do the best we can, with what choices we have.'

'Bravely spoken, Cat. You are a daughter any man would be proud to acknowledge. I cannot help but feel that Corinna would be proud of you as well, and that it would please her to know we two had found each other at last and stood together now side by side.'

'Perhaps she does know,' his daughter answered. 'Who can say? But I, too, rejoice in having found you, Father. Whatever dangers await us, I am glad to be facing them with you.' With an impulsive movement, she leaned close and pressed her lips to his cheek in a girlish kiss, light and fleeting, gone almost before he could register it.

He had ample reason to flinch from that kiss. Her touch had stirred him before in unwelcome ways. But this proved different. The warm pressure of her lips lingered, settling in his heart and bringing with it a flood of tender feeling painful in its intensity, yet somehow pleasurable, too, as if his heart were being stretched into a new and better shape. He turned away, wiping his eyes with a grey-gloved hand. More than anything, he wished to protect this young person, to shelter and comfort her, and to make safe her way in the world, though he knew there was no safety where they were going now, or indeed anywhere else below the ground . . . or, for that matter, above it. And what protection could he offer in any case? What need, after all, did she have for a father . . . especially such a poor father as he must be, coming so late to the role, with no experience to guide him and no particular wisdom to draw on? Yet he was determined to be worthy of her, this gift that had come to him all unlooked for out of a past he had thought irretrievably lost.

Just outside the stair-master, a collection of torches long since pre-pared for use leaned against one rocky wall. He took one and lit it from the candle, then, holding it upraised before him, and feeling like some obscure allegorical figure, proceeded into the crevice, which gave every sign of having been cut by a natural sundering of stone from stone and not by any effort of human hands.

The way down was gentle, the path worn smooth by what once must have been a stream, though far from straight: it zigged and zagged, the walls sometimes drawing so near to each other that they were forced to edge through sideways, while the roof often dipped so low that they had to stoop. The only sounds were the scraping of their boots over the stone and the breezy flutter of the torch's flames, both of which, weirdly distorted and amplified, suggested the presence of others, so that Wichcote and Cat were forever looking over their shoulders as they descended. The ragged light of the torch seemed less to illuminate the passage than to carve it.

After about ten minutes, the way widened moderately, and they were able to continue abreast rather than single file. Still they did not speak, though they clasped gloved hands as they went. The slope increased, the cold air grew colder, and side passages began to appear, marked with symbols carved into the stone: arrows, Xs, Ys, and other signs whose meaning was not immediately clear. Wichcote took the third of these passages, and after that point followed no obvious route but rather a labyrinthine succession of branching tunnels. If Cat was

145

bewildered by this maze, or made apprehensive, she did not show it, but strode step for step beside her father.

At last he drew to a halt. They stood in a space as wide as any they had yet encountered, and almost twice their height. The path curved out of sight before them. Lord Wichcote spoke softly. 'Ahead lies a great vaulted chamber – an anteroom of sorts to the kingdom of the Morecockneyans. This entrance was discovered and mapped by my grandfather – your great-grandfather, dear Cat. As far as I know, its existence is a family secret, not known to the Morecockneyans. Yet it would be foolish to assume their knowledge of these places is less complete than my own. We dare not continue farther by torchlight.'

Suiting action to words, he extinguished the torch. A profound darkness fell.

'You may wonder how we are to make our way with no light,' he continued. 'There is a species of mushroom native to this soil that is cultivated by the Morecockneyans. It produces what, to our eyes, is a faint but noticeable glow; but to eyes that have never seen the sun, it fairly blazes with radiance. Thus have the Morecockneyans marked the highways and byways of their realm, and if we but let our eyes adjust to the dark, we, too, shall be able to discern those marks, however faintly, which I have learned to read.'

'That is well,' she said, her voice pitched as softly as his own, 'but not necessary. I do not require light to see. Even such dark as this is no hindrance to my sight.'

'How can that be?'

'Just as the light of the mushrooms you mentioned is faint when compared to the sun, so, too, is the light of the sun faint in comparison to another kind of burning: that which goes by the name of time. It is that radiance by which I and all my fellow Risen see. There is not darkness enough, even at the very centre of the Earth, to blind us.'

'What is it like to see this way?'

'More beautiful than I have words to describe,' she said. 'And more sad, too. Every sight glimpsed by the light of sun or candle comes at the cost of what burns, does it not? Whether we behold a face we love or a stark mountain peak or a wide, shimmering sea, we owe that sight to

146

the decay and death of what shines upon it. To behold a thing is to be present at a sacrifice. That is true also of time, but more so, for every object in this world that Doppler brought into being by the exercise of his sovereign will, every single thing here, whether animate or inanimate, quick or dead, shines with an inner burning, if you could but see it as I do. Humans shine most brightly of all; indeed, it hurts us to gaze upon you, yet you are so beautiful that we cannot look away. We love you and mourn you at once. We envy you and pity you.'

Lord Wichcote shivered to hear these words addressed to him from out of the dark. 'But you are half human, Cat,' he protested, as if to claim her, or some part of her, for his own. He clasped her hand more tightly than ever.

'When lesser and greater are mixed together, the lesser can pull the greater down. Yet it can also happen that the greater absorbs the lesser, and the lesser dissolves into the greater. I am half human, it is true, and I am proud of that – proud to be your child. But in every way that counts but one, I am Risen.'

'What is that one?'

'Unlike my grandfather and the rest, I was born with a measure of time. To them, time is foreign, a substance to which they have grown addicted and now must have at any cost to preserve their eternal lives. I cannot become addicted to time, because it is already part of me. In that sense, I am immune to time – but only in that sense. For though my life will be a long one by human measure, it will not be eternal. I, too, am time-bound. That is how I can be here.'

'I do not understand,' he said, feeling as if he might cry.

'Once the Risen could travel freely to this world, and did so – but no longer. To do so now is to become trapped here for ever. Only one such as I can travel freely between both worlds, belonging fully to neither. That is the reason you were brought to Märchen, Father. To mate with my mother and sire a new breed of Risen – a soldier in our dreadful war able to fight on this distant battlefield and, it was hoped, turn the tide by a rearguard action, so to speak.'

'Tell me this is not true, Cat,' he said, voice trembling. 'For surely it must be too terrible for any father, even Doppler, to use his daughter

147

so meanly. Or if it is true, then at least tell me in the light, so that I might see your face, for I cannot bear to hear these hard truths in darkness.'

'It is all true, Father,' she said, and he felt the soft touch of gloved fingers on his cheek. 'But do not be sad on my account, nor on my mother's. She loved you – this I know. And I love you. I regret nothing of who I am or how I came to be, and nor should you.'

'But you will die,' he said. 'Thanks to me, you were born into a death sentence.'

Her gentle laughter struck him like a blow. 'Why, so were you, and so are all human children! There is no tragedy in that. No wrong. To be alive at all is a gift beyond compare, and I will not fear death as the Risen do. I will not let that fear warp me into its likeness as it has my grandfather, who introduced time into the universe that he might become the master of all, and instead became a slave to what he had created. I will not become a slave of time. Or a miser, storing up a treasure house of stolen time. No, I will use what time remains to me to burn as brightly as I can – not for the sake of the Risen, who will warm themselves at my bonfire, but for myself and those I love – my mother and father, my friends. It is for their sakes that I fight alongside Tiamat to topple the tyrant.'

'You make me ashamed,' said Wichcote.

'You spoke out of love for me. What shame can there be in that?'

He did not trust himself to reply without shaming himself further with tears. But in the silence that followed Cat's words, in which he struggled to command himself, Lord Wichcote heard a noise that at once achieved what he could not have otherwise accomplished half so quickly. It was a faint sound, the merest scrape of leather over stone. A moment earlier, and he would not have heard it at all. A moment later, and it would have been too late. As it was, he had only time enough to utter a warning – 'We are not alone!' – and draw his blade . . . though his eyes had not yet fully adjusted to the dark, and he could see little more than a vague hazy glow where, long ago, in emulation of the Morecockneyans, he had painted mushroom powder onto the stone to light his way.

He heard the chiming echo of Cat's blade sliding free of its scabbard even as he felt her hand slide free of his grasp.

'What a pretty little speech,' said a voice he knew all too well. 'Like to 'ave broke me 'eart.'

Lord Wichcote sighed. 'Hello, Cornelius.'

'Well, well,' came the reply. 'I wouldn't 'ave thought the great Lord Wichcote knew me from Adam. So that's 'oo's been under that mask all these years, eh? 'Oo'd've guessed it? Grimalkin and Lord Wichcote – one and the same! I 'ope yer don't mind if I presume on our old acquaintance and just go on callin' yer Mr G.'

'Not at all,' said Lord Wichcote easily, though in fact he was chagrined that his secret, after having been kept for so long, had been so easily spoiled.

'It's been right crowded with Grimalkins 'ereabouts lately,' Cornelius continued. 'Yer can't 'ardly throw a stone without 'ittin' one. But this is the first time I've encountered a *lady* Grimalkin. I take from what I could not 'elp over'earin' that this be yer daughter, eh, Mr G? Cat, is it? A name as charmin' as 'tis fittin'!'

'Catherine,' corrected Cat. 'Only my friends may call me Cat.'

'Why, I am yer friend, Cat, or mean ter be,' said Cornelius with a rumbling laugh. ''Ere now – put up them pig-stickers, and no one needs ter get 'urt. Last time yer got the jump on us, Mr G, I'll give yer that, no offence taken. But it's more than just two o' us now. And I don't think you and your daughter 'ere can 'andle six – not even if she's twice the man you are . . . or anyways used ter be.'

'He's right,' said Cat. 'We can't beat them all.'

By now Wichcote's vision had adapted sufficiently to show him Cornelius's distinctive blockish shape, aglow with its dusting of mushroom powder, which the Morecockneyans applied indiscriminately to their flesh, hair, and clothes with all the restraint of a palsied barrister adding powder to his wig.

If ever there was a man suited to life below ground, it was Cornelius, who looked like one of the giants of old, a son of the earth. He resembled a boulder with arms and legs and a smaller rock for a head – a rock that sprouted thick moss from the lower end, was bare at the top, and had a third rock, the smallest yet, and shaped rather like a potato, for a nose.

It was also evident that Cornelius was speaking the truth. He had five men with him – none of whom Wichcote recognized.

'Where's your better half, eh, Cornelius?' he asked to buy some time. He was not as ready to surrender as his daughter, no matter the odds. Nor could he quite believe that she was as ready as she seemed. He recalled quite clearly how quickly she had dispatched three of his best men on that night in his attic when she had first appeared to him dressed as Grimalkin – looking so much like him, in fact, that he'd almost felt as if he were gazing into a mirror: at least until that mirror image had pressed a sword point to his throat.

'In all the long years of our acquaintance, Mr Cornelius,' he continued now, 'and I hope you'll agree that they have been marked by mutual respect if not always friendship, I don't believe I've ever seen you apart from Mr Starkey. Where there was Starkey, there too was Cornelius. Where there was Cornelius, Starkey was ever to be found. Yet here is Cornelius – and no sign of Starkey! Why, it's like encountering a man without his shadow! Or, rather, a shadow without its man. I'm thrown, sir, positively thrown.'

'Don't yer worry none about Starkey,' said Cornelius in a gruff voice. ''E's gone in fer a spot o' travel, 'as ol' Starkers.'

'Has he now. Never struck me as the travelling type.'

'It do improve the mind, they say.'

'Do they? How extraordinary. Well, in his case there is a lot of room for improvement. He'll be gone for some time, I expect. Months. Years, even. Where was it you said he'd gone again?'

'I didn't,' growled Cornelius and rubbed briskly at the warty potato of his nose. 'But I don't see no 'arm in tellin' yer. 'E's off ter Frog Land, is Starkers. Dispatched by 'is Majesty, don't yer know. On a very important mission, 'e is.'

'That mission wouldn't have anything to do with a Mr Aylesford, would it?' put in Cat.

''Ere now!' said Cornelius. 'I never said that! Yer never 'eard it from me!'

'I'll take that as a yes,' Wichcote said. 'This new king of yours is making a mistake, Cornelius. He's got you backing the wrong horse.'

'I didn't realize there was 'orses involved. Don't know much about 'orses meself. Not got much use fer 'em down 'ere, don't yer know. But I reckon you'll 'ave the chance ter tell 'is Majesty yerself, Mr G, fer it's ter 'im that I'll be takin' the two o' yer. 'Is Majesty is most interested in meetin' yer. Now if yer don't mind – toss them swords on the ground. I won't be askin' again. And in case yer thinkin' o' tryin' somethin' fancy out o' yer bag o' tricks, Mr G, think again, fer there be two crossbows aimed at yer pretty daughter's pretty 'eart.'

Cat was the first to comply, throwing her sword down at Cornelius's feet. Wichcote followed suit.

'If you harm so much as one hair on her head, I'll kill you, Cornelius, even if I have to come back from the dead to do it,' he said.

'Why, yer cut me ter the quick,' Cornelius replied. 'D'yer take me fer some lowlife ruffian? I be a Morecockneyan born and bred, and I knows 'ow ter treat a lady with the proper respect. I do assure yer, madam,' he added, addressing Cat now, 'that yer 'ave nothin' ter fear from me or my men.'

'I never imagined I did,' Cat said.

'Why, that's fairly spoken,' said Cornelius. 'Dingle, Grimsby – bind the lady's arms now. Not too tight, lads, but not too loose neither. There be no tellin' what the daughter o' Grimalkin might be capable of.'

Cat did not resist as two young men – boys, really – came forward and bound her arms with a length of rope. Lord Wichcote, however, was barely able to restrain himself from striking them down where they stood, though they took no liberties whatsoever and in fact treated their prisoner with marked deference, as though they sensed there was something special about her, something other.

'How did you know you would find us here?' asked Wichcote as his own arms were being bound – rather more roughly and tightly than his daughter's had been, though he could not fault Cornelius for that.

'We 'ave a man in the Worshipful Company o' Clockmakers,' said Cornelius. He gave his nose another brisk and satisfied rub.

''E learned that the Old Wolf 'ad secured permission from the king ter raid the 'ouse o' the great eccentric, Lord Wichcote. I were sent 'ere ter catch 'is lordship should he attempt ter escape by the back door, as it were. And 'ere yer are. Little did I dream I'd catch Grimalkin, too – two birds with one stone! And now, Mr G,' he continued once Lord Wichcote's bonds were secure, 'there is a little bit o' unfinished business between us. I owe yer for what yer done ter me and Starkers on yer last visit 'ere. Yer know I do. No 'ard feelin's, all's fair *et cetera*, but a man's got ter pay 'is debts.'

'I would expect no less,' he said. 'Cat, I'm sorry you have to see this.'

'Mr G 'as the right o' it, miss,' said Cornelius. 'Yer might wish ter avert yer eyes.'

'I shall keep watch,' said Cat. 'The better to judge the debt you are now incurring – a debt I shall pay with interest.'

Cornelius smiled grimly. 'Aye, she's yer daughter right enough, Mr G.'

With those words, the beating began.

4

Rebirth

AGONY WAS ALL HE KNEW. IN THAT PAIN WAS NO ROOM FOR ANYTHING BUT ITS own perception: no name, no memory, no thought, nothing. It was as if his skin had been flayed from his body, and what remained was a single raw nerve exposed to a blistering flame – a flame that burned without consuming. If he had been able to think, he would have figured himself in hell. Indeed, he might have suffered for an eternity already. He had no more notion of time than he did of self. He knew only pain, and that pain, as in some twisted philosophy, was his sole measure of existence: *doleo ergo sum*.

Then came a refinement to his torment: intervals of oblivion in which he knew a blessed relief from the rack of pain on which he hung like a body from its own barbed bones. Or not *knew* – for he knew nothing at all during those times; only when he emerged from them, waking suddenly, as it were, in the very heart of hell's inferno, did he remember that something existed other than the agony he was.

He held on to this idea, which offered a kind of cool comfort, a shred of hope. But this hope was itself a torture, for there was always the fear that the oblivion he did not so much remember as infer would fail to return, and it was this fear, this apprehension, that first caused him to separate himself from the pain. He was something other than pain. Pain was not his natural state. And nor, it seemed to him, was the oblivion he so desperately craved – for that was no more than a response to pain, a blind recoiling.

153

He began to conceive of himself as something acted upon. He swung between extremes of pain and its surcease. What was he – who was he – in the intervals between those extremes? He did not know the answer to that question. But he felt sure there was an answer, and that answer would come to him in time.

Time! That was his next great discovery. As he swung from pain to no-pain and back again, a conviction grew in him that this action provided energy to drive some sort of forward movement; that he was not simply oscillating back and forth in pointless repetition but also progressing through a regular sequence of intervals that, however identical they might be, nevertheless would leave him in a different place from where he'd started. From this arose the notion of a history: a past that has gone before, a present that slips away even as it is embraced or, in his case, helplessly endured, and a future that lies ahead, unknowable until it arrives, awaited with both eagerness and dread. He had a past, though he did not remember it. He had a present, though he did not desire it. And he must have a future, though he could not imagine it.

These wound-up thoughts – for by now they fully merited that name – conjured strange yet familiar images in his mind . . . and with those images came names, and with those names came other bits of knowledge like the flotsam of a shipwreck washed up on a distant shore, there to be picked over and wondered at and perhaps even pieced back together by clever and diligent hands. Pendulum. Pinion. Escapement. Remontoire. These were all parts of devices built to record the passing of time. Clocks. Watches. He saw their shapes, saw their functions sketched out on the blank parchment of his mind. He had built such devices himself, with his own two hands . . . just as a clock had two hands. And a face, as he had a face, though he could not picture it. Was he then a kind of clever clock? Something built to record the passage of time? He felt that he was . . . but also that he was more, much more.

Thus passed the first epoch of his awakening.

The second, like the first, was born in pain. It was a different pain from that which had preceded it – not lesser, exactly, but other. This epoch was punctuated by light and dark, and by noise and silence. All were equally unpleasant, in whatever combinations they occurred. Light was a flail of images that could not be dodged or deflected but which struck him full in the face no matter where he turned. It was stained glass ground fine as sugar and then rubbed into the jelly of his eyes – yes, that was what they were called! – until they bled colour. Dark was a heavy hammer wrapped in a smothering pillow. It was a dull, throbbing ache that echoed down the shattered corridors of his bones. Noise was something shrill and senseless and full of terror. It was meaningless sounds pelting him like stones. It was his own voice, raw and vomitous, unspooling in a continuous idiot scream. Or not quite continuous, for silence was the space between screams, in which some deep-seated instinct compelled him to break off and like a drowning man draw into his lungs the very substance already killing him. At least it felt that way – as it must to a newborn that imagines itself drowning in this harsh medium of air. For he was newborn, or as good as, though of course he didn't know that yet.

Thus passed the second epoch.

The advent of the third and final epoch was marked by the assemblage of these sensory derangements into patterns that yielded to understanding. It happened suddenly, without warning, as if he had been locked away in a cell whose bars, translucent as glass, yet more permeable, distorted all that passed through them – light, sound, everything – making him believe himself irredeemably mad, when in reality it had only been necessary to find the right key in order to restore him to his rightful senses. The key found, whether by chance or design, the tumblers clicked into place, the bars dissolved as if they had never been, and chaos at once gave way to order.

Of course, the pain didn't go anywhere. That cell was not to be escaped in an instant, or even a lifetime, though he didn't know that yet, either.

The first thing he saw, or rather the first thing he recognized, was the face of an elderly gentleman gazing down at him with concern. That is, he did not recognize the man, but only that he was a man. This nevertheless seemed miraculous to him, and he gazed in a kind

155

of awestruck rapture at the by no means handsome face, as if he had never beheld anything so beautiful. It almost made him forget the pain that had sunk its poisoned claws into every square inch of his body, but of course there is no forgetting that kind of pain, not for an instant. You don't even get used to it, though it's a constant companion, with unvarying habits. That, too, he had yet to learn. But at least he was no longer screaming.

The face gazing down at him was unnaturally pale, as though its owner were deathly ill, and very finely wrinkled, as if the skin might tear if touched too roughly. The lips were thin and bloodless, the nose rather regal though webbed with a delicate tracery of veins that contributed the only touch of colour apart from blue eyes that blinked owlishly but not unkindly behind thin-framed gold-rimmed spectacles. Tufts of white, featherlike hair clung to the man's head as though he were in the process of moulting.

'Can you understand me?' asked the man in a tone that indicated he had posed this question a number of times already. His voice had that high and querulous pitch peculiar to very old men and castrati.

'Yes, of course,' he answered – or anyway tried to. But what emerged was a croak that would have done a raven proud. He tried to nod instead but found he could not move his head. Or, indeed, any other part of himself. This did not strike him as a good sign, and he felt himself verge perilously close to screaming again. The only thing that gave him the strength to resist was the fear that, once started, he would never be able to stop.

The man appeared to be aware of his precarious state and made an attempt to soothe him. 'There, there,' he said, laying a hand more bone than flesh upon his forehead. 'Hush-a-bye, my boy. Everything will be all right.'

And strange to say, though by every objective measure he should have felt the very opposite of soothed, as if he were being pawed by a ghoul, there was something in the man's voice and actions, his touch, that calmed him.

'Good,' the man continued, nodding over him even as he stroked his brow. 'Excellent. There is some disorientation, no doubt. But it will pass, don't worry. There is pain, as well, I know. That cannot be helped. It will lessen but never entirely pass. Your injuries were too severe, my boy. Nearly every bone in your body was broken. Your internal organs were crushed and ruptured. Your skull was fractured in a dozen places. That is why you cannot move – I have bound you in place while your body heals. You must be patient. But you will live! I have saved you! I have put you back together like a broken toy!'

That seemed as good a reason to scream as any, and he would have screamed, was set to scream, was in fact already screaming inside, when the man smiled. His face changed utterly with that smile. It transformed him from ghoulish to grandfatherly. Here, now, was a man to be trusted and relied upon. A wise healer who would do no harm. As he watched, a tear spilled from the corner of one blue eye and dispersed at once into the network of wrinkles there. The man seemed not to notice, gazing down as if he were looking at the dearest thing in the world to him, continuing to stroke his forehead all the while.

'Dear boy,' he said. 'My dear, dear boy.'

Who was this man? Did he, should he, know him? He could not remember ever having seen him before. Yet the man spoke as if he knew him. And something in him responded from beyond the reach of memory.

'Sleep now,' the man continued, his dry fingers moving lightly, rhythmically, across his forehead, seeming to inscribe some obscure design there. 'I have work to do. Sleep and dream and remember. When you wake, we will talk again, you and I. For I have much to tell you, Daniel Quare.'

Quare. Yes, that was his name. He remembered now. Remembered everything. His orphan childhood. His apprenticeship with Mr Halsted in Dorchester. How Master Magnus had appeared one day like a grotesque guardian angel or rather devil with his huge head, hunched back, and twisted legs of unequal length . . . appeared out of the blue and fetched him back to London and the Worshipful Company of Clockmakers. His years of study there, marked by steady advancement in his craft and in the estimation of Magnus, from apprentice to journeyman. His induction into the secret ranks of the regulators, and his training in arts he had never thought to master: the arts of the thief, the assassin, the swordsman. He recalled his first mission, to the town house of Lord Wichcote, and how he had surprised the thief Grimalkin there and taken from him – or, rather, as he would soon learn, *her* – the pocket watch that had since snared him in its web . . . snared all of them: Grimalkin, Magnus, Wichcote, Sir Thaddeus Wolfe, Thomas Aylesford the murderer and spy. The whole wide world tangled in that web.

The web of the hunter.

It is just what you have called it: a hunter. It hunts. That is its secret, or one of them.

Who had told him that?

Tiamat the dragon. Denizen of the Otherwhere.

It is a weapon, a very great weapon – too great to be left in the hands of men.

Tiamat, who in human form walked the Earth as a young woman, the same young woman he had encountered on that London rooftop, disguised as Grimalkin, though he hadn't known that then – neither her true identity nor that of Grimalkin, who had turned out to be Lord Wichcote of all people . . . or, as he found it more natural to think of him, for he had first met and come to know him thus, Longinus, former regulator, sham servant at the guild hall, and spy for Master Magnus.

It was Longinus who had told him of the Otherwhere, that realm of godlike beings who were at war with each other just as England was at war with France and her allies; indeed, the war on Earth was but a reflection of the war in heaven, or so he had been assured. Or not precisely a reflection but rather the same war spilled past its original borders and into distant lands, just as England and France clashed both in Europe and across the wide Atlantic, in the American colonies.

Like the savages of that godforsaken wilderness, employed as proxies by the two European powers, those same great powers, whether they knew it or not, were in the employ of greater powers still: Doppler and Tiamat and their respective followers, some of whom he knew by name from Longinus's account of his time in

Märchen, the Alpine town that served as a gateway between the two worlds, higher and lower: Adolpheus the dwarf; Inge the buxom innkeeper of the Hearth and Home; fair Corinna, beloved of Longinus; severe Doppler, her jealous father; one-eyed Hesta, who appeared as both dog and dragon, guardian of the place.

And Dr Immelman, who had, by some science indistinguishable from magic, given Longinus a wonder-working foot to replace the foot of flesh and bone mangled by the gear train of Märchen's magnificent and perverse tower clock – Wachter's Folly, as it was called, after the brilliant but eccentric clockman who had made it. And apparently Immelman had been Wachter, too. It sometimes seemed that everyone but himself had an alias or two! Only Immelman, according to Longinus, had claimed to be human like Longinus himself, a prisoner in Märchen, held against his will, for reasons he did not dare to disclose. He had tried to warn Longinus, had wanted to help him escape whatever fate had been prepared for him . . . but there had been no time. Yet Longinus had escaped, aided by Corinna, who had stolen the hunter from her father and entrusted it to her lover's keeping before they entered the Otherwhere and went their separate ways.

The Otherwhere! Longinus had conducted him through the insane labyrinth of that place, in which all possibilities were attainable if one but had the will and knew the way or could make it. They had travelled in a single step impossibly prolonged, yet over in the blink of an eye, from Wichcote House to the rooftop, a mile or so away, where he, Quare, had first encountered Tiamat in the guise of Grimalkin. As strange as that had been, even stranger was the fact that, beyond the revelation of such a miraculous mode of travel, which upended everything he understood or thought he understood about natural science, the actual experience hadn't been strange at all. An unsuspected instinct lying dormant in him had awakened, and he'd found himself able to influence their direction . . . and then to wrest control of it entirely from Longinus, much to the latter's surprise.

No doubt that unexpected ability was a result of his exposure to the hunter.

It has drunk your blood and left its mark upon you.

Tiamat, again.

Later, Longinus had led him through the subterranean vaults of the Morecockneyans and to the guild hall in quest of the hunter, which the Old Wolf had claimed for his own following the death of Master Magnus. By then he'd known better the danger of examining the timepiece. He'd seen how thirsty it was for human blood. And not just human, for the hunter had killed all of Magnus's beloved cats in an instant, left them drained and desiccated husks . . . and then, scant hours later, taken Magnus himself. Yet the watch did not only kill. It could protect as well. He himself had survived what should have been a fatal wound – the treacherous thrust of Aylesford's dagger between his shoulder blades and into his heart – thanks to the action of the watch; in fact, he was convinced the two were linked as intimately as cause and effect: that the price of his survival had been the death of Master Magnus. The watch had used him, used all of them. It cared only for its own survival. Or, rather, for the survival of what it held, for he had learned that the watch was an egg, and inside that egg a dragon was gestating, a creature of the Otherwhere nurtured on mortal blood and semen, both of which carried in concentrated form that nectar most precious to the gods of the Otherwhere (if they were gods): time.

And so they had come to steal back the egg before the Old Wolf, in his clumsy meddling, could inadvertently add his own store of time, or that of others, to the mix, and thus bring to pass, or at any rate hasten, the moment when the dragon would hatch, hungrier than ever. But instead Sir Thaddeus, cunning as always, had been waiting for them and had captured them all in an instant: himself, Longinus, and poor Gerald Pickens, whom he could not bear to remember, yet – in this curious dream state, in which memories were not so much rising up in him of their own accord as being somehow set down from outside, like plants from one garden transferred to another whose soil has been prepared to receive them – could not forget.

He recalled now with perfect clarity the icy thrill of the scalpel passing through his flesh and bone – felt again the pain, sharp yet also distant, as if even then he had been remembering rather than experiencing it, saw his cleanly severed finger lying upon the dark wood of the Old Wolf's desk as blood spilled from the wound in a thin red stream that was drawn into the hunter like thread being swiftly wound onto a bobbin.

He had been drawn after it. Suddenly the hunter was in his hand. Then nothing. He hadn't known if he were alive or dead, hadn't even guessed where he was until the voice of his master spoke to him – Master Magnus: not dead after all, or only his misshapen body, which no one, least of all Magnus himself, would mourn, but his mind or soul, the vital essence of his genius, remained intact, translated into a new and better housing – the dragon's egg. Or, more accurately, into the dragon taking shape within that egg, for now that he, too, had been sucked inside, he understood that the essence of every living thing consumed by the hunter was present and contributing its portion, however small, to the great production of time that would culminate in the dragon's birth. Yet he had not been similarly absorbed into that collective – a collective whose leading voice belonged to Magnus but whose underlying nature had nothing human about it at all. The dragon, though yet unborn, was already ancient beyond measure, and wise beyond human ken, and while it might permit itself to be guided by Magnus in certain things, and might take from its prey whatever attributes suited it, like a woman trying on foreign styles, in the end it would remain a creature of the Otherwhere. Magnus had boasted of his influence over the dragon, but in fact, as far as Quare could tell, it was the dragon that had influenced Magnus, using his own ideals against him, his pride and his resentment, his iconoclastic intellect and his shrivelled, stunted heart, turning him from a man Quare had looked up to and admired as a kind of surrogate father (knowing nothing of his true sire), and yet pitied, too, for what he might have been, the greatness denied him by what- ever accident of nature had bent his spine and clubbed his foot, into a man he feared had lost his sanity and, with it, all moral compass. Even more, Quare had feared that he would be similarly corrupted.

But his corruption, when it came, had been of a different order. For he found himself returned to his body, the hunter fused to his maimed hand, the voice of Magnus – and, looming behind it, the shadowy alien presence of the dragon – resident in his mind. His will was no longer his own. His limbs no longer obeyed him. So it was that he could only watch aghast as his traitorous hand methodically and without a shred of malice behind it slew every last man in the Old Wolf's den, with the exception of the Old Wolf himself and Longinus – not excluding Gerald Pickens, his friend and fellow journeyman, whom he had saved from one impending death only to deliver over to another. He had cut a dozen throats . . . yet not a single drop of blood had splashed him or stained his clothes. The clockwork egg had sucked it all up. But most shameful and unforgivable of all was the tribute the dragon had demanded from him, and which he, or rather his body, had willingly supplied. For it was not just the blood of others that spilled; as it did, his own seed was milked from him in paroxysms of poisoned pleasure he burned with humiliation to recall. He had sobbed then in helpless anguish and horror, and it seemed to him that he must be sobbing now, sunk in sleep. But there were not tears enough, even in dreams, to wash him clean of these crimes.

The memories came fast and furious now. How he had stumbled, half blind with grief and revulsion, out of the guild hall, retracing his steps to the caves of the Morecockneyans. Aylesford had been waiting there, and with a single stroke of his sword had freed him at once from hand and hunter. Later, in the dungeons of the Morecockneyans, as he lay burning from infection on a bed of foul, louse-infested straw, he'd learned that Aylesford had taken the hunter to France, where he meant to put its infernal powers in the service of England's mortal enemies: Louis XV and his whore Madame de Pompadour, and Pompadour's lackey, the duc de Choiseul, chief minister of the king. But the hunter, he knew, would serve only itself, seeking out the battlefields of Europe for the feast of blood that would provide the nourishment necessary to trigger the dragon's apocalyptic birth. But what could he do? He was sick, dying – and in any case would soon be tried and convicted by the Morecockneyans, and immediately after that put to death. There was a part of him, already defeated, weighed down with despair, that welcomed this fate, as if it were no more than the just requital of his sins. But another part, clinging to life, was not so ready to give up the ghost and instead had called for help, invoking a promise made to him by the dragon Tiamat when she had pressed him, all unwilling, into her service. He did not trust her but needed her now.

She came to him dressed in the garb of Grimalkin, as she had appeared to him once before, though he had not known then, on the moonlit rooftop, whom or rather what he was truly facing, and if he had known would not have believed it. Now, of course, he had learned to believe many impossible things. She'd freed him, this Tiamat who in manner as well as aspect seemed so different from the dragon who had so cruelly toyed with him and casually exulted in her power over him. Perhaps, in shedding the shape of a dragon, she had shed its qualities, too, for in human form she seemed more, well, human, and in her attitude towards him there was no cruelty but instead a gentle concern and tender, teasing humour that, along with her mastery of the blade, which he found rather stirring for the way it testified to a certain suppleness of form, might have made him love her just a little had she been in truth the young woman she appeared to be. But he knew that was just another disguise, no more to be relied upon than the grey costume that gave her the look of Grimalkin. Still, he preferred her this way.

Together they'd escaped through a gateway of standing stones guarded by tongueless brown-cassocked men with teeth filed to wolfish points. As they passed between the stones, and into the Otherwhere, Tiamat had transformed from fierce young woman into a dragon fiercer still, a creature so large that it could hold him loosely caged within the talons of one great forepaw. They had flown for what might have been days above an ever-changing surface of land and sea while in the sky overhead strange stars and suns went spinning by. He did not know where she was taking him, or if she even remembered that he was there. He called to her but she made no reply. Or if she did, he could not hear it for the wind. In any case, he was still feverish, starving and parched besides, and did not trust his eyes or other senses.

Then Tiamat was attacked by a dragon bigger still, a great black beast, and in their savage mutual mauling he, forgotten, had fallen from her grasp. Tumbling head over heels through the enormous, empty air, he'd reached out with the same sure instinct that had served him so well when Longinus had introduced him to the Otherwhere. He'd chosen a path, opened a door – or so he conceived of his actions, though at the same time he knew, dimly, that these were but clumsy metaphors to express concepts no sane human mind could other-wise entertain – and fallen like a star dislodged from its place in the firmament, fallen ablaze with fever or perhaps some other fire, fallen fast as ever lightning fell and landed as hard, with a shattering impact that extinguished every attendant flame and spark but which now, in memory, kindled them anew, so that even as he reached the end of one history he seamlessly began another and awoke mid-scream, feeling his broken body straining against whatever bonds held it fixed so rigidly in place, bones grinding against bones, torn muscles freshly tearing. It was as if he were both mother and child, self-generated, with agony the midwife of this miraculous rebirth.

What, then, did that make the elderly, bewigged man who stood near by, a candle in one hand, watching from behind the glint of gold-rimmed spectacles with an expression in which rapt interest mingled with suffering? It took Quare some time to become aware of him, pre-occupied as he was by his own rather more immediate suffering, and because the man's dark clothing merged imperceptibly into shadow. But at last, when his screams had faded to whimpers, and they to gasping sobs such as a child might make, he – feeling very much like a child, the child he had been once upon a time, with no father or mother to protect him, at the mercy of every hand and will stronger than his own, unable now to even wipe his eyes clear of the tears that streamed unchecked down his bare cheeks and splashed across his bare chest – addressed the heretofore mute witness in a whisper too feeble to carry any freight of anger or accusation but only sincere curiosity. It was not that he had exhausted his voice but that he had learned to fear even what little movement was occasioned by the use of that instrument.

'Why do you torture me?' For what else could it be? Though he could not move so much as a finger, and his head, like the rest of him, was locked in place, he could perceive that his body – naked, as far as he could tell, though he was not cold; if anything, he felt rather too warm – was not recumbent but propped upright and spread-eagled, pinioned to a hard and unyielding frame. The room he was in had no visible windows, but there were a handful of scattered candles burning, and by their meagre light he was able to make out vague shapes that put him in mind of torture implements: racks and screws and wheels. Funny how he had never considered until now how alike such devices were in their underlying mechanical properties to devices employed in the manufacture of clocks, as if there were some sinister affinity between horologists and torturers! He saw, too, sunk in shadow behind the old man, assorted figures looking on in silence, like a crowd of apprentices intently studying the work of a master.

'My dear boy!' exclaimed the man in an injured tone, as if feeling himself unjustly accused. 'It tears my heart to see you suffer so – never doubt it! But grave injuries require grave measures. Pain is the doctor's friend, for it tells much that even the most intelligent patient cannot sensibly articulate. I know it is uncomfortable – not to mention undignified – to be restrained in this fashion, naked as a newborn babe, but it is necessary, I assure you. Your body could not bear the weight of even the finest silk at present, and immobility is essential for your fractured bones and nerves to mend.'

'Are you a doctor then, as well as a torturer?'

'I am not a torturer at all.' He stepped forward and made a curt bow that seemed utterly out of place in this chamber of horrors. 'My name is Immelman. And yes, I am a doctor, among other things.'

Quare had already guessed his location, but now he was certain. 'So, this is Märchen, is it?' he asked. 'I suppose that means I am a prisoner of Herr Doppler.'

'Prisoner? Ach, curse me for a fool!' the doctor cried and hurried about the room as fast as a slight limp would allow, lighting other candles from the one in his hand.

Bit by bit, the shadows peeled back, and though Quare could not turn his head, and the light, though far from bright, hurt his eyes, grown used to darkness, still he grasped soon enough that what he had taken for instruments of torture were instead parts of a massive clockworks. Some bits were in perfect condition; others were damaged. And rather than an audience of silent apprentices watching worshipfully as their master put a prisoner to the test, the figures he had seen, or thought to see, were no more than crudely carved and painted automatons. Many of these, too, were damaged, some quite severely, as if they had seen battle.

'The clock,' said Quare as understanding dawned. 'We are inside Wachter's Folly!'

'Yes, that is right,' said Dr Immelman sadly. He set the candle down upon a small table and gestured expansively with both hands. 'This is all that remains of my second greatest masterpiece. Like the town itself, it has been destroyed by this terrible war. So much has been destroyed! And for what? It is madness!'

'But didn't Doppler bring me here?'

Immelman shook his head. 'Doppler and all the rest left this place long ago. It is a ruin now, deserted, forgotten by everyone except me. But I knew you would show up sooner or later, dear boy. I found you lying outside, in a pool of your own blood, unconscious and near death. You had fallen from an immense height; it was the awful thunder of your body striking the ground that announced your arrival – the impact set the tower bell ringing, as if the ruined clock had been restored to strike a fateful hour! I carried you inside – here, to my old workshop – and laboured hard to save your life, but it is you who came to Märchen. You brought yourself here, through the Otherwhere.'

'How can that be? I've never been here before. I don't know the way.'

'You know it. But you do not know you know it.'

'I don't understand.'

'Do you not, Daniel?'

'And that is another thing. How is it you know my name? I am certain we have never met before. At least, I have no recollection of it.'

'It would be a wonder if you had, for you were a mere babe at the time. You were born here, Daniel. This is your home.'

Quare was at a loss to reply. He had known nothing of his mother beyond a name, and of his father, not even that. Now, it seemed, he might learn at last the truth of his parentage, his history . . . and perhaps his destiny, too.

'How?' he croaked at last. 'Do my parents yet live? Tell me of them, I beg you!'

Dr Immelman appeared to consider his request with care. 'Very well,' he said. 'But I must first relate how I came to this cursed place – why I was brought here and how I was used. Tell me, my boy, how old do you think I am? Do not worry about offending my vanity. I have none left, I assure you.'

Quare answered without hesitation. 'I should say you were a hundred or more. Indeed, I do not believe I have ever seen a man as old as you.'

'Hmm,' said Immelman, and snorted. 'So old? Perhaps I have not set the sin of vanity aside after all! I had flattered myself that I did not look a day over ninety. On a good day, eighty. But in fact I am more than twice that. I was born in the year 1555, by the Roman calendar. That makes me two hundred and four years old – at least by Earthly measure. But time, as you will learn, dear boy, is wilder here, and does not respect any calendar.'

'I thought there was no time in the Otherwhere.'

'That is not precisely true. The potential for all things lies within the Otherwhere. All that is needed to bring them forth is to imagine them – and by that I mean rigorously, fully, with close attention to the most minute details – with sufficient force of will. Of all the Risen – for so the denizens of this place name themselves – Doppler has the most rigorous imagination and the most forceful will. It was he who created time, calling it forth from that cauldron of infinite possibilities and making it real. But he did not pour his creation into this world. No. You see, he built another world to contain it – the world that we call Earth. Earth and everything on it, animate and inanimate, living and dead, are receptacles for time.'

'Longinus told me as much. He said that time was a kind of drug for the Risen, and that it matured in humans like wine in bottles.'

'Longinus?'

'You knew him as Michael Gray. He has many aliases. Some know him as Grimalkin. Others as Lord Wichcote. But everything I know about Märchen and the Otherwhere, I learned from him.'

Immelman nodded. 'A good man. I liked him – and pitied him, too, for he was to become my apprentice, and then my replacement. But Corinna had other ideas about that. Still, I helped him as best I could. And he helped me.'

'The last I saw of him, he had been gravely wounded,' Quare said. 'I do not know if he is alive or dead. He fled into the Otherwhere.'

'Ach. That is bad. To enter the Otherwhere in a weak or confused frame of mind is to risk becoming lost for ever.'

'Perhaps, like me, he will be fortunate enough to find his way to safety.'

'Fortune had nothing to do with your arrival here,' Immelman said. 'You have always known the way. It is your birthright.'

'So you say, but as yet I've heard nothing to convince me of it.'

'That is because you keep interrupting! We will get nowhere if you continue thus.' With an exasperated grunt, Immelman stepped close to Quare and reached up – Quare hung suspended a foot or so above the floor, and Immelman, though normally only an inch or two shorter than his patient, was in effect rendered much shorter by this circumstance – to touch his forehead with his index finger. This he brushed briskly across Quare's skin.

Earlier Immelman's touch had been soothing, but not this time. Quare felt as if his skin were being peeled away from the bone. He cried out . . . or tried to. But his voice was gone. He had been silenced.

'There,' said Immelman, drawing back with a satisfied smile, as at a job well done. There was nothing overtly malicious in his expression; he did not seem to be aware of the pain he had inflicted, or, if aware, to accord that pain any importance, despite his earlier words on the subject. 'Now, to continue. But first, a chair, Corinna, if you please.'

To Quare's astonishment, there was a stirring at these words from the group of automatons, and one of them strode jerkily forward. It had been given the appearance of a young woman with rosy red cheeks and two wings of stiff blonde hair emerging from beneath a blue kerchief. Like most of the others, it had been damaged in whatever calamity had befallen the tower clock. One of its arms was missing, and the pretty painted features were cloven by a deep gouge, as from an axe. Its legs were charred like willow saplings after a fire.

Immelman did not so much as glance towards the approaching figure. Rather, he began to lower himself as if into a chair . . . but there was no chair. And then, suddenly, there was, for the automaton, without pausing in its advance, began to contort itself as no human being, not even the most supple acrobat, could have done. Its blackened legs bent unnaturally; its torso swivelled and, as it were, unhinged; its lone remaining arm rotated and descended backward to the floor. Horribly, its mutilated head remained up, facing forward even as, like some cross between a spider and a sofa, it scuttled into place beneath the old man's lowering posterior.

Quare wondered if he had gone mad.

Leaning back with a sigh, Immelman stretched out his thin legs in their black breeches and grey stockings, crossing them at the ankles. 'You asked about time,' he said, returning to his subject as if there had been no unusual interruption. 'Doppler created time in order to bend the other Risen to his will. He knew the novelty of it would prove irresistible to their jaded appetites. And so it was. In those days, when the Earth was young, the Risen often travelled there to taste time in all its potent varieties. They came via portals – natural gateways placed there by Doppler or erected by their own formidable wills. But later, with the arrival of human beings – for we were something of an afterthought in the mind of Doppler, my boy – these portals ceased to function and were replaced by manmade monumental structures – standing stones, pyramids, and the like, all of which had one thing in common, despite their differing appearances: they served as crude devices for the measurement of time. Thus our savage forebears were taught by Doppler and others, in their Earthly guises of gods, monsters, and heroes, to take note of certain periodicities attending the celestial pageant and evident even to the naked eye: the relative motion of stars and planets and their satellites, the portentous appearance and reappearance of fiery-tailed comets, the awesome spectacle of lunar and solar eclipses, and so on, all tied in one way or another to the progression of the seasons, the turning of the years, the emptying of the storehouse of a man's life from birth until death.

'To measure something is to harness it, and to harness something is to enslave it. Yet to become the master of a slave is also to become a slave. And so it was that the Risen, including Doppler himself, became dependent upon time in ways that even he had failed to foresee. Thus did time escape the constraints he had sought to place upon it and, stealing between the worlds like a plague that leaps between cities, infect the Otherwhere. This is the cause of the great war that has divided the Risen into two implacable armies and which continues unabated – indeed, more fiercely than ever – to this day.

'No doubt you are wondering what this has to do with me, for after all I set out to tell you the story of your birth, not the whole history of this place. But you will see that the one cannot be told without the other.'

5

Dr Immelman's Tale

I WAS BORN IN THE CITY OF PRAGUE, TO A PROSPEROUS BUT BY NO MEANS wealthy family of artisans. In those days there were many Jews in Prague, men and women whose lives were so often invisible to us Christians. We considered ourselves, by virtue of our religion, to be the only true citizens of the place, the rightful rulers, ordained as such by almighty God. Thus was even the lowest Christian stableboy greater than the richest Jewish merchant or the wisest, most venerable rabbi. And if there should be any doubt of this, as indeed there sometimes was, especially in the face of adverse circumstances such as sickness, natural disasters, wars, or calamities of other kinds, why, then the remedy was as close to hand as the Jews themselves, those perpetual foreigners in our midst, who dressed and spoke so strangely, and whose ancestors had, after all, or so we were taught, put Christ to death.

At such times, a kind of festival spirit would grip the city, and what had been invisible would become not only visible but impossible to ignore, like a provocation, until everywhere one looked there were Jews, and behind every sickness and bankruptcy more Jews, and behind all the vicissitudes of life more Jews still, a sinister cabal of string-pullers that stretched beyond the borders of any one nation, extending even into the innermost councils of Rome.

Well, Rome was far off, no doubt, safely beyond our reach and retribution, but not so our neighbours, who strutted about our streets as if they owned them, dressed in their queer black clothes like so many carrion crows picking the flesh from our bones and the gold from our purses.

Now, it so happened that in 1588 I became acquainted with a wealthy Jew who had recently moved with his family to Prague, there to take up a prestigious rabbinical position. This man had six daughters, each more beautiful than the last, and I confess that I found myself admiring these girls, the eldest of whom was no more than twenty, if that, while the youngest, twins, were already of marriageable age. At thirty-three, it was long past time for me to settle down, but in truth I felt no urgency, despite the increasingly desperate entreaties of my mother, who wished to see a grandchild before she died, so I felt quite free to admire these girls, and more than that, to wonder if I might enjoy their favours, for I well knew that Christian girls, even the most seemingly devout, were often not as chaste or reserved as they liked to pretend to be, and I saw no reason to assume things were any different among the Jews.

I was curious that such ripe beauties as these were not already spoken for, married off to respectable husbands and with children of their own, but it appeared that certain vile calumnies had been spread about their legitimacy which, notwithstanding their father's exalted position, kept potential suitors at bay. Perhaps their father was glad enough to keep his daughters close and, as it were, unspoiled – there are such men in the world, misers who can conceive of no better fate for their daughters than to ornament the garden of their old age.

At any rate, I took advantage of the opportunity to strike up a conversation with the rabbi when he came into my shop one day – I was known throughout the city as a broad-minded businessman who would serve Jews as well as Christians, provided they paid in advance.

'Herr Immelman,' he said, all but swallowed up in his dark robes, with his ridiculous hat perched upon his head like a baker's confection and his long grey locks dangling down to tangle in the riot of his peppery beard. He had a face like a monkey's, all pushed in, great craggy brows, and a nose that proclaimed him, even if nothing else had, an elder of the tribe of David. He smelled, not unpleasantly, like old books and incense.

'Rabbi,' I said. 'Tell me how I may serve you.'

'Everyone says there is only one man to be seeing in all of Prague when it comes to time, and that man is you, Herr Immelman.'

His accent was so barbarously thick that it took me some time to decipher this statement. When I had, I merely smiled and inclined my head, as to say, 'Who am I to argue with everyone?'

He approached the table on which I had been laying out certain of my choicest wares. Reaching into his robes with one hand, he rummaged around as though groping blindly in a sack of the kind children believe Sinterklaas carries on St Nicholas's Eve – a sack whose inside is bigger than its outside. It was comical but also a bit unsettling, for the thought had popped into my head, I know not from where, that the rabbi was nothing more than his robes, and that if I were to tear them away, I would behold only empty space, with that little monkey face floating mockingly in mid-air. But of course I did no such thing, and in another moment he had produced a small clock of the type that wealthy gentlemen and ladies of those days carried upon their persons.

Perhaps you have seen such timepieces in your guild hall, dear boy, kept as historical curiosities. They are crude, bulky objects, little boxes made to be worn, with their keys, on a chain. There is a protective ornamental casing and, within, the clock itself. In need of frequent winding, their calibration upset by the slightest motion, these clocks are notoriously inaccurate and, in fact, of so little practical use as to be mere objects of jewellery. It is something to be proud of, is it not, how far horology has advanced in just two centuries!

'Can you mend it?' the rabbi asked, handing it to me.

'A beautiful piece.' It was hideous. Some knave with no taste and less skill had crafted the outer case of gold-plated tin in the image of a lion with two intertwined tails. I suppose one tail was not grand enough! I turned the object over in my hand but could see no obvious injury, and the same was true when I opened the case – the lion's jaws swung apart to reveal the face, nestled in the neck of the beast, as if it had tried to swallow the clock and choked to death instead. Time

173

may fly, but it is not easily digested, I find. The hands had stopped at three-fifteen precisely. I looked up. 'What is the matter with it?'

'It does not keep the correct time. I am forever coming late to appointments because I cannot tell when is the proper hour.'

'Yes, I can mend it,' I assured him, though he would have done better to throw it away and rely instead upon a sundial, for any repairs I made would be undone as a matter of course in a day or so by the unavoidable indignities of city life: the jarring of carriages on cobblestones, the countless small collisions that occur during any walk from here to there, people jostling you in the street, in front of stalls, in shops, everywhere and anywhere. To say nothing of pickpockets. I named a price, somewhat above my usual rate for such work, knowing, as I did, how the Jews love to haggle. But to my surprise, the rabbi agreed at once. I explained my policy of requiring full payment in advance, and the rabbi did not object to this either, counting out the money with fastidious attention from a purse he retrieved from his robes rather more easily than he had the clock. I confess that I was conceiving a certain fondness for the man.

'How are you finding our city so far?' I asked him.

'There are many Jews here,' he said, bobbing his head like a pigeon . . . a bearded and be-hatted pigeon. 'I do not think there could have been more in Jerusalem in the days of King David.' He had come, I had heard, from a smaller town in Moravia, where Jews were less plentiful than in Prague.

'Many suitable husbands for your lovely daughters,' I suggested with a wink.

He visibly deflated at this sally. 'Ach, Herr Immelman,' he said sadly. 'If only families could be mended as easily as clocks!'

'Why, can they not?' I essayed, hoping to salvage something yet, in spite of the disappointing start, my eyes still on those nubile daughters – all six of them, one for each day of the week, with the Sabbath, of course, set aside as a day of rest! 'Surely such repairs are not beyond your skills, Rabbi.'

'Ach,' he repeated. 'There is only so much a father may do. Young people today do not listen to their elders. They think they know everything. And there is something that plagues us Jews. A terrible, pernicious practice – *nadler*. Lies and rumours have been spread about my daughters. God knows the truth, but men are foolish and believe the worst.' He shrugged his shoulders – assuming he had any under those robes, and the robes were not lifting of their own accord. 'Well, what can be done? God does not send us what cannot be borne.'

'God helps those who help themselves,' I said. 'That's the Christian way. You should try it, Rabbi. Speak out against these liars. Don't let them get away with their slander.'

'Yes, yes, no doubt you are right.'

'You must do it for the sake of the girls,' I persisted. 'They are innocent, after all. One need only look at them to know that they are capable of nothing but goodness. They are angels come to Earth.'

He looked me in the eye then, and his own eyes were shining with emotion. I had not noticed how blue they were, like a windswept autumn sky. They seemed out of place in that pinched monkey face. 'You see more clearly than most, Herr Immelman. You have a father's thanks.'

After he had gone, I reflected that I had made a good start, for when it comes to daughters, there is no surer way to end with a father's curses than to begin with his thanks. Thus encouraged, I decided that I would press my advantage by delivering the repaired clock to the rabbi at his home the next morning, rather than waiting for him to come back to the shop to claim it two days hence, as we had agreed. Perhaps I would catch sight of one of the daughters, engage her in light conversation, and one thing would lead to another.

I closed early and turned my attentions to the clock. In those days, dear boy, the art of clockmaking was in its infancy, the province of blacksmiths and other metalworkers, as well as cabinetmakers and similar artisans in wood. There was not yet a clockmaking guild in Prague to order and regulate those of us who practised this upstart trade; hence, every man had his own precious store of knowledge, his own secrets and methods, even his own tools, self-developed and jealously guarded. Needless to say, the quality of the work varied widely.

My father was a cabinetmaker, like his father before him. And so, nominally, was I. But from boyhood I had been obsessed with clocks, whose ingenious mechanisms, marvels of practical engineering, seemed to herald a new and brighter age, one in which reason and natural science would hold sway over ignorance and superstition. I cannot tell you how many hours I spent taking clocks apart and putting them back together again, or roaming around within the works of the larger clocks that had begun to adorn public buildings and churches, learning the principles by which they functioned, and how they were made. I found them beautiful in every respect. Soon I was building my own timepieces, using cast-off pieces of other clocks, as well as wooden parts that I fashioned myself. I was young, and the world itself seemed so: full of promise, a place where a boy might achieve great things by dint of his own efforts. My father's generation viewed clocks with suspicion, indifference, or superstition, but to me they represented everything that was fresh and new, all the promise of a better world, as well as a rejection of the hidebound world of my father and his father, going back, it seemed, to the beginning of time. No doubt it seems thus to every young man with an ounce of spirit and ambition. Yet there are hinges of history, so to speak, pivot points at which the world may take a new direction, if only sufficient force is applied, and it seemed to me then, and seems to me still, that I was living in such a time.

I don't mean to give the impression that I was a grim and studious boy, forever hunched over a worktable or with my nose buried in books. I had my duties in my father's shop to keep me busy, as well as opportunities for adventure and mischief in the perpetual carnival of Prague's colourful streets. There I found love as well, or anyway women whose bodies, if not precisely their affections, were available for a price even I could afford to pay, and often for no price at all, given freely, out of the sheer exuberance of desire, for I was not bad to look upon in those days, and what I lacked in experience I more than made up for in enthusiasm. There are women who enjoy a good tumble as much as men do. That was not the least valuable of my youthful discoveries!

But the truth is, everything about clocks came easily to me. I understood them intuitively, and very often, when I took a timepiece apart to examine its insides, I would discover that what I had seen already, in my mind's eye, was either present now before me or, on the contrary, constituted a superior design to what the clockmaker had actually employed. I began not only to repair clocks but to improve them, and to build clocks of my own design, using techniques and parts of my own invention, often entirely of wood, for that was the material closest and easiest to hand. You can build a very fine clock out of wood, sturdy and surprisingly dependable, though of course for precision there is no beating metal.

I mention all this by way of preparation, so that you can better comprehend the shock I received upon opening the rabbi's clock. I prised apart those lion's jaws like some Hercules of horology and then opened the clock face to get at the interior mechanism. But there was none. The clock was empty. A hollow shell!

I wasn't sure what to make of this. Was I the victim of an elaborate practical joke? It was difficult to conceive of the rabbi, a man of immense dignity, playing such a joke, either on his own behalf or at the behest of others. I decided that it was he who had been the victim. Whoever had sold him the clock had swindled him good and proper. I had to admire him, whoever he was, this anonymous trickster who had swindled a Jew! I couldn't help laughing, imagining the rabbi dutifully winding his clock and painstakingly setting the hands to the correct hour and minute, only to find, when he next checked the time, that the clock had stopped again! It struck me as a most excellent joke.

But then it occurred to me that perhaps the rabbi was testing me. That he knew perfectly well the clock was an empty shell, and he was interested for some reason in seeing what my reaction to this discovery would be. The Jews, I reminded myself, are an odd people; that the rabbi might test me with an ethical dilemma such as this did not seem by any means impossible, though I could not imagine his reasons for doing so. By what right, in any case, did he or any Jew test a Christian man? Still, I had to tread carefully, for if I hoped to speak to his daughters, let alone seduce them, I could not burn any bridges with their father.

The more I thought about it, though, the angrier I got at the old rascal for sticking me in this quandary. Of course, the simplest response would have been to return the clock to the rabbi, tell him what I had found, or, more accurately, hadn't found, and commiserate with him over the sad state of a world in which unscrupulous men could prey with impunity upon honest rabbis. I might even bring along some timepieces of my own to offer for sale and thus squeeze more profit from the whole sorry affair.

But this course of action didn't appeal to me, for two reasons. First, the rabbi had paid in advance. If I returned an empty casing, he would no doubt expect his money back. And if word of that got around, then, whether or not he or anyone else had intended for me to be the victim of a joke, I would become a general laughing stock. Herr Immelman, bested by a Jew! Why, I would never hear the end of it. Second, and weighing even more heavily on my pride, was the fact that, as with every clock I examined, a detailed image of the interior mechanism had arisen in my mind's eye before I opened the face – and that image did not vanish simply because I had discovered the clock to be a hollow fraud. On the contrary, it burned brighter than ever, and I found that I could not resist the challenge of turning that image into reality. Not to try would have been an act of cowardice. Besides, I could not help but imagine the look on the rabbi's face when I handed him a clock that was in perfect working order. His expression would tell me in an instant whether or not he had known of the clock's true nature. I laughed to think that I would thus turn the tables on him, and that he would be the one put to the test.

Rubbing my hands together in gleeful anticipation, I set to work.

By morning I had contrived to pack the shell with all that was necessary to turn the sham clock into a real one. I set the hands to the proper time, inserted the key and wound the mechanism, listening with contentment to the constancy of the ticking, then closed the gaping jaws with a snap. I felt very pleased with myself. It was now a clock to be proud of; indeed, I should not have hesitated to present it to the emperor himself.

I cleaned up, put away my tools, locked the clock in my wall safe with my other valuables, then climbed the stairs to my room – I slept above the shop – and lay down in my bed, still dressed, exhausted after my labours. I had intended to sleep for an hour or two only, but when I awoke it was midday, the sun shining brightly through the narrow window to illuminate a universe of dust motes swirling in the air. But it was not that which had awakened me. Someone was pounding at the door to my shop.

Imagine my surprise, dear boy, when I opened the window, stuck my head out, and beheld a woman on the stoop below me dressed in the distinctive garb of a Jewess, an unusual sight so far from the ghetto. She was hammering at my door as if it were a matter of life and death, drawing curious stares from passers-by, of whom there were many owing to the time of day. No one stopped to ask her what was the matter, however, no doubt wary of becoming involved in some tawdry business. I would have felt the same had it not been my door. I did not mind it being generally known that I served Jews in my shop, but I did not want things to go too far, and for my business to become known as a Jewish shop. I could not afford to have every stray Jew in Prague show up at my door!

'Stop!' I thundered at her. 'Stop at once, do you hear?'

She looked up as if Jehovah himself had addressed her.

Imagine now my further surprise when I beheld the rabbi's eldest daughter, Rachel.

'Please, Herr Immelman, I must speak with you,' she cried in evident distress.

'I will be right down,' I replied and ducked back inside. My head was awhirl; was this a dream? I pinched myself hard but did not wake up. Very good! I smoothed my hair and moustache – yes, I wore a moustache in those days, a bristling affair that rather resembled a spitting cat, with its back up and fur as spiky as the quills of a porcupine, most impressive! – and straightened my sleep-rumpled clothing as best I could in a handful of heartbeats. Then I plunged down the stairs two at a time and flung open the shop door.

'Please come in,' I said. 'You have already given the neighbours quite enough to gossip about, I think.'

At this she blushed most becomingly and stepped past me into the

179

shop. I caught a whiff of incense as I closed the door behind her, as if the smoke of all the secret midnight ceremonies of her race had woven itself into her hair and clothes.

'What can I do for you, Fraülein?' I asked. Though I had admired Rachel from afar, strolling the streets in the company of her equally admirable sisters, this was the closest I had ever come to her. Her presence was intoxicating. Her lingering blush, her downcast, long-lashed eyes, her dusky olive complexion, all affected me like the perfume of some exotic desert flower, so that I felt dizzy with desire. 'What did you wish to speak with me about?'

'It is about my father, Herr Immelman,' she said. 'I believe he came here yesterday and left a clock with you for repair?'

I affirmed that he had, though to tell the truth, Rachel's visit had so distracted me that I had completely forgotten about the rabbi's clock!

'Have you started to work on it yet?' she asked rather timidly.

'In fact, I have finished,' I told her. And it struck me suddenly that it was she, and not her father, who was being subjected to a test. Only, I was ignorant of the terms of this test, even though I was the one administering it. 'Shall I fetch it for you?'

She shook her head no. Then burst out, 'Oh, Herr Immelman, what will you think of us!' She began to cry, burying her face in her hands and turning away from me, as if she might rush out the door.

I grabbed her by one arm, just above the elbow, to keep her from going, but she had not been trying to flee after all, and instead of pre-venting her exit, as I had intended, my action had the effect of drawing her sharply back, so sharply that she stumbled into my chest. Rather than pull away, she leaned there, as though resting against the trunk of a tree, her hands covering her face, her firm body, whose outline I could feel even through her thick clothing, racked with sobs. I could not help putting my arms around her, and still she did not pull away, though she must have felt me pressing against her.

'Why, what is the matter, child?' I asked softly – though she was no child but a woman of twenty-odd years, not so very much younger than me. I wanted to comfort her at that moment more even than I wanted to seduce her. 'Here – dry your eyes!' I drew a handkerchief from my pocket and pressed it upon her.

She took it and only then stepped away. I let her go. A moment later, when she turned to face me, she had brought herself under control, though I could see the streaks of the tears she had shed glistening on her cheeks, and unshed tears pooling in her glossy brown eyes. She gave me a self-conscious smile and laughed lightly, with embarrassment, but I could see, too, that she was grateful for my gentleness and concern.

'Now, Fraülein,' I said, taking charge of the situation, 'what is the meaning of all this?'

She took a deep breath, and for an instant I thought she might start to cry again. But she did not, and instead spoke softly but clearly, my handkerchief clasped in her hands just below her chin. 'We are but recently arrived in this city, Herr Immelman,' she began.

'Yes, this I know,' I said encouragingly.

'Perhaps you do not know that there are many things we Jews are prohibited from doing for ourselves during the Sabbath – necessary things that our religion forbids us but which it is hard and perhaps even dangerous to do without.'

'I have heard this,' I told her. 'It seems foolish.'

'Perhaps all faiths have their bits of foolishness,' she replied somewhat sharply, but then, before I could answer, went on: 'But you are right – it is foolish. Did you then also know that we Jews employ the services of what we call a "righteous gentile" to do for us during that time those things we are forbidden to do for ourselves, lighting candles and suchlike?'

'This I did not know,' I told her, feeling my eyebrows rise in consternation. 'Jews make servants of Christians?'

'It is not like that,' she said. 'It is a *mitzvah* – a good deed, like the charity you Christians preach and sometimes even practise. But our religion directs that we pay something, usually only a token amount, but perhaps more, and this we do, meaning no insult by it.'

'I see,' I said, though I did not. 'What has this to do with me?'

'My father has heard from many Jews that Herr Immelman is a fair man, a man that one can do business with, who does not try to cheat Jews as others may do.'

I nodded for her to continue, pleased to hear myself spoken of in such glowing terms.

'So my father, he decides to put this information to the test by bringing you for repair a clock that has no insides. If you are an honest man, you will return the clock, and his fee paid in advance, and then my father will know that you are indeed a righteous gentile, and he will ask you to come and help us during the Sabbath – for which he will pay handsomely, for, as he says, a righteous man is a pearl without price.'

I could not help it; I began to laugh.

'What is so funny?' she demanded.

'Why could he not have simply asked?' I said. 'Why did he have to set me this ridiculous test?'

'My father has his own ways of doing things,' she said ruefully. 'I did not feel it was fair, this test. And so I came to warn you. And to ask that you not judge him too harshly, for he is a good man, really. A very good and wise man.'

'He is going to be a very surprised man when he sees that clock,' I told her, still chuckling. 'For as I told you before, I have finished with it. It is mended.'

'But it is not even broken! It is only the shell of a clock, like a child's toy. How can you mend that?'

'I will show you.' There were a number of clocks in my shop, wall clocks and mantel clocks, all of them showing the same time, right down to the minute. An impressive feat even in your day, let alone two hundred years ago! 'Pray regard the hour on these clocks,' I told her.

'I see that it is nearly two of the clock,' she said. 'What of it?'

Only a woman could be so imprecise about the time. But I let it pass. Instead, I went to my wall safe, opened it, and took out the rabbi's clock. I returned to her and held it, dangling by its chain, up to her ear.

Her eyes widened, but she said nothing.

Then I opened the jaws of the lion, revealing the clock face . . . which showed five minutes until two – the same time indicated on the other clocks.

'This is no trick,' I told her. 'I simply turned this clock into what it had been pretending to be all along.'

'But why?' she asked. 'Why go to all that trouble?'

I shrugged, closing up the clock and slipping it, chain and all, into my pocket. 'Perhaps because I do not like to be tested.'

She considered this for a moment, then shook her head. 'No, I think there is more to it than that, Herr Immelman. I believe you *do* like to be tested. It is to fail the test that you do not like.'

I could not in good faith dispute this point. 'What of your father, Fraülein? What will he say when he sees the clock? Will he consider my actions to be those of a righteous man?'

'As a righteous man himself, how can he not? And what, then, will you say when he asks you to help us?'

'What would you like me to say?'

At this she blushed again. 'Can you not guess, Herr Immelman? I did come to warn you, after all. I have seen you looking at me. You, too, are pleasant to look at.'

'There are more pleasant things than looking,' I said.

Her blush deepened, and she turned her back to me. 'You mustn't say such things.'

'Why, we need not speak at all,' I assured her, and went to her, placing my arms about her as I had before. I could feel her trembling like a leaf. As for me, I would surely burst if I did not have her. But it was not to be, for at that instant someone else began knocking at the shop door.

Rachel turned to me, a stricken expression on her face. 'No one must see me here!'

'It is a bit late to worry about that,' I pointed out as the knocking persisted, even growing louder. 'Half of Prague must have heard you hammering at my door!'

'Please,' she said, and I could see that she was genuinely afraid. 'What if it is my father?'

'Come,' I told her, and hustled her into the back room. 'You may leave by this door, which opens into an alley behind the house. Just turn the key.'

She nodded and made for the door. I did not have time for another word, or even to steal a kiss. But our eyes spoke, and kissed, and then she was gone.

I hurried back into the front room and wrenched open the door, in a foul mood, as you may well imagine, dear boy.

Standing there was the rabbi's second-eldest daughter, Ruth.

'Herr Immelman, I must speak with you,' she said.

Numbly I stepped aside, and she entered the shop.

Ruth was a year or so younger than Rachel. Whereas Rachel was like a fruit at the very height of ripeness, a plum whose outer blush testifies to a juicy inner sweetness, and whose whole existence constitutes an offering of itself to the eye and to the mouth, practically begging to be bitten into, and awaiting only an outstretched hand to fall, Ruth had just entered into the first flush of mature ripeness, and she glowed with the still-fresh awareness of her beauty and health, feeling herself the cynosure of every eye and basking in that universal regard, as if the world were a mirror before which she might preen without consequence, like a pretty girl in the privacy of her sitting room. Rachel's every gesture, every word, was an invitation, whether or not she knew it, but Ruth fancied herself complete, self-contained, in need of nothing from others beyond their worship, as natural and unremarkable to her as sunlight. That is the kind of beauty, my boy, that a man cannot help but view as a challenge, a provocation.

'What can I do for you, Fräulein?' I asked.

She had been looking about my shop with keen interest, taking in the timepieces and the various samples of my cabinetmaking and woodworking skills, seemingly entranced by their delicate beauty, no doubt imagining them as ornaments to her own. She turned to me now as if she had forgotten me entirely, and only the sound of my voice had recalled my existence to her mind. 'Herr Immelman,' she said briskly, bestowing on me – or, rather, upon her own reflection – a sweetly chiselled smile. 'My sister has been here, has she not? Don't bother to deny it – I know it to be true.'

'I deny nothing. Why should I? Many people come to my shop, Fräulein. Indeed, you are here yourself! What of it?'

'Forgive me,' she said with another, similar smile. I confess that it was a particularly winning smile. It caused her whole face to light up most becomingly, even if it was no more than artifice. But under the artifice, I thought to see a flicker of something real, like a fire burning beneath a layer of ice. There was passion in this girl, if only one could free it. To do that, of course, one would have to melt the ice . . . or break it. That was a pleasure that could fall to but a single man, and I saw no reason it should not be me.

'Why, there is nothing as yet to forgive,' I told her.

'I am glad of it,' she said, 'because I have come in friendship, to do you a good turn.'

'That is most kind of you,' I said. 'I should very much like to be your friend.'

'And I yours,' she said. She seemed at a loss to continue, however, and I was reminded that, artifice aside, here was a girl of eighteen or so, whose experience of men was as yet more theoretical than real, and who had been sheltered, moreover, in the severe tabernacle of her faith, so to speak, and so was considerably less worldly than she took such pains to appear.

'You mentioned a good turn,' I prompted.

At this she blushed, and that involuntary response was more attractive to me than all her carefully rehearsed charms; indeed, at that moment I desired her even more than I had her elder sister. 'Why did my sister come here?' she asked.

'That is confidential,' I replied.

'Very well, then I shall tell you, so that you need not betray any confidences. My sister came to warn you of a test our father has subjected you to, without your knowledge or consent. She explained that the clock he gave you is an empty shell, and thus impossible to repair. And that he waits to see if you attempt to cheat him or, instead, will act the part of an honest man, in which case he plans to ask you to be of service to our family as a righteous gentile. Is that not correct?'

'What if it is?' I asked in turn.

'Why, it is a lie!' she exclaimed.

I confess I had not expected to hear that. 'A lie?' I echoed stupidly.

She smiled with satisfaction to see the effect of her words. Indeed, she nearly licked her lips. 'My sister is most wicked,' she confided with relish.

'But the clock . . . it was empty, just as she said!'

'Only because Rachel herself, unbeknownst to Papa, removed the insides.'

'For the love of God, why would she do that?'

'Because she wishes you to fail the test.'

'But did you not just tell me there is no test?'

'I did not mean to give that impression,' she said. 'It is true that Papa heard from the other Jews that you are a righteous man, and he wished to determine that for himself before asking you to assist our family as a righteous gentile. Thus he brought you a broken clock – a clock he had broken himself – to see whether or not you would cheat him. But Rachel, you see, would like him to choose someone else for the task.'

'Who?'

'Can you not guess? A man she is in love with!'

I was stunned by this revelation of Rachel's duplicity. In fact, I was not entirely certain I believed it.

Ruth rushed on regardless. 'When you tell Papa that the clock cannot be repaired, he will think you a cheat, and choose Rachel's lover, bringing disgrace upon our family!'

'But I *have* repaired the clock,' I told her. 'See for yourself.' And I drew it from my pocket and displayed it for her just as I had her sister. 'If what you say is true, then your father will be expecting me to mend the clock, since he does not know of Rachel's trickery. Thus, he will judge me a righteous man.'

'I don't understand,' she said, gazing at the watch as if it were a severed head. 'How did you do this?'

'I rebuilt it,' I said with a shrug. 'It's what I do. So, you see that there is no cause for concern. Either way, your family's honour is safe.'

'You've mended it,' she said, as though still not quite believing the evidence of her eyes. 'You have already mended it.'

'Yes,' I said, laughing, 'I'm afraid I have.'

'You idiot!' she cried. 'You've ruined everything!'

I confess I did feel rather like an idiot as I stood there, gazing at her open-mouthed, the clock dangling from its chain in my hand.

But then, suddenly, something became clear to me, though I did not yet understand it. 'You are the one who removed the workings of the clock, not Rachel!'

She shook her head.

'Yes,' I persisted. 'But why? Why remove the workings . . . and then come to warn me of exactly that . . . only seek to cast the blame for it on your sister?'

'I never,' Ruth said indignantly, brown eyes flashing, and for an instant I felt the heat of her passionate centre threatening to break through the ice of her habitual self-regard. Pride was the key to this lock, I told myself. What satisfaction it would be to compel the submission of this proud young Jewess, to shatter the mirror and make her see me as I was! And then, in a flash, I knew.

I clasped her by the arms, but did not draw her to me, merely let her feel the strength of my hands, my arms. She looked at me as if she were at last beginning to see me clearly. 'Do you know what I think?' I said. 'I think your sister is in love with a gentile . . . and I am he.'

A wild look came into her eyes. 'No,' she said, and began to struggle a bit, trying to pull free.

But I was not ready to let her go. 'What's more, she is not the only one. You, my dear Ruth, are in love with the same man. You want me to become a trusted guest in your house . . . but at the same time to discredit your rival – your own sister! So you scooped out the insides of the clock, and then came to warn me of what you had done, blaming Rachel, while yet giving me time to mend the clock, for, as you must know, your father is to come here tomorrow to retrieve it. Only, I had already repaired it, so your warnings were all for naught, and your attempt to discredit your sister a dismal failure.' As I spoke, I brought my face close to hers, so close that I could feel the hairs of my moustache stirred by the moist heat of her panting breaths and smell their sweet perfume. 'I'm right, aren't I? Admit it!'

Instead of answering, she pressed her mouth fiercely to mine in a kiss at once passionate and chaste, for her lips remained tightly shut, as did her eyes, which I could plainly see since my own eyes were open wide in astonishment. Then, before I could react, she pulled free of my grip and ran from the shop.

I felt dazed, weak in the knees. I staggered to a nearby chair and collapsed into it. My lips still burned from her kiss. My head was spinning from the same cause, and also from all that I had heard. Everything that had seemed so clear an instant before, now seemed hopelessly muddled. I didn't know what or whom to believe. I only knew two things for certain. First, the rabbi's household was a snakes' nest of intrigue and duplicity unmatched since the days of the Borgias. And second, I would do whatever it took to gain admittance to that snakes' nest, even become a righteous man. Thus I might, under the blindly benevolent gaze of the rabbi, deflower his two eldest daughters, each of whom seemed quite willing to be deflowered!

'Herr Immelman . . .'

I glanced up. It will not surprise you, I think, to learn that I found myself faced by the rabbi's third-eldest daughter.

'The door was open,' she said. 'So . . .'

She trailed off, for I was gazing at her in absolute horror.

'Are you well, Herr Immelman?' she asked at last.

I shook my head and gasped as if emerging from a dream of drowning. 'Yes, yes, quite well.' I got to my feet and gave her a polite but weary – and, truth be told, wary – bow. 'Esther, is it? The rabbi's daughter?'

'Yes, I am Esther,' she said and smiled fleetingly, as if pleased that I had taken the trouble to learn her name.

Oh God, I thought. Not another one. I don't know if I can handle three!

I needn't have worried.

If Rachel was a succulent, tempting plum, and Ruth an ice sculpture with a heart of fire, then Esther was whatever the Jews have instead of nuns. She was about seventeen, her body no longer that of a young girl, yet not quite that of a woman. She had that pleasing pink plumpness about her that suggests baby fat but is really more a token of the womanliness lying ahead than of the girlhood being left behind – soft rolls of flesh that will migrate and swell into ripe breasts, pillowy hips, and ample thighs like blood sausages. I have noticed that while some girls of this in-between age embrace their burgeoning bodies with pride, eager and even impatient to enter into, as it were, their full inheritance, others attempt on the contrary to reject the ripening that is taking place, or, rather, if not to reject it exactly then to restrain it, as if there is something in that ripening which cries out for restraint, as perhaps there is, for it cannot be a coincidence that so many girls of this age are already married and nursing babies of their own. But there is a certain type of girl, often unusually devout, who embraces restraint with the fervour that other girls reserve for husbands and lovers. Indeed, they are like those saints and ascetics who see themselves quite literally as the brides of Christ and reject all Earthly partners for a passion whose consummation is not of this world. Such a girl was Esther, though of course she was not Christian.

She dressed like her sisters, only more severely, and though she shared the hallmarks of their beauty – the doe-like eyes, the full lips, the voluptuous nose that, at least in the females of the race, seems almost a reproductive organ itself, like the pistil of a flower (or so it has always seemed to me) – she took no evident pride in them, and indeed seemed to hold her beauty in a kind of contempt, for she squinted constantly and smiled but rarely, and then for no longer than it took her to notice, reprove herself, and correct the error. Despite her youth, which she could not hide, try as she might, she held herself like an old person, and moreover like an old man – an old rabbi, to be precise.

'Let me save you the trouble,' I said. 'You have come to warn me about a test your father has seen fit to impose upon me in order to determine whether or not I am a righteous man, or rather gentile. This test involves a certain clock he brought me yesterday and hired me to repair – a clock that, upon examination, proved to be hollow inside, a mere plaything, though whether your father knew of this or not is a matter of some contention, apparently, between your sisters, as is the identity of the person responsible, if any. At any rate,' I continued, 'I must either report to your father that the clock is an empty shell and hence not reparable, in which case I must give back the money he paid in advance, or, assuming your father is of the conviction that the clock he gave me is not empty but, on the contrary, merely broken (and leaving aside for now the question of who broke it), then I must return the clock to your father in good repair. But as I have already repaired the clock' – I dangled it before her – 'I suppose that I must pass the test no matter what, for I mean to tell your father that I found it empty but felt myself nevertheless moved to mend it, or rather reconstruct it, if for no other reason than the simple fact that I possess the skill to do so.'

Esther took this in like a judge listening to a long complaint, nodding occasionally, unsmiling, her squinty eyes fixed on my lips. When I had finished, she nodded once more and said, 'That is not the test.'

'What?'

'The test is the daughters, not the clock.'

I fell back into the chair. 'The test is the daughters . . .'

'Yes,' she affirmed. 'My father wishes to know whether you will tell him all that transpired between you and his daughters. He does not care a fig about the clock. If only you report truthfully about our visits, he will know that you are a righteous man.'

'But if I tell him everything that happened . . . That is, he . . .' I was not in the habit of regaling fathers with tales of my conquests of their daughters, even if those conquests were as yet more theoretical than actual.

'You may be assured that anything any one of us has said or done has been at our father's express instructions, as part of the test.'

'Including what you are telling me now?'

'Yes, including what I am telling you now.'

'And I need not fear compromising you or your sisters, because everything you've said and done has been part of the test devised by your father.'

'That is correct.'

'Why?'

'Why what?'

'Why in the name of God almighty and all the saints and prophets has your father gone to so much trouble in order to determine whether or not Gustav Immelman is a righteous man? Let me save him the trouble! I will tell you right now that I am not a righteous man and what's more have no desire to be! Let him find someone else to torture! I wash my hands of the whole business!'

'Only a righteous man would speak so.'

'Please go away,' I said, rubbing my forehead.

'Remember that when my father comes tomorrow, you must tell him the absolute truth.'

'I won't,' I said. 'I told you, I'm through with this business. I'll lie to him through my teeth until he proclaims me the least righteous man who ever lived!'

'That would be a shame,' she said.

I glanced up at her through my fingers. 'Why?'

'Because a righteous gentile may know the daughters of a Jew without any sin accruing on either side.'

It took me a moment to register that I had just heard the seventeen-year-old daughter of a rabbi, who might as well have been a rabbi herself, act as a procuress for herself and her sisters. 'You're mad,' I said. 'The lot of you, up to and including your father. He is the maddest of all.'

'He is a wise and just man,' she said. 'I hope you will consider carefully everything I've told you, Herr Immelman.'

'Just answer one question,' I begged her. 'Why me? Why, of all the Christians in Prague, did your father settle on me?'

'Because all the Jews of Prague say that you are a righteous man.'

'I don't believe you. There has to be something more.'

'That you must ask him,' she said, and left the shop, drawing the door closed behind her.

I sat for what seemed a long time in the creeping shadows, for I had lit no candles, and it now lacked twelve minutes of five of the clock. Dear boy, I had no idea what to do or even what to think. I looked at the clock in my hand, that absurd gold-plated lion with its two tails, and I wished with all my heart that I had turned down this commission when the rabbi offered it. I even came close to dropping the beastly thing on the floor and crushing it beneath my heel, but I had poured some of myself into it and could not bear to see it destroyed. I have always been too tender-hearted for my own good.

At last, when my clocks chimed the hour, I rose and began to light the shop, less in expectation of customers than because I felt oppressed by the encroaching dark, which reminded me unpleasantly of the rabbi's robes. That done, I started to wind all the clocks in the shop, which I did every evening at about this time. I had not finished this task when there came another knock at the door.

By now I knew what to expect.

Sure enough, there stood the fourth-eldest daughter. I judged her to be fifteen, perhaps sixteen at the most. She was a slip of a girl, willowy as an elf, not an ounce of fat on her, as if someone had taken a plump ten-year-old girl and rolled her out like dough. But the way her clothes hung on her left no doubt that, underneath them, time had begun to knead her rising body into its future fullness. Yet she seemed entirely ignorant of these changes – not, as with Esther, seeking to restrain them by an act of will, but instead blissfully unaware that she was no longer the girl she believed herself to be. There was something infinitely alluring in that innocence, as if she were asleep within her own body like some fairy-tale maiden cursed by an envious fairy's spell – a spell that could only be broken by a kiss. Or so I had thought on previous occasions, admiring her as she flitted about the streets of the city. I had imagined her seated on my lap, my lips on hers, the two of us exchanging kisses like children in a carefree game. Now she stood before me, near enough to embrace, had I wished it, but her lips did not seem quite as tempting as they once had. Or perhaps it was just that I was not in the mood.

'What is your name?' I asked, barring the entry and very much aware of the glances that passers-by were casting our way.

'Rebecca,' she said.

'I suppose your father sent you?'

'No.' She shook her pretty head, then pouted up at me. 'Aren't you going to let me in?'

'I don't think so,' I said. 'What business do you have with me?'

'I have come to warn you.'

'Then by all means do so.'

Her gaze shifted left, then right, before fixing on me again. She leaned closer and dropped her voice to a confiding whisper. 'Do not listen to my sister.'

'Excellent advice. Which one?'

'Esther.'

I sighed. 'Do you mean I shouldn't tell your father everything that has passed between me and your three other sisters?'

'Or me. Papa would skin me alive if he knew I was here! You won't tell him, will you?'

'I don't know,' I said truthfully. 'What do you think I should do, Rebecca?'

'Didn't Papa bring you a clock for repair?'

'He did.'

'Why, then repair it.'

'As simple as that?'

'Yes, of course.'

'And that's the test, is it?'

'I don't know about any test, Herr Immelman. I only know that Esther is a wicked girl who thinks she's better than everybody else and is always trying to get the rest of us in trouble. Whatever she told you, don't believe it, or you might get in trouble, too.'

'It is too late for that,' I said. 'I am already in trouble, I think, and sinking deeper all the time. In any case, thank you for the warning, Rebecca.'

She blushed and made a little curtsy. 'You're welcome, Herr Immelman. I did not like to see Esther work her mischief on you. I have seen you watching us, my sisters and me. I can tell that you are a good, kind man, even if your moustache is rather funny and must tickle your nose ever so dreadfully.'

'Yes, I suppose it does tickle sometimes, at that. Perhaps I will shave it off. Would you like that?'

'I don't know,' she said, cocking her head to examine me intently. 'It is sometimes quite pleasant to be tickled, after all.'

With that, she giggled and ran off, merging into the flow of people strolling along the street. I watched until I couldn't see her any more. Then I closed the door and bolted it behind me. I went around the shop, extinguishing all the candles. All I could think was: two more. God help me, there are still two more to go.

I would rather have faced an army of Turks than those two remaining girls.

Well, I thought, they could not find me if I were not at home. And so I hastily drew on my coat and hat and left by the back door – the door by which, in an earlier and more innocent time, mere hours previously, Rachel had departed.

They were waiting there, both of them.

Two girls, no more than thirteen years old, exactly alike in every respect, gazing up at me with blank moonish faces and the shining eyes of demons. I made the sign of the cross and slammed the door in their faces. I had no interest in hearing whatever they had come to say. I hurried to the front door, unbolted it, and made my escape.

Or tried to. But the rabbi's two youngest daughters were there already, blocking my way. Or perhaps two different daughters, identical to the pair stationed at the back door. I did not stop to inquire more deeply but slammed the door and re-bolted it.

A moment later, the knocking began. From the front door and the back, simultaneously.

'Go away!' I cried. 'Go away in the name of Christ and leave me in peace!'

The knocking continued. There was no urgency to it, as there had been with the older sisters. Instead, it was as slow and measured as the beating of a drum at a dirge, or the tolling of a dreadful bell. As if those girls had all the time in the world, and knew it. I felt terror then such as I had never experienced before – terror and helplessness, for though it might have seemed the simplest thing in the world to force my way past two thirteen-year-old girls, I found myself quite unable to contemplate the idea of coming into contact with them, as if their touch, however slight and incidental, even the touch of their clothing, would burn like hellfire, which, as we are taught, burns eternally without consuming what it feeds on.

I had no place to flee but up, and so I hastened up the stairs and into my room, where I threw myself down on the bed, drew the covers over my head, and lay curled and shivering in the dark while that baleful knocking counted out the minutes and hours like the impossible ticking of a vast, hollow clock.

*

I must have fallen asleep at some point, for when I awoke the knocking had stopped. It was morning, to judge by the light; the clocks in my room could not be relied upon for a more precise indication of the hour, as, in all the excitement, I had neglected to wind them the previous day, and they had now either stopped or were no longer in agreement. In those days, dear boy, timepieces had to be wound daily, and sometimes more often still. It must seem terribly primitive to you, I know. But it was not so long ago, after all, and who can say but that a day will come when the clocks and watches that seem the very height of sophistication to you now are viewed with condescension, as crude instruments long since surpassed in every way.

I rose and, not without trepidation, and as furtively as a thief, crept to the window and peeked down at the stoop below. It was blessedly empty. But were the visitations over, or was this just a brief respite? Either way, I was resolved to be finished with the rabbi and his daughters this day. I had had enough of tests and torments to last a lifetime. I no longer cared to be judged a righteous man. And the prospect of bedding those odd and indeed uncanny girls filled me with dread rather than desire.

I performed my morning ablutions, dressed in fresh linens, and breakfasted on bread and cheese and beer before winding the clocks I had not got to the day before, setting them all to the proper time. Then I opened the shop for business. I confess that I was on pins and needles, waiting for the rap of knuckles upon the door that would announce the return of the final two daughters, worse than all the others put together, those mute twins whose faces had been wiped clean of human emotion but whose glowing eyes had nevertheless seemed to wish me ill.

When a brisk knock finally sounded, I nearly jumped out of my skin. I found myself unable to move and so called out for the knocker to enter, in as bold a voice as I could counterfeit, which I'm afraid cracked rather shamefully, as though the shop were tended by a smooth-cheeked boy of thirteen.

The door opened, and in flowed the rabbi. I did not know whether I should be relieved at the sight of him or, on the contrary, made more anxious than ever. I stammered a good morning.

He wished me the same, continuing to move towards the counter, behind which I stood frozen in place. He seemed not to walk but rather to glide across the floor, his black robes billowing in a manner not entirely consistent with the hypothesis of flesh and bone beneath them. He wore the same high black hat he had worn before, which did not so much sit atop his head as sprout from it like a giant mushroom. His bearded monkey face, with those incongruous blue eyes, seemed to float between the hat and the mass of robes as if suspended within an inky cloud.

'Are you well, Herr Immelman?' he asked with grave concern when he had drawn up to the counter and had a better look at me.

'I slept badly,' I told him. I was unsure whether to say more. Should I mention the visits of his daughters? Had Esther told me the truth? Or Rebecca or Ruth or Rachel? Or, for that matter, the twins, though I shuddered to think what their message might have been. In the end, I opted for silence, which stretched between us until the rabbi spoke.

'I have come for my clock.'

'Yes, of course,' I said. Here, then, was the moment of truth. It was ridiculous, really, I could not help reflecting, that I, a good Christian man, should stand trembling with fear and indecision before a Jew! And over what? A test that might not even exist, and, if it did, need be of no concern to me. What did I care if the rabbi judged me to be righteous or not? Was it not of more import how I judged the rabbi? And even if he proclaimed me to be this paragon of righteousness, that in itself could not obligate me to serve him on the Sabbath! After all, I was perfectly free to refuse him, was I not? Of course I was!

Greatly reassured by this line of reasoning, which had come to me all unlooked for, as if God had whispered into my ear, I let out a sigh of relief and fished the clock from my pocket. 'I have not yet wound it today,' I told him, and I proceeded to do so under his interested eye.

As I turned the key, feeling in the nerve ends of my fingers the tightening internal resistance that would power the timepiece for an interval of hours, I was struck by the conceit that I was simultaneously winding something in myself, the very spring of my heart.

The veneer of reassurance vanished. I grew dizzy and afraid, as though an abyss had suddenly yawned open at my feet, into which I might fall for ever without touching bottom. Or, no, the abyss was in myself, and it was that which I was opening with the key, wider and wider, until it must swallow me. I set the clock down on the counter, unable to continue.

'You are not well,' said the rabbi. 'I will summon a physician.'

I raised a forestalling hand. 'No, no. It will pass. Give me a moment.' I closed my eyes and took a deep breath, then another. My heart was plunging like a tethered horse that has caught the scent of a wolf. Nothing like this had happened to me before. My shirt was drenched with a fearful sweat.

Then, as quickly as it had come over me, the affliction lifted, and I was myself again, though weak as yet, my heart still racing but steadily slowing, returning to its proper pace. For the first time in two days, I could think clearly, or so it seemed to me. All my fears, all my doubts and hesitations in this matter of the clock, seemed suddenly absurd, like elements in a dream that take on inflated importance and significance, casting portentous shadows over every aspect of our lives, dire as fate or destiny, only to dwindle back into their ordinary selves when we wake, astonished to recall how terrified we were of a dog or a hairbrush or, yes, a common clock. Now, at last, I had awakened. The spell had broken; the dream was over. I opened my eyes to see the rabbi just closing the jaws of the lion.

'You surprise me, Herr Immelman,' he said, depositing the clock deep into the folds of his robe.

'Do I?' I managed.

'The clock I gave you two days ago was empty, useless. A false thing. You have turned it into a true one. Why?'

'It bothered me,' I told him, as no doubt I should have done from the first. 'So I mended it. Don't worry – there will be no extra charge. But why did you give me such a clock, rabbi?'

'Did Rachel not explain to you?'

'She did,' I replied, 'but then again so did Ruth and Rebecca and Esther. Rabbi, all your daughters visited me yesterday, one after the other, to tell me a different story about why you had given me that clock, and to advise me about how I should respond to the test – for it was a test, wasn't it?'

The rabbi laughed. It was a deep, rumbling laugh, full of infectious good humour, all the more unexpected as it transformed that pinched monkey face of his into something shining and almost beautiful. I couldn't help but join in, as if that transformation were itself a kind of joke, and the two of us laughed together for a long while.

'Yes,' he said at last, wiping his eyes with the sleeve of his robe. 'Of course it was a test, Herr Immelman. What else but a test?'

'Yes,' I said, and shook my head sheepishly, still grinning. 'What else? But what of your daughters? Were they, too, part of the test?'

'Ach, Herr Immelman, daughters are always a test to their father. A test and a trial. I do not know what they told you, my beauties. I will not ask. That is between you and them. They are headstrong, those girls. Fond of mischief. But they are good girls all the same. I indulge them, I know. I cannot help it. They are dear to me, you see.'

I nodded, though privately I thought that the future husbands of those girls would have little cause to thank the rabbi for his indulgence.

'Well,' said the rabbi. 'Come by tomorrow, Herr Immelman, and I will show you what you must do.'

'Yes,' I heard myself saying, as if everything had been arranged openly between us, a contract negotiated and signed to our mutual satisfaction. 'I suppose I might as well.'

I had been into the Jewish ghetto but rarely, and never to the house of a Jew. I did not know what I would find there and in truth was hesitant to go. The previous day, after the rabbi left the shop, I had wondered at my easy acceptance of his invitation – which hadn't even been an invitation, really, but more in the nature of a command. I felt that he had got the better of me in business, and it was not a pleasant feeling. I was used to coming out on top, bending the other man to my will, and though the Jews have a deserved reputation as shrewd bargainers, I could honestly say that no Jew had bested me yet . . . until now.

It was that laugh of his that had done it, I finally decided. There had been something magical about that damned laugh. You couldn't hear it and not join in. It made you feel glad just to be alive. Because of it, we had not discussed what services, exactly, he wished me to provide, much less the terms of payment. How could you broach such tawdry subjects with a man once the two of you had laughed together like brothers? You couldn't. It was a dangerous thing, that laugh.

But once the glow of it wore off, I found myself regretting everything. I began to worry that, if my service to the rabbi became generally known, it would be misinterpreted, people being what they are, by and large, which is to say vicious, double-dealing bastards out for themselves, and so my fellow Christians would start to think of me as a Jew-lover, disloyal to his own kind. My business would dry up, and I would become an object of pity or derision, snubbed in the streets, if not actually kicked and spat upon. Why, I might as well pack up and move to the ghetto myself!

So it was that, while I had little enough desire to go, I set out for the rabbi's house the next morning determined to break things off before any permanent damage was done. He had given me directions, but I soon found myself lost in the welter of tight and twisting streets and alleys of the ghetto, which seemed to lie in a different city entirely, as though I had crossed beyond the borders of Prague and entered into some obscure quarter of old Jerusalem.

Everything was strange. To be surrounded by so many Jews, all of them dressed in their doleful costumes, scurrying about their business in their self-important way, as if there could be nothing so needful in the world just now as their own particular errand – because it had been ordained and sanctified by the Almighty – made me feel silently but roundly rebuked for some moral failing. I could feel their eyes on me, curious and judgemental yet ultimately dismissive, for I was but one gentile in a sea of Jews and thus presented neither a danger nor an opportunity. I did not hear a single word of good, honest German but instead the jabbering tongue of the Israelites on every side. I imagined them discussing me, wondering at the reason for my presence, perhaps even mocking me, as we Christians mocked the Jews in our sections of the city. I glared at them as I stalked past, shouldering my way roughly through knots of men gathered here and there in vigorous debate, or so it seemed from their raised voices and vehement gestures. Some of them called after me challengingly, but I ignored them. The Chosen People, indeed! I had not chosen them.

The place was even more offensive to the nose than to the eyes and ears. A miasma of stenches arose on every side: the smells of human shit wafted up from the open sewers that lined the streets, mingling with the aroma of horse manure and the waste of the animals that crowded every yard and roamed freely underfoot: bleating cows, squawking chickens, barking dogs, every winged, hoofed, and furred creature, it seemed, but pigs, which the Jews – in common with the heathen Mohammedans – disdain. It said much, I thought, and none of it good, that the Jews should reject the pig as an unclean animal when they themselves lived in such filth and squalor!

From every open window – and they were all open – poured a mix of scents among which, on the occasional breeze, one might sniff something wholesome and recognizable – a whiff of tobacco, perhaps, or the savoury smell of a roasting chicken. But these individual strands, as it were, came together in and were overwhelmed by the general stink of the ghetto, which hung over everything like a noxious cloud, a haze that even obscured the light of the sun, or such was my impression as I hurried along in increasing discomfort. I had thought to hold my handkerchief to my nose and mouth, not just to blot out the unpleasant odours but to ward sickness away, but only after I failed to find it in its accustomed pocket of my coat did I recall having given it to Rachel the day before. She had not returned it. And so I progressed deeper into the maze of the ghetto with my cloak held up before my face, for all the world like some theatrical villain skulking across a stage.

'Herr Immelman!'

I stopped and looked around me, utterly at a loss. It was as though I had been addressed by a single ant amidst a swarming anthill.

'Herr Immelman, hello!'

I saw a waving hand and only then recognized Rebecca standing among a group of girls her age and younger, all of whom were whispering to each other now as if scandalized by my presence or by

Rebecca's greeting or both. She left them without a word or glance and came skipping over to me.

'Have you come to see Papa?' she asked.

'I have,' I told her. 'I'm afraid I am lost.'

'I will conduct you,' she declared and, taking me by the hand, began to pull me down the street. I followed, feeling rather ridiculous yet at the same time charmed by her thoughtless trust, which put me in mind of the kissing games I had imagined the two of us enjoying. What was it she had said? *It is sometimes quite pleasant to be tickled, after all.* Yes, I thought now, quite pleasant indeed. A shame I would have to forgo that pleasure.

As it turned out, my wanderings had brought me closer to the rabbi's house than I had realized. Rebecca and I turned a corner, and the squalid street underwent a miraculous transformation, becoming wider and cleaner and quieter – in short, becoming a respectable thoroughfare that very nearly might have belonged in one of the more genteel neighbourhoods of Christian Prague. The buildings on either side were two- and three-storey houses with painted wooden doors, glass windows that glinted like clear water in the sunlight, and tiled roofs. Smoke drifted from brick chimneys, and what odours there were had precious little of the barnyard about them. Some of the windows had painted boxes with flowers set outside. It was a street of confident prosperity, even wealth, though without a shred of ostentation. The sun seemed brighter here.

'Come,' said Rebecca excitedly. Slipping her hand from mine, she ran to one of the houses, neither the most nor the least impressive, but somewhere in the middle, just as it was set towards the middle of the street. I followed her up worn stone steps to a wooden door on which was carved the same two-tailed lion I knew from the casing of the rabbi's clock.

'What is the significance of this lion?' I asked her.

'Oh, it is our family crest,' she explained proudly. 'The lion of Judah, you know. That is Papa's name. Judah, I mean, not lion.' At which she giggled and threw open the door. 'Papa!' she sang out. 'Mama! Herr Immelman is here!'

I stood on the threshold, feeling that I should not enter until formally invited. There was a narrow entryway that led to a door and a staircase and, to the right of the staircase, an opening that appeared to lead into an adjoining room. There were tapestries on the walls whose colours had been dulled by time and whose subjects I could not make out in the light of the single candle that burned on a narrow table beside the far door. There must have been a window on the stairs, for I could see the fall of its light on the bare wooden steps, though that light did not reach all the way to the bottom.

Rebecca had vanished behind the door. Now she emerged from it again, preceded by a stout and dignified Jewess of forty years or so whom I knew by sight as the rabbi's wife but had not met before.

'Herr Immelman,' she said with a grave bow. 'You do us honour by your visit.'

I smoothed my moustache and inclined my head in acknowledgement. 'Thank you, Frau—'

'Ach, call me Pearl. We do not stand on ceremony here, you will find.'

I inclined my head again, though I did not invite a reciprocal intimacy.

'Please come in, Herr Immelman. Judah is in his workroom; I will fetch him directly.'

I entered the house. Rebecca slid past me to close the door while her mother gestured me into the adjoining room I had noticed earlier. It proved to be a small but comfortable sitting room, with rugs on the floor, oil paintings on the walls, and two windows that admitted a flood of light. A wooden candle wheel depended from the high, moulded ceiling, but none of its candles were lit. There was a fireplace as well, also unlit, though kindling and logs had been stacked in readiness. Upon the stone mantel was an unexceptional clock I judged to be off the proper time by a good forty-five minutes, though its ticking was loud and regular. On the opposite wall, a low shelf contained what in those days was a real rarity: a handful of leatherbound books. There were two padded chairs and, between them, a slender wooden table whose dark top was inlaid with lighter woods in a simple floral pattern. The room smelled pleasantly of old fires and older books.

So far the furnishings and general comfort level of this house exceeded those of my own home – with two exceptions. First, the cabinets and tables I had seen were inferior to those I kept in my shop and home, which, of course, I had made with my own hands. Second, and for exactly the same reason, my own clocks far outstripped the poor example upon the mantel. All the same, I was impressed. I suppose I had expected to find myself in some garish or even barbaric setting right out of the Old Testament, with straw on the floors and camels wandering through the rooms. Instead, the house was indistinguishable from a Christian abode. Indeed, I had been a guest in the houses of important Christians who could not boast as much, or as fine, as this Jew.

I sat down in a padded chair while Pearl went in search of her husband. Rebecca, suddenly shy, lingered in the opening.

'Where are your sisters today?' I asked her.

She shrugged.

'Are they at home?'

Another shrug.

'Why, has the cat got your tongue, Rebecca?'

At this, she poked out the cherry tip of her tongue as if to assure herself, or me, that, no, the cat had not got it, after all. I confess the sight was a tempting one, and for a moment I considered the wisdom of trying to entice her onto my lap. But before I could make up my mind, fate intervened in the person of her father.

I heard a heavy tread on the stairs. Rebecca glanced back over her shoulder and up, and broke into a smile such as men like me will never receive, nor deserve to. 'Papa!' And she was gone, though I could hear her lighter tread as she flew up the stairs.

'Rebecca!' came the rabbi's rumbling voice.

A moment later he entered the room as if borne on the cloud of his billowing robes, his own smile stoked to beaming by his daughter's; she, however, did not return.

'Herr Immelman,' he said, and his smile altered to one of mere pleasure at the sight of me. The hat he had worn at our previous meetings was gone, exposing hair as grey and thick and unruly as his beard. Indeed, it was difficult to say precisely where the one ended and the other began. Hair ringed his face like an aged lion's mane. How had I ever thought this man resembled a monkey?

'Thank you for coming,' he said. 'I was afraid you might have changed your mind.'

I rose to my feet. 'As to that—' But before I could go on, a veritable avalanche of footsteps came crashing down the stairs. One by one, in swift succession, Rachel, Ruth, Esther, Rebecca, and the twins appeared in the opening behind their father, crowding each other in an attempt to get a look at me yet seeming unwilling to be the first to enter the room.

The rabbi's smile changed again as he regarded his daughters with a kind of prideful fond annoyance. 'Ach, you know my girls, I believe, Herr Immelman.'

'I have had the pleasure,' I returned.

'Then perhaps you do not know them after all,' he said.

'Papa!' protested the pretties in their various voices – all save the twins, who were as silent as they had been the day before, though, I was glad to see, less ominous in aspect; indeed, they seemed not a whit demonic, just deeply shy.

The rabbi's infectious laugh boomed, and though I tried to steel myself against it, I couldn't help but chuckle along. 'Well, you have seen him, daughters,' he said. 'Will he do?' And to my astonishment began to poll them individually.

'Rachel?'

'Oh, yes, Papa!'

'Ruth?'

'I suppose we could do worse.'

'Esther?'

'He seems satisfactory, all things considered.'

'Rebecca?'

Giggles behind an upraised hand signified, I supposed, a yes.

'Sarah and Sadie?'

The twins nodded their moonish faces in solemn accord.

'Good! It is decided! Off with you now – Herr Immelman and I have much to discuss.'

Dismissed, the girls trooped up the stairs, not without casting backward glances over their shoulders that left me decidedly less resolved to break my arrangement with their father. But what, after all, was that arrangement? I supposed it couldn't hurt to listen a while longer.

The rabbi gestured for me to take my seat, and, when I had done so, sat opposite me in the remaining chair, which, like his own body, was immediately engulfed in his robes and, as it were, swallowed up in them, as if that garment possessed an insatiable appetite. 'I see that you are surprised I would solicit the opinions of my daughters in this matter.'

I did not deny it. 'It is not the custom in Christian households. There children are expected to be silent and obedient.'

'Indeed?' he said, a twinkle in his blue eyes. 'Silent and obedient children – why, it is almost enough to make one convert!'

His laugh rang out again, and, again, I was pulled along in its wake.

'I suppose my daughters must have mentioned to you the business of the righteous gentile,' he said after a moment.

I affirmed that they had but added that I did not fully understand the concept in theory, or, for that matter, how the practice of it would work.

'Good,' he said. 'Then I need not disabuse you of any misunderstandings. The truth is, Herr Immelman, we do not require a righteous gentile in this house. I already employ the services of a poor Christian lad in this regard, an orphan. He is entirely satisfactory and, in any case, needs the money more than you do.'

'I see,' I said, though of course I did not. 'Why, then, the test? And why ask me here today?'

'Because of all the clockmakers I have given that empty clock, only you have made it whole. Only you, Herr Immelman, had the wit to see what was required and the skill to carry it out. Even one of these attributes is rare. To find both together in the same man is extraordinary.'

'So you have tested others this way,' I said. 'How many?'

'More than you would believe,' he answered. 'Not just in Prague but in many lands.'

'To what purpose?'

'A great work of time.'

'Do you mean a clock?'

'Of sorts,' he said. 'Come, I will show you.' And he made to rise.

But I hesitated, and he sank back into his chair. 'What troubles you, Herr Immelman? Speak frankly, I beg you.'

'Very well,' I told him. 'I am a Christian man, Rabbi. I will not risk my immortal soul in any witchcraft or blood magic such as, I have heard, you Jews do sometimes practise.'

'Any such claims are libels,' he replied at once, calmly but with an edge of steel in his voice I had not heard before. 'Calumnies spread by enemies of the Jews who envy our knowledge and wealth. It is not the Jews who in their worship drink blood and eat flesh.'

I bristled at this, but before I could say anything, he went on.

'Peace, Herr Immelman, peace! I say nothing against your faith, whose roots, after all, are sunk in the same holy soil as my own. We are two branches of the same tree. We must be friends, you and I, not enemies. Together we may accomplish a great and holy thing.'

'What is that?'

'Will you not come see?'

I confess I was intrigued, dear boy, but also wary. 'First tell me what you can, and I will judge whether it is something I may see without sin or peril to my soul. If you cannot do that, Rabbi, then I must take my leave.'

'As there is nothing sinful or perilous in it, I will speak. But give me a moment to marshal my thoughts, as I had not thought to come at the matter in this oblique way.'

I nodded, and he sank into a heavy silence, his blue eyes focused on the fireplace as if he might kindle the wood into flame by attention alone. The only sound in the room was the ticking of that abominable clock and noises from the street beyond.

At last, feeling anxious, I essayed a joke of sorts. 'For someone concerned with a great work of time, Rabbi, your taste in clocks is awful! What you have to tell me may not be sinful, but this mantel clock most certainly is. Whoever made it will have to justify himself before his maker on the Day of Judgement, I doubt not.'

I had expected at least a smile in response to this sally, and a lightening of the sombre mood, but instead the rabbi grimaced as though I had touched a sensitive spot. 'Ach, you have the right of it,' he said. 'That unfortunate man is me.'

'You!' I said, surprised. 'You are a clockmaker?'

'I do not deserve the name,' he said sadly and, it seemed to me, bitterly. 'You have heard of men who are tone deaf, no doubt, who cannot carry a tune.'

'I am one of them,' I confessed.

'I am what you might call time deaf,' he said.

'Time deaf?' I repeated. 'What in the name of heaven do you mean by that?'

'I have no sense of time. One minute is the same to me as any other. I do not perceive the passing of the hours, the days, the years. Oh, I can look in the mirror and see that I grow older, and see the same evidence of time passing in my wife and daughters, but all of it seems unreal to me, an illusion. To me, there is no past or future, only a present that has always existed and always will exist, an eternal now.'

'I have never heard of such a thing,' I said, amazed. 'Or met a man who suffers from such a queer affliction as you describe.'

'In many ways, it has brought me closer to God. But we human beings are meant to be creatures of time. And as such, we are meant to come to God through time. That I have not done and, indeed, cannot do. I have tried. That clock you justly criticized is but one of my efforts to equip myself with the sense of time that all other men are born with. Just as a blind man will tap his way along with a cane, so, too, have I sought to build myself a kind of helper, a device that I may lean upon to guide me through this time-bound world, so I may come to God as others do, minute by minute, hour by hour, day by day, and in that way lead others more surely along the same path, as a good rabbi must do.'

'You taught yourself the art of clockmaking.'

'I tried to. But though I can grasp the principles readily enough, the mathematics, I cannot translate any of it into a practical time-piece that will serve me in the manner I have described. My clocks always run slow or fast, and, because of my condition, I do not even notice they are doing so. I am like a blind man using a cane that he cannot see is defective in some way.'

'Then why not use a clock built by another man?'

He shook his head. 'Alas, my affliction, as you so aptly term it, infects any timepiece in my possession, whether I carry it on my person or keep it in my house. No matter how well made, it begins to go awry from the moment it comes to me. Indeed, for all the good they do me, all my clocks might as well be as empty as the one I gave you for a test.'

'And that clock, too, I suppose, has been, as you say, infected?'

'Now, that is a strange and wondrous thing,' he said, brightening. 'A circumstance that makes me more certain than ever I have chosen rightly in seeking you out. For the clock you repaired or rather built for me has not yet been infected. Since you presented it to me yesterday, and wound it yourself in my presence, I have wound it again once, and, despite this, it is unaffected by the curse of my affliction.'

'But how can you know that,' I asked, 'if, as you have said, you cannot tell if a clock is running fast or slow?'

'I do not know how I know it, but I do,' he answered with a smile. 'And that is the most wondrous thing of all. For that, Herr Immelman, I am greatly in your debt.'

'I am glad to have been of service, though I confess I do not understand what I did or, indeed, how I did it. I simply did what I always do, which is to make the best clock I am capable of making. But I suppose God works in mysterious ways, as the priests are fond of saying.'

'That is it exactly!' the rabbi exclaimed. 'But let me ask you this, Herr Immelman. Should men seek to understand the mysteries of God? Should we seek to master them? Or is it, rather, impious to do so?'

'I am no theologian, Rabbi, but I suppose it depends on why a man might wish to understand and master those mysteries, whether for his own profit and power or for the benefit of others.'

'In this we agree,' he said with a satisfied nod. 'Have you heard of the Kabbalah?'

'No. Who is he? The head rabbi?'

'The Kabbalah is not a he but an it – a part of the Torah. Do you know the Torah?'

'That's the Jewish word for the Bible, isn't it?'

'Not just the Bible – that is, what you Christians call the Old Testament – but the whole tradition of Jewish teachings. Some of these teachings are for everyone, young and old, male and female, even righteous gentiles like yourself. But other teachings are more secret, esoteric, reserved for rabbis and holy sages. These are the teachings that seek, from pious motives, to understand and master the great mysteries of God. That is the Kabbalah.'

I frowned. 'It sounds like magic.'

'Was it magic when Aaron bested the sorcerers of Egypt?'

'No. That was God, working through Aaron.'

'Just so. And God works through the Kabbalah in precisely the same way. Magic is evil because, through it, the magician seeks to bend higher or lower powers to his will. The Kabbalah, on the contrary, teaches submission to the will of God, which is eternal love. A man wise in the wisdom of the Kabbalah is like a pipe through which the pure water of God flows into the world. In himself, he is nothing, a hollow tube of clay. Yet through him flows a wonder-working power that glorifies God. Rabbis and sages have studied the Kabbalah for many hundreds of years, Herr Immelman, adding to it, refining it, seeking always to submit themselves to its hard wisdom and thereby make themselves worthy to serve as conduits for God's love.'

'I take it, Rabbi, that you are such a man.'

'I would like to be,' he said. 'I have tried to be. In some small way, perhaps, I have succeeded. But not so well as you.'

'Me!' I couldn't help laughing at this. 'I am no sage, and certainly no rabbi! I know nothing of this Kabbalah of yours or, indeed, any Jewish teachings at all, beyond what the priests have told me – and much of that, from what you say, cannot be trusted.'

'Perhaps not. But I do not impugn your faith. Indeed, Christ himself was called rabbi, was he not? One need not believe he was the messiah, as you Christians do, to acknowledge his goodness and humility, and to see him as worthy of emulation. For if ever a man was a conduit for God's love, then surely it was he.'

'I confess I am surprised to hear you say so. I thought you Jews hated Christ. You killed him, after all.'

'I had thought that was the Romans,' said the rabbi dryly. 'But be that as it may, the ancient enmity between our peoples has harmed and degraded us both, I think. I cannot imagine that this endless cycle of pogroms is pleasing to God. Can we not, at least in this room, for now, set that enmity aside and call each other friends?'

'Within this room we may do anything we like, Rabbi,' I said. 'But outside these walls, we have the world to contend with, and that world has a long history behind it – a history that is not so easily forgotten, or, for that matter, forgiven.'

'True, but what if it could be?'

'That would take a miracle indeed!'

'And what else is a miracle but God's love flowing into the world, by one conduit or another?'

'You are speaking of the Kabbalah?'

'I am speaking of the great work of time.'

'Go on.'

'A man may spend his whole life studying the Kabbalah, Herr Immelman, yet never experience what it is to feel the grace of God acting through him. Another man might spend his life otherwise, in trivial or even sinful pursuits, and yet suddenly feel the spirit of God take hold of him and make use of him.'

'An edifying parable, Rabbi!' I smirked at its transparency. 'I suppose that I am meant to be the man who has spent his life in trivial pursuits, while you are the other?'

'God made us both as we are,' he said. 'And He has seen fit to bring us together, that we may complement each other and, in so doing, glorify Him in this world.'

'And how, exactly, are we meant to do this?'

'I am a man without an inborn sense of time. In a way, I inhabit eternity – and to inhabit eternity is to know God. That is God's gift to me. But when God gives with one hand, He often takes with the other, lest we grow too prideful, and so it has been with me. For though I know God, I do not know humanity. How can I, when I lack the very thing that makes us human? Not merely the knowledge of

210

our mortality, but its daily experience. You, Herr Immelman, possess that knowledge, that experience. But do you know God? Do you know eternity?'

'I don't suppose I do,' I felt compelled to admit, then added defensively: 'I don't suppose many people do.'

'All do,' the rabbi said, 'sooner or later. For death will teach that lesson if life does not. But because He loves us, God wants us to learn it while we are yet alive.'

'Perhaps you are right,' I said. 'Perhaps not. I am a simple clockmaker, Rabbi. I am content to serve God by making the best clocks I can.'

'Yes. That is why God has chosen you, whether you realize it or not. There is no lack of clockmakers in this world, Herr Immelman. Yet only one – you – responded to my challenge by filling an empty clock with the needful parts to make it work. And what's more, only one – you – has given me a clock that does not fail or degrade in my presence. A clock that I may rely upon at last as a blind man relies upon a trusted cane. This is a sign. And, in its way, a test. Yes, God is testing me, Herr Immelman, just as I tested you! For He has not come to me directly, but instead through you, a Christian ignorant of the Kabbalah and of much else besides. A worldly man, if I may term you so without offence, for I do assure you I mean none.'

'It is no more than the truth,' I said. 'I have never pretended otherwise.'

'God cannot be compelled,' the rabbi said, and it was as if he were speaking to himself rather than to me, reciting some prayer or incantation peculiar to his faith. 'He cannot be seduced. He acts where He will, for His own reasons, and His choices are as sovereign as His will. We can only respect them, bow to them. Embrace them, if we can, in a spirit of submission.'

With that, as though throwing himself off a cliff rather than a chair, he dropped heavily to his knees before me, knocking over the small table between us. Dear boy, I nearly fell over myself from sheer surprise! The sight of the dignified old Jew abasing himself at my feet filled me with a sense of shame as unexpected as the act that had precipitated it.

211

'Get up!' I cried, jumping to my feet and endeavouring to help him stand. 'What do you mean by kneeling to me? Get up, I say!'

'I am not kneeling to you but to the God in you,' he responded stonily. He might have been made of stone, for all the success I had in moving him.

'Get up in any case,' I implored. 'It's not right!' I was terrified that his wife or one of his daughters would walk in on us. What would I say to them? How explain this grotesque scene? The odd thing is that, had a friend described a similar situation to me, I would have howled with laughter, picturing the old Jew abasing himself upon the floor. But there was nothing funny about it at the time, and it is not pleasant for me to recollect even now. Indeed, I would sooner kneel to any man alive than be knelt to.

At last I managed to wrestle the rabbi back into his chair. He was breathing heavily, his face flushed. His blue eyes had a dazed look to them. 'I will get Pearl,' I told him. It seemed plain to me that he had experienced an attack of apoplexy – though I had not yet, at that time, taken up my medical studies.

'No,' he said, and, when I rose to go regardless, clamped a hand about my wrist in a grip I could not break. 'Sit down, Herr Immelman.'

His voice was unwavering, his gaze as commanding as his words had been. Here, again, was the lion I had glimpsed earlier: the lion of Judah, as Rebecca had called him. I sat down.

'Will you come with me now?' he asked, his eyes boring into mine, his hand squeezing my wrist as if he meant to grind the bones to powder. 'Will you look upon my great work of time?'

'Yes, anything!' I blurted out, hardly knowing what I was saying.

He released my wrist and smiled. 'You shall be the first to see it,' he said. 'I will be glad of your opinion.'

With that, he stood easily – all trace of the attack, if it had been an attack, gone – and led me out of the room and up the stairs. The change in him was profound; if I had not witnessed the preceding moments, I would not have believed they had taken place. Indeed, I began to wonder if, once again, he had bested me in a bit of business. At any rate, he seemed again the man he had been, dignified but affable. He described his home to me with pride as he conducted me through it.

'Here are my daughters' rooms. Each has her own, save for Sadie and Sarah, who share a room, and a bed, as they do most things. Pearl and I sleep downstairs.'

'You are indeed an indulgent father,' I said. 'What a luxury, to give each girl her own room!'

'Ach, I spoil them, I know. But I am a wealthy man, thanks be to God and an inheritance from my father. It is a hard enough life, to be a woman. I will make it easier for them while I can.'

I saw no sign of the girls, nor heard any hint of them either, as we climbed through the large house, which was of three storeys, plus an attic. At last we stood outside the attic door.

'Here is my holy of holies,' the rabbi said. 'No man, nor woman either, has seen what you are about to see – only God has seen it.'

I said nothing to this. What was there to say?

The rabbi hesitated, seeming as if he might speak again, but then fished inside his voluminous robes and produced a key that he fitted into the lock of the door. A sharp click, and the door swung inward onto darkness. Without a word, stooping slightly, he entered. I hung back, wary of the dark. Then a light flared, and I saw the rabbi's face cowled in light and shadow as he raised a fat tallow candle. Never had he looked more the lion.

'Come and see,' he said.

I entered, stooping rather more than the rabbi had. It was a large, cavernous space, with high ceilings of bare wooden beams. It was stiflingly hot. The close air smelled of damp earth and resin, as if we had wandered into a mine rather than an attic. There were windows on the walls, but they were closed and had been painted black to keep out the light. Thus the only illumination came from the lone candle in the rabbi's hand, which he held up now to direct my attention to the centre of the room, where loomed an altar-like stone slab. I approached with curiosity and trepidation.

Upon that slab – not stone after all, I realized, but wood covered with hardened clay – lay a clock such as I had never before seen or imagined. The casing, a rectangular box lying on its back, rather like an open coffin, had been sculpted out of clay, and so had the gears and the rest of the works that filled it. It had all been done in the most slapdash manner imaginable, as if by a disturbed child. There was no precision to it, no artifice. The various pieces of the clockworks were not distinct from each other but rather part of the same block of clay, so that they appeared to be melting together, or perhaps emerging from a common mass. It was rather like looking into the exposed chest cavity of a dead man – as I have since had occasion to do – to see the organs and muscles embracing in lax and sloppy promiscuity, like offal floating in a vat, dead things lacking only a breath to make them live again.

I glanced at the rabbi, wondering if he were playing a joke on me, or if he had gone mad, but his expression in the light of the dancing flame was both proud and serious as he gazed upon his handiwork. I turned my attention back to the clock.

Lying beside the casing was the clock face, which had also been sculpted from clay. It was square and of a size to fit at one end or the other of the rectangular box, which, I supposed, would then be stood up like a mantel clock, though it seemed evident that the damp clay could not possibly support itself in that position, and the whole edifice, so to speak, must come oozing down. I had not realized until that precise instant that horology was a religion to me. I knew it because I understood instinctively that what I was seeing was a species of blasphemy. I knew it in my gut. I felt as if I was going to vomit.

Then I saw the numbers that had been painted in black onto the clock face, which as yet had no hands. They were no numbers in any system I knew, not Roman or Arabic or anything else even remotely recognizable.

'What numbers are these?' I asked in a small, strangled voice.

'None at all,' the rabbi answered. 'They are *shem* – letters in our alphabet associated with the many names of God.'

I turned to him. 'What is it you are attempting to do here, Rabbi?'

'This is my great work of time,' he said, as if that should be obvious. 'It is a clock built to the specifications of the Ark of the Covenant, using the esoteric wisdom of the Kabbalah. It will allow all mankind to experience eternity, just as I do. It will bring God to all men, and all men to God.'

'But you must realize . . . I mean, look at it! It is nothing but clay!'

He nodded. 'Of course. Clay is the divine medium par excellence. It was what the Lord God used to fashion the first man. There is no substance better suited to embody the divine spark. You see, this will be a living clock, Herr Immelman. With each hour, it will invoke one of the blessed names of God, until, at the end of a single day, the last day, God will be made manifest in this Earthly sphere. Time will be snuffed out like a candle flame, and blessed eternity will descend for ever and ever.' His voice was fervent, his blue eyes visionary. He turned those eyes on me now, and they were terrible in their fierce conviction. 'I am not mad, Herr Immelman. This clock will do what I say it will do.'

'Rabbi,' I said gently, horror giving way to pity as I realized the depth of his delusion, 'this clock cannot do anything. It does not – indeed, cannot – work. Surely you can see that!'

'Of course it doesn't work,' he said, and chuckled as if I were the mad one. 'That is your job. You will make it work, Herr Immelman, just as you made this clock work.' And he pulled the lion-cased clock from his robes, dangling it before me like some heathen talisman.

Without thinking, I struck at it, knocking it from his hand. It flew, a blaze of gold in the attic gloom, and fell into the open coffin of the Kabbalah clock. I had turned instinctively to follow its flight. Now, in a searing flash, the images penetrating my brain and fusing themselves into my understanding for ever, I saw how to make the thing work.

This would not be a clock of wood or metal but of clay . . . of clay made flesh. Flesh and blood and bone, with organs serving as clockworks. The clock would be alive as a human body is alive. Yet that body would also be a mechanism, as a clock is a mechanism.

To see this, to understand it, to hold the design together as its crisscrossed lines wriggled to escape into insanity, was indescribably painful to me. It was not a knowledge my mind had been made for. So my mind shattered. It seemed that my skull had shattered. The self inside my head, the clockworks of consciousness, flew all over the attic, splashing up into the timbers of the ceiling, dripping down the black glass of the windows, mixing with the moist clay of the clock, even spattering the lion's face of the rabbi. But then the same awful knowledge that had broken me kicked in again and started putting me back together, drop by drop, piece by piece, cog by cog, for the law of creation is the reversal of the law of destruction, until I was myself again, only there was more of me. And that was more painful still. You think you understand something of pain, my boy. And you do. You do. And will come to understand more yet before you are done.

But you will never understand it as I do. Remember that, if you can, and be comforted.

For me, there was no comfort.

All this took place in an instant. It happened and was done. A world ended and began anew in the blink of an eye. There was not even time to scream. It is ever thus to be born.

Afterwards, I stood trembling in the ecstasy of what I knew, the beautiful abomination I and I alone could bring forth here, would certainly bring forth, did not dare to bring forth. The rabbi was laughing that infectious booming laugh of his, only this time it wasn't quite as infectious, or maybe I didn't see the joke, or maybe I saw the joke all too well. At any rate, I didn't join in. Instead, I walked over to the Kabbalah clock and pulled the rabbi's gold-plated timepiece out of its squishy insides. I could tell just from the feel of it how its works had been knocked awry and how to fix it so that it would never lose another second from now until Judgement Day. But there was no point in doing so, because that was how I sensed everything just then, and one clock was as good as another.

I handed it back to the rabbi, who grinned as he tucked it into his robes.

'When shall we get started, Herr Immelman?' he said, rubbing his hands together in anticipation.

I said, 'Never.'

And walked past him out the door of the attic like an automaton escaping from a clock.

He followed on my heels. 'You can't do this,' he said as we descended the stairs. 'You know that I'm right. You see it, I know you do. You *see* it!'

'That doesn't mean I have to make it,' I said.

'It does mean that,' he said. 'You just don't understand that yet.'

'I never will understand it,' I said at the foot of the stairs.

'You will. And when you do, you'll be back.'

'I'm not coming back,' I told him from the doorway, and then left the rabbi's house, or so I thought, for ever.

But to escape from one clock is not to escape them all, or so I realized as I made my way through the streets of the city. Earlier, the ghetto had appalled me with its crowds of Jews and their animals, its riotous clamour, as of an Oriental bazaar, its stench or rather stew of stenches, its unapologetic otherness, which yet offered cringing apology, its intense self-absorption, as if the ghetto were the most brilliant jewel in Prague's glittering crown or were instead the only Prague that mattered or indeed existed, everything else just another, larger ghetto, a second-rate ghetto, in fact, since it lacked Jews. But now everyone and everything I saw struck me as occupying its ordained place, in its ordained way, so that there was no action or expression or conversation that could surprise or delight or disgust me. Nothing was real. Or, to put it another way, everything was real to the exact same degree, people and animals and buildings, the stones on the street, flowers, weeds, all of them built up out of the same clay and then breathed into by God, or what I assumed must be God, for that was the one thing I could not see clearly. But I could see His name, or rather names, like the signature of an artist, on the foreheads of the Jews, on the sides of their animals, on the stalks of flowers, the leaves of plants and trees, the stones of the street. Shining there, as if written in fire, the same exotic symbols I had seen on the rabbi's clock face, what he had called *shem*. The holy names of God.

When I passed before a shop window, I saw that my forehead, too, had its shining mark. I was no different from anyone and anything else, or different only in that I could see what others were blind to. But I was as much an automaton as they were, my steps as ordained as theirs; I saw this clearly: all of us, down to the smallest stone, the last blade of grass, essential elements in a single vast clockworks, a great work of time.

Passing out of the ghetto and into Christian Prague was like stepping from one clock into a bigger one, as if the world were a system of concentric clocks, clocks containing clocks containing clocks, and so on ad infinitum in every direction imaginable, every mote of dust a clock, and every far-flung star, and the universe surrounding them all, and whatever surrounded that. I wanted to fall on my knees and weep at the beauty of it. And, simultaneously, scream in horror. But I did neither. What would have been the point? To demonstrate that I had free will? Of course I had it. Everyone did. But it didn't matter. It had been taken into account. And, so to speak, corrected for, like variables in a mathematical equation that cancel each other out. For instance, had I stopped to harangue passers-by with all that I knew, all that I saw, pointed out the incandescent name of God ablaze on their foreheads, I would have been ignored or derided or beaten or locked away in the madhouse. I would have given anything to rid myself of this dire knowledge, to go back to how I had been before, but I knew that wasn't possible. My eyes had been opened. Even if I plucked them out, I would never be blind again. I cursed the rabbi for what he had done. I cursed God for having permitted – indeed, abetted – it.

As I hurried home, retreating like a wounded bear to its cave, a certain pattern began to impose itself on my perceptions. It was there in the curving lines inscribed by birds upon the air, in the slow, majestic sweep of clouds, and in the watery creep of their earthbound shadows. I saw it in the trajectories of individuals on the street, in the grander collation of crowds, heard it in the mingling of voices, the cries and calls of animals, the grinding wheels of wagons and carriages. I smelled it in the smoke of countless cook fires. It was written plainly in the steaming ordure of horses, of pigs.

Pogrom.

It would break upon this mild day like the sudden turning of a season. What people would cling to as causes before and after the fact, explaining this or that by what had gone before, by what had been said or done by this person to that one, or, on the contrary, by what had not been said or done, were, I saw, not causes at all but parts of the same phenomenon they only seemed to give rise to, in the same way that a gust of icy wind that comes as the outrider of a blizzard may be mistaken, by simple or superstitious folk, as the breath of some boreal god that by magic, or perhaps in answer to a prayer, swirls itself into the storm that follows, or rather seems to follow, on its heels. Just so do many otherwise sensible people mistake the striking of the hour as an effect caused by the passing of all the minutes that preceded it, as if those minutes have accumulated somewhere within the mechanism of the clock, like so many grains of sand, and have finally grown weighty enough to pull some trigger that releases some hammer that in turn strikes some bell, thus causing the clock to chime. But that is to confuse a metaphor with the thing itself. After all, my boy, a clock, useful as it may be, however elegantly constructed, is but a metaphor, is it not?

In those days, in that part of the world, pogroms were like queer Christian festivals that sprang up of their own accord from time to time, unpredictable and hence more to be savoured than those marked on the calendar. They were wild festivals rather than tame ones, if I may use that figure, perfect little whirlwinds in which all was permitted, provided you dared take it. Murder, rape, torture, theft, arson – all were laid out in the ghetto streets like so many courses in a banquet, rare dishes that one did not often have the chance to sample, here presented without charge, absolutely free for the taking! Small wonder if some men stuffed themselves to sickness, as unrestrained in their appetites as gluttons. Others, whose palates were more refined, or more jaded, contented themselves with a taste of this, a nibble of that, washed down with a fine bloody claret. I fell into neither of these categories myself, yet I must confess, with shame, to taking some advantage of the liberties presented, especially in my younger days.

Now, however, the imminence of just such a festival did not put me into a festive mood. Much as I would have liked to forget my troubles and blow off some steam as I had in the past, I couldn't forget what I knew or dismiss what I saw everywhere I looked; even if I shut my eyes against it, there it was in the darkness. It *was* the darkness, just as, when I opened my eyes again, it was the light. I felt as I had earlier, when the rabbi had knelt to me or, as he'd put it, to the God in me: ashamed. But whether I was ashamed of myself, of those around me, or of God himself, I could not say. Perhaps all equally.

The worst of it was that I began to discern, in the various *shem*, the fates of the ones who, unknowing as cattle, bore them like a brand. Jews and Christians alike, their destinies were written so clearly upon their foreheads that it seemed impossible I was the only one who could see them. I will not say all that I saw there. I do not like to think of it. But I saw which ones would die, and how they would die. There was nothing I or anyone else could do to save them, or even a reason to try. It was all inevitable, yet senseless, as if the enormous clock whose meticulous workings were manifest everywhere around me, and in me, meshing with such precision that to witness it demanded not merely admiration but worship, had been designed and built by a bloodthirsty lunatic genius.

When I got home at last, wrung out as a dishrag, I locked myself inside and went up to my bedroom. I didn't bother to wind the clocks in the shop or anywhere else; they were clumsy, inferior creations, as if an ape had tried to build itself a soul out of its own excrement, worthy only of destruction, but I was too weary and disheartened for that. Upstairs, I pulled the curtains shut, crawled into bed, and drew the covers over my head. That didn't change anything, of course. The idiot ticking of the clocks was just as loud. Maybe louder. But I thought, or rather hoped, I might fall asleep, and so escape what was coming. I recalled that I had a bottle of wine, but the effort involved in fetching and opening it, much less drinking it, was overwhelming to contemplate, as if it lay at the top of a mountain and not on a table just a few steps away.

The ticking of the clocks was unbearable. Really, what a maddeningly stupid sound a clock makes! How had I ever been able to stand it? The beating of my heart was no better. It, too, was an inferior timepiece, at least compared to the one that had revealed itself to me on the table in the rabbi's attic, the secrets of which had not faded from my mind, or ever would. I seemed to hear it now, pulsing in the dark, calling to me to build it, to birth it, to bring it fully into the world.

You see it, I know you do. You see it!

That doesn't mean I have to make it.

It does mean that. You just don't understand that yet.

But no, it was no clock, but someone pounding at the door to the shop.

'Herr Immelman! Herr Immelman!'

I groaned, for I knew that voice.

'Herr Immelman! Let me in!'

And the pounding grew louder.

But I did not rise from the bed. I did not go to open the door. I did not call out for Rachel to go away, to hurry home as fast as ever she could and gather her sisters and parents and take refuge in the deepest cellar of the house. I did none of those things.

The pounding continued, rising in a frantic crescendo, and she called my name once more before her voice, and the door, fell silent. I bestirred myself then and crept to the window and peered like a soldier over the parapet of an enemy wall in time to see two dark-cloaked figures hurry around the corner at the far end of the street, hand in hand, a larger and a smaller, Rachel and Rebecca.

Even after they had gone, I lingered at the window, watching the groups of agitated men who had begun to materialize outside in obedience to a law of which they were ignorant yet bound to follow, like birds impelled to fly south each autumn in their vast flocks that darken the sky. There, too, in the glass, I read the reflection of the *shem* upon my forehead, a pale and ghostly fire. And then, dear boy, I wept.

I rushed out into the already swarming streets. An ever growing flood of men, and some women too, even children out for a bit of fun – or, curious, come to see the commotion only to find themselves swept away by currents too strong to fight, and now carried along willy-nilly, their tears or cries of terror or shouts of supplication ignored or even mocked by their elders, who might easily have intervened then to save them, although not later – were streaming in the direction of the ghetto as if drawn there by some force of attraction impossible to resist. From all over the city they came, the Christians of Prague, converging on the ghetto. The festival had begun.

I saw men whose faces were contorted with anger as they shouted themselves hoarse. 'Death to the Jews! Kill the Christ-killers!' Others wore expressions of childlike glee or eagerness. Some sang and danced, capering like drunks, and indeed many were drunk or well on the way to being so though it was but early in the afternoon.

I saw women whose flushed faces reminded me of the stone gargoyles at the cathedral, more demonic than human. They laughed and leered, licked their lips lasciviously, bared their teeth as though they would bite anyone who came near.

Yet terrible as this carnival of faces was, expressing as they all did in their various ways the basest emotions stripped free of every civilized veneer, more terrible still was what blazed upon each forehead, for people's *shem* were not altered by the expressions underneath them. Those expressions might change as rapidly as the flames of a fire that seem to take on a succession of likenesses, moving fluidly from one grotesquerie to the next, but the *shem* burned with a constant and unchanging fire that illuminated only the eternal truth of that person, his or her fate, if you like, which had been written there at the beginning of time by the moving finger of God. And the gap between that eternal truth, writ in holy fire, and the ephemera below it, writ in flesh, was one that could not be measured in numbers or expressed in words or reconciled by any effort of the human mind or heart that I then knew how to make.

I forced my way forward, looking for the dark-cloaked figures of Rachel and Rebecca. I passed through pockets of fighting that spread like fire or died out suddenly for no more apparent reason than they had started. I was grabbed, shoved, punched, whirled, embraced. I was cursed, exhorted, harangued, laughed at, spat upon. A woman old enough to be my mother pulled me to her with one hand and grabbed between my legs with the other. When she thrust her tongue into my mouth, I bit down hard enough to draw blood. I passed a boy industriously beating a cat to death with a stick. Another, older boy had his breeches open and with a look of immense satisfaction was pissing on the placid face of a man who lay stretched out motionless in the gutter, whether dead or unconscious I could not tell and did not care. Urine glistened in his beard like dew. Always and everywhere was the lively, indistinct hum of voices, and woven through that hum, now rising, now falling, as if some great beast were rampaging through the streets, drawing nearer and then moving farther off again, the noise of breaking glass. And I had not yet even reached the ghetto.

Finally, at the end of an alley that opened into a courtyard, I saw a ragged length of black waving in the bright sunlight from the blade of a pike held above the heads of a crowd that was not as large as other crowds I had seen but was nevertheless big enough to do what it had done, though of course it does not need a crowd for that. A single person will suffice.

I knew at once that strip of cloth had been ripped from Rachel's cloak. And though I knew, too, what I should find beneath it, for I had heard it in her voice, and read it in my *shem*, I hastened towards the pike and its fluttering standard. The crowd was thickly packed, ringing some display of interest, people in the back craning their necks to see over the heads of those in front of them. I heard laughter, whistles, cat-calls. Something or someone was being passed or rather thrown roughly from hand to hand at the centre of the circle, but I could see no more than an occasional flash of black.

Kicking and punching, I bulled my way to the centre, or tried to, but people were not so willing to give up their places, and I found myself in the middle of a brawl. Blows rained down on me, and it was all I could do to keep my feet. Suddenly I was pushed into an open space. I stumbled over something and fell, to hoots of laughter.

It was Rebecca, or what was left of her. She lay upon the bloody stones like a broken doll. I could not see her face, for her head was turned away, as if in shame or shyness, but I knew it was her, had always known.

It is sometimes quite pleasant to be tickled, after all.

With a sob, I clutched her to me, though I knew it was too late. But I cradled her on my lap just the same, and kissed her battered face as though I could in that way restore what had been stolen from her. The *shem* on her forehead blazed as brightly as ever. I could not tell why. Yet beneath my lips her skin was as cool and smooth as clay.

Then someone cried my name, and, raising my head, I saw Rachel.

223

She too had been beaten severely about the face, though her *shem*, like her sister's, was undimmed. Her robes were torn, her breasts, spattered with blood, exposed. She could not cover them, for her hands were being held behind her back by two men. Another man worked with a knife to cut her robes away. He was none too careful, and his blade drew yet more blood.

Laying Rebecca's head down on the stones as gently as I could, I got to my feet. All the while, people were spitting at me, cursing me, jeering. My fellow Christians at worship. Once I had been like them. One of them.

'Jew-lover!'

'He is one himself!'

'Christ-killer!'

I thought that if this was what it was to be Christian, then perhaps I was a Jew at that. 'Yes, I am a Jew!' I said. 'What of it?' Then I addressed the men holding Rachel. 'Let her go. She has done nothing.'

The man with the knife seemed to listen intently. Then he took a step towards me and stabbed me in the side. I felt hot blood gush from me. I staggered but did not fall, and he came for me again, his face still wearing that same expression of intent listening. As he closed with me, I reached up and touched his *shem*. I had not known I could do this. But now it was as if I had always known. I wiped it away with a gesture, brushed it off like a stain. Snuffed it out.

He fell at once to the cobblestones and did not rise.

At this, the crowd seemed to take a collective breath. In that space, I did the same to the two men holding Rachel's arms, one after the other. Then she was at my side, holding me up, or I was holding her up, it was difficult to say which.

The crowd was gone, blown away like so much chaff, its bonds broken, its individual elements scattered and dispersed. They ran in terror of what they had seen. Of what they had done.

Together, Rachel and I made our way to her father's house. She carried her sister's body in her arms, for I was too weak to bear even that small burden. I had lost too much blood. We did not speak. We did not have the heart for it.

The pogrom had outstripped us, and we were not molested again.

*

The rabbi's street was no longer clean and well ordered. It was filled with debris, smashed furniture, broken glass, scraps of clothing. At the near end, a bonfire had been built out of still more furniture, fence posts, and a wagon; it smouldered now, glowing red in places, leaking a thin trail of greasy smoke into the sky. A general haze hung over the whole city, bringing an early twilight. As we passed the bonfire, I saw a charred form there that might have been a human body or perhaps the remains of a chest of drawers that had collapsed in on itself. I looked away. Dogs skulked along the edges of the street, eyeing us mistrustfully.

The windows in the rabbi's house had been broken, the door spattered with what I knew from past experience of such things to be pig's blood and faeces. But it did not appear that the house had been entered. We climbed the steps, and I knocked as loudly as I could upon the profaned door, using the haft of a dagger that must have come from the first man I had killed; I hadn't realized I had taken it until that moment.

At last I heard movement behind the door. It was pulled open by the rabbi. Anger and anguish warred in his leonine features, but no *shem* burned upon his forehead. Briefly I wondered if this was due to his strange affliction, that time-deafness of which he had told me. But then Rachel pushed past me with a howl and hurled herself, and her sister, into the old man's arms. I threw the dagger away, as if to carry it across the threshold would be a further violation, a deeper cut, then followed Rachel inside and slammed the door behind me and bolted it.

When I turned from this, Rachel and her father were regarding me. The rabbi held the limp form of Rebecca in his arms. Tears were streaking his cheeks, but his arms did not tremble. Nor did his voice.

'So, you have come back,' he said. 'I knew you would.'

'I did not mean . . .' I trailed off uselessly.

'You know what you must do,' he said, then added in Latin, as if only that language, long dead yet enduring past death, was fit for the moment, '*Facta non verba.*'

225

Deeds, not words.

I nodded and, wordlessly, pushed past them and climbed the stairs to the attic. I heard them following me but did not slow or look back.

Once in the attic, which had been lit with candles, as though in preparation for my coming, I went straight to the slab or altar in the middle of the room, where the rabbi's Kabbalah clock lay just as it had the last time I had seen it. It reminded me of nothing so much as the clocks in my shop – it fell so far short of what it aspired to that it was fit only to be destroyed. But the effort to do so seemed beyond me, weak as I was, feeling the blood dribble sluggishly from the wound in my side as if pushed out by the weary beating of my heart.

I scooped a handful of clay from the insides of the clock and pushed it into the hole in my side. Then I took my bloody hand and plunged it into the clock, mixing my blood with the moist clay until there was nothing left of the clock at all but just a pile of clay that might be shaped into anything.

I set to work in earnest, growing stronger as I worked. But I did not sculpt a clock.

No, it was a person I gave shape to, a girl. Her form was rough, her features rougher still, two thumbprints for eyes, a pinch of clay for a nose, a deeper hole for a mouth. When I was done, I turned to the rabbi. 'Give me something of hers. Anything.'

Rachel, who stood beside him, tore a strip from Rebecca's cloak and handed it to me.

This I took, reverently folded, and placed as gently as a communion wafer into the hole of the mouth.

Then, upon the forehead, I traced a particular *shem* whose shape and meaning came to me at that moment as if the Almighty had whispered into my ear.

The mouth hole closed. The eye holes opened. The clay girl sat up, forehead ablaze.

'Take my message to the Christians of Prague,' I said, and the girl who rose from the slab was not a girl of clay at all but rather one of flesh and blood, or seemed so. She giggled as she skipped past her sister and down the stairs.

Thus did I send Retribution into the streets of Prague.

Afterwards, the rabbi addressed his daughter. 'Bring your sister to your mother, that she may be prepared in the proper manner.'

Rachel nodded, but before taking the body from her father's arms, stepped close to me and handed me something: a white square. It was the handkerchief I had given her, freshly laundered. Even now there was not a spot on it.

I took it numbly. I have it still.

'I had thought to return this to you,' she said. 'Rebecca begged to come too, and at last, just to get some peace, I permitted it.'

'It is not your fault,' I told her. 'You couldn't have known.'

She nodded. Tears glimmered in her brown eyes but did not fall. 'Didn't you hear us knocking at your door, Herr Immelman?'

'I heard,' I said.

'Why didn't you answer? Why didn't you let us in?'

What could I say? How could I explain the *shem* and what they had shown me? How tell her of the change I had undergone, whose cause and purpose I did not understand myself?

'Leave him, daughter,' said the rabbi. 'He has burdens you do not know.'

Rachel looked to her father. 'Do you know them, Papa?'

'I do,' he said.

This seemed to comfort her. 'He called himself a Jew,' she told her father as he laid Rebecca into her waiting arms. 'When he saved me from the mob, he said he was a Jew like me.'

'He is nothing like you,' said the rabbi, and leaned forward to kiss Rebecca's forehead one final time. Then he kissed Rachel in the same spot, with the same tenderness, and at that, somehow, I knew.

'You made them, didn't you?' I asked after Rachel had gone, bearing her sad burden. 'You sculpted them out of clay and wrote upon their foreheads one of the names of God.'

'I did,' he said, as if pleased at my deduction.

'And they don't know,' I went on. 'They don't know what they are.'

'None of them do,' said the rabbi. 'Of all that I have made, none know the truth of it but you, Herr Immelman.'

And then I understood why he and he alone of everyone I had seen did not bear a *shem* upon his forehead. I fell to my knees before him, as he had fallen before me.

'Forgive me,' I said.

Again that infectious laugh boomed out. 'Get up, Herr Immelman,' he said, and extended a hand to me. 'Herr Immelman, who calls himself a Jew. We have much to do, you and I, in this great work of time.'

In the days and nights that followed, we laboured feverishly, the rabbi and I, on the Kabbalah clock. Only on the night it was done at last, and set in motion, did I understand that its true purpose was quite other than what he had told me. I was not to learn of this purpose until later, but that it was not a clock to 'bring God to all men, and all men to God', as he had put it, became clear to me the instant I left his house that night and found myself not in the familiar streets of Prague, as I had of course expected, but in another place entirely, an Alpine village I would come to know as Märchen: my home and my prison from that time until this.

That, my boy, was the first lifting of the veil.

Others followed in swift succession.

The citizens of this town, like the rabbi, had no *shem* upon their foreheads. Thus did I learn of the Otherwhere and its denizens, the immortal Risen, whom at first I took for angels in the service of the rabbi I still thought of as God.

But, of course, he was no more God than he was a rabbi or, for that matter, a Jew.

At least, he was not the God that I had heard of, read of, and worshipped for all my Earthbound life. He called himself Doppler, and he told me that he was the first and greatest of the Risen, that he had created the Earth and all that existed there in order that he might have a storehouse in which to collect and ripen the divine nectar known as time, which is to his kind as the most potent wine is to mortals. Everything on Earth, animate and inanimate, is a repository of time, he told me. But only in human beings can time reach its full exquisite potential.

On his Earthly sojourns, he liked to create a family for himself and live unsuspected among them, as one of them, sometimes as the father, sometimes the mother, sometimes a child, so that he could give his utmost attention to shaping even the most seemingly insignificant details of their lives, for only in this way could he ensure that the time maturing within their mortal frames reached its optimum potency and flavour, its full complexity. He had been about this business when I had met him, and he assured me that Rebecca, and Rachel too, had been especially fine, exquisite, in fact, worth every bit of the considerable effort he had lavished on their cultivation. I should add that he wept as he reminisced about Rachel and Rebecca. He seemed genuinely to have loved them. Though what love might mean for such as he, I did not and do not know, unless eternal beings can only love that which is unlike them: the ephemeral productions of time.

Why did he need me at all, this god in all but name? Why could he not have built the Kabbalah clock himself?

The answer was that time is not just a drug but also a poison to the Risen. Their exposure to it had to be delicately measured, or they would become enslaved to its delights and as much bound to it as any mortal. Indeed, they could, it seemed, lose their immortality by immoderate consumption or prolonged exposure . . . or, if not lose it entirely, then render it contingent upon continued and increasing doses. And this in fact is what has happened in the last two hundred years, since I have been here.

Doppler had created time in order to impose this fate deceitfully upon his fellow Risen, so that his dominance would be assured for eternity. When the others realized what he had done, they rebelled against his rule, or at least some of them did, led by Doppler's wife – if such terms have any meaning here – Tiamat. That was the cause of the war among the Risen that continues to this day without quarter or mercy.

But Doppler was caught in his own snare, and it was for this reason that he conceived the Kabbalah clock – though, as I later learned, there was nothing of the Kabbalah about it, not even the fiery symbols that I had been told were *shem*. Those things, like all Earthly things, were as flickering shadows cast on the wall of Plato's cave, distortions of the reality that lay behind them: the will of Doppler working upon the raw stuff of the Otherwhere.

Think of it, dear boy – the mighty Doppler, first and greatest of the Risen, a spider caught in its own web! His exposure to his own creation, over tens of thousands of years in the bosom of his countless families, had served only to debase him from connoisseur to addict. Think of his awful dilemma! Without access to sufficient time, he would lose his immortality and become mortal. The same fate awaited him if, on the contrary, he consumed too much of the ambrosial elixir. Only by measuring out his doses with the finest precision could he maintain the immortality that was his birthright as one of the Risen. Yet this precarious equilibrium was not sustainable indefinitely, for in order to enjoy the intoxicating effects of time, and maintain his immortality, he had to gradually increase the dose, as he became acclimated, and sooner or later he must reach a point where there would not be time enough in all the vast storehouse of the universe to satisfy his need. Then the universe would end, sucked back into the Otherwhere from whence it had come, and Doppler would end with it.

All this Doppler realized during his sojourn as the rabbi. The Kabbalah clock was his first attempt to manage the addiction that, as he had come to understand, must ultimately cost him his immortal existence. The purpose of that clock, then, was simply this: to generate more time – so much more that he need never fear running out of it or reaching a point where his need for it outstripped his supply. Such was his great work of time – an addict's attempt to ensure for himself an endless supply of his poison!

It was, of course, a failure. For time, once created, cannot be added to or subtracted from. It exists in its entirety right from the start; its end is in its beginning, and its beginning in its end. Or so I do believe, having made what study of it I can.

Since then there have been other attempts, other clocks. I have built them all. That is my purpose, or one of them. Doppler requires an intermediary to do what he cannot, a mortal for whom time is no foreign substance or medium but the very stuff of existence, for such a one may be exposed to time without temptation. We mortals are proof against its intoxicating effects, and it is already killing us. For this, then, Doppler made me as I am today. Opened my eyes and brought me here, to Märchen, to serve as his hands. Here, in my workshop at the very centre of the great tower clock that grew up around me, which is both clock and portal through the Otherwhere, I build his clocks. And I measure out the doses of time that he and his followers must ingest to sustain themselves.

Or did, until the war came to Märchen and destroyed it. Then Doppler and the others fled to fight elsewhere, leaving me behind in the ruins of my workshop, forgotten, it seems. Perhaps, one day, he will return. Or perhaps he has found another mortal to take my place, as he had always intended to do. I do not know.

All the clocks I built for Doppler to end or ameliorate his addiction failed, save one. Can you guess it?

Yes, dear boy, the hunter. It is the most terrible of them all. For by its working, Doppler plans to survive the death of this universe and be reborn in another – a universe shaped entirely by his will, without the flaw, or rather mistake, of time. That is why he is so desperate to retrieve it. Without it, he is doomed. Nor can he build another, for he has poured too much of his will into this one.

Though Doppler raised me above other mortals, I was still mortal. I aged more slowly in Märchen, but still I aged, and at last the time came when he saw that he must provide me with an apprentice, a mortal I could train to take my place in his service. So it was that, at Doppler's direction, I scattered a trail of timepieces across the Earth – unusual, eccentric creations sure to pique the interest of any man or woman with a nose for time. I signed these with the enigmatic intials JW, for Jozef Wachter, a name that meant nothing to me but which had some significance for Doppler, though he never explained it beyond saying that as I had seen fit to call myself a Jew, it was only right that I take the name of one. Whoever followed that trail to Märchen would be my apprentice. For a long while, no one came. But then, one snowy evening, my apprentice-to-be arrived.

Michael Gray, the man you call Longinus.

By then the war had been going on for some time. Tiamat and her followers had fled Märchen; where they had gone, no one, not even Doppler, knew. But from their secret refuge they lashed out with fearsome weapons – devices that delivered concentrated doses of time, doses sufficient to deplete and even drain entirely the immortality from any of the Risen unfortunate enough to be struck. Doppler himself could not withstand more than a few such wounds. I had built these weapons under his direction, for use against his enemies, but Tiamat had stolen the secret of their making and turned them against us.

Tiamat's response to the fact of her addiction was quite different from Doppler's. What Doppler cared about above all else was that his existence and his power continue unchecked and undiminished for ever and ever. He would destroy everything that was, so long as he might emerge from the ashes, phoenix-like, the lord of a new and better creation.

None of that mattered to Tiamat. Even her own existence meant little to her in itself. Rather, she conceived the belief that time was not a poison at all, nor was it a drug. It was, instead, to her way of thinking, a force or power greater than that of the Risen. Greater even than the Otherwhere that had given birth to it under the impetus of Doppler's will and desire. Thus, she reasoned, time was not to be feared. It was not to be destroyed. It was not to be stored up and selfishly savoured. It was, instead, to be worshipped like a god. And, like a god, submitted to.

Tiamat and her followers longed to submerge themselves in time. They wished to lose themselves in it, merge with it, become one with it. The only way for them to do that was to become mortal, for only mortals can truly know time. And only mortals can disperse their essences through time, dying to themselves yet living on in their progeny, generation upon generation, until time itself unravels.

Was that not, as Doppler scornfully said, to embrace their own extinction?

Not extinction, Tiamat answered, but a higher form of immortality, collective rather than individual, leading ultimately to an end she didn't know or need to know: a revelation that awaited them all at the end of time, which could only be reached through time.

Delusion, said Doppler.

Faith, answered Tiamat.

It was an answer that appealed to more than a third of the Risen. Others joined with Tiamat not from shared belief but simply out of a desire to be revenged upon Doppler, who had betrayed their trust.

Pity poor Michael Gray, who walked unsuspecting into the midst of this civil war!

By then, Doppler had conceived of a new use for him besides being my successor in his service. He was to mate with Corinna, his daughter by Tiamat, who had remained loyal to her father – or so it was believed. The fusion of mortal and immortal, thought Doppler, might confer immunity or resistance to the pernicious effects of time. Such unions had once been common enough on Earth, giving rise to various creatures of human myth and legend, but they had never taken place in the Otherwhere, for no mortals had ever been brought here before me – or, for that matter, at least until the arrival of Michael Gray, after me. There had been no need of it.

Doppler had thought at first to mate me with Corinna, or another of the Risen, but, alas, I was too old, and so saturated with time from my long years of service that any of them who might lie with me would risk their immortality.

Michael Gray, but newly arrived in Märchen, was as yet unspoiled.

The Otherwhere is no fit abode for humans, my boy. No mortal can long survive here, not even in Märchen, where the walls between the worlds are at their thinnest, or at any rate were, until the destruction of the great tower clock that served as the central portal between the Otherwhere and Earth. Now but a single portal remains, and it is far indeed from here, all but inaccessible, in fact.

Any mortal brought here must inevitably sicken and die, unless his mortal substance – flesh and blood and bone – be tempered with the stuff of the Otherwhere. That is what had been done to me in

233

the rabbi's attic: the change I had experienced as the opening of my eyes to the underlying reality of God's presence in the world – though of course it was Doppler's presence that I really saw. Actually, it had begun when I crafted the rabbi's clock: I had quite literally, though entirely unbeknownst to me, poured something of myself into that clock, as I did with all my clocks, and that bit of time-infused essence was used by Doppler to trigger the change, when the clock came into contact with the undiluted stuff of the Otherwhere, which I had taken for the mere clay of the Kabbalah clock.

But no matter, dear boy – this is only by way of explaining why it was that, soon after Michael Gray's arrival in Märchen, his foot was amputated and replaced by a prosthetic. That new appendage, built by me to Doppler's specifications, had the marvellous effect of allowing him to access the Otherwhere, to come and go along its tangled highways and byways almost as easily as one of the Risen, for among his future duties would be frequent travel to Earth, there to oversee Doppler's vineyards. But its real purpose was quite other: to inoculate him, as it were, against the poisons of this place, and thus permit him to remain here, first as my apprentice, then my successor, for the rest of his natural – or, rather, unnatural – life.

Of course, that was not to be. Corinna had long since gone over to the side of her mother, and had lingered in Märchen only as a spy . . . and so that she might, given the opportunity, make off with the hunter – as, in fact, she did, entrusting it to Michael Gray, for whom she had conceived, I believe, a true affection, insofar as such human emotions may be said to be present in the Risen, who after all are not human, however cleverly they can counterfeit it in appearance and action when they care to.

I suppose I resented Michael Gray. And envied him, too, a bit. Yet above all I felt sorry for him. I pitied him deeply, as only I could, knowing, as only I did, what lay in store for him. Not once in all my long years of service to Doppler had I attempted to sabotage his work. I had not added to or subtracted from his allotted measure of time, but poured it out with a steady, incorruptible hand. I had been a trustworthy steward in every way. But now a strange mix of emotions roiled up in me. I felt as if Doppler had betrayed me as he had his fellow Risen, lifting me above my fellow mortals, yet only to a height from which the distance I must inevitably fall seemed more stark and terrible than ever. Despite everything, I was still mortal. Death was my lot, and it was drawing uncomfortably near . . . in the presence, it seemed, of this innocent young man who was to become the heir to my kingdom, such as it was, without being of my flesh and blood.

And it was not only that. It was the knowledge that everything I had undergone, all the joys and sorrows, the loves and the losses – at the very centre of which, like a sacred wound, was the precious memory of Rebecca – had been purposefully chosen for me by Doppler, not for my own sake but rather so that the time maturing in me, when it was at last decanted, might deliver some novel taste to that infinitely jaded palate. It angered me. Even more: it offended me.

At first I harboured notions of escape. I thought I might assist young Michael Gray, who, in turn, would assist me, and together we would flee Märchen for the sanctuary of Earth. Or I might return alone to Prague and live out the remainder of my life there in peaceful solitude.

But these were merely pleasant fantasies, and soon enough it was too late even for that: the amputation performed, the prosthetic attached, nothing left to do but dispose of the gory original.

Yet I hesitated.

First I took the mangled foot and mended it – easy enough for one whom Doppler had gifted with clear sight and steady hands. Then, using the same store of clay I had used to sculpt poor Michael Gray's new foot, I moulded a new body to go with his old foot – as I had moulded the bodies of so many automatons for the tower clock and other timepieces about the town. Into this body I poured all the knowledge I had amassed during my years in Märchen. Everything I had learned about the human body and about clocks, and the fusion of the two, from my work on the Kabbalah clock to my work on the hunter, went into that lifeless clay. And more. I poured myself into it as well, dear boy – poured everything that Doppler was so eager to despoil . . . and everything I longed to atone for. I all but emptied myself.

When I was done, what lay upon the bloody table where, hours earlier as such things are measured elsewhere, I had operated upon the unconscious Michael Gray was, to all appearances, the selfsame man, albeit worked in clay.

I knew a moment of fear then, amidst the headlong exhilaration that had been driving me on as if I were drunk on fumes of stolen time. I realized that my creation would be immediately detected, whether by its original or by Doppler or Corinna. I had been a fool to make this thing. The only sensible course of action was to destroy it.

Instead, I traced a glowing shape upon its forehead. The same shape I had traced on another forehead that long-ago day in Prague. When I lifted my finger, what was underneath was no longer clay but flesh, human flesh. Only it was not the firm flesh of a man in the full flower of youth but instead that of a babe no more than a few weeks old, soft and rosy pink and glowing with health. A babe sunk deep in peaceful slumber.

Still I was not through. Now, working more quickly than ever, I sculpted a woman of twenty or so years. I wrote upon her forehead the bare scraps of a history. And the name of a girl I had known once, and loved in my thoughtless way.

I woke her and placed the sleeping babe into her ready arms. Why not? She had always wanted a child of me! Then, before I sent her through the portal I used in my work, I whispered a name into her ear. Can you guess it, dear boy?

For it was your name.

Daniel Quare.

6

Malrubius Takes Command

'I MUST ONCE AGAIN PROTEST THIS OUTRAGEOUS INTRUSION!' SAID THE WOMAN who had identified herself as Mrs Bartholomew, Lord Wichcote's housekeeper.

'Must you really, madam?' Malrubius sighed. Since invading the house an hour ago at the head of a squad of redcoats – a sign of improved relations with Mr Pitt following the handover of Boxer, who'd clung to life just long enough to have it snatched away at the end of a rope on Execution Dock, an example to smugglers and traitors everywhere – he had set up a headquarters of sorts here in the sitting room, from whence to direct the search of the premises, but unfortunately this harridan of a housekeeper insisted on plaguing him with her tedious objections. He did not dare to treat her with the discourtesy she merited – the Old Wolf's instructions were explicit on that point: no harm was to come to Lord Wichcote or any member of his household; this directive had originated with the king himself, who, despite everything, apparently retained a certain fondness for his scapegrace cousin. Nor did Malrubius wish to let the woman out of his sight; he did not trust her and did not like to spare any men to watch over her: the house was huge and, as his men had already discovered, riddled with secret rooms and passages, all of them no doubt well known to the housekeeper, who might vanish as thoroughly as her master seemed to have done. 'I suppose if you must, you must. But I am afraid this latest protest will make no more difference than those that preceded it – or, for that matter, those that will, I feel sadly confident, follow.'

'When His Majesty learns—'

'Madam,' he said, cutting her off, 'as I have explained already, I am here on orders of the king. I have shown you the writ. Was it not plain enough? All I do here is by royal command. You may, if you wish, lodge a protest with the government. Perhaps Mr Pitt will entertain your objections. I will not. Now, if you wish me to be gone, you need only tell me where I may find your master.'

'Even if I knew, I'd not tell you.'

'Rest assured – if he is here, we shall find him. If he is not, then I will arrest you, madam, and see you put to the question in such manner as befits your protection of a traitor to king and country.'

'His lordship is no traitor!' The woman, who had been pacing relentlessly before the fire, turned towards him with such a hate-filled expression on her ugly, pockmarked face as to make him fear a physical attack. But even as he stepped behind a table and nearer to the door, she sank into a chair and began, silently but vigorously, to weep into the caul of her upraised apron, shoulders heaving.

Malrubius watched for a moment, suspecting a ruse. Women were deceitful creatures as a rule, full of tricks, who put on emotions as they did paints and other fripperies, to catch men in their coils. They always wanted something. This homely housekeeper, for instance. What airs she gave herself! It was plain that she had Wichcote wrapped around her little finger. But if she thought her wiles would work on him, she would soon learn otherwise. He did not doubt that she was involved in her master's conspiracy right up to the eyeballs, and he itched to prove it.

But that was for later. What mattered now was finding Wichcote.

There had been no news as yet from France of Aylesford and the hunter. Doubtless information would come to light, and sooner rather than later, for Pitt had his spies in high places, and Malrubius spies of his own in lower ones – whose testimony he trusted quite a bit more – but for now his only lead to Aylesford and the hunter was Wichcote.

Wichcote, who Sir Thaddeus believed was also the master thief Grimalkin.

And who – again according to Sir Thaddeus – possessed an ability as extraordinary as any demonstrated by the hunter: that of vanishing into thin air. Privately, Malrubius had been highly doubtful of the first belief and entirely dismissive of the second, putting it down to the Old Wolf's having been drugged and on the verge of losing consciousness when he'd seen what he'd seen – or imagined himself seeing. But now that Wichcote seemed to have vanished right out from under their noses, Malrubius was beginning to wonder if Sir Thaddeus did not have the right of it after all. Certainly there was something odd about Wichcote House and its elusive master.

'Master Malrubius, sir,' came a voice from the doorway.

Turning, he saw the lieutenant in command of the redcoats. 'Yes, what is it?'

'We've found something.'

'About bloody time.' He looked at Mrs Bartholomew, who had raised her tear-stained face at the interruption. 'You see, madam? I told you we would find him.'

'It's not that, sir,' said the officer.

'What then?' snapped Malrubius, angered by the triumphant smile that had appeared on the woman's face.

'You'd best come see.'

Malrubius sighed. 'Must I do everything myself? Very well, Lieutenant, detail a man to guard this prisoner.'

'Very good, sir.' The officer ducked out of the room and returned a moment later with another soldier. 'This is Private Matthews, sir. A trustworthy man.'

'Matthews,' said Malrubius, 'this woman may appear to be harmless, but I assure you she is not. She is the servant of a traitor, and very possibly a traitor herself. She is not to be trusted. You are not to let her out of your sight even for an instant. Is that understood?'

'Answer the gentleman,' said the lieutenant.

'Aye, sir. I understand, sir!'

'Good. Lead on, then, Lieutenant – let us see what you have found.'

The lieutenant led him upstairs to a room containing two items of immediate interest. The first was a daybed that had clearly been in recent use; the bedclothes showed every sign of having been thrown hastily aside. The second was a false section of wall: a door disguised as a panel. This now stood open, flanked by two soldiers. Within, a small, square chamber was lit by a single candle.

'Why, this is a stair-master!' Malrubius exclaimed.

'A stair-master, sir?' inquired the lieutenant.

'The guild hall has a number of these ingenious devices, invented by one of our late masters, a cripple, to aid him in getting about, for he had great difficulty in climbing stairs, or, for that matter, in walking at all. I am both surprised and alarmed to see one here. These devices are the property of the guild and may not be built elsewhere. The list of Lord Wichcote's crimes continues to grow!'

'What does it do?'

'You shall see for yourself,' said Malrubius decisively. 'Come with me, Lieutenant. You two as well,' he added, motioning to the two soldiers as he stepped between them and into the stair-master. 'Grab hold of the railing, gentlemen,' he advised when they had crowded in. 'And be ready to draw swords. I know not where this leads – but I suspect we shall find Lord Wichcote there.'

With that, he tugged sharply at the bell pull in one corner, and the room, with no warning, dropped. The lieutenant and two soldiers cried out in terror, their faces ashen in the light of the single candle. Malrubius laughed heartily, enjoying their distress. 'Fear not, gentlemen,' he said. ''Tis perfectly safe!'

'God save us,' said the lieutenant, clutching the rail with both hands. ''Tis witchcraft, sure!'

''Tis science, sir,' Malrubius answered scornfully.

'God save us from science, then!'

Malrubius glowered but said nothing; in truth, he expected no better from the common herd. Soon the stair-master began to slow, then came to a stop.

'We have arrived,' Malrubius announced in a low voice. 'I do not know what we shall encounter beyond this door—'

'Just open it, for the love of God!' demanded the lieutenant loudly, one hand on his sword.

'As you have already alerted whoever might be on the other side, why not?' Malrubius pulled the door open, then stepped aside to give the others a clear avenue of escape. They wasted no time in taking it, blundering past him and into the room beyond, which was dark save for what little illumination was provided by the candle within the stair-master. After waiting long enough to be certain the men had not rushed into an ambush, Malrubius lifted the candle from its sconce and followed them into the room.

'Gorblimey,' said one of the soldiers softly, his sword drawn, turning in a slow circle as he looked at the walls. 'What is this place?'

Malrubius did likewise, the candle upraised; its light showed walls hung with grey clothing and assorted weaponry. 'Gentlemen,' he said, 'I believe we have found Grimalkin's lair.'

'Grimalkin?' asked the lieutenant. 'D'you mean the thief?'

'Is there another?' Malrubius inquired.

'But what would the likes of him be doing in Wichcote House?'

'Is it not obvious? Wichcote and Grimalkin are one and the same. In fact, I had suspected as much. He must have fled here to arm himself when we entered the house – you can see that there are weapons missing from their places on the walls.'

The lieutenant nodded.

'He came here to arm himself, as I said – but then he must have used the stair-master to transport himself elsewhere.'

'Where?'

'That, gentlemen, is what we shall now find out.'

'I'm not getting back in that thing,' the lieutenant said.

'I had not thought to find cowards among the king's soldiers,' said Malrubius.

At this, the three redcoats exchanged glances, and Malrubius wondered if he had gone too far. The men might murder him here, after all, and lay the blame at Grimalkin's feet. 'Besides, Lieutenant,' he added quickly, 'that thing, as you call it, is the only exit from this room. If you wish to remain here, be my guest. But duty demands that we do our utmost to track this traitor down.'

The lieutenant swallowed heavily and nodded. 'Right you are, sir. We'll do our duty. In you go, lads.'

The other two soldiers did not look happy, but they obeyed the lieutenant and stepped into the stair-master. The lieutenant followed, and Malrubius brought up the rear, after first choosing a rapier for himself from Grimalkin's armoury. Once inside, he replaced the candle in its sconce and shut the door.

'Gentlemen,' he said, 'prepare yourselves.' And then he tugged the bell pull.

The stair-master resumed its downward course. If anything, it moved more swiftly than before. Or so it seemed, at least, to Malrubius, though he kept his thoughts to himself.

'How far down does the damned thing go?' whispered the lieutenant. 'To hell itself?'

'Enough of that talk,' said Malrubius. 'No doubt the traitor has prepared a bolt hole. But we will take him there like a rabbit in its burrow. The important thing, gentlemen, is to keep your nerve.'

'Grimalkin is said to be the best swordsman in all England,' remarked one of the soldiers.

'Perhaps he was, once,' said Malrubius. 'Now he is an old man of seventy-odd years. Do you honestly think the four of us cannot best him?'

'What if he is armed with pistols?' asked the same soldier.

'What if he has confederates with him?' chimed in the other.

'Damn your eyes!' exploded Malrubius. 'Give me no more of these what-ifs! Why, what kind of pettifogging soldiery is this? We are four. He is one. Let that be the end of it.'

'Master Malrubius has the right of it, lads,' said the lieutenant. 'The next man who speaks out of turn will be flogged for it when we return to quarters.'

They continued on in a glum and resentful silence. But at last the stair-master began to slow, and finally it drew to a halt. Malrubius lifted the candle from its sconce and surveyed the faces of the others. 'Gentlemen,' he whispered, 'in the heat of battle, it is easy to lose track of one's objectives. But we must try to take Lord Wichcote alive if at all possible. And not just alive: he must be fit for questioning.

242

This man is the key to a conspiracy that threatens the life of the king and the survival of the country itself. Is that understood?'

'Aye, sir,' said the lieutenant. The other two soldiers nodded.

'Very well,' said Malrubius. 'Good luck to us, then, and may God watch over us all.'

So saying, he pulled open the door.

There was only blackness beyond.

The soldiers advanced. Malrubius followed cautiously, upraised candle pushing back the dark.

'Why, we're in a sort of cave, I think,' said the lieutenant. He spoke in a hush, as if they were interlopers in a cathedral.

'Look, sir,' whispered one of the soldiers. 'Torches.'

Indeed, a number of torches were stacked neatly by the door. Malrubius took one of these and lit it with the candle; it flared to life, throwing the rough walls into sharp relief and revealing as well the only way forward: a narrow, jagged crevice cut into the rock.

'I'll go first,' said the lieutenant, assuming a tone of business-like command that Malrubius was quite content to indulge for the moment, feeling as he did a certain uncomfortable awareness of how deep they were below the ground, how suddenly, like the light of the torch, his existence might be snuffed out in the dark.

'Give me the torch, sir, if you please,' the lieutenant said. 'In fact, everyone take a torch – we may be glad of spares. Private Lockhart, you'll follow me, then Master Malrubius. Hedges, you'll bring up the rear.'

'Aye, sir,' chorused the men as Malrubius nodded, his mouth too dry for speech.

They set off into the crevice.

'In other words,' said Sir Thaddeus, glaring up from the handwritten report on his desk to the sweating face of its author, 'you lost him.'

Malrubius winced. The effects of the beating he'd received from Quare and his cronies that night at the guild hall were still visible on his face, if much reduced. The black craters around his eyes had dimmed to shades of purple and yellow that suggested sickly flowers; his nose had nearly returned to its former size, though the same could not, and never would, be said of its shape, which no longer resembled a tuber but instead, thought the Old Wolf, a smashed toad. Hard as it was to believe, the man was uglier than ever.

'It was impossible to track him,' Malrubius whined. 'The passage we were following started to branch in different directions, marked by symbols scratched or painted onto the walls – symbols whose meanings were ambiguous if not entirely obscure. To wander at random, deep underground, with no supplies and only a handful of torches . . .' He gave a shrug of resignation.

'So you retraced your steps,' the Old Wolf supplied. 'You rode the stair-master back into the heart of Wichcote House. And what did you find there?'

'Nothing,' admitted Malrubius sheepishly. 'The man I left to guard the housekeeper was unconscious. The housekeeper was gone.'

'Vanished,' said the Old Wolf. 'Into thin air. Just like her master.'

'But Lord Wichcote did not vanish into thin air,' Malrubius pointed out. 'He vanished by means of a stair-master. And a search of the sitting room revealed that the housekeeper must have vanished in the same way. It's all there in my report, Sir Thaddeus.'

The Old Wolf took the sheet of paper on the desk before him and slowly ripped it in two, never breaking eye contact with Malrubius, who looked as though it were some part of his own anatomy being torn. 'That is what I think of your report, sir,' said the Old Wolf, continuing methodically to reduce the paper to shreds. 'I dispatch you upon a simple task – to storm Wichcote House and arrest its master. Instead, by other testimony, not contained in this self-serving compendium of excuses' – here he tossed the scraps of paper into the air – 'you wasted precious moments in a vain dispute over command of the operation.'

'Your orders plainly gave the command to me,' Malrubius said. 'That noxious lieutenant—'

Sir Thaddeus interrupted forcefully: 'My orders, sir, entrusted operational command to the professional soldier – that is, the lieutenant. You, sir, were entrusted with the search of the house and the questioning of the captive.'

'Yes, but the overall command lay with me. I simply wished for the lieutenant to acknowledge that basic fact before we committed ourselves. Successful operations require a clear chain of command, Sir Thaddeus.'

'Perhaps so,' Sir Thaddeus said, 'but there is a time and a place to resolve such disputes, and it is not in plain sight of the very house you are preparing to enter! Small wonder that Lord Wichcote had time to flee. But that was not the last nor the least of your errors. You established yourself in the sitting room – yet never thought to subject that room to a thorough search! Had you done so, you would have found the stair-master by which the housekeeper made her escape right from under that mashed toad you call a nose! Yet disaster might have been averted in any case had you simply detailed a man to conduct the housekeeper here to the guild hall for questioning! I am disappointed in you, Malrubius. I thought I had trained you better than this. After the death of Magnus, you begged to be allowed to administer the Most Secret and Exalted Order of Regulators on my behalf. I see now that I was mistaken to entrust you with the respon-sibility. You are not ready for it. I am taking the reins back into my own hands.'

Malrubius's face flushed crimson, but his voice was steady and controlled. 'Give me another chance, Sir Thaddeus. You will see that I am ready.'

'I thought you might feel that way. Very well, you shall have your chance at redemption. But your days of command are over for now. This time, Malrubius, you will follow, not lead.'

'I will not disappoint you, Sir Thaddeus.'

'See that you do not. Mr Pitt was most interested to learn of the passages you discovered beneath Wichcote House. He confided to me that there is a vast network of such passages and even larger caverns under the city, home to the worst sort of criminals and riff-raff. That was not news to me, as the guild archives refer to such things. But I had not realized the caverns were so extensive . . . or so populous. According to Pitt, there may be thousands of miscreants down there. It is to this subterranean gang of thieves and murderers that Wichcote has fled in his hour of need. No doubt, as Grimalkin, he commands them all . . . and has infected them with his treasonous ideas. In the past, Mr Pitt has tolerated their presence, as we tolerate the presence of rats in the sewers. But no more. Not with the war going against us and the French, as our spies report, preparing to invade. Thus Pitt has decided to launch an expedition against these vermin – a full-scale military operation, with the purpose of exterminating them utterly, before they rise up quite literally and exterminate us, or assist the French in doing so. You will be attached to this operation as my representative, to observe and assist as requested.'

Malrubius looked decidedly uncomfortable. 'I am to go back underground?'

'Is that a problem?'

'Not at all,' he replied unconvincingly.

Sir Thaddeus studied the man before him. 'Malrubius, are you by chance afflicted with a fear of tight spaces? The presence of such a man could jeopardize the mission.'

'I am no coward,' came the reply.

'That was not my question,' said the Old Wolf. 'Such fears are instinctual and not a matter of cowardice. I have known brave men who cannot bear high places, for instance. It is no cause for shame. The shame, and the cowardice, would be in refusing to admit to a fear over which one has no control. So I ask you again, sir, and advise you to reply with care: will you be able to keep your wits about you down there in the dark?'

'I will,' said Malrubius.

'So be it,' said the Old Wolf. 'I take you at your word. But take care not to disappoint me again, Malrubius. I assure you, it will be the last time you do.'

7

Needful Things

AYLESFORD OPENED HIS EYES IN A SOFT, DRY BED, IN A ROOM WARMED BY A peaty fire. He lay without moving for a while, half asleep, remembering like the drowsy ebbing of a dream how he'd cast himself into the storm-racked sea, trusting in the power of the relic, or rather the god within the relic, to bring him safely to shore. That act of faith had been rewarded, it appeared, yet he had no memory of how he had come to be here . . . or where, for that matter, he was. Yet this caused him no anxiety; he felt sure somehow, wrapped in warm contentment as he was, that the missing details would surface as sleep receded. All he need do was wait. And it was so pleasant to wait, to drift on idle currents of fancy that barely rose to the level of thought, as if he were again a wee bairn rocked to sleep in the sweet and loving arms of the mother he had never known.

Daylight streamed through cracks in the closed shutters of the single window and past chinks in the rough stones of one wall, pooling on the packed dirt of the floor. The wind gained entry likewise, circling the room like some small curious mammal with a cold nose drawn by the warmth of the fire yet too restless to settle down. The wind outside was bigger, wilder, noisier, though also curious in its way. It moaned and whispered and sighed. It whistled and boomed and buffeted. It rubbed its flanks against the sides of the house, sharpened its claws upon the stones. It was never silent or still.

The room's ceiling was a peculiar mix of bound rushes, planks, fishing nets, and bits of stitched-together sailcloth. A spider had built a web in one corner, and evidently did not lack for flies. It hung there, patient and plump and prosperous as any innkeeper on the road to London; he felt comforted by its companionable silence, which seemed welcoming somehow. On the floor was a wooden chest – not, Aylesford saw at once, his own – and some mismatched pieces of furniture – a chair, a cabinet, a dressing table with a mirror attached (only shards of which remained in the oval frame, filled now with fractured slivers of the ceiling) – that appeared, judging from their state of general disrepair, to have been salvaged from a succession of shipwrecks.

He hurt. It was that which finally roused him from his torpor. A distant throbbing ache, like the far-away crashing of surf, uncomfortable yet soothing in its rhythmic way, was all at once too near and insistent to ignore. Suddenly there was no part of him that didn't register its painful protest. It hurt to breathe. It hurt to think. It hurt to be alive.

Wincing, and with a low, involuntary whimper such as might escape a suffering animal, Aylesford peeled back the bedclothes and regarded the naked body beneath. He felt like weeping. He did not recognize himself in this discoloured, swollen flesh, so deeply bruised, banded in livid streaks of purple, yellow, red and black. He might have been looking at the painted body of an Iroquois warrior who had fallen in battle. Like all orphans thrown to the tender mercies of their fellow men, Aylesford had received his share of beatings down the years. Maybe more than his share. But never one like this.

It was the sea had done it. That and everything preceding his final desperate leap of faith: from the battle on the beach at Hastings to the mutiny aboard the foundering *Pierre*. All had contributed a blow here, a bruise there, before the sea had taken over as if to demonstrate how it was really done. But it seemed to Aylesford that his god had also taken a hand in beating him. He had been saved, yes, but also punished. Why?

How have I failed ye? Tell me, and I'll remedy it, if I can, or pay whate'er penance ye ask o' me!

The silence was answer enough. He knew at once, and his heart sank at the knowledge.

The relic!

He had lost the relic!

He threw back his head and howled.

'Awake, are ye? Good!'

He turned, startled into silence by the vigorous, unheralded voice. The speaker had entered the room by a door that Aylesford had not noted, sunk as it was in shadow. He might have been anywhere from seventy to one hundred. His face was a weathered map of tortured lines lost amid a wild eruption of shoulder-length snow-white hair that did not appear to have ever been brushed. His beard was just as white and long and unruly, falling nearly to his waist. Twigs, grasses, and bits of food were visible there, along with assorted unidentifiable debris; indeed, Aylesford would not have been surprised to see a spider sitting in its web, or even a bird's nest.

The man was of middling height, a good five inches shorter than Aylesford, but his shoulders were unbowed, and his stout form, beneath a shirt of stained white linen, silk breeches that might once have been blue but were now as washed-out as his eggshell eyes, and torn grey stockings, seemed as vigorous as his voice. He had the look of a hermit or a madman, or both, but one who, like a monk, welcomed the hard work of every day.

'Awake and alive, God be praised,' the man continued, smiling as he approached the bed; what teeth he had were white, white as bleached shells or stones, but there were not many of them. Aylesford thought that it was not so much a mouth as the ruins of one.

'Did ye,' he asked now, pain and apprehension giving his voice a thin, querulous edge, 'happen tae find a queer relic o' sorts when ye rescued me – if, that is, ye are the one I have tae thank for fishin' me from the sea?'

'Oh, aye, that were me right enough,' said the man, who had reached the bottom of the bed; he stood there with his large, grubby hands – hands seemingly too large for his body, as if they had kept on growing after the rest of him stopped – held palm down above the bedclothes, making small circling movements as if smoothing the air, or tasting it. 'Caught ye in my nets, I did, lad, like some creature o' legend, half man and half fish, or so I thought at first, by the size o' ye!'

'What o' the relic? Did I have aught in my hands or about my person? Think, man!'

The man's brow furrowed, and he raised a dirty hand to scratch vigorously in his white mane. 'A relic, is it? What sort o' relic? Like o' a saint, d'ye mean?'

'Never ye mind what sort,' said Aylesford. 'Ye'd know it by sight.'

At which the man laughed boisterously, displaying rather more of the ruinous cavern of his mouth than Aylesford cared to see.

'Bless ye, lad,' he cried. 'That I would not do! I am blind, lad, stone blind – I could not see the relic o' a saint unless o' course it cured me.' His face took on a sudden expression of interest, almost of cunning. 'Were it that kind o' relic, d'ye reckon?'

Aylesford did not like that look. 'In point o' fact,' he said, 'it was a watch – a hunter, tae be precise. O' nae more than sentimental value.'

'There weren't no watch, lad,' said the man decisively. 'Leastways not on your person nor tangled up with ye in the net. Ye were all alone. Naked as the day ye were born. A miracle, it is, that ye survived! God be thanked for it. A shipwreck, was it?'

Aylesford nodded glumly. He believed this mad old man. The hunter was gone, lost in the storm, swallowed up in the vast expanse of the ocean. He wished that he had been swallowed along with it. 'Aye, a shipwreck. The *Pierre*, out o' Hastings. She went down with all hands – unless, that is, ye rescued anyone else, or have heard o' other survivors.' He thought of Starkey, swept off the deck as the two of them tried to make their way to one of the crew boats; if anyone could have survived that dreadful maelstrom, it would have been the resourceful and obstinate Morecockneyan.

'God rest their souls,' the man said piously, crossing himself with a single slurred motion of his right hand. 'I found no one besides yourself, lad, but I wouldn't give up hope,' he added. 'I live alone here, on my island. No one else comes here. I don't talk to no one, and no one talks to me. Might be as some o' your shipmates have found succour elsewhere. Mayhap that watch o' yours, too. Anyway, like as not it'll show up here one day, in my nets. Most needful things do, I find, if I but wait long enough.'

Aylesford felt ashamed. The man was right. He had no business giving up hope. He had been saved for a reason. His destiny was still before him. He couldn't quit now.

'I need to get off this island,' he said.

'Not so fast, lad,' said the man. 'I pulled ye from the sea, true enough, but the sea is not done with ye yet.'

'What nonsense is this?' demanded Aylesford.

'A man can drown on dry land, lad, never doubt it! I have known it to happen many a time. A man is pulled half-drowned from the sea. High and dry he is, or thinks himself to be. Thanks God for a narrow escape. A week later, he is in the ground. Why? From the pneumonia, lad. Sea water in the lungs. That's what does it. The sea has left a bit o' herself inside him and has clawed him back. She is greedy that way, the sea. Does not easily give up what she has once laid claim to.'

'Nonsense,' Aylesford repeated. 'Why, I'm fit as a fiddle. A bit sore, I grant ye. But I am nae invalid, and I shall prove it.'

So saying, he swung his bruised legs out of bed and stood, holding the bedclothes draped around his shoulders like a cloak. The pain involved in the simple act of standing took his breath away. The bedclothes seemed to weigh a thousand pounds. His legs were trembling in a way he did not recognize. Sweat poured from every inch of his skin. It ran down his face, into his mouth, and it struck him that it was as salty and cold as the sea.

'Easy, lad, easy,' said the old man, his useless eyes darting about as if searching for their lost sight. 'What are ye about?'

'Stand aside,' he said through gritted teeth. 'I told ye I mean tae leave this island.'

'But ye can't go now,' the man protested, reaching towards him with his big blind hands, a giant's hands, slow and stupid, fingers heavy and blunt as cudgels, however kindly their intent. ''Tis madness!'

Aylesford lurched past him with a curse. His legs wavered but stayed loyal to the Jacobite cause, carrying him through the door and into the larger room beyond, which appeared to be where the old man cooked and slept. It, too, was crammed with incongruous flotsam and jetsam, but Aylesford paid none of it any heed. He spied a door that must lead outside, and he waded towards it, feeling as if the tide had come in when he was not looking and was dragging him back now, so that he had to fight for every step.

'Damn ye,' he muttered. 'I'll see ye in hell! Do ye not know who I am?'

It seemed to him that he was once again addressing Captain Bagot.

At last he reached the door. There was no sign of the Frenchman. He must have fled like the coward he was. He heard someone shouting at him in English, but he could not make out the words. Was it Starkey? A light was shining from behind the door, which was held shut by a length of rope looped around a post in the wall. It took him a few tries, but at last he got it open and stepped out into the day.

Brightness struck him like a blow. It was as if his beating were not done after all, and now the sun wanted to get a few licks in. Struck blind, he staggered and nearly fell, would have fallen if not for a strong arm suddenly bearing him up.

'I've got ye, lad.' The voice of the old man rose above the keening of gulls and the moaning of the cold wind that buffeted Aylesford from all directions, filling the bedclothes and making them snap as smartly as sails. 'Ye best come back inside and have a lie down.'

Aylesford wept from frustration and pain. He felt weak as a kitten. 'Lost,' he sobbed, clutching the bedclothes to his shivering frame. It seemed that he could hear the rattling of his bones, like dice in a cup. The sound filled him with horror. 'All lost! I dinnae want tae live!' He sagged against the old man's rigid arm.

'Belay that talk, lad. Ye've a patch o' rough seas ahead, that's all. Ye'll get through 'em all right, if ye behave sensible like and take to bed.'

He nodded bitterly, less in agreement than defeat. He could fight no longer. His vision, clearing at last, showed him for the first time something of his surroundings: a flat, windswept, dull green sod littered with lichen-covered rocks and scrub brush extending to an abrupt horizon, beyond and far below which the vacant blue-grey sea heaved and spangled like the flexing coils of a huge serpent, here and there feathered with thin lines of white ruff, delicate as cloud. Gulls scythed the air or soared on outstretched prayerful wings. The plateau – for so Aylesford judged it: a flat column jutting starkly up from the sea – was crisscrossed by lengths of rope threaded through eyelets bored into wooden posts that had been sunk into the ground, and which made convenient perches for gulls. The taut ropes hummed and sang in the wind, rattling against the eyelets in the wood, and it was this sound, he realized with a feeling of relief so welcome it brought a smile to his lips, that he had taken for the rattling of his bones. It was the last rational thought he was to have for a very long time.

Later, Aylesford was able to calculate that he had lain abed in the stone hut for nearly three weeks before his fever broke and reason began a fitful return. It was another two weeks of slow recuperation before he felt himself able to try to leave the island. During this time, and for those first three weeks especially, he did not feel himself to be in the world at all. At least, not in any world he knew. It was, instead, a world cut loose from time and space as he understood them, in which the past mingled promiscuously with the present, memories consorted with dreams, and dreams bled over into hallucinations that were indistinguishable from reality, assuming such a thing existed any longer, which he tended very much to doubt. It was a world governed by no natural law but rather the fancies and fears and perverse imaginings of a madman.

He might, for instance, be conversing with Starkey in a bouncing carriage one minute, only to find himself in bed the next, looking by moonlight into the wide eyes of Arabella, the barmaid, while plunging his knife between the shoulder blades of Daniel Quare, who turns to him then with a hideous smile and smothers his screaming mouth with his own.

Or he might be back aboard the *Pierre*, not as that ship had been when he had so briefly known her but as she is now, sunk at the bottom of the Channel. He has been pulled down with her, tangled in a hawser, and he drifts there, at the mercy of secret tides and currents, nibbled upon by eels and fishes, the corpses of the crew surrounding him in companionable silence – what, after all, remains to be said between them? They are all friends now, even Captain Bagot, restored posthumously to command . . . And there, again, is Starkey, his darting glance made of darting silver fish, an eel for a tongue, motioning him closer with the lazy crook of one half-severed finger, as if eager to impart a confidence, or more likely a cynical, sardonic joke, which he bends obligingly to hear, only to find himself facing Grimalkin, who without a word stabs him through the heart, at which he wakes screaming into the small room with its peat fire and watchful corner spider that now begins to move towards him, a spider with a human head and a wild mane of white hair.

Or he is a boy again, lying limp as a drowned thing beneath the alternating thrusts and grunting prayers of Father Aylesford, like being simultaneously fucked and catechized, smelling the whisky on the priest's hot breath and feeling himself split open by the steel of his erection and wondering if there will be blood this time, dreaming meanwhile of the day that he will slit the priest's throat like the whoreson pig he is, and suddenly reliving that day, or living it for the first time, the old man sprawled in the confessional, head thrown back in bliss and cassock raised to give prodigal Aylesford easy access to the fatted calf between his legs . . . *Nay, nay, it did nae happen so!* But perhaps it did, after all, and anyway didn't a part of him wish it had, hadn't he in fact, as the priest always claimed, led him on with his wickedness?

Ye'll end up in hell, sure enough, Thomas Aylesford. It's roasted by devils on a spit ye'll be!

That was it, surely. He was in hell, literally in hell, suffering torments that he richly deserved, punished by the god within the relic, whose express commands he had failed to follow, whose trust he had betrayed. To the extent that he was able to reflect on what was happening to him, Aylesford gave himself up to the punishment gladly, with a heart full of repentance, though he had neither expectation nor hope of forgiveness.

But mostly he was not able to reflect, but only to experience. And what he mostly experienced was stark unreasoning terror. The same basic situations repeated themselves over and over again, only with infinite sadistic variations, so that he never knew what to expect, was never able to let himself be lulled by the familiar unfolding of dream or memory or hallucination or whatever it was, could not take comfort in the sameness of even the most awful of them, with Father Aylesford, for example. One might think the actual event, or rather the memory of it, bad enough to satisfy any god or devil intent on making a man suffer for eternity. But apparently not, for he might look over his shoulder while being buggered to see his own face leering back at him rather than that of the priest, or perhaps the face of Daniel Quare, or Starkey, or Captain Bagot, or Grimalkin, or even the old man who had rescued him, so that he wondered in some cool cellar of his mind whether this wasn't happening to him now, in the stone room with the peat fire and the watchful spider whose presence no longer seemed quite as welcoming or companionable as it once had. And sometimes it was he who was fucking the priest in the arse, and it would be the priest who looked back, tongue out like a panting dog's, his throat slit like a pig's. Or he might see his own face there, or Quare's face, or that of the white-haired old man, suddenly obscenely fat, his rolls of wet slapping flesh threatening to swallow Aylesford up, suck him down, drown him like a sailor in the sea.

The most terrible of all, however, was one that didn't involve him directly. He was not a participant but an observer, watching from somewhere out of the scene as Quare's severed hand, still holding the hunter, which shone with a faint blue light, crawled along the ocean floor like some ghastly glowing crustacean. It seemed to be looking for him, and for some reason, though he mourned the loss of the relic and wished for nothing more than to get it back, the sense he had was not that of being reunited with a beloved or valued object but instead that of being the prey of a remorseless hunter. Yes, that was it: the thing was hunting him. It crept across the graveyard floor of the Channel with excruciating slowness, dragging itself along with what fingers it could, while gripping the hunter with the others, pausing every so often as if to satisfy itself somehow that he was not near, perhaps orienting itself with the watch, using it as a kind of compass, a compass whose true north was himself. It did not speak to him in the dream, if it were a dream, as it had spoken to him before. It did not seem to be aware of him watching, but only of his presence somewhere ahead, drawing it inexorably on. And he did not call out to it, either, or attempt to draw its attention in any way, but rather held himself motionless, as quiet as quiet could be, gripped by a visceral dread so strong it was like an instinct, as if he were a rabbit hunkering down at the nearness of a wolf, until the dream, if it was a dream, passed on, and he awoke to more understandable and immediate horrors.

But at last there came a day when he looked up at the down-turned weatherbeaten face in its cowling of white hair and did not in the next heartbeat or the one after that find himself at the bottom of the sea sharing jokes with Starkey or being diddled by the dead priest or stabbed through the heart by Quare. It was as if a cool breeze had blown through his brain, sweeping its cobwebbed corners clean. Dream and memory, fact and fancy: none of that could torment him any more. He was free of all of it, blessedly free.

'Thirsty,' he managed to get out past lips that felt as if they had forgotten their use and purpose.

The old man's blind eyes seemed to lock on his at that, and he laid a big hand, the palm coarse as sailcloth, across Aylesford's forehead, an intent expression on his face, as if he were listening for strains of far-off music. 'Well, ye're back,' he said a moment later with evident satisfaction. 'The fever's broke, God be praised. Thirsty, are ye, lad? I expect ye're hungry, too.'

He ran his parched tongue over his cracked lips. 'The hunter.'

'Hunter? Oh, aye, the watch ye mentioned. Nay, lad. I've found no sign o' it in my nets or anywhere hereabouts.'

He closed his eyes, relieved. Then it had not found him. He was safe, for a while yet, anyway.

But why safe? That is nae real, but some lingerin' poison o' the fever only. I want it tae find me. I want tae be found!

So thought the rabbit cowering in its burrow.

At first he could not keep even broth down – at least not the brackish stuff brought to him by the old man, made from mussels and seaweed. Water he fared better with, though the old man doled it out stingily, explaining that there was no natural source upon the island, and he was therefore dependent upon rainwater collected in barrels, which supply he had always rationed carefully and would need to be even more sparing of now that the same amount must satisfy the needs of two men. But gradually Aylesford's stomach settled and he began to crave solid food.

The old man, who gave his name as Hubner – surname or given name, he did not say – brought cooked fish and shellfish, gull's eggs, and a flat, hard sort of bread baked from the grains of island grasses and seaweed. It was amazing how well he had adapted to life on the island, blind as he was.

'It's my home, lad,' Hubner replied with a dismissive shrug when Aylesford said as much. 'I've learned my way around, is all. Ye will, too, in time.'

'Why, I dinnae mean tae tarry here,' Aylesford said.

'No more did I,' said Hubner. 'But ye'll find it is not so easy to leave.'

'We'll see about that,' Aylesford said. 'How long have ye been here, Hubner?'

'Years, lad. In truth, I've lost count.'

'Don't ye wish tae leave? Go back tae your home?'

'This is my home,' he repeated obstinately.

Aylesford tried a different tack. 'Were ye blind when ye came here?'

The old man nodded. 'Oh, aye.'

'Were ye shipwrecked, like me?'

Hubner's normally affable features darkened at this, and he shook his head vigorously. 'I were marooned,' he said. 'Cast upon this rock and left to live or die by my own brother. 'Twere he what blinded me.'

'What happened?'

''Tis a sad story. In truth, I do not like to think o' it.'

'Do ye not crave justice? Revenge?'

'I might have dreamed o' it once, long ago. Not any more. What's the use? What's done is done. My brother is far away, beyond my reach and power. Besides, I were in the wrong. Let's talk no more o' it, lad.'

Aylesford nodded, strangely moved by the old man's words yet unsure how to respond.

'What of yourself, Tom?' For he had shared his name as well, in the course of things. 'Do ye not have a wife or sweetheart out there in the wider world? Brothers and sisters? A mother and father who love ye and e'en now do pray for your safe return?'

'I have no one,' he said. 'I never knew my parents. A priest raised me, and gave me his name, but he is dead now.'

Hubner nodded, sadly, it seemed. 'Ye're alone, then. Like me.'

'I need no one and never have,' Aylesford declared. 'I have something better than any sweetheart or mother that ever was. I have a cause, a destiny.' But then he remembered that the relic was gone. Without it, he had no cause. No destiny. He had nothing, was nothing. How had he forgotten? All the strength ran out of him, and he sank back into the soft mattress stuffed with seaweed and dried rushes, weak as a babe. He felt it shift beneath him like a raft, as if he were far indeed from dry land. 'Or thought I had . . . All of that seems so distant now, like a dream . . .'

'I've tired ye out with all this talk,' Hubner said apologetically. 'I'll let ye sleep.'

It was still there, in his dreams. Coming for him across the ocean floor.

He woke in a cold sweat, panic in his breast.

From its corner, the spider gazed patiently down, or seemed to.

'How long have I been here, Hubner?' he asked one day, when he was feeling stronger again. There was a beard on his face now, though not so thick or unruly as his host's.

The old man gave an indifferent shrug. 'One day is much the same as any other. The sun rises, it sets. The wind blows. The ocean flows. The birds fly and cry.'

258

'Have ye nae way o' keepin' a calendar? Nae clocks o' any kind?'

'Why ever should I want such things? To be reminded o' my exile, my punishment? Is it not better to live without recourse to clocks or calendars, in blessed innocence, like Adam and Eve in the Garden? What are they but chains that bind us? I've had my fill o' time! I mean to escape it, Tom.'

'Ye cannae escape time, Hubner. It'll find ye out, even here. It has turned your hair white and left its marks upon your face.'

'Has it? Then I am glad to be blind. If I cannot escape it, I will ignore it.'

'But it will nae ignore ye.'

'Why, then I'll fight it. I do fight it. Indeed,' he confided with the utmost seriousness, 'I consider myself to be at war with time.'

'Do ye now?' asked Aylesford, laughing. 'And how, pray tell, do ye wage this war?'

A sly look came over the old man's features. He leaned closer above the bed, his voice dropping to a whisper. 'Shall I tell ye?'

'I'd like tae hear it, aye.'

'I smash 'em up!' Hubner said, his ruined mouth gaping open in childlike glee.

'Smash what up?'

'Clocks, o' course! They come into my nets, ye know, from time to time.' He chuckled at this witticism. 'Everything does, sooner or later, Tom. I cannot see 'em, but I know 'em by their shape and feel, and by their sound, too, for a clock will come sealed tight in a chest betimes, dry as—'

Here he broke off, for Aylesford's hands were at his throat . . . or as near to it as they could get through the dense wilderness of beard.

'Is that what ye did tae the hunter?' he growled. 'Smashed it up?'

'Nay, nay,' the old man frantically demurred, his big hands fluttering to either side of his head like a moth's wings. 'I have not found it. I told ye so!'

'Aye, but did ye speak truly?' Aylesford gave him a shake.

'I did! I swear it!'

Aylesford released him, his strength expended. He lay back

259

wearily. 'That watch is precious tae me,' he said, half apology, half threat. 'I mean tae have it back.'

Hubner rubbed his neck. 'That was ill done, Tom,' he said reproachfully. 'To strike a blind man so.'

'I'd like tae see these nets o' yours, Hubner. I've an itch to get out o' bed and explore a bit o' the island.'

The old man brightened at this. 'Are ye strong enough?'

'In a day or two, aye,' he said.

The next day, Aylesford left the hut for the first time since his illness. The trunk containing his clothes had been lost with the *Pierre*, but there was no shortage of replacements – Hubner had enough clothing, salvaged from shipwrecks, to outfit a small army. The variety was astonishing, as if a collector had meticulously assembled a comprehensive sample of fashions worn over the past century, from the garb of common seamen to that of naval and merchant officers to that of passengers of every social class.

Yet Hubner evidently cared not a fig for any of it. The clothes, most of them badly damaged by exposure to the elements, and quite probably stripped from the drowned corpses of their original owners (Aylesford wondering briefly, with a shiver, whether he had, after all, as Hubner claimed, really arrived in his nets as naked as the day he was born, or had, instead, merely left them that way), were crammed willy-nilly into travelling chests and chests of drawers, divided between the two rooms of the hut, that had themselves been salvaged and were much the worse for wear. Hubner dressed himself, he said, from these clothes, guided by touch alone – which, thought Aylesford, explained why his outfits evidenced no harmony of style, colour, era, or condition. On more than one occasion, in fact, he had appeared in the sickroom in the clothing of a woman!

Yet as it turned out, Aylesford was able to do very little better for himself. He found linen, breeches, stockings, shirt, coat, and tricorn, even a pair of leather boots that fitted, more or less, but at the end of it, examining himself in the mirror shards of the dressing table in his room, he had to confess that he cut but a sorry sight, more jester than gentleman.

He had looked for a sword but had seen no weapons of any kind;

he wondered if Hubner had hidden them following his outburst of the previous day. Or perhaps the madman simply 'smashed 'em up', as he apparently did as a matter of course with any clocks that drifted into his nets. Aylesford decided to say nothing but to keep his eyes open. He would have a sword, if there were one to be had in this hellhole. Even a dagger would be welcome.

The bruises had by now largely faded from his skin, but much of his skin, it seemed, had followed. He was thin as a scarecrow, and felt scarcely stronger than one, which was why he wanted the reassurance of a sword at his side, even if, as he ruefully supposed, he would be incapable of wielding it with anything like his former skill.

Once dressed, he was led by Hubner – the blind leading the infirm, as he jokingly remarked, to his host's immoderate amusement – out of the hut and into a bright and bitingly cold day. The wind immediately snatched the tricorn from his head and sent it whirling away like some new breed of gull. Had Hubner not been there, grasping him by the arm, Aylesford felt certain that he would have followed, borne up into the air and carried out over the serpentine ocean languidly flexing its coils and flashing its bright scales beyond the island's severe edge. Perhaps he might even have made it to France that way, a second, more successful Icarus.

'Watch yourself, lad,' Hubner said, or rather shouted. 'The wind do like to play its tricks!'

'I'm afraid I've lost my hat,' he said as the tricorn dwindled with distance, a black speck, like a spider sailing on a silken thread to nowhere. 'Still, that's one way tae escape the island!'

'True, lad, true!' laughed Hubner. 'But it'll find its way back into my nets sooner or later just the same. All needful things do!'

'And some not sae needful, I suppose.'

'Aye, Tom. Ye have the right o' it there. Come, let's walk a while, if ye feel up to it.'

'I'd like tae see these nets o' yours, Hubner. They must be a wonder, right enough.'

'I'll take ye, never fear.'

Aylesford nodded, hunching his shoulders against the wind. His memory of standing here before was a vague one, but now it came back to him strongly as he walked beside Hubner towards a central wooden post, as tall as a man and as wide around as the trunk of a mature oak, from which a dozen or more ropes fanned out in all directions save one: that leading back to the hut from which they had come. These thick ropes, threaded through a whole network of smaller wooden posts extending into the distance, buzzed and hummed in the tireless wind, rattling against the sides of the eyelets cut into every post.

'Each one o' these ropes leads to a different part o' the island,' explained Hubner, laying a big hand against the smooth wood of the post. If Aylesford had not known he was blind, he would never have guessed it, so surely did the old man move around his hut and its immediate environs. 'They let me make my way, blind as I am, to my nets, and to other places as well.'

'Did ye make all this yourself, then?' he asked Hubner, shouting to be heard above the wind, though the man was at his side, still clutching his arm.

'Nay,' he said. 'All this were prepared and waitin' when I were set down here by my brother.'

'Thought o' everythin', did he?'

'He is a most thorough man.'

'Sounds a right bastard.'

'He left me everythin' needful to live, or the means to acquire it, save one. He did not mean me to die here but rather to live and suffer in the absence o' that one needful thing.'

'What's the one thing, then?' He smirked. 'A woman?'

'Nay. My son. He were the last thing I ever saw, but newly born. Ah, what a beauty he were! I'll never forget the sight o' him as I held him in my arms. It were more than I have words for, Tom, not in this crabbed tongue or any other. He let me drink my fill o' that sight, my brother did. Then he blinded me.'

'The blackguard! And what o' your boy, Hubner? What became o' him?'

'That only my brother knows. But he swore to me that I would not clap eyes on him ever again, nor so much as hear his voice, but it mean my own death.'

'But why? What had ye done tae make him take against ye so?'

'He blamed me for the loss o' his daughter.'

'Is she dead then?'

'I'll say no more,' Hubner said. ''Tis too painful to speak of.'

'Fair enough,' said Aylesford. 'I'll not ask again. But it's sorry I am for all o' it, Hubner. Ye've been done a terrible wrong, that's plain. I dinnae see how ye can stand it. Were ye nae tempted tae throw yourself from yon cliffs when ye first got here?'

'Aye, and many times since. But what if my boy should come, then? Or rather the man he must now be? What if he were to wash up in one o' my nets, and me not there to find him?' Tears spilled from the old man's sightless eyes; they were whisked away at once by the wind, leaving his furrowed cheeks dry.

'But is the boy nae with your brother? How should he come tae be here?'

'All needful things come here, Tom.'

'Save that one, ye said.'

'Aye, but I must have hope, mustn't I? How else could I live on this island without goin' mad or killin' myself?'

'Why, hate will serve as well as hope for that,' said Aylesford, though privately he thought it was bit late for the old man to worry about going mad. 'Many's the time I have been laid low and full o' despair, and it has been the thought o' revenge that has spurred me on.'

'Is that what drives ye now?' asked Hubner with what seemed to be genuine curiosity.

'I dinnae know,' Aylesford answered truthfully, taken aback by the question. 'I have lost somethin' I held dear, more dear tae me than aught else in the world, or so I thought. But now that it is gone . . .' He shook his head, suddenly confused and feeling near to tears himself. What was wrong with him? Was it just the sickness, or rather its after-effects? Had the fever burned something needful out of him – burned out the hate? He had been sick aboard the *Pierre* as well, he suddenly remembered. Sick not from the heaving of the sea, as he'd supposed, but from the absence of the relic, which he'd grown used to. Had this been the same thing? Not pneumonia at all but rather his body, his very soul, freeing itself of a malign influence, an evil dependency? As if from a dream, he recalled the words that Grimalkin had addressed to him on the beach at Hastings: *Already it has a claim upon you. What is left of your life will be warped by a longing that can never be fulfilled.*

'Are ye all right, lad?' came Hubner's voice.

He wiped angrily at his eyes. But this time, when he laid a hand on the old man's shoulder, there was no anger in it. 'I'll take ye with me off this island, Hubner, I swear it. Ye've saved my life twice over, and I'll nae forget it.'

'Well, as to that, lad, there's no hurry, is there, weak as ye are? Best take it day by day. The island is not goin' anywhere, nor the world beyond it. What d'ye say, then? Would ye like a look at my nets?'

'Maybe tomorrow,' he said. 'I dinnae feel up tae it just now.'

The brief excursion brought on a mild relapse, and it was not until three days later that Aylesford – wearing the same clothes as before, though hatless this time, having learned his lesson in this regard – stood with Hubner beside the central wooden post. It was another clear, cold, windy day, with clouds like high-masted schooners scudding through a sky so blue it hurt to look at. He felt strong and clear-headed, as if the last dregs of his sickness had been squeezed out of him.

For the first time, he had not dreamed of the relic. Did that mean he had escaped it? Or was it still out there somewhere, at the bottom of the broad, ever-churning sea, making its tireless way towards him like some vengeful ghost? God knew he had enough of those on his trail already! What was one more?

Why, on this last trip to England alone, he had killed at least eight men in cold blood, nine counting the priest, which had been a personal matter, ten counting Quare, who, stabbed through the heart, had perversely refused to die – protected, as he now understood, by the relic, kept alive by it against all reason, just as it had protected him, kept him alive. And if the deaths aboard the *Pierre* were added to his account . . . why, then the sea must be teeming with ghosts, whole packs of them a-hunting Thomas Aylesford!

But no – the men on the *Pierre* had been eaten by the relic's ravenous god. He'd seen their spilled blood sucked into the hunter, felt their souls pulled along as well. He need not fear those ghosts, at least. There was nothing left of them to fear. Would that have been his fate, too? The god had promised so much. *You have climbed high, Thomas Aylesford. Higher still shall you climb in my service.*

He had been chosen. He, rejected by all men, had been the one man chosen above all others! He was to be prophet and warrior both, wielding the hunter like a scythe amid the battlefields of Earth, there to reap a bloody harvest.

There is a hunger in you like a faint echo of my own. It has carved you out, made you a fit vessel for my purpose. Serve me well, and great shall be your reward, an eternity spent at the highest pitch of love's groaning ecstasy.

Eternity in love! Even now his body thrilled to the memory of the merest foretaste of divine caresses endlessly prolonged. He had lain for a brief forever in the god's all-encompassing embrace, simultaneously penetrated and penetrating, poured out and poured into, shuddering in an agony of bliss that transcended all understanding. To know that completion again, even for an instant . . . What matter if the price were another man's life, or the lives of a thousand men, ten thousand even? He would pay all that, and more. The only man's life he had ever valued was his own.

How many human beings had he cut down in his short life? Twenty? Thirty? In truth, he had lost count, just as Hubner had stopped counting all the years of his imprisonment. Those murders had taken place before he'd severed Quare's hand and thus come into possession of – or rather come to be possessed by – the relic. So it hadn't corrupted him, just made use of the man he already was: a man skilled in murder, who took pleasure in killing, however much he might tell himself the deaths were necessary, debts of honour, for instance, or orders he was duty-bound to execute, all sanctified by one cause or another, whether his own or that of the Bonnie Prince.

And was he still that man? Did he want to be?

Or had he been given a chance to change? Perhaps the old Thomas Aylesford had died on this island, or in reaching it, and the body

Hubner had fished from the sea was, like that of a newly baptized infant, washed clean of all past sins. Why not?

Maybe he could be free of all of it. Free of the hunter and the grim ecstasy of its hold on him. Free of the shining god and its sanguinary appetites, its promises and its love. Free even of himself.

Of himself most of all.

And what then? What would be left to begin again?

'As long as ye follow these ropes, ye'll come to no harm,' said Hubner, taking one of Aylesford's hands in his own and placing it on one of the ropes, thick as a hawser, slick with moisture and vibrating with a fierce intensity, as though its other end were yoked to the ocean itself, or, rather, hooked into the leviathan said to sleep fitfully in its gloomy depths, amid the forgotten foundations of the world.

'And do ye have the map o' it all in your mind?' asked Aylesford.

'Aye, that I do, lad,' said Hubner. 'And a right tangled map it be! Why, many a time, in my first days and weeks here, before I had freed myself o' the foul habit o' keepin' track o' such things, I would lose my way, mixin' up one line with another, and that with another still, until I were turned all about, mayhap even hangin' upside-down for all I knew, a sorry spider lost in its own web! Sometimes I would not find my way back home for days, as drenched and miserable as if I had crawled up from the bottom o' the sea!' He shook his head and chuckled as at some fond reminiscence, as people do when recollecting trying circumstances from a safe distance. 'O' course, ye'll not have such troubles yourself, Tom, blessed as ye are with the sight God gave ye.'

'I shall be glad o' 'em all the same,' said Aylesford. 'They will give me somethin' tae grab on tae in this damned whoreson wind.'

Hubner laughed outright at this. 'Why, this be but the most gentle o' zephyrs compared to what ye might call a real wind hereabouts, Tom. Aye, when such winds do blow, ye'll need these ropes for sure if ye venture out o' doors. The most sensible course then be to stay inside, or get there as quick as ever ye can, for ye do not want to be caught out in a real blow, by which I mean a storm like the one what sank your ship and brought ye here.'

266

'Do ye have much warnin' o' such storms, then?'

'Oh, aye, warnin' enough. I can feel a storm comin' on in the twitch and wiggle o' these ropes. And hear it in the keenin' o' the gulls – for the birds are the wisest o' all God's creatures in the ways o' weather, bein' closest to heaven as they are. Even the wind itself do give fair notice to them what knows what to listen for. But ye have not the ears for it, lad, listen howe'er ye will. Until ye learn, I will be your ears and give ye what warnin' I can.'

Hubner indicated a particular strand, and this they began to follow. It led straight across the top of the plateau, effectively bisecting it, heading for what Aylesford, from his starting perspective, had assumed to be the edge of a high cliff overlooking the ocean. At intervals along the way, other strands branched out, skilfully woven into the original, so that it seemed they were traversing a gigantic net that had been laid down over the entirety of the island. He marvelled more than ever at the sheer scope of the construction, and at its flawless execution: all testimony to the character of the man responsible: Hubner's brother, architect of an appalling revenge.

Aylesford found he hated this man not only for what he had done to Hubner but because he, Aylesford, had become entangled, through no fault of his own, in the sadistic web. He meant to get out, one way or another, and to take Hubner with him. And if Hubner's brother got in the way . . . well, he wouldn't shed any tears over one more body added to his count. Not many men merited murder as much as this one did. To keep a man from his son . . . To steal him away, raise him up in ignorance of his true self . . .

He felt a connection to Hubner's son, though of course his own situation was quite different. He had never thought the priest was his true father, for instance, as Hubner's boy no doubt believed about his uncle, and he knew that his parents had not wanted him, for they had given him to the church, as indeed happened with many unwanted children. His own story was ordinary enough. But all the same, he felt for the boy, and for his father, too. They were like two sides of himself.

The rope reached its terminus in a wooden post sunk into the stony ground; a big grey and white gull perched there, eyeing them contemptuously, but flew off as they approached, dropping precipitously out of sight. Two more ropes emerged from the post, to the left and right, running along the edge of the plateau and thus constituting a railing of sorts. From this vantage, the wind gusting stronger than ever, as if seeking to shove him over the edge, Aylesford, hands clutching the taut rope for dear life, saw that his original surmise – that the plateau ended abruptly in high cliffs towering above the ocean – was accurate enough yet at the same time pathetically inadequate.

They seemed to be at least a mile above the water. It was difficult to judge the distance more precisely, however, because the drop was so sheer, and nothing grew along the face of the cliffs but a few hardy shrubs that had somehow taken root in crevices and clung there as obstinately as barnacles. Though when he looked more closely, or tried to, it seemed to him equally likely that they were huge trees dwarfed by the blank expanse of surrounding stone. The base of the island was lost in a pale misty haze thrown up by the constant crashing of surf against the rocks, whose booming reached Aylesford like the beating of a monstrous heart. Farther out, the sea rolled on and on in its immense and awful monotony, utterly empty of any sail. Nor was there so much as a hint of land.

The cliffs extended to the left and right, gently curving out of sight after what he guessed to be a few miles. He wondered what the circumference of the island was, and if he could walk around it.

'Does the rope encompass the whole island?'

'Aye, it does,' answered Hubner, his hair and beard flapping wildly, as if they might tear themselves loose. 'Ye can walk it in a day.'

'I have never heard o' any island like this,' he said. 'With walls so sheer and high.'

'Is it very high, then?' asked Hubner with interest. 'I thought it might be. Aye, it has the sound o' it.'

'We are a mile up, or more. Indeed, there are clouds below us, or so it seems! Why, we might be on Olympus itself!'

'Where, then, are the gods, lad? They seem to have forsaken us.'

'Aye, 'tis a forsaken place, true enough. I would sooner expect tae find the bones o' a dead god here than tae meet a livin' one. Your

268

brother could nae have devised a more hellish prison if he had built it himself.'

'He has a nose for such places. They remind him o' himself.'

'What is his name?'

'He goes by many names. I do not know what he may call himself today. Keep clear o' him, Tom, if ye can.'

'Mayhap it's he who should be keepin' clear o' me.'

Hubner smiled at this, but there was no humour in it. 'Do ye think ye'd fare any better against him than I did?'

'He's older now.'

'Aye, he is that. But age does not always mean weakness or infirmity. My brother is no ordinary man.'

'Why, neither am I, as it happens. There be more tae me than meets the eye, Hubner.'

'I'm afraid I'll have to take your word for that, lad.'

Hubner conducted him along the rightward strand for a few hundred yards, past three branching points, then took the fourth. From there the ground began to slope gradually downward; this declivity grew steadily steeper, the walls rising up until they were above Aylesford's head, the sky a narrowing sliver between. The wooden posts gave way to iron bars hammered at regular intervals into the stone face of one wall; the rope continued smoothly and without interruption from the former to the latter, still at the height of Aylesford's waist: chest-high on the old man. The wind was louder but less forceful. The light faded by slow degrees to a dingy gloaming. Then all at once the open space overhead was gone, and with it the light. They had entered a cave.

'I dinnae suppose ye have any torches?' Aylesford asked, halting.

Laughter barked and echoed out of the dark. 'Nay, lad! Ye'll have to make your way as best ye can, just as I must do.'

'Is the whole island filled with such caves and passages as this, then?'

'Aye, it is. But remember to keep hold o' the rope, Tom, for ye do not want to stray. Your sight will not help ye here.'

'I shall make some torches that I may explore these tunnels.'

'If ye like.'

A thought suddenly occurred to him. 'What o' the nets? Will I be able tae see 'em?'

'Why, do ye know, I cannot say!' Hubner sounded more amused than upset. 'I confess I did not consider the question until now. After all, no one has ever come here before but me.'

'Have ye not fished other men out o' the sea?'

'Aye, I have – but she has always clawed 'em back.'

'Ye mean I am the first tae live?'

'Aye, lad, ye are. Well, would ye like to go on?'

'I'd best make some torches first, I suppose,' Aylesford said after a moment's thought, though in truth he hated to turn back. But he didn't want to get to the end of this passage only to find himself still in the dark, which seemed all too likely. He berated himself for not having thought of this trivial but essential detail. He should have quizzed Hubner more thoroughly about their route; had he done so, he would be prepared now. It appeared he had not recovered as fully as he wanted to believe. The sea might claw him back yet if he were not careful.

'I'll show ye more o' the top o' things, then, shall I?' asked Hubner.

'Aye, we've light enough for that, I suppose.'

They retraced their steps. As Aylesford emerged out of the furrow in the ground, he marvelled at how well concealed it was. From just a few feet away, there was no hint that the slight slope might lead any deeper into the earth, much less to a cave. Looking around – one hand on the thrumming rope at his side while, before him, Hubner trudged ahead as stolidly and timidly as a turtle – it struck him that there were dozens of such declivities in the immediate area, visible only because he could trace the descent and disappearance of the ropes that had been strung so meticulously to help Hubner find his way. It seemed impossible that nature could have constructed such a landscape. Yet even more impossible to seriously entertain was the idea that the landscape was an artificial one, the gentle furrows as much the cunning product of human effort as the system of ropes that, as it were, had caught the whole island in a net. No man, not even Hubner's mysterious brother, for all his evident wealth and power, could transform the surface of a barren island plateau this way. The engineers of Versailles could not have done it. And yet, Aylesford reasoned, if the declivities had been cut with the art and purpose that they appeared to exhibit, then what of the caves they led to? What of the tunnels that Hubner had spoken of, leading downward to his nets?

What of the island itself, rearing a mile high out of the sea? Would not such an island be the wonder of the world? It would be visible, he thought, from the coast of England. And yet it was not visible. It was not spoken of. He felt very certain of a sudden that it was not to be found on any charts of the Royal Navy.

But this was not the strangest and most unsettling aspect of the matter. For even supposing that the island and everything on it had been built by human hands – never mind whose, exactly – that did not in itself answer the question of why.

Aylesford kept these ruminations to himself – in truth, he preferred to forget them, so disturbing were they, enough to make him question his sanity and thus call into further doubt the extent of his recovery – while Hubner conducted him over more of the island's surface.

As there was not daylight enough to walk the whole perimeter, they cut across the island instead, moving from the east side – to judge by the sun – to the west. Later, back in the warmth and safety of the hut, he would estimate that their journey had taken three hours or so – again to judge by the sun, for there was no other means available to Aylesford for assessing the passage of time – and that the island, at the point of their crossing, measured somewhere in the vicinity of seven miles wide. He could have covered this distance much more quickly, of course, had he not been forced to proceed at the snail's pace set by Hubner. Or perhaps not.

In any case, it was fascinating, if frustrating, to watch the old man navigate his way around the island. Whereas within the confines of his home, and in its immediate environs, he moved with an easy assurance that would have fooled all but the most acute observer into believing him sighted, once forced to rely upon the system of ropes his movements became tentative and slow, as if he did not trust the ropes to take him to the same places they always had in the past, the map in his mind no longer congruent with the world outside it. A fearful expression played continuously over his features. He seemed to be straining with every remaining sense to detect something – perhaps the first faint warning of an imminent storm. Whenever they reached a branching point, Hubner would stop, and his blunt fingers would quest along the surface of the ropes in all possible directions, like blind insects, before he decided, with every indication of deep misgiving, upon the route. This was sheer torture to observe, for Aylesford could see that the way before them was as safe and diligently roped as that behind.

'I can see the way plain, Hubner,' he said once. 'Take my arm and I'll lead ye.'

'Nay, lad,' said Hubner from out of his windblown mane in a voice that brooked no argument. 'We must keep to the ropes.'

Only when the two men stopped to rest, or to answer the call of nature, or to sip sparingly from a water skin the old man carried, did Hubner emerge from the shell of his tortoise-like concentration.

There was scant variety in the terrain they covered. Mile after mile of the same flat, peaty sod, strewn with lichen-covered rocks and stones, with small stands of stunted, scraggly bushes sprouting here and there as if seeking comfort in numbers and not finding it. There were no trees at all.

'Are there nae other creatures here?' asked Aylesford. 'Apart from the birds, I mean.'

'Nay, Tom. Not so much as a mouse.'

'Dae ye nae find that odd?'

'Odd? How d'ye mean?'

'I should have thought there would be mice at least. And rats. Men fetch along suchlike willy-nilly when they come tae a place. Why, the island should be rife with 'em!'

''Tis a hard place,' said Hubner with a shrug.

'What o' your nets, then? Have ye nae found such things in your nets betimes, clingin' tae the wreckage o' a ship?'

272

'Oh, aye, that I have,' said Hubner. 'I do find all manner o' creatures.'

'Well, then,' said Aylesford. 'What becomes o' these creatures?'

'I eats 'em, o' course.'

'But ye cannae eat 'em all, surely!'

'I gets hungry,' said Hubner, and grinned his gap-toothed grin.

'E'en so,' Aylesford persisted, looking away, unsettled by the sight of that ruined mouth, 'blind as ye are, some must escape ye.'

'I gets *very* hungry,' was the reply, and Aylesford decided to drop the matter.

After an hour or so, a grey-green bulge appeared on the horizon, and this bulge grew slowly as they approached, resolving finally into a hill – the only one that Aylesford had yet seen on the island.

'Why, there be a hill ahead!' he exclaimed when it was still far off; the sense of novelty was such as might better have befitted a mountain.

Hubner stopped. 'Aye, 'tis the highest spot on the island.'

'What is that upon the crest? I cannae make it out. Ruins, is it?'

'Stones,' said Hubner. 'A circle o' standin' stones set upon the brow o' the hill like a kind o' crown. Who set it there, and for what purpose, I cannot say. It were here when I arrived, and I dare say it will be here when I am gone. What are ye about now?'

For Aylesford had ducked beneath the rope and was loping across the open ground beyond. 'I'm for a closer look,' he called as he ran.

'The ropes'll bring ye!' the old man cried. 'Come back, lad! Keep to the ropes!'

'I'll meet ye there!' he shouted, then ignored the old man's continued exhortations to return. Soon enough, his frantic cries were lost in the wind.

God, it felt good to run, his shadow stretched out before him, leading the way! How long had it been since he'd done aught but creep along like a bug? Not since the beach at Hastings had he stretched his legs like this, and there he'd been driven by sheer panic, desperate to escape death or capture. Now he ran not away but towards something that tugged at him with a kind of familiarity almost, as if he knew it from somewhere, had seen it, or something like it, before. But he couldn't remember. He needed to get closer, to climb the hill and stand among the stones he could see more clearly now, vertical slabs arranged in a rough circle, some of them fallen, leaving gaps like those between the teeth in Hubner's cratered mouth. Yet here, too, it was plain how far he had yet to travel on the road to recovery, for in no time at all he was out of breath, his heart flopping like a fish out of water, as if he'd run for miles and not a couple of hundred yards at most. *I'm nae the man I was,* he thought grimly, slowing to a walk, half bent, one arm clenched to his heaving sides. *Or e'en half that man.*

He heard it first, a rush and rumble in the air, like an avalanche tumbling down upon him from out of the clouds. Then he saw its shadow gliding across the uneven ground before him, a dark undulant ribbon that flowed like water, as if a river in raging flood were pouring down the slope of the sky. He turned; he couldn't help turning; he was small and afraid and helpless in the face of whatever it was. But he saw nothing. Perhaps the faintest ripple in the air. And then, with a roar, it was upon him.

He was engulfed in noise and movement, bowled off his feet, swept up into the air for all he knew. He could see nothing but smeared shapes and colours, as if everything were happening at a fantastic speed, faster than human sight could follow or thought contain. Airy coils enwrapped him, went slithering by, the feel of them slick yet dry, passing him in windy loops as if through a flexing tube or tunnel, until he emerged or rather was expelled onto the hard ground, where he lay gasping for breath, racked with shudders. His clothes were shredded, his senses likewise in tatters. He turned on his side and vomited as if he might turn himself inside out and find some shelter there.

A booming overhead drew his attention. There it was again, that impossible flicker or ripple of light, vanished in the very instant of seeing it. But the ground displayed what the sky concealed: a shadow like the shed skin of some airborne serpent lazily drifting earthward. It was coming for him again.

Aylesford scrambled to his feet, desperately looking for shelter.

There was a length of rope a hundred feet away. He made for this at a dead run, hearing the dreadful thunder at his back, buffeted by gusts of hot air. He lunged for the rope, fell upon it like a drowning man upon a lifeline, clung to it with every drop of strength remaining in him.

The roar was as loud and encompassing as before, but this time whatever made it did not swallow him; instead, he felt it veer aside. The fierce wind of its passage drove him to his knees but did not break his fiercer hold upon the rope. Then it was gone, booming back into the sky, into the highest canyons of the clouds.

He was still hunched there, shivering, afraid to so much as raise a finger, when Hubner reached him.

'Are ye hurt, lad?' the old man called as he drew near, hauling himself hand over hand along the rope as slowly and deliberately as if hoisting himself above the deck of a pitching ship. Aylesford fully understood his caution now.

'What was that thing?' he whispered, afraid even to raise his voice.

'I told ye to keep to the rope! I warned ye!'

'Ye might have mentioned the consequences o' failin' tae heed that warnin'!'

'Would ye have believed me if I had?'

Aylesford grimaced and spat. 'Believed ye? I scarce believe it myself, or know what it is I'm not believin'!'

'Did ye see it, then?' Hubner inquired keenly.

'I saw nowt,' said Aylesford. 'Only a writhin' shadow upon the ground. But nothin' o' what cast it.'

''Tis the guardian o' this place,' the old man confided. 'The warder o' this prison, placed here by my brother to enforce his will. Watcher o' the skies, I call it. If ye keep to the ropes, it will not trouble ye.'

Aylesford shook his head as if to clear it. 'How came your brother tae have command o' this demon, for such it must be – there is nae creature like it on God's earth, I'll warrant.'

'I told ye, my brother is no ordinary man.'

'Is he a man at all is what I'm wonderin'! I'm thinkin' that this is no more an ordinary island than your brother is an ordinary man.'

'Aye, ye have the right o' it, Tom. 'Tis an unnatural place. A conjuration o' the blackest magic. A place o' torments devised for the punishment o' one man.'

'Conjured by who – your brother?'

'Aye. Or infernal powers subject to his will. 'Tis much the same.'

Aylesford was silent for a moment. Then: 'D'ye know what else I'm thinkin', Hubner?'

'Nay, what?'

'I'm thinkin' that if there is aught else ye have omitted tae mention, 'tis now ye might be mentionin' it!'

Hubner frowned as if thinking deeply. Finally he shook his head. 'Ye know everything now.'

'Nae more nasty secrets? Nae more unpleasant surprises? Nae more beasties skulkin' aboot? Is it certain ye are, now?'

'Nay, I swear it. But now ye know why there is no escapin' this island. Ye asked me if I'd ever thought o' pitchin' myself o'er the cliffs – I've more than thought it, lad. I've done it a dozen times or more. But that damned thing will not let me fall.'

'The watcher o' the skies,' Aylesford said bitterly, like a curse, looking up fearfully meanwhile for any sign of the thing. But he saw nothing, just the first blush of sunset bruising the soft white undersides of the clouds.

As Aylesford lay abed that night in his dark and toasty room, listening rather more alertly than in past nights to the noisy coursing and carousing of the wind, it suddenly came to him why the circle of stones atop the hill – which he had never reached, insisting instead that Hubner lead him directly home while there was yet light enough to see by – had struck him as such a familiar sight, and moreover had exerted such an irresistible attraction, drawing him towards it like a moth to a flame.

He had visited that hill, or one very much like it, in the vision vouchsafed him by the god within the hunter. In that vision, he had climbed a hill crowned by a circle of strangely shaped standing stones. There, floating above the stones, had been a silvery orb whose pale, flat, moonish surface had shimmered like a puddle of water reflecting the moon. From out of that orb, the god had addressed him. And more than that. It had reached out to him and swallowed him up, sucked him into itself.

When it had done so, Aylesford had realized, or rather understood, that the vision was more than just a vision. It was as real as anything, or actually quite a bit realer, and just as the vision was taking place within his mind, so, too, was his mind somehow being held inside the hunter that was itself held in the stony grasp of Quare's severed hand. It was there, in that infinite inner space, where reality was no more nor less than the god's will made manifest, that the god had revealed its plans for Aylesford, giving him a taste of the eternal bliss that awaited him upon the successful completion of his labours, before expelling him rudely back into the outer world.

Now, lying in the double darkness, as it were, of room and mind, it occurred to Aylesford that the reason he had seen the hill of standing stones upon the island was quite simply that the island – which obviously existed nowhere on Earth, as he had reasoned out for himself earlier in the day; though, badly shaken by this deduction, he had failed to follow the chain of logic to its inevitable conclusion until now – *existed within the hunter.*

Which meant that he had not lost the relic at all.

Instead, the relic had consumed him.

That was how the god had saved him after he had flung himself into the sea.

By swallowing him, as the whale had swallowed Jonah.

All of this – the island, Hubner, the watcher of the skies, the hill with its crown of stones, all of it – had been created by the god on his, Aylesford's, behalf . . . just as Hubner believed that the island had been created by his brother on his, Hubner's, behalf. It was dizzying to contemplate, like a hall of mirrors endlessly reflecting each other, and not just mirrors but warped or shattered ones, so that they distorted their own reflections, and then further distorted those reflections, over and over again, for ever and ever.

Reflections . . . yet as real as the god could make them. Which was as real as real could be. And yet everything here was not equally real, or, rather, not real in the same way. Aylesford was different. He knew, as Hubner presumably did not, could not, that Hubner and everything else here was the creation of the god within the hunter. Everything but Aylesford, because he came from the world outside the hunter, and would presumably be returned there, for it was that world, Aylesford's world, that the god had chosen to be born into, hatching out of the egg of the hunter, and it was Aylesford's task to prepare the way for that divine birth, by providing the hunter with everything needful for its incarnation.

But Aylesford had not been returned to the outer world. Instead, he remained trapped within the inner one. Trapped within the hunter.

Why?

Perhaps because the god could not yet return him. He had dreamed of the relic dragging itself across the ocean floor, and though the dream had not recurred for some days now, could it not have been a true glimpse of things? In that case, the god could not return him to the world until it reached dry land; otherwise Aylesford would drown.

But as he considered this, tossing and turning in his bed, tangling himself in mad loops of fevered logic, he decided it made no sense. If the god could protect Quare from a dagger thrust to the heart, then surely it could protect Aylesford from drowning. No, the god had not needed to draw Aylesford into its shell to save him – he saw that now. If he had been drawn bodily into the hunter, as he no longer doubted, then there must have been another reason for it. And that reason was not hard to find.

The island was not a prison devised by one man for the punishment of another.

It was a prison devised by the god for the punishment of Aylesford.

He must be blind as Hubner not to have seen it before now!

He had failed or displeased the god in some way, and the god had made the island, and everything on the island, from Hubner to the watcher of the skies, to punish him for that offence.

But not just to punish him. He had not been put here merely to suffer. He had to believe that. The god was testing him. Teaching him. Yes, there was a purpose to these torments – the seemingly endless parade of horrors, in sickness and in health, each worse than the last. It was all meant to teach him a lesson. If he failed, he would remain here for ever. But if he passed, he would be returned to the world, having proved himself worthy to serve the god.

It was the hill with its crown of standing stones that convinced him, that gave him hope of escape. For that detail could only have been placed here to awaken Aylesford to the truth of his situation. And while that awakening no doubt was meant to serve as a refinement of his punishment, one more twisted reflection in that cruel hall of bent and shattered mirrors, it also served to remind him of all that the god had promised.

But what was he supposed to learn?

And how had he offended the god in the first place?

Maybe that was it, he thought. Maybe he needed to understand his sin before he could begin to atone for it.

And not until he had atoned would he be set free.

Set free to serve the god.

But did he, any longer, wish to serve? When he had awakened here, believing himself saved, he'd thought the relic lost. He'd grieved that loss with a grief beyond anything his crabbed life had prepared him to feel. It had ripped something out of the heart of him. Yet at the same time, and increasingly over the days and weeks that followed, he'd felt relieved to be rid of it. As if he'd been given a chance to start over, to become a different man, a better man.

Aylesford was not yet that man. He knew that. But neither was he the other. Not any more. He had changed. Even locked within the prison of the hunter, he had drifted away from the god. Perhaps that was his sin. Not something he had done or failed to do but instead that potential for change. Perhaps the god had sensed that potential in him, sniffed it out, and had decided to put him to the test now, rather than risk it happening later. Perhaps Aylesford, like any good sword, required tempering.

Now he must either break or emerge stronger than before. And to emerge stronger could not be to forsake the god. Thus it seemed to Aylesford that if he wished to escape the island and return to the world, his world, he must first find his way back to the god. He must become again the man he had been. The murderer.

And how could he do that? Why, there was but one way, as obvious as it was terrible to contemplate. There was, after all, only one other person on the island.

Hubner.

He must murder Hubner, the man who had saved him, whom he, in turn, had sworn to bring safely off the island. That was the test set him by the god.

The logic seemed unassailable as he lay there in the darkness. Again and again, Aylesford tried to knock it down. But it withstood every assault.

Yet why should he hesitate? Why feel guilty? Hubner had been created by the god to serve this purpose, had he not? He had been made in order that Aylesford might murder him. That was the meaning and purpose of his life. What did it matter if Hubner understood this, so long as Aylesford did? What matter if he had memories of his own, memories of a life as real to him as Aylesford's life was to Aylesford, a life filled with event and emotion, a son he had loved and lost, and mourned still, a niece whose loss was also to be mourned, a brother whose trust he had betrayed, it seemed, and whose righteous wrath must be stoically endured?

As real as all of that was, it was indisputably less real than Aylesford, because none of it existed outside the world within the hunter, as he did. Hubner was part of the prison the god had made to hold Aylesford – a very specific part.

He was the key.

The key that would unlock the prison gates.

A key that could only be turned by murder.

Why, then, did Aylesford not rise now and creep into the next room, where Hubner lay asleep, the rattle of his snoring audible even above the wind? Why did he not pad on tiptoe up to the old man's bed and, with his two skilful hands, an assassin's clever and quiet hands, well used to such work, choke those snores into silence?

For the life of him, he could not say.

The next morning, after selecting new clothes for himself, Aylesford rummaged through Hubner's bottomless stores of salvage to fashion a dozen torches. He contrived a sack from some petticoats in which he might carry the torches slung across his shoulders and over his back. Then he took a tinderbox from a supply that Hubner kept beside his fireplace, where he did his cooking. Thus equipped, after a breakfast of gull eggs gathered by Hubner, the two men retraced their steps of the day before. This time both of them crept along the length of the rope like snails, and Aylesford's eyes kept roving across the sky, looking in vain for some sign of the watcher. A dirty tide of clouds had rolled in overnight, and a light snow was falling, the first that Aylesford had seen on the island. Whipped by the wind, the flakes stung his exposed face and hands, clung melting to his beard.

'Will there be a storm?' he wondered aloud.

'Mayhap,' said Hubner, 'but not till later – we have time enough to visit the nets.'

For that was their destination. Aylesford's assessment of the situation had not altered with the dawn, but as he had not yet been able to steel himself to the necessary action, there seemed no alternative but to accompany the old man as planned. It was not that he thought he might see or learn something thereby which would make it easier for him to act, or, on the contrary, render action unnecessary. He simply wanted to postpone the moment as long as he could, like a child who tries to put off an unpleasant duty, even knowing the delay will make that duty all the more unpleasant.

Now, following along behind Hubner's stout figure, Aylesford coldly sized him up as an adversary. Old as he was, he was hale and hearty, and he must outweigh Aylesford by fifty pounds or more – much of it muscle. If they should come to blows, Aylesford, still weak from his ordeal, was not confident in his chances, to put it mildly. Had he possessed a sword or other weapon, he would have felt more

281

sanguine. But he had no weapons – except for the cudgel-like lengths of wood he had used for the torches. A few blows to the back of the head with one of these would lay Hubner flat. The problem would be getting close enough to deliver those blows without subjecting himself to retaliation from one of the man's huge fists. He would have to strike without warning, when Hubner was unsuspecting and vulnerable, to have any real chance of success.

Is this nae such a moment? he asked himself. All Hubner's attention was focused on the rope. Aylesford was behind him, unobserved. He might easily stop long enough to take one of the torches from the sack, creep close, his movements covered by the snow and wind, and club Hubner down.

But the man's ears were so infernally sharp! To say nothing of his sense of touch. The way those blunt fingers teased out entire encyclopaedias from the slightest tremors in the ropes was positively uncanny. If he stopped now, the old man would sense it. Who would have thought it would be so damned bloody difficult to murder a blind man?

And what of the watcher in the skies? Would it allow him to kill Hubner? The watcher, like Hubner himself, was a creation of the god, which meant that its reality, like Hubner's, was subsidiary to Aylesford's. But that did not mean the watcher would not intervene if he attacked Hubner. For all Aylesford knew, the interference of the watcher was another part of the god's testing of him. And if he attacked Hubner now, in the open, and the watcher intervened, then Hubner would be alerted to his intent, and would come after him. In which case Aylesford would fail the god's test and remain here, or in some fresh and worse hell, for ever. No, this was neither the time nor the place. He would have to wait.

But even as he coldly, with professional objectivity, assessed his chances and plotted how best to maximize them, as he had done on dozens of previous occasions, for instance that London evening at the Pig and Rooster prior to neatly dispatching eight men in the confusion of a brawl instigated by himself – the very night, as it happened, that he'd met and, indeed, murdered Daniel Quare, or would have, if only Quare had had the common decency to die when stabbed through the heart like anyone else – some other part of himself, which had been silent on each of those previous occasions, now spoke up in a small voice to ask: *But what harm has he done ye, Thomas Aylesford? Why must ye kill him at all? What gives ye the right?*

And there his philosophy was silent.

Once they reached the cave, Aylesford kindled the first of the torches. The scraps of torn clothing burned with a low bluish flame that guttered in the wind but stubbornly refused to go out. The flickering light sent the shadows of the two men jumping over bare rock walls whose wind-and-water-smoothed contours glistened damply. They seemed to be grappling there, fighting hand to hand, as if the shadows were not cast by the present light but rather backward from a future already written, as it were, in stone.

'Are ye ready?' asked Hubner.

'Lead on, Hubner. I'll follow ye.'

'Keep to the rope, lad. The watcher'll come for ye as soon here as under the open sky.'

The back of the cave narrowed into a tunnel just wide enough for the two of them to walk abreast. But Aylesford, mindful of the warning, which he had not in any case needed after his experience of the previous day, stayed behind Hubner, one hand holding the torch, the other gliding along the rope that was their constant companion. Try as he might, he could glean no knowledge from the vibrations of the rope as it passed under his fingers. If there were messages there, he could not read them. The light of the torch could not dispel every darkness.

Reminded of his time in London's netherworld, Aylesford wondered again what had become of Starkey. He had grown unexpectedly fond of the acerbic Morecockneyan. He missed the man's unflappable competence. What would he have made of the island and its blind tenant, to say nothing of its swift and keen-eyed watcher?

'How far till these nets o' yours?'

''Tis a long way, lad – all the way to the bottom o' the island.'

'Did ye bring me up this way, then, after ye fished me from the sea?'

'That I did, slung o'er my shoulders like a lamb.'

'And must ye haul every bit o' salvage up the same way?'

'Aye. 'Tis hard work, and no mistake.'

They continued on, the ground sloping steadily underfoot, the tunnel zigzagging on its downward course. The first torch sputtered and went out; Aylesford lit another.

'I have heard ye mention God, Hubner.'

'Aye, why should I not? 'Tis a comfort to me.'

'Do ye pray for an end tae your torments?'

'Nay, lad. For the strength to endure 'em.'

'But ye told me ye tried tae end 'em by takin' your own life.'

'That were long ago. I do most sincerely repent o' it now.'

'What changed?'

'I did.'

'How?'

'Ye're full o' questions today, Tom.'

'I thought only tae pass the time. But if ye'd rather nae answer . . .'

'Nay, nay. How did I change? I suppose I came to understand that I had wronged my brother, and that my punishment, however harsh, is a just one.'

'Just? How can ye say so, trapped as ye are in this ungodly place!'

'God is here, Tom. Never doubt it.'

'He is a wicked god, then, tae allow such a place tae exist.'

'Merciful, rather.'

'Why, ye've been blinded by your own brother and jailed upon an island conjured up by infernal powers at his command! Where's the mercy in that?'

'My brother took my sight, but he left me my life. What is that if not mercy? And though I am blind, I have learned other ways to see. My nets do bring me every needful thing . . . but one. And I may yet have hope o' that.'

'What hope can ye have?'

'In time, perhaps, my brother will forgive me. He will free me once my penance is done, and let me know my boy. He may even

restore my sight, God willing. He may, if he chooses, restore everything I have lost.'

'I dinnae understand ye, Hubner. If ever there were a man with a
claim tae revenge in this world, it's ye. I dinnae care what ye did. Only
God himself may condemn a man tae hell. Your brother has nae the
right!'

'He does have the right.'

'Then mayhap it's tae him ye should be prayin', nae God.'

'My brother is God. Did ye not ken that, Tom?'

This reply put an end to Aylesford's questions for the moment,
and the two men continued on in silence. Was Hubner mad? Or
was it possible that, in the universe within the hunter, there could
be a small god ignorant of the existence of the larger one? What
if Hubner's brother, after all, had created the island, and everything
on it, believing he was acting out of his own omnipotent will, never
suspecting that his real purpose had been directed by another, higher
hand? The man – or god, rather – might imagine himself to be self-
created, the architect of all that was, is, and shall be . . . but that
did not change the fact that Aylesford knew better. Aylesford knew
that it was not Hubner's brother but the god within the hunter who
had created everything here, including Hubner and his brother both.
Everything but Aylesford himself.

Then Aylesford had a most disconcerting thought. One of those
revelatory thoughts that seems to lift a set of blinkers from the
mind's eye, letting in a dazzling and, in retrospect, glaringly obvious
truth.

What if Hubner's brother was the god within the hunter?

The more he considered it, the more he imagined it must be so.
Was it not neater, more parsimonious, to hypothesize the existence
of a single god, rather than a hierarchy of gods in which those below
were ignorant of those above?

And did that not explain his absence? For this, too, was part of the
test Aylesford had been set. Not only to find his way back to the god,
but to name the god.

But what, then, did that make Hubner?

Were there other gods within the hunter, a whole pantheon of which Hubner's brother was merely (merely!) the first and most powerful, like Zeus sitting at the head of the Olympians?

And if that were true, could Hubner, a lesser god of this place, be murdered by Aylesford, who was, after all, only mortal, though his origin was quite otherwise? He decided that the answer must be yes. That the god within the hunter might permit anything at all here by the exercise of his sovereign will, even the death of his brother and fellow – though inferior – god.

And indeed, that must have been his plan all along, for Hubner had, in some as yet unspecified way, sinned against his brother. Aylesford had been brought here, then, and placed on the island in order to execute the death sentence pronounced against Hubner, and, by doing so, demonstrate his worthiness to serve as the god's prophet. That was the remainder of the test.

In other words, he realized – hardly able to tell any longer whether his reasoning was sound, yet drunk on it nonetheless, carried away on its intoxicating draughts to a conclusion he could not dispute yet felt strangely hesitant to endorse, like a philosopher who has just proved the impossibility of his own existence – he had come back to his starting point. Everything had changed, yet nothing had.

But what harm has he done ye, Thomas Aylesford? asked the small voice, returning to its vexing catechism.

None.

Why must ye kill him?

Tae be free o' this hellish prison.

What gives ye the right?

The god within the hunter. 'Tis he gives me the right.

What o' the god outside the hunter? 'Tis he ye must answer tae.

Then let him free me from this cage.

Another torch had flared and died, and doens of switchbacks been put behind them, before Aylesford spoke again. 'I know ye dinnae like tae speak o' it, Hubner, but as I am a prisoner here myself, with a share in all your hardships and torments, I feel I have the right tae know. How did ye come tae earn the enmity o' your brother?'

'Nay, I'll not speak o' it, Tom. Ye'd not believe me if I did.'

'Nae believe ye! Why, after so much, is there aught I would nae believe?'

The ensuing silence stretched for so long that Aylesford took it for a rejection. But then, out of nowhere, Hubner began to speak.

'How do I appear to ye, Tom?'

'As a man o' seventy or eighty year. Blind, tae be sure. But hale and hearty as a man half that.' Though he could wish it otherwise.

'Blind I be, right enough, but in all other respects ye are wrong.'

'What d'ye mean? Wrong how?'

'For one, I am older by far than seventy or eighty, or even seven hundred and eighty.'

Aylesford's mouth had gone dry. He swallowed, but it did not help. 'Are ye then a god, like your brother?'

'Something like, aye. I was. But no longer. I am as mortal as yourself now, Tom.'

For a while, the only sounds were the moaning of the wind through the tunnel, the scrape of their boots along the ground, and the flutter of the torch in Aylesford's hand. Then: 'For one, ye said. What else?'

'I were not always as ye see me now. Once I wore a different shape. A woman's shape.' Here Hubner laughed, and to Aylesford's astonishment, he heard, or thought to hear, the trace of a woman's gay, carefree laughter buried in the sound. 'If ye'd but seen me then, lad, in all my glory! Why, there was none could hold a candle to me! Tiamat, Hesta, even Corinna – lovely as they were, I were more so. *More* – aye, that's the word. Whatsoe'er the others had, I had more o' it! My tits were bigger, my thighs bigger, my belly bigger, my cunt bigger – a man might get lost in there, as in one o' these caves, and ne'er find his way out again . . . or care to!'

More laughter followed this declaration. Not from Aylesford, though. It had begun to seem to him that not only could he hear the trace of a woman's voice braided into Hubner's but also see a woman's shape, grotesquely fat, yet somehow all the more desirable for it, cast upon the walls of the tunnel by the play of torchlight over Hubner's squat and stolid body. Indeed, it seemed to him that his shadow and that of the old man, or rather woman, were not fighting at all, as he'd earlier imagined, but rather fucking with wild abandon.

'D'ye not believe me, lad?' asked Hubner, as if offended.

Aylesford found his voice. 'I'll not call ye a liar, nae after all I've seen. But I am nae god, only a man, and such things are strange tae me.'

Hubner seemed to find this acceptable, for he continued with his story. 'My brother had a daughter, the apple o' his eye. That were Corinna, out o' Tiamat. He had decided, for reasons that are none o' your concern, to marry Corinna to a mortal man, and this man, all unknowing, were enticed across the boundary what separates the mortal world from the immortal. Now, before this time, there had been matings o' mortal and immortal, lad, but ne'er on the immortal plane – the Otherwhere. Corinna would be the first o' us Risen – for so we call ourselves, though I have been cast out and am fallen now – to lie with a mortal man in the Otherwhere and bear his child. No one, not e'en my brother, knew what the result would be. But 'twas hoped the child would prove able to restore our race to its former potency, for a sickness o' sorts had taken hold o' the Risen and were sappin' our strength and vitality. As ye might expect, it were a great honour to be chosen for this task – to be the mother o' the saviour o' our race. It were an honour I lusted after, Tom. I wanted it to be my child, my son, what saved the Risen! But my brother forbade all but Corinna from lying with the mortal, whose name were Michael Gray. Do ye know that name?'

'Nay. Should I?'

'I thought, bein' mortal, that ye might know him.'

'There are rather a lot o' us mortals,' he said. 'We dinnae all know each other.'

'Do ye not? How strange! All the Risen are known to each other. Indeed, we are all related, brothers and sisters, parents and children, though such terms are o' course but poor attempts to render into mortal tongue what cannot be so rendered.'

'O' course,' Aylesford said, feeling that he had slipped back into one of his fever dreams. Finding the activities of the shadows on the walls too disturbing to look at, he kept his eyes fixed on the mane of white hair at the back of Hubner's head, trudging along dutifully a step behind him, his left hand never lifting, even for an instant, from the rope, his right clenching the haft of the torch as if it were his own sanity.

'Ah, but he were fine to look on, were Michael Gray! I knew when I first clapped eyes on him that I would wrap him in my coils one night and compel the tribute o' his seed! Aye, I would wring the very juice out o' him! I knew I would be takin' a great risk by goin' against my brother's express command, but I couldn't help it, Tom, for I were a creature o' boundless appetites, and restraint were not in my nature.'

'So you lay with the man whom your brother had chosen to be his daughter's husband.'

'Aye, I did – and got with child by him. So did Corinna. Well, you might think if one is good, two is better. So did I think, and so did I tell my brother when his wrath fell hard upon me. But he did not listen, because by that time Corinna had fled to where he could not follow. Fled beyond his reach. Fled to her mother, his great enemy. And there she gave birth, or so I have heard, though I do not know if the child lived or died. Meanwhile, time came hard upon me, and I were delivered o' a son.'

'But how did ye end up here, Hubner, and as ye are?'

'I'll tell ye, lad, though it wring my heart. No one, not e'en my brother, knew what would happen should an immortal give birth to a mortal's child in the Otherwhere. I know not how it went with Corinna, but as for me, my immortality were shed with the afterbirth, and when I rose from my childbed, I were fixed in the shape o' a man: a mortal, though yet endowed with some shreds o' my former self, bits o' cast-off glory clingin' to me after the fall. That were when my brother reached out his hand and wrote revenge into my flesh. He made me old, he did, and ugly, as ye see me now. He took what were straight in me and bent it crooked, so that my thoughts are tangled and slow, and e'en my words come out wrong, twisted up somehow, as ugly as the rest o' me, harsh to my ears as the screechin' o' gulls. Then he blinded me and took my son away and exiled me to this island, where I have been e'er since, crawlin' along these ropes, more like a spider than a man. 'Tis a wonder I have not gone mad.'

''Tis a wonder indeed,' said Aylesford, feeling more than half mad himself. How much of Hubner's story was true? How much the ravings of a madman? And this was the test the god had set him! This the victim whose sacrifice would buy his freedom: this shattered husk, this pitiable but harmless lunatic!

'I'm sorry for ye, Hubner,' he said, and swung the torch down with all his might.

Or tried to. For it seemed that something had taken hold of his arm. He looked up wildly to see a strand of rope where there had been none before. It was looped about his wrist, holding it fast. With a choking cry, Aylesford brought his left hand to the aid of his right . . . but that, too, was caught, stuck to the rope along which it had been, until now, effortlessly gliding.

Hubner turned, his mouth spread wide in a grin that was terrible to behold, like a cave fringed with boulders, out of which a foul stench wafted. And all at once, the rest of Hubner was of a size with his hands.

The hands of a giant, or an ogre.

And he was like a spider, too, for he hung there, borne up by the same ropes that bound Aylesford, yet in no way hindered by them.

'Do ye like my nets?' he asked, and laughed, his mouth opening wider still, as if it might swallow Aylesford whole.

Aylesford screamed. Not just from the nearness of that gaping maw and its graveyard reek, but because he suddenly perceived that he had not, after all, been following the twists and turns of a tunnel cut into the solid rock of the island, as it had seemed, but instead tangling himself hopelessly in the sticky strands of a web. His feet hung above a yawning chasm, into which he could see other ropes descending until they vanished into darkness.

Nor were those ropes empty. Stuck to them was debris of every sort – the wreckage of what must have been dozens or, no, hundreds of ships . . . and all those who had sailed aboard them. Some of the latter were but skeletons now, or portions thereof. Others had the look of living men and women, though they hung as limply as the skeletons. Still others were alive, squirming in their bonds, their voices hoarse croaks, either wordless or unintelligible. Hundreds or perhaps thousands had been caught in this gruesome harvest. All without even a stitch of clothing upon them.

The torch dropped from Aylesford's nerveless fingers and fell, illuminating as it did still more of Hubner's nets. They were, he saw now, in the last feeble glow before the spinning torch winked out, sunk not in darkness but in dark waters – as if trawling tirelessly through the lightless depths of all the world's oceans to bring Hubner every needful thing.

'That were ill done, Tom,' came Hubner's voice out of the dark. 'To strike a blind man so.'

And then he cackled, as at some private joke, while Aylesford struggled fiercely but uselessly against his bonds. He did not know if he were screaming or not. There was no room in him for the awareness of anything beyond his own limitless terror. He had forgotten all that he had so painstakingly reasoned out. There was no comfort in reason now. There was no comfort anywhere. Only madness.

'Don't worry, Tom,' came the voice again. 'I'll not eat ye. Nay, I've a better use for ye. For I know ye, Thomas Aylesford. Aye, from the first I knew ye. I smelled it on ye. I smell it still! Ye have held my brother's watch, filched by his faithless daughter. And more than held it. Aye, the hunter has drunk from ye. Ye are bound to it now.'

'I dinnae have it!' he gibbered. 'I dinnae know where it is! I lost it, I told ye!'

'Hush now, lad. What's lost may be found again – why, ye never know when a lost thing may turn up! 'Tis for that reason I were set here – to comb my nets for the missin' hunter. That be my punishment. Aye, and my chance o' redemption, too! I will give ye to my brother. He will know how to reward the gift! Long has he sought the hunter. Far and wide has he bent his will towards the findin' o' it! But without a glimmer o' success . . . till now. Corinna hid it well. But now, at last, it has awakened. It has tasted human blood, and that taste has set its inner works in motion. Aye, it must run now as it were made to do; it has no more choice in the matter than an egg to hatch, a clock to chime, a man to age and die. Only them what secure a place within it will survive what is coming, Tom. They alone will be born anew in the next world, that world born free o' the taint and curse o' time! The gift o' ye will win me my place. Thanks to ye, I shall be again what I were, and more, restored to the ranks o' the Risen. For my brother will know the value o' ye. Aye, he will know how to put ye to good use.'

There followed a colossal boom Aylesford recognized with horror, and then a sensation of movement, swifter than swift, in the course of which darkness gave way suddenly to light, though a light that revealed nothing but blurred streaks of white and grey. Then he was, as he had been before, extruded. He lay on his back, blinking up into a swirl of snow, listening to the boom of the watcher returning to its home beyond the clouds. *Nae Hubner's jailer,* he realized, or rather some part of him realized, a very small part that was not either numb or screaming. *His servant.*

'Can ye stand?' came Hubner's voice.

All at once the old man was there, extending a big hand from out of the heavily falling snow. The hand caught hold of Aylesford by his coat and dragged him up with a strength he could not have resisted even in the full flush of health.

And I thought tae murder him!

The notion was so absurd that he broke into helpless laughter.

'Alas, what a noble mind is here o'erthrown,' said Hubner, again chuckling as at some purely private amusement. 'Not to worry, Tom. My brother will straighten ye out. He will make everything right.'

'What then will be left?' Aylesford inquired, giggling.

Hubner did not respond to this but instead opened that ghastly mouth of his and exhaled a roar. So gargantuan was the sound, so out of proportion to the mouth that made it, even Aylesford was shaken. The noise penetrated his madness and cowed him into silence. He looked around fearfully, flinching as the inhuman roar stretched on. It was, he thought, a sound better suited to a dragon than a man, even such a man as Hubner.

Amid the driving snow he made out the shapes of the standing stones. The watcher had brought him to the hill. It seemed to him that the stones were spinning – the entire circle rotating around them, faster and faster, like figures in a dance, until the individual stones melted into a single blurred line. Dizzied, he fell onto his backside.

A boom split the air, a crack of thunder that dwarfed the roar emerging from Hubner and made the noise of the watcher seem puny. When it had faded, Hubner had fallen silent. The only sounds were the keening of the wind and the smooth, soft, somehow soothing hiss of the snow. Aylesford noticed that he had pissed himself at some point. He began once more to giggle.

'Hush, you fool!' came Hubner's anxious voice.

'He is mad, and cannot help himself,' a new voice rang out. 'Thus he is blameless before me. I cannot say the same for you, sister.'

Hubner dropped to one knee, bowed his head. 'Brother, I give ye Thomas Aylesford, but lately the bearer o' the stolen hunter!'

'I should rather have the thing itself. Where is the hunter now?'

'It has drunk o' him – can ye not smell it?'

'I can, but what of that? I do not seek the smell.'

'Aylesford is bound to the hunter – and the hunter to him. My eyes are useless, but yours see more clearly than any o' the Risen. Look upon the face o' this mortal – mayhap ye can see written there what I cannot: the secret history o' the hunter. Mayhap there will be a trail there for ye to follow!'

'And if there is? What boon would you ask of me?'

'Why, to be restored to my former place, o' course. To be rid o' this foul, constrainin' form and be once again Inge Hubner, with hearth and home my rightful domain. To have my sight restored, and my boy.'

'What I can do, I will,' said the voice. 'I did not make you mortal, sister. That was the work of time, which you brought down upon yourself, and as such is beyond my present power to undo. Nor, for the same reason, can I make you Inge again, though I can give you a woman's form easily enough. And your sight I can restore, too, if you merit these rewards.'

'What o' my boy?'

'That is beyond me. For I have sworn an oath – perhaps you remember it.'

Hubner grew pale. 'Ye swore that I should not clap eyes on my boy again, nor so much as hear his voice, but it mean my death.'

'My will is supreme,' said the voice. 'Even I must bow to it. That is the way of things with us, sister, as you know very well, or did know, once, before you fell so low.'

'Well do I remember it,' Hubner said bitterly. 'Then one more boon would I ask o' ye, brother, and that is a place within the hunter when ye recover it. For though I be but mortal now, if it were time that did make me so, then mightn't it be that in the world to come, purged o' that vile infection, I will be restored to what I were? And mightn't it also be, in the new world, that oaths sworn in the old, e'en by such as yourself, will be naught but memories, with no more power to compel us?'

'It may be so,' said the voice. 'Or not. But you shall have a place within the ark, sister – if this mortal leads me to the hunter.'

'I can't ask no fairer than that. Come and look upon him, then, brother. Study him close.'

At this, Aylesford, lying curled and shivering in the snow like a beaten dog that has learned no reason to expect anything from the world but more beatings, saw a man appear where there had been no one before. He did not so much stride out of the snow as coalesce from it. He wore a military uniform of somewhat antiquated appearance, though Aylesford was no expert at such things even at the best of times, which this wasn't, obviously, and had a full white beard like Hubner's, only in much better trim. In fact, the man looked something like Hubner – or, rather, Hubner looked like the man, as if he had been modelled upon him. The resemblance was plain, though Hubner fell far short of the original.

Oddly, the wind did not appear to be touching the new arrival, nor the snow. He occupied a pocket of still air that the storm was helpless to perturb. His features were flushed, as if with emotion, and his eyes were the bluest that Aylesford had ever seen.

'I'm Doppler, lad,' he said. 'Don't be afraid. I just want a closer look at you.'

Nor, at that, was Aylesford any longer afraid. It wasn't the words but rather the tone of the man's voice that immediately soothed him. Had he possessed a tail, he would have wagged it, or maybe just the tip of it.

The man stepped close and looked with interest at a point between and above Aylesford's eyes. Then, unexpectedly, he began to laugh. It was deep and infectious, this laughter, utterly spontaneous, and Aylesford found himself quite unable to resist joining in, though of course he had no idea what the joke was. But he didn't care. It just felt so damn good to laugh like that, from the belly, and to hear Doppler laugh, also from the belly, but, as it were, from the belly of the whole wide world. He felt such love for him then, this blue-eyed stranger, that he would have laid down his life for him without hesitation. When he realized that he not only had an erection but was actually spurting inside his breeches, he laughed all the harder.

'What's so funny?' spluttered Hubner, who had stepped close to his brother. 'What d'ye see, brother? Is it the hunter?'

'See for yourself, sister,' he said and, reaching up, appeared to brush something off the other man's forehead.

Hubner retreated a step, as though his brother had shoved him; but he hadn't shoved him, had barely even seemed to touch him. He was blinking furiously, as if even the muted daylight suffusing the snowstorm was too bright for his eyes. Then, with one big hand upraised to ward off the worst of the snow, Hubner gazed at Aylesford. Looked long and hard. An expression of disbelief stole over his features, and he crumpled to his knees. 'No,' he croaked. ''Tis not possible . . .'

'Meet your mother, lad,' said Doppler jovially, beaming at Aylesford in a grandfatherly way.

Aylesford looked from one to the other in utter incomprehension.

'Ye did this,' Hubner said meanwhile, still on his knees, looking up at Doppler with an expression of impotent rage. 'Ye made this happen!'

'I have more important things to worry about just now, sister,' he said with a smile. 'I took your boy, but I did not keep him, for, unlike Corinna's child, he had nothing of the Otherwhere about him, but was a mere mortal. He was useless to me. So I gave him to his own kind. I did not bother to keep track of him. What would be the point?'

'But he came into my nets! Ye said that my nets would bring me every needful thing save one!'

'But I did not say what that thing was, did I, sister? You assumed it was your son. No. It was something quite other.'

'What?'

'Forgiveness.' And at that, his expression hardened. Gone was the jovial grandfather, as if he had never existed. The blue eyes that just seconds earlier had twinkled with merriment grew dead as chips of ice. 'Ye have heard his voice,' said Doppler with grim satisfaction. 'And clapped eyes on him again.'

Hubner shuddered. 'Please, brother . . .'

'Nay, sister. 'Tis out of my hands. What has been said cannot be unsaid.'

With a groan, Hubner rose to his feet and took a staggering step in Aylesford's direction, his arms held out imploringly. Aylesford cringed away.

A snowy whirlwind ghosted between them. When it lifted, there was no sign of Hubner but an impression in the snow.

'Come, lad,' said Doppler, holding out a hand to Aylesford.

Aylesford took the proffered hand in his own and was lifted to his feet.

Now he, too, stood within the bubble of still, dry air.

'What to make of you?' mused Doppler, studying him closely again. Then, without giving Aylesford a chance to reply, he touched a finger to Aylesford's forehead and seemed to scribble something there.

Madness fell from Aylesford like so many cobwebs blown away. All the events of his past life, without in any way fading from his memory, suddenly seemed but half real. He was no longer the man who had lived that life, done those things, though he still carried him inside.

'Why, ye're nae the god within the hunter,' he said.

'No, lad. I am he that made the hunter. As I made all things.'

'What is it then, the hunter?' he asked. 'And the thing inside it?'

'Imagine a ship of sorts. A ship with a mind of its own. But no captain to guide it. I am the rightful captain of that ship – that ark of a new covenant. Without me, it is but a mad thing. Mad and dangerous.'

'I served it,' he confessed. 'Willingly, I served it.'

'You chose the wrong master, nephew. Many do, and never learn to repent of it.'

'I do repent,' he said. 'Most earnestly. I would serve ye now, uncle, if I can.'

'Glad am I to hear it, for as it happens I have need of someone trustworthy here,' said Doppler. 'Here at the bottom of the world. Someone to tend the nets and all that drifts into them. Most of all, I need someone to keep an eye out for the hunter, for it will come here sooner or later, willy-nilly, as all needful things do.'

'I am your man,' said Aylesford.

'I thought you might be,' said Doppler with a wink, and strode off into the snow, which was falling more heavily than ever now.

Aylesford watched him walk between two of the standing stones, after which he did not see him any more. Then he turned and walked out of the circle in the opposite direction. He looked briefly for the impression left by Hubner's body, but he couldn't find it. The space had already been filled.

8

Wheels Within Wheels

'ALLOW ME TO CONGRATULATE YOU ON YOUR GOOD FORTUNE, *MONSIEUR l'ambassadeur*,' said the duc in his excellent English as Starkey was shown into the room.

'Good fortune?' queried – also in English – the room's sole other occupant (apart from the liveried servants positioned like pilasters along the panelled walls). This gentleman, of impressive girth and largely artificial height, wore a powdered wig whose stiff upturned curls added an extra three inches to his frame, a dazzlingly blue coat with gold braid on the sleeves, a ruffled white shirt, pale blue breeches, white stockings, and elaborate shoes whose purpose seemed more to elevate the wearer than to transport him. He stood before the roaring fire, where he had been warming himself, and gazed at Starkey with a bovine expression that suggested his question had been perfunctory and in truth he had no curiosity whatsoever about Starkey's fortune, good or bad, or, indeed, about much of anything else in the world. This, Starkey knew, though he had not met the man before, was Marshal Belle-Isle, the French minister of war, a man of serene temperament and unflappable self-regard. 'Zat is a strange zing to say of a man 'ose arm is in a sling.'

'Do you not know ze story, *mon cher*?' asked the duc de Choiseul with feigned surprise as he impatiently gestured Starkey forward with his plump hands, for all the world like a *maître d'hôtel* signalling a tardy waiter to refill a glass, and not the foreign minister of a great power. His wig was more modest than the marshal's, though even whiter; his coat was of a rich burgundy hue, with abundant gold braid. His breeches of creamy yellow and pale grey stockings enclosed plump, shapely legs of which their possessor was evidently – and quite justifiably, Starkey had to admit – proud. His small feet, like springtime flowers yet enfolded in their leaves, were shod in silk slippers of the palest green. 'Why, it is all ze talk at Versailles! Jeanne-Antoinette pronounced it *un miracle* today at her afternoon *salon*. Monsieur Starkey, you must tell it. I insist! *En français*, if you please, for *monsieur le maréchal*'s English is not so good as mine.'

Starkey smiled and sketched as gracious a bow as he could manage with his left arm, indeed, in a sling. He understood very well that the duc had absolutely no interest in his tale, no more than did Belle-Isle, but had simply wished to advertise his close friendship with Madame de Pompadour, the king's mistress, and to underscore Belle-Isle's exclusion from the innermost court circle, to which Choiseul, long a favourite of Pompadour's, belonged.

He knew, too, that there was another reason behind the duc's request – the desire seemingly lodged at birth in the breast of every Frenchman to humiliate the English at every turn. Not that he was English. Though he lived beneath that country, he was not of it, as his diplomatic credentials testified, albeit somewhat damply. But that was too fine a distinction for the duc to make. Starkey spoke English; ergo he was English. Though in point of fact, there were Englishmen aplenty who would consider his accent so barbarous as to deny that they spoke a common language at all. Of course, to a Frenchman like the duc, English was by definition a barbarous tongue no matter who spoke it or how – though presumably a French accent was the preferred method. Still, the duc knew that Starkey's French, which was serviceable enough to be sure, displayed the same accent that, so to speak, bent his English out of true. It seemed to give him a perverse satisfaction – nor was he the only one of his countrymen and women of whom this peculiarity was true – to hear his beautiful language mangled by a foreigner, and an Englishman in particular. It elevated the listener and degraded the speaker.

Life among the French could seem like little more than a succession of such petty slights and trivial cruelties, Starkey reflected, not for the first time, as he launched into his tale – one he had related so often by now, though he had been in Paris for barely two days, that he himself was already bored with it.

But no sooner had he begun than Belle-Isle, with a horrified expression, interrupted, raising a hand that dangled a white handkerchief as though in abject surrender. '*Mon dieu, monsieur!* Desist, I beg of you! Continue *en anglais, s'il vous plaît*. I had rather limp along in your language zan be a party to ze murder of mine.'

'As yer grace pleases,' said Starkey through gritted teeth while the duc looked on with beaming satisfaction, an anticipatory gleam in his dark eyes, as if things had turned out far better than he had dared dream, and he now cherished hopes that they might continue better still.

'*Monsieur le duc* is good enough ter ask about my recent crossin',' Starkey resumed, deciding *en passant*, as it were, to dash those hopes and thereby inform *monsieur le duc* that Richard Starkey was nobody's fool. ''Twere aboard the *Pierre*, a fine ship out o' Le 'avre, what lifted me and my companion, Thomas Aylesford – a Scotsman 'ose name yer grace might know, as 'e were dispatched ter England in the service o' 'is lordship the duc 'ere – from off the coast o' the town o' 'astin's. Mr Aylesford were carryin' on 'is person a watch o' sorts – but no ordinary watch, please yer grace.'

At this, Choiseul interrupted, beaming no longer, his eyes flashing. 'Zis is not to be spoken of, monsieur!'

But Belle-Isle, the wily old commander, saw his chance for a flanking action and took it. 'What is zis, *mon ami*? 'Ave you go behind my back again wiz your plots and scheme?' He wagged a scolding finger. '*Le roi* will not be please!'

'Calm yourself, *mon cher*,' responded the duc, still looking daggers at Starkey, his English deteriorating, Starkey noticed with relish, by the word. 'I 'ave go behind no back! It is *le roi* who 'ave command zis. Zis cretin' – he caught himself – 'zis Christian gentleman 'as spoke out of turn.'

'I do 'umbly beseech yer lordship's pardon,' Starkey said.

'I give you my zanks instead,' said Belle-Isle. 'Now ze cat is, 'ow you say, out of ze sack. *Monsieur l'ambassadeur*, I would 'ear more of zis watch. Unless, zat is' – addressing the duc now, his tone dripping with irony – 'ze minister of war is no longer ze minister of war. 'Ave you, perhaps, *mon ami*, a letter from *le roi* to zis effect? If so, present it, I beg you!'

'Of course it was always my intent to share zis information,' said Choiseul soothingly, regaining control of his temper and his tongue. 'But zis is not ze time or ze place. Our ozzair guests will arrive soon, *mon cher*. Let us wait till zey 'ave left. Zen you will 'ear all, I swear it.'

'Our guests are not yet arrive,' Belle-Isle pointed out after gazing about the room, seeming to seek for them in the corners and under the tables, even upon the ceiling, as if they might be clinging there among the painted cherubs. 'I will 'ear now.'

Choiseul bowed his head, the battle lost, and gestured for Starkey to proceed.

'Right. Like I said, yer grace, this were no ordinary watch. Fer one thing, it were not made ter tell the time – leastways, not like no watch I ever saw. It 'ad no numbers on its face, just odd symbols, all mystical and obscure like, such as I never seen anywhere before. And it were 'eld in a severed 'and.'

'*Excusez-moi*,' said the marshal. 'I do not believe I 'ave understand zis.'

Starkey raised his right hand and mimed cutting off his left hand, cradled in the sling, at the wrist. '*Coupé*,' he said. '*Complètement*. I were there meself when Aylesford chopped it off a Englishman wot 'ad stole it from the Worshipful Company o' Clockmakers – *la Corporation des maîtres horlogers de Londres*,' he added helpfully, to which Belle-Isle nodded with an 'Ahh'.

'The fingers o' that severed 'and could not be prised off o' that watch. Indeed, the 'and were more stone than flesh – like marble it were, cold and 'ard. Or so Aylesford did tell me. I were not keen ter touch it meself, as yer might imagine.'

'Most curious,' said Belle-Isle. 'But zis is important 'ow?'

'I'm gettin' ter that, yer grace. It appears as this 'ere watch 'ad been sought after fer some time by both the English and you lot.'

'*Pourquoi* – why?'

'I reckon *monsieur le duc* could tell yer more about that.'

'Rumour,' said Choiseul, wriggling his plump fingers in the air in a manner suggestive of smoke. 'A clue 'ere, a 'int zair, enough zat *la Corporation des maîtres horlogers* came to me and zaid, "If 'alf of what we 'ave 'ear of zis watch is true, zen to possess it is to win ze war." And I ask, "'Ow is it a watch can win ze war?" "Because it is no watch." "What is it, zen?" "A weapon." "'Ow does it work, zis weapon?" "We do not know. But if zair is such a weapon, better it belong to France zan England, *non*? Bring it to us, and we will learn 'ow to use it." As to all zis, *mon cher*, I do not believe or disbelieve. But I make discreet inquiry of our friends *en Angleterre*, and I learn zat ze English are indeed seek zis watch. Zis *'untair*. And so I go to Louis and tell 'im, and 'e say, "Bring me zis 'untair, but tell no one." Zat is why I 'ave not told you, *mon cher*, till now.'

Belle-Isle inclined his head with grave dignity, as though Louis himself had accompanied the mention of his name.

'In accord wiz ze command of *le roi*,' the duc continued, 'I decide to send a spy across ze Channel, a native Englishman 'oo is loyal to France. I put about zat I am seeking such a man, and soon I 'ear from ze aide-de-camp of ze Scottish prince, Lieutenant-Colonel Grant. "I 'ave just ze man you want," 'e tell me, "a brave lad 'oo do not blink at bloody deeds and is a loyal subject of ze rightful king of Scotland." And zis is 'ow I come to send Thomas Aylesford to England in search of ze watch zat is no watch.'

'And Monsieur Aylesford, I take it, met wiz success in 'is mission?' asked Belle-Isle.

'In a manner o' speakin',' Starkey answered, picking up the tale. 'In fact, 'e met with too much success, as yer might say.'

''Ow "too much", monsieur?'

'Yer won't believe me when I tell yer. I were there, and I scant believe it meself. Yer see, the 'unter be a weapon true enough, but it be no weapon crafted by 'uman art or science. It be a cursed device, a right devil caught in a cage o' glass and metal! It be alive, I tell yer. I did behold it glowin' with a spectral fire. A eerie blue glow it were, sickly as the glow what do rise from graveyards betimes. I seen it drink blood, aye, human blood! It killed every man aboard the *Pierre*, it did. Sucked 'em dry like so many empty bottles! And then it did not glow blue no more, yer grace, but red as the very eye o' Lucifer! I care not if yer believe me or no – but it kindled a storm as well. Aye, a storm so fierce that the *Pierre* were battered ter pieces by it! Only Aylesford and I were left alive by then. Why the thing spared me, I do not know. I felt it, yer grace, rummagin' about in me mind. I felt the evil o' it. The bottomless 'unger. And I knew then that it were not content ter remain within its clockwork prison. It desired above all else ter be free. Ter be born inter the world. And ter rule it.'

The marshal had grown pale while listening to this, and now hastily crossed himself. 'Where is 'e now, Thomas Aylesford? And where now is ze watch?'

'Dead,' said Starkey. 'Drownded, the poor sod. As fer the 'unter – swallowed by the sea. Aye, 'tis with Davy Jones now, and long may that gentleman keep hold o' it! I were picked up the next day by a French cutter out o' Le 'avre, clingin' ter a bit o' wreckage with my good arm, 'alf drownded and 'alf froze and 'alf out o' my mind with terror – and if that do seem too much by 'alf, yer've the right o' it! That were a week ago, yer grace. I came ter Paris as soon as I were able and presented meself ter the duc as the ambassador o' the Morecockneyans. 'E brung me to Versailles fer a private audience with the king, and it were there that I did 'ave the 'onour o' relatin' a somewhat expurgated version o' my exploits ter Madame de Pompadour, after which that lady did me the greater 'onour o' callin' my survival a miracle, which I did not and do not dispute.'

'*Incroyable*,' said Belle-Isle, and turned to Choiseul. 'Do you believe zis fantastic tale, *mon ami*?'

The duc de Choiseul shrugged eloquently. 'We know from our friends *en Angleterre* zat Messieurs Starkey and Aylesford were indeed picked up by ze unfortunate *Pierre*, and mention was made in ze report of a strange relic in ze possession of Monsieur Aylesford – a relic just such as Monsieur Starkey 'as describe. As for ze *Pierre*, *elle a complètement disparu*. Gone wizout a trace. Monsieur Starkey is ze sole survivor of zat tragedy. Upon 'is rescue, a letter was found upon 'is person, wrapped in oilskin, zat bore ze signature and mushroom seal of *le roi sous la terre*. Zis letter named Monsieur Starkey ze *ambassadeur* of zat subterranean nation which, as you well know, *mon cher*, is so essential to ze 'opes and plans we 'ave gazared here tonight to set in motion at last.'

'*Je comprends bien,*' said Belle-Isle.

At which Starkey smiled. Always with the French there were wheels within wheels. *Why,* he thought, '*tis a veritable clockwork nation!* 'I find I am somewhat parched, yer lordship,' he said. 'I wonder if I might trouble yer for a bit o' wine?'

Choiseul motioned with those plump fingers, the pilasters on the walls moved in swift obedience, and soon the three men were seated in a semicircle around the fire, a glass of red wine in hand, each lost in his own thoughts, or in the hypnotic dancing of the flames. So they remained until two more guests were announced.

'*Messieurs,*' began the duc de Choiseul, who had led the others from the sitting room into a small dining room where another fire blazed and a late supper of roasted quail, sweetmeats and pastries had been laid out English-style, along with more bottles of wine, and more silent pilasters lining the walls, and silent paintings, too, great gold-framed oil portraits of men in martial splendour who gazed down haughtily on the figures below, as if in doubt that their puny deeds would ever win them ascension to the august pantheon of these already overcrowded walls, 'I 'ave arrange zis small repast—'

'Capital!' interrupted the grander of the two new arrivals, and rushed, or rather waddled hurriedly, to the table holding the food, where he began at once to help himself to sweetmeats, stuffing them into his mouth as though he had not eaten in days. This man – evidently somewhat inebriated – had been introduced to Starkey as Prince Charles Edward Stuart, rightful heir to the throne of Scotland and – following the retirement to Italy of his father – the unquestioned leader of the Jacobite cause, otherwise famous – or infamous – as Bonnie Prince Charlie, who in 1745 had landed in Scotland, mustered an army of Highlanders to his banner, and embarked on a quest to win back his father's plundered kingdom . . . in the process inciting raw terror in the breasts of all right-thinking Englishmen.

He had stood on the brink of success . . . but it had all come crashing down in an ill-considered throw of the dice at Culloden, after which the would-be conqueror had fled back to the succour of France, disguised, or so it was said, in women's clothes.

The fourteen years since had not been kind to the prince, 'bonnie' no more but instead an obese, middle-aged caricature of the dashing figure who had rallied a subjugated nation to his cause and still commanded, from afar, the passionate devotion of tens of thousands of deluded Scotsmen. Better he had died in the Forty-Five than to have lingered on, a living martyr to his own myth. Or such, anyway, was Starkey's opinion, formed mostly, until this moment, from his acquaintance with certain of the prince's fanatical followers, among them the late and not entirely lamented Thomas Aylesford.

Even Aylesford, he thought now, would have regarded with horror and shame this fallen hero attacking the roasted quail with a zeal that had been conspicuously absent on the battlefield at Culloden. The duc de Choiseul and Marshal Belle-Isle were momentarily struck dumb, watching aghast as the prince, grunting and slurping like a sow, consumed two quails in quick succession, barely pausing between them, like the Cyclops in his gory cave, to let the bones fall to the floor, or rather to the Aubusson carpet that covered the floor.

The second of the new arrivals, Lieutenant-Colonel Grant, the prince's aide-de-camp, a hefty man with an expression of impenetrable sangfroid on his smooth-shaven, heavy-jowled face, must have been taken aback by the speed at which the prince had launched himself into the fray, for it was only now, as his charge reached for a third quail, that he gathered his wits and advanced.

'No doubt Your Highness wishes to hear the report of the French ministers,' he said in a firm tone, laying two fingers lightly, and as it were deferentially, upon the prince's elbow, whereupon, without seeming to exert any particular force, he somehow steered him away from the victuals.

'Eh?' said the prince, turning ponderously. He held a quail in one fat white hand; the other he wiped negligently on the front of his resplendent coat, leaving a trail of grease. His fleshy face, flushed a pleasant shade of pink, like the insides of a baked ham, glistened with perspiration and shone with affability. The eyes, glittering with insatiable hunger, struck Starkey as surprisingly intelligent, though quite mad. 'Reports, is it? Capital!'

Lieutenant-Colonel Grant, meanwhile, his touch as light as ever, continued to propel the prince forward, like a mahout guiding an elephant, towards a large round table covered with maps showing the coasts of France, England and Scotland, around which the others stood as if paralysed.

'I am most eager to hear the details of my family's long overdue restoration,' the prince continued, his intonation leaving no doubt, though of course he would not offend the sensibilities of his hosts by stating it openly, as to whom the blame for this delay must attach, as well as the responsibility for correcting it.

'*Oui*, Your 'ighness,' said the duc from behind a frozen smile as, at the twitch of a finger, a liveried pilaster separated itself silently from the wall to expunge all evidence of the prince's appetite from the carpet. 'If you will be so good as to 'ave a seat, I will explain everyzing.'

Other pilasters had meanwhile stridden forth to pull back the chairs around the table. They might have been invisible for all the notice that was paid them.

'Capital!' exclaimed the hope of the House of Stuart as, with small grunts of exertion, and with the assistance of Grant, he lowered himself into a chair that Starkey, for one, had grave doubts would prove capable of supporting him . . . especially since, at the last moment, his legs and the lieutenant-colonel alike abandoned the struggle, and the prince fell heavily the remaining six inches or so. But the chair held, a glance of relief was shared around the table, and the prince, in need of refreshment after his efforts, tore a mouthful of flesh from the quail, set its greasy corpse down upon one of the duc's pristine maps, just off the coast of Normandy, and loudly called for wine.

This was swiftly produced, and the others seated themselves.

Good God, thought Starkey, who found himself across the table from the prince, *pity the poor 'orse what 'as ter carry that load! Why, 'twould be too much fer an ox – 'e would 'ave ter ride inter battle on a elephink, like a bleedin' 'indoo!*

At which Starkey noticed the prince was staring at him in the most discomfiting manner, as if he had somehow overheard his thoughts. He essayed a weak smile.

The prince blinked his hungry eyes. 'You are the first of your nation I have met, Mr Starkey,' he said. 'Indeed, until recently I did not know any of you existed. Imagine – right under our noses all this time! Living in caves and tunnels and such. Quite extraordinary! I confess you appear surprisingly civilized for a troglodyte.'

'We Morecockneyans be an old folk, Yer 'ighness,' he replied. 'The city o' London raised itself above us; we was there first, and we shall be there after. Why, 'tis our influence what 'as civilized the topsiders, as we call 'em, as much as t'other way around.' He thought he might have gone a bit too far there at the end, but the prince seemed to find it amusing, perhaps because his words seemed to apply exclusively to the English, and Londoners in particular, for neither of which did the Stuarts profess any great love. *'Twould be a wonder if they did*, thought Starkey.

'When I am king,' said the prince after draining his wine glass and holding it up negligently, as if the ether itself must produce wine in answer to his need (and wine was indeed by some miracle produced), 'I should like to visit your country and acknowledge in person the contributions of your people and my brother king.'

'My royal master will make yer right welcome, 'e will, Yer 'ighness,' Starkey declared.

'Capital! Grant, make a note of it!'

'Your Highness,' said Grant.

Again the prince's glass was drained, raised, and miraculously refilled. 'Tell me of my countryman, Thomas Aylesford, with whom I am told you travelled, and who, or so I understand, met a tragic end in my service. Did he acquit himself bravely and with honour?'

'That 'e did, Yer 'ighness,' Starkey attested.

'What else can you tell me of him? I should like to send something to his family.'

''E didn't have one, Yer 'ighness. Tom were an orphan, or so 'e did tell me, raised by a priest what stood ter 'im in the relation o' a lovin' father. 'Twas 'e what gave 'im the name o' Aylesford and

307

taught 'im ter love Christ. I gather 'e's dead now, God rest 'is soul.'

'Another martyr to the English zealots, no doubt.'

''E loved Yer 'ighness, did Tom. 'E were a stalwart champion o' yer cause in all company. I 'ave never seen a better man with a blade, unless it be but one, and 'e no gentleman, like Tom, but a thief and blackguard. 'E faced 'is end with bravery and courage. Why, if it were not for Tom, I would not be sittin' 'ere today. 'E saved me life, 'e did!' Again, Starkey wondered if he had gone too far. But again, it appeared not.

The prince, having set down his wine glass beside the roasted quail, more or less upon the port city of Le Havre, produced a perfumed handkerchief from the voluminous sleeve of his coat and proceeded to dab his eyes; the spicy scent of pomander instantly pervaded the room. 'Ah, the poor laddie! Sacrificed himself, did he? The noble nature of the true Scotsman will always show itself! An orphan, you say? No! A son of Scotland, rather! I will do something in his memory, when I am king. Grant, make a note of it.'

'Your Highness,' said Grant.

'Mr Starkey, I have decided to reward you for your service, since Mr Aylesford is beyond my reach.' As he spoke, the handkerchief now tucked back up his coat sleeve – though a few overlooked inches yet protruded – the prince tugged at a thick gold ring upon the forefinger of his left hand. 'This – *unh* – ring – *unh* . . .' A little grunting exhalation accompanied each tug. 'Was – *unh* – given – *unh* – me – *unh* – by – *unh* – my – *unh* – father – *unh*!'

At which, to everyone's surprise, including his own, the ring flew off his finger. It struck Marshal Belle-Isle, seated beside Starkey, in the forehead with a sound like a bullet hitting home, and the marshal slumped back in his chair, apparently stunned, if not dead. The ring, meanwhile, lay gleaming upon the table. But all eyes were on the prince, who, in the recoil attending the ring's liberation, had fallen backward out of his chair with a crash that completely drowned out the noise of the ring striking the marshal. As he toppled over, the prince, flailing for balance, had struck his wine glass – refilled by the same miraculous process as heretofore noted – with the protruding end of his handkerchief, thus knocking it over, with the deplorable effect that the duc de Choiseul's maps were inundated in a spreading red stain that quite obliterated every carefully inked and coloured line like the advance of an unstoppable army.

No one moved. Not the duc, who somehow found himself holding the remains of the roasted quail, which he gazed at in something like horror, as if it were a severed head, while his own wine glass, upended by the prince's, added its contents to the flood. Not Starkey, who was unsure whether helping the prince to his feet would constitute a crime of lèse-majesté. Not Belle-Isle, who looked as if he might never move again in this life. Not Grant, whose normally blank expression had grown even blanker, as if his mind had vacated his body. Not the pilasters, who kept to their posts, having received no order to do otherwise.

Only the prince moved. He squirmed on the floor like an upended tortoise, calling over and over again for Grant.

At last the repetition of his name seemed to penetrate whatever interior fortress of the mind or soul Grant had retreated to. Blinking placidly, he set his glass of wine down carefully, without spilling a drop, and went to the aid of his chief. He appeared quite well versed in this sort of operation, and Starkey watched with interest and admiration as the lieutenant-colonel first rolled the prince over, then helped him to all fours, thence to his knees, and from there, with the aid of the chair, which he had righted, to his feet. Starkey felt like applauding when the operation was complete and the prince stood erect again, breathing heavily, his pink face even pinker than usual, his eyes even hungrier and more mad.

These were the eyes that now fixed upon the table.

'Who has spilled my wine?' asked the prince in a tone of barely suppressed anger.

Again, Grant proved himself equal to the task. 'Your pardon, Your Highness, but it is my wine that has spilled, through my own clumsiness. Here is your glass.' And he handed the prince his own wine glass, which the prince accepted and drank off at once.

This seemed to calm him. Now he scrutinized the table with a more exacting gaze. 'What are you doing with that quail, Choiseul?'

Choiseul gave a start, as if he had forgotten about the quail in his hands, or only now noticed it for the first time. He jumped to his feet and threw the roasted bird spasmodically to the carpet. 'My beautiful maps!' he said with a groan. 'Zey are *ruinées*!'

'I say, is that my ring?' asked the prince, indicating the ring upon the table with his now empty wine glass.

Everyone looked over.

'What is wrong with Belle-Isle?' the prince demanded.

Starkey bent close. ''E appears ter be asleep, Yer 'ighness.'

'What, passed out, is he? Too much to drink, I suppose. A man has got to be able to hold his liquor, Choiseul, especially us military men!' He sighed and shook his head, then raised his empty glass to the ether in an expectation not long disappointed. He drank again and belched. 'Damn good wine. One thing you French do right, I must say. But see here, Choiseul! What kind of talk do you expect to have with Belle-Isle soused and no maps to speak of? This whole evening has been a waste of time, apart from meeting the ambassador. Come, Grant! Let us go in quest of more amusing play-fellows, eh?' He winked broadly and laughed, setting the wine glass absently upon the table. 'Do let me know when you are ready to discuss battle plans, Choiseul. Don't forget the ring, Mr Starkey! Wear it in good health – it was my father's, you know.'

With that, he sallied forth from the room.

Grant lingered behind. '*Monsieur le duc*,' he said, speaking in flaw-less French. 'The prince is a man with heavy burdens, as men of destiny so often are. He must be permitted his little foibles, eh? But I assure you, when he is called upon to act, you will not find him wanting. With a sword in his hand and an army at his back, he will raise all of Scotland as he did in '45 . . . and this time, lead them to victory!'

Choiseul replied, also in French, 'He is a buffoon and a drunkard, monsieur. I would not trust him with a flock of sheep, let alone an army.'

'Nevertheless,' persisted Grant. 'I saw enough of the maps to grasp your design. It is a clever and audacious plan. But you cannot succeed without the prince. You know it, I know it, and he knows it. I give you my word of honour that the prince will be sober and fit enough to sit a saddle when the time comes. As for the military end of things, leave that to me and to any commanders you care to appoint. But let me remind you again: for your plans to succeed, Scotland must rise. And Scotland will not rise without Bonnie Prince Charlie.'

'The fleet will sail for Scotland by the end of March,' said Choiseul after a moment, with the air of one bending to painful necessity. 'See that the prince is ready.'

'*D'accord*,' said Grant and bowed. Then, turning to Starkey, he held out his hand palm-up and said in English, 'The prince is a generous man – too generous for the state of his purse. The ring, Mr Starkey, if you please.'

Starkey, who had picked up the heavy object and had been turning it in his fingers admiringly while following the conversation in French as best he could, now handed the ring to Grant with a regretful sigh.

'When the prince becomes king,' said Grant, pocketing the ring, 'I'll see to it that you receive something, Mr Starkey. Indeed, I shall make a note of it.'

With that, he bowed and followed the prince out of the dining room.

The duc de Choiseul sank back into his chair with a groan that was echoed feebly by Marshal Belle-Isle, who had regained consciousness and now sat up, gazing about in perplexity.

'What 'as 'appen?' he asked, rubbing his forehead with one hand. '*Où est le prince?*'

The duc gestured helplessly at the table, as if there were no words sufficient to convey the enormity of all that had occurred.

'*Je ne comprends pas*,' said the marshal, groping for his wine glass and draining its contents at a swallow. '*Ouf, j'ai mal à la tête!*'

'Yer picked a fine time fer a nap, Yer Grace,' said Starkey.

'Nap?' he repeated in English.

'*Oui*,' said the duc, adding with some asperity: 'Ze man zat cannot 'old 'is wine should not pick up 'is glass, *mon cher*.'

'Not 'old . . .' Comprehension awoke in the befuddled features, followed swiftly by indignation. 'You zink I am *bourré*? I am sober as ze judge!'

'In zat case, perhaps you are too old for ze demand of your position!'

311

The marshal pushed back his chair and stood. 'But not too old to 'ave forget ze demand of 'onour, *mon ami!*'

'Do you imply zat I 'ave forget?' inquired the duc, standing himself.

'Gentlemen,' interrupted Starkey before things could deteriorate further. 'Do yer want ter do the work o' the English? 'Tis they are the enemy!'

The two men glared at each other. Then:

'*Monsieur l'ambassadeur* is right,' said the duc, resuming his seat. 'Sit down, *mon cher.*'

The marshal did so stiffly.

'Zat man,' muttered the duc, shaking his head. 'Sometimes I zink 'e is ze real enemy.'

'At least in Scotland 'e will be out o' the way,' said Starkey.

'True,' said Choiseul.

'Zen 'e 'as take ze bait?' inquired the marshal, brightening somewhat.

'*Oui,*' said the duc, motioning to a pilaster. 'Henri, clear away zis mess and bring the ozzair maps, *tout de suite!*'

The mess was cleared, new maps brought, and the three men sat down again.

'*Bon,*' said Choiseul. 'Ze ozzair maps, *monsieur l'ambassadeur,* as you may 'ave notice, and as Lieutenant-Colonel Grant did most *assurément* notice, showed ze plan for ze landing in Scotland of an army of some twenty zousand, supported by ze French fleet. Zis is ze plan to which you 'ave 'ear Monsieur Grant agree. Ze prince will sail wiz zis force. But in truth, zis is, 'ow you say, a *divertissement.*'

'Diversion,' Starkey supplied, once again thinking *Wheels within wheels.*

'*Exactement,*' said the duc. 'By ze time ze prince 'as land and raise ze 'ighlandair against ze crown, ze real war will be ovair. 'E may 'ave Scotland, ze prince, and much good may it do 'im. But England, she will be a zorn in ze side of France no more. Ze real zrust of ze attack will commence 'ere.' He pointed to the port city of Le Havre. 'It is 'ere zat we 'ave build anozzair fleet, a fleet of flat-bottom *bateaux* design to ferry one 'undred zousand men across ze Channel. Zat we

312

shall do, monsieur, and land 'ere.' And he pointed to the town of Hastings on the English coast – the same town from which Starkey had sailed aboard the *Pierre* just over a week ago.

'And what o' the British fleet, yer lordship?' asked Starkey. 'Yer think yer can just sail them flat-bottomed boats o' yers past the fleet patrollin' off o' Brest? Them ships be under the command o' Admiral Edward 'awke, a sailor who lives up ter 'is name, I do assure yer. 'E will not scruple ter sink them boats. Nor will he show yer sailors a shred o' mercy. It'll be the Spanish Armada all over again.'

'Not zis time,' said Belle-Isle, whose forehead had sprouted a dark bruise, as though he had been anointed with ashes by a careless or drunken priest. 'Zis time, Admiral 'awke will be in pursuit of ze French fleet and ze prince, leaving ze road to England open. *L'armée de la France* will land unopposed and win a great victory, ze greatest *coup de guerre* since *le cheval de Troie!*'

''Tis a bold plan, yer grace, I'll give yer that,' said Starkey. 'But what if 'awke don't take the bait?'

''E will take it,' said Choiseul with serene confidence. 'Ze English, zey are mad about ze prince. *Absolument fous.* Zey 'ave build 'im into annozair Alexander. 'E is zair *idée fixe*, zair *bête noire*. Admiral 'awke cannot resist zis bait, monsieur. *C'est impossible.* Once 'e 'as 'ear zat ze prince 'as sail for Scotland, 'e must fly after 'im *tout de suite.* 'E will 'ave no choice. Even if 'e wish to remain, Monsieur Pitt will not permit it. 'E will not be allowed to permit it.'

'I reckon yer right,' said Starkey. 'But what o' the weather? *Le temps?* Look at what 'appened ter the *Pierre*, yer lordship – and she were a true seagoin' craft, built ter ride out a good blow. Them ships o' yers – them flat-bottomed barges – why, they might do fer a sail up the Thames, but will they be able ter ride out a storm?'

Belle-Isle shrugged. 'Zey will not need to. Wiz calm seas and a fair wind, zey can make ze crossing in a day. Even if we lose 'alf ze boats, we will still land fifty zousand men *en Angleterre*, wiz no one to oppose us but ze militia – old men and farmairs. And no one will expect us to sail until spring at ze earliest. We will take zem by surprise.' He sniffed contemptuously and snapped his fingers. '*Non, monsieur l'ambassadeur*, zair is no one 'oo can stop us once we 'ave land.'

'Maybe not,' said Starkey, 'but they can slow yer down long enough fer London ter raise 'er defences. And if yer 'eld up outside the city gates, yer grace, and it comes ter a siege, why, with the passin' o' time the Bonnie Prince might take it inter 'is 'ead ter come down from Scotland wif 'is army, and yer might find 'im not quite so grateful a ally as yer 'ad 'oped, nor so inept a commander as 'e 'as 'eretofore appeared. 'E wouldn't be the first Stuart ter find the throne o' England a prize impossible ter resist. Which is why yer need our 'elp, I do believe.'

'*Exactement*,' acknowledged the marshal. 'Even as ze French army is land on ze coast, your countrymen, monsieur, are rise up from below ze ground to take control of *Londres* in a *coup de main*. Afterward, ze victorious Louis will proclaim *le roi sous la terre* as *prince de Londres*, and *le prince* will declare 'imself ze vassal of Louis. Zese terms are already agree between us, *non*?'

'Well,' said Starkey, leaning back in his chair, a smile on his face, and, in his mind, wheels within wheels within wheels turning most pleasantly, 'as it 'appens, yer grace, I 'ave been dispatched by my royal master with, 'ow shall I put it, an amendment o' terms.'

Some hours of hard bargaining later, a drained but well-satisfied Starkey returned by coach to his lodgings in an unobtrusive *hôtel particulier* on the left bank of the Seine that had been provided for his use by the duc de Choiseul. All the terms he had been instructed to obtain had been agreed to by the duc on behalf of the French Crown – chief among them the establishment of London as an independent city-state, with the King Beneath the Ground recognized by Louis as a co-equal monarch and not a vassal, yet with the security of the new city-state nevertheless guaranteed by the French. A secret memorandum detailing the new agreement, bearing the signatures of Starkey and the duc, had been dispatched by French courier and should reach London – or Londinion, rather, as the city would become officially known, and as the Morecockneyans had always named it among themselves – in a matter of days.

Yes, the King Beneath the Ground would be pleased, thought Starkey, and with good cause. In a few short months, after the war was won and the Morecockneyans had emerged from long millennia of concealment to claim their rightful place among the nations of the world, the marvel of all mankind, he, Starkey, would receive his just reward: a special dispensation to admit him, despite being only a third-generation Morecockneyan, into the highest – that is to say, the lowest – of the mysteries of the one true faith. He would descend into the depths of Londinion, to the holy of holies, said to be older than time itself. There, in the company of the priests, he would enter into communion with the first and greatest god, he who had created the heavens and the Earth and all things visible and invisible. The god who had revealed himself to the ancient ancestors of the Morecockneyans and chosen them as his people, whose name it was forbidden to speak above the ground.

Doppler.

9

Retribution

9

Retribution

QUARE WOKE NAKED AND SHIVERING ON A WOODEN TABLE IN DR IMMELMAN'S
ruined workshop. Patches of slate-grey sky showed through ragged
holes in the roof. Even that meagre light hurt his eyes. Wincing, he
sat up, only then noticing that his restraints were gone.

'Hello?' he called weakly. 'Dr Immelman?'

The words ghosted through the cold air.

He swung his legs over the side of the table, wincing again at the
movement. His bones ached to the marrow. His body – what he could
see of it in the gloom – was webbed with scars. It was as if he had
been sliced apart, then crudely stitched back together. Yet apart from
the ache, itself a kind of scar, he felt strong and fit, recovered from his
injuries – more fully than seemed possible, in fact, for his left arm no
longer ended in a stump, but in a hand. He flexed it wonderingly.

Like the prosthesis Dr Immelman had grafted to the maimed leg of
Longinus, Quare's new appendage was made of an ivory-like substance
joined seamlessly to the flesh. It responded to his will as naturally as had
the original and felt as much a part of him. It was smooth as marble
yet pliant and sensitive. He recalled how Longinus – Lord Wichcote,
rather – had opened a panel in his prosthesis, revealing flesh and blood
threaded with gears and wires. He looked but could find no similar
point of access in his new hand, but when he pressed the cupped palm
to his ear like a seashell, he heard faint clicks and whirs from within, the
sounds stirring a queasy flutter in his gut.

The question, however, was: would it give him access to the Otherwhere in the manner of Lord Wichcote's appendage? Could he reach out with this new hand and open the door to that place, escape this prison and find his way home?

Earlier – how much earlier he didn't know, for he had no sense of how long he'd been bound to Dr Immelman's worktable, the subject of surgeries he was glad to have no memory of (if only he could say the same about the tale Immelman had told him; but he would not think of that now!) – Quare had stood beside Lord Wichcote on a London rooftop and sensed the Otherwhere all around him, had known instinctively how to enter its warped spaces and navigate them as effortlessly as any winding London street. But that instinct was dead in him now. If there was a door, he did not know how to grasp it, much less open it.

He pushed himself off the table and stood, hugging his chest against the cold. Scars abraded scars. It seemed they were all that was holding him together.

The shadowed figures of automatons stood amidst the wrecked machinery of the workspace. Quare approached them cautiously, remembering how they had stirred to life, or its semblance, at the doctor's command.

They seemed to be watching him, aware of him in some way. But as he drew near, his bare feet scraping across the cold, bare floor, he saw that, however lively they had once been, they were dead things now. They did not respond to his voice or touch. They were empty, broken vessels. Their painted wooden features, cracked and blistered from long-guttered fires, were frozen in expressions of agony, as if they had felt the life being burned out of them.

My brothers and sisters, he thought mockingly. But that mockery was muddied with other emotions, less easily labelled.

If Dr Immelman were to be believed, he, too, was a made thing that had been invested with life, or its counterfeit. He was not a human being but an imitation of one, sprouted from the amputated limb of Longinus like a plant from a cutting. Immelman had built him. Breathed life into him, like a god. And put something of himself inside, too, or so he'd insisted proudly: poured his secret heart and soul into the receptacle that had become Daniel Quare.

What does that make me?

All his life he had wondered about the identity of his father. Had dreamed of finding him, or at least of discovering the name and history of the man who had sired him. Only then would he know who he truly was. Only then would he be whole. Now, unless Immelman had lied to him – and in his heart, or whatever he possessed that passed for one, Quare knew the doctor had not lied – it seemed he had not one but *two* fathers: Lord Wichcote, who had unknowingly provided the raw materials, as it were, and Dr Immelman, who had shaped them. He might look like a man, and indeed feel himself to be a man, filled with desires and sensations, stirred by thoughts and dreams, but he was not of woman born. He was no more alive – though, perhaps, also no less – than his new hand.

Quare's breath steamed in the cold air. Scars wreathed his body, thorns his bones. He felt frightened, alone. Dr Immelman had told him too much . . . yet not enough.

Why was I made? To what purpose?

Immelman had said that he'd spoken a word while tracing the *shem* upon the yet lifeless clay of Quare's forehead, the same word he'd spoken over the golem of the little girl he'd sent into the streets of Prague centuries earlier.

Retribution.

Quare shuddered. He must go in search of answers, for there were none to be found here.

Nor was there a stitch of clothing, or anything to wrap himself in against the cold. But what did cold matter to one not truly alive?

Woodworking tools were scattered about the shop, and from these he took an adze – not much of a weapon, but he felt safer with it in his hand. Thus armed, he left the workshop by a door behind the automatons.

Outside, winter waited. Snow drizzled from a grey, windless sky. Frozen drifts blanketed the ground. It was easy to believe, as he had heard, that time was a different thing here in Märchen. He couldn't tell if he stood on the threshold of day or night. Perhaps there was only a single hour here, sunless, lifeless, stretching out for ever. Far away and high above, looming over the entire town, was an immense glacier that seemed more a part of the dirty sky than it did of the land below.

He turned slowly, taking in the devastation around him. Collapsed buildings, homes shredded by cannonballs and consumed by fire. The wreckage of Wachter's Folly, from which he had emerged as naked as a newborn from the womb. He recalled Lord Wichcote's description of the intricate carvings that had covered the façade: the figures of men and women suffering the torments of the damned, and the sinuous shape of the great dragon running through them like a sea serpent sporting among the floundering victims of a shipwreck. Only splintered fragments remained, images of a more immediate hell. The proscenium, where Wichcote had watched a parade of automatons resembling the citizens of the town and seen with horror his own doppelgänger striding among them, was gone entirely. The clock face was still present but as pocked with holes as a Swiss cheese, the iron hands twisted out of true. A lone bell remained in the campanile, pinging tunelessly to the patter of snow.

Quare turned his back on the tower and made his way through the square. The drifts were high, frozen into a slippery landscape over which he was able to scramble, though not without falling from time to time, sliding painfully on bare skin. Scraped raw, his flesh bled; but was it really blood? So what if it had the look of blood: the feel and the taste, too? That proved nothing. After all, he had the look of a man.

Wichcote had told him how Märchen's citizens had built a network of covered passages that, over the course of the interminable winter, came to be buried under the snow, so that they functioned like a warren of tunnels linking the dwellings of the town. These, too, had been destroyed, but bits of them remained, gaping pits in the snow. He kept well clear of them.

Instead, he entered the wrecked buildings – vacant homes of a vanished citizenry. He saw no one, heard no human sound. Given the degree of destruction, he had expected to find corpses, or what was left of corpses, but there was no sign of any remains, human or otherwise. The town was empty alike of the living and the dead.

In one of the first homes he entered, Quare encountered his reflection in an ornately framed mirror. Startled, he thought the mirror was webbed with cracks, only to realize an instant later that the glass was smooth, and the cracks were on his face: a tracery of scars that gave his head and shoulders something of the look of a porcelain bust that had been shattered into a hundred pieces and then painstakingly glued back together. After that, he avoided mirrors.

The townspeople might have gone, but they had left clothes behind. Quare salvaged breeches and a belt, stockings, shoes, a shirt and coat, even gloves and a battered tricorn, enough to keep the raw edge of the cold at bay. He found a scarf, and this he wound about his neck and lower face, trying to hide as much of his fractured visage as he could. He kept an eye out for a blade but found nothing. He would have to make do with the adze, which he tucked into the belt.

Masked now, after a fashion, he could not help but remember his ill-fated mission with Lord Wichcote and Gerald Pickens, the three of them garbed as Grimalkin, alike as peas in a pod . . . until the Old Wolf had sprung shut the jaws of his trap. Moments later, Pickens was dead, Wichcote wounded, perhaps mortally, fled into the Otherwhere, and Quare himself was minus a finger and in the thrall of whatever hybrid entity inhabited the hunter: his old master, Magnus; all the men and women whose blood the hunter had swallowed; the cats it had killed when he'd first examined the cursed thing in Magnus's workroom . . . and behind and above them all, a dragon, or something that his senses could only stretch far enough to perceive that way. A creature of the Otherwhere, quickened with the blood and essence of timebound life. One of the Risen, he supposed, nameless as yet, eager to be born into the world – the better to feast upon it.

His guts clenched at the memory of the thing's iron will clamping down over his own, taking command of his limbs, his voice, his very thoughts. He would have given up more than just his hand to be free of it.

But *was* he free? Quare searched inside himself for any hint of its presence but came up empty. Still, he worried that it might be lurking deep within, waiting for the chance to reassert control. He would have to be on his guard.

At last he came to what could only have been the Hearth and Home: the inn where Lord Wichcote, in the guise of Michael Gray, had passed his time in Märchen. Quare entered through a broken first-storey window – the door on the ground floor was buried under a snowdrift – to find himself in what, for all he knew, might have been the very room that Wichcote had stayed in: where he'd lain abed after his injury and operation; where he'd seduced or been seduced by Doppler's daughter, Corinna; where he'd been interrogated by Doppler; and where Corinna and Inge Hubner had shed their human semblances and fought over him on the night that he and Corinna fled, taking the hunter with them.

Now the room, open to the elements, was almost as wrecked as the town without, and this was true of the rest of the rooms on the first floor as well. Wandering through them, Quare felt like a ghost haunting someone else's memory.

The stairs were intact, and he followed them down to the common room, wishing for a candle to dispel the gloom. But there was light enough to make out the fireplace before which the dog Hesta had lain, warming herself; it was filled now with ash-coloured snow. A soft, steady knocking drew his attention to the long bar at which Doppler and Michael Gray had sat and talked; there he saw the cuckoo clock whose tiny dragon automaton had so astonished Gray with its lifelike qualities. It appeared undamaged; indeed, the brass pendulum was swinging: the source of the knocking he had heard.

Quare slipped behind the bar and approached the clock, eager to examine it. The hands that had made the hunter and Wachter's Folly had made this timepiece. If he could learn something of its secrets, perhaps he might learn something of himself as well, of his origins and purpose.

The clock was evidently a study for the tower clock outside. Here were the same hellish figures, only executed hastily, it seemed, in the first flush of inspiration. The half-formed bodies, striving to separate themselves from the dark wood, or, on the contrary, being pulled down into it by a force impossible to resist, made him think of how Doppler and the other Risen had emerged from the Otherwhere . . . and how they feared, above all else, dissolving back into its embrace.

The clockmaker had memorialized the birth of the Risen and their ultimate demise. Even the war that had come to divide them was represented in the design: the figures were engaged in a titanic struggle not only against the engulfing medium of the wood but against each other as well. It was a battle of all against all, set against the backdrop of a hostile universe seeking to devour its children.

Quare gingerly tapped the tiny door at the top of the clock, recalling how Michael Gray had been harried by the waspish dragon within . . . but nothing emerged or, as far as he could tell, stirred. The pendulum swung undisturbed, a touch of the familiar amidst so much that was strange. Yet it struck him as strange, too, that the clock should have escaped the general destruction. It was a testament to the skill of its maker . . . and perhaps to more than that. For the hunter, too, was not easily destroyed or even damaged. He would have to be careful: this clock might have similar wards in place, similar protections.

Similar appetites.

It came down easily from the wall, surprising him with its lightness. Quare regretted the absence of his tool kit, then realized that Dr Immelman's tools were readily at hand even if the doctor was not. Thus, after first wrapping the clock in a ragged blanket pulled from one of the beds upstairs, he climbed out the window through which he had entered and made his way back to the workroom, the blanket slung over one shoulder.

As before, the presence of the automatons was disconcerting; he couldn't shake the idea that they were spying on him. But there was no sign that anyone had disturbed the workshop in the hour or so – as best he could judge the time – he had been away. More as an act of bravado than anything else, he placed his salvaged tricorn upon the bare head of one of the automatons, whose chiselled and painted features suggested a crude likeness of Dr Immelman himself.

'A hat for you, sir,' he said, sketching a bow.

Moving to the table on which he'd awoken, whose surface bore gouges and dark stains he preferred not to associate with himself in any way, Quare set his burden down, unwrapped it, and tossed the blanket aside. Then, marvelling afresh at the facility with which his new hand served him, he gathered what tools he could find.

Though he discovered a number of candles as well, he saw no means of lighting them. He thought of moving to a better-lit location, but on consideration could not be sure of finding one and so decided to remain where he was.

He expected to have difficulty opening the clock. The hunter, after all, had been locked up tighter than an oyster in its shell. But the back of the clock was easily unscrewed and lifted away.

Nestled within, the size of a clenched fist, was a heart.

Quare recoiled with a cry, dropping the screwdriver and the back of the clock, both of which clattered to the floor. Yet almost immediately, drawn by a curiosity he couldn't resist, he leaned in for a closer look.

He cursed under his breath in fear and wonder. Not a heart, but a snake curled into itself, its scarlet coils so tightly knotted that it gave the illusion of being a single lumpy mass. But now he could make out the tracery of cracks where the sinuous edges of its slender body came together like fused metal. A palpable heat rose from it, as though it were wrapped about an incandescent coal. He smelled the tang of limes; that was a scent he knew. He had last smelled it in Lord Wichcote's house, when Tiamat had appeared to him while he lay half asleep in the bath, projecting her essence through the Chinese screen that had somehow acted as a kind of window into the world.

Not a snake, he thought. *A dragon.*

There was nothing else inside the clock. None of the mechanical works that by right and reason should have lain exposed. He had thought to learn its secrets, but what was there to learn from this? That he had come to a place where natural law, as he had always understood it, held no sway – a place governed by other laws entirely . . . or by no laws at all, only chaos and madness? He already knew that.

Was the creature asleep? Sunk in hibernation? Quare had no wish to learn the answer. Stepping back, his own heart knocking so loudly against his breast that he thought it must certainly wake the dragon, he stooped to retrieve the items he had dropped: the screwdriver and the back of the clock. He would seal the dragon in its prison, or what he hoped would serve as one.

323

The cover of the clock had fallen so that its inner side faced up, and from that side a faint glow emanated. It came from an engraving of a golden gear that, even as he watched, began to turn . . . or perhaps it had always been turning. At any rate, as it turned, the light brightened, until it was as if dawn had come to the room.

Quare picked it up, feeling sunk in a dream, for what he held in his new hand was not the wooden backing he had removed from the clock, but the leather-bound cover of a book.

Dazed, he sank to his knees and, with his flesh-and-blood hand, opened it.

Printed within: line after line in a language he did not know . . . a sinuous black script that for all its incomprehensibility did not repel his gaze but rather pulled it in and carried it along like a leaf in a stream. He felt a sense of panic then and tried to look away but could not. Nor could he shut his eyes. He could not even blink. He made to fling the book away, but that, too, was beyond him; his new hand had betrayed him and clung stubbornly to the book, as if fused to it . . . as his lost hand had once been fused to the hunter.

The headlong rush of fathomless language swept him away. A roaring filled his ears, yet he thought to hear speech in it, though he understood not a word. Dimly Quare recalled that Lord Wichcote had spoken of reading such a book as this, or rather of being read by it . . . and he wondered if that was happening to him now. There came a sudden sickening lurch, as if the bottom had dropped out of the world, and he with it, and in the aftermath of that earthquake, everything had changed.

He was at rest, no longer moving; but the script on the page flowed faster than ever, a dark blur like the thread of blood that, in the Old Wolf's den, had unspooled from his wounded hand and disappeared into the hunter's insatiable maw. Just so were the inky words of the book, like a river running uphill, or an army of swarming ants, pouring into him now, into his artificial hand, which was no longer white as marble but black: a shining, blinding obsidian.

In this darkness, there was no division between inside and out, between the words rushing into him and everything Quare knew or believed himself to be. Lord Wichcote had told him how the contents of the book had revealed themselves to him as parts of an intricate machine that was simultaneously itself and a description of itself, but Quare's experience was quite different; the words of the book seemed to be describing him, defining him, moulding him to their shape, filling him with their purpose . . . a purpose he didn't know but felt, as it were, pregnant with.

How long he knelt there, holding the book open like a devout soul lost in prayerful ecstasy, he didn't know. But the onslaught ended as suddenly as it had begun. In an instant, he could see again . . . and what he saw chilled him: instead of a book, the wooden back of the cuckoo clock, bare of any ornament or shine. The hand that held it, which a moment ago had been black as pitch, had faded to a dull grey, and now, as he watched, that colour swiftly ebbed until the hand was restored to its former chalky whiteness. No trace remained of stain or shadow. Whatever had been absorbed or channelled was gone. He carried it inside him now.

Quare dropped the thing as if it had burned him – his new hand once again his faithful servant. He had no time to stand, barely enough to rip the muffling scarf away, before sickness roiled up and spewed onto the cold, dirty floor. On hands and knees he convulsed and coughed, insides clenching, his body seeking to drive out the foreign substance. But though a rank liquid pooled beneath him, he could tell that he had not purged himself of the invader. He felt it inside, a restless energy squirming through his veins. He could *hear* it, a far-off hissing that held whispers of a knowledge he hadn't sought, didn't wish to know. It was changing him, writing itself into his blood, his cells.

Quare groped for and found the scarf, wiped his lips, tossed the soiled fabric aside. Then stood, all atremble. A bearded figure in a tricorn leered at him from the shadows, and in his confusion and fear he thought that someone – Dr Immelman, or perhaps Doppler himself – had crept up on him. Fumbling at his belt, he drew the adze and brandished it.

'Stay back – I'll not warn you again . . .' But even as he spoke, he recognized the automaton upon which he had placed his scavenged hat. He lowered the adze with a shaky laugh, then retrieved the tricorn from that venerable old gentleman and set it on his head. 'Your pardon, sir,' he said, and sketched a bow whose very ridiculousness gave him a puffed-up kind of courage.

A hiss from behind, as of steam escaping a kettle. Quare spun to face the sound, the adze coming up again.

As wide as his index finger and as long as his arm from the tip of that finger to his elbow, the dragon floated above the clock like an open wound in the air. The slow and steady lashing of its tail, regular as a pendulum, seemed to keep it aloft and hold it in place.

A flat, triangular head regarded Quare languidly through eyes of cloudy jasper. The jaw unhinged; a flickering tongue darted out like a dancing flame; another hiss sent Quare stumbling backward, until he bumped against what must have been the automaton of the old man. The scent of limes was suddenly overpowering, just as it had been when Tiamat made her appearance in Lord Wichcote's house and laid her *geas* upon him, commanding him to bring the hunter to her once he had liberated it from Grandmaster Wolfe. And so he would have done, had not the hunter seized control of him and bent him towards a darker purpose. He was heartily sick of the Risen – why could they not leave him alone? But he knew the answer to that. He had a part to play in their damned war. It was his reason for being. The purpose for which he had been made.

Retribution.

Gladly would he wreak retribution upon the Risen! He would see the whole lot of them expunged from the universe like a nest of vermin from a nursery. Well, perhaps not *all*; despite everything, there was something . . . appealing about Tiamat in her human form – the blonde-haired young woman he had first met upon the rooftops of London and who had rescued him from a Morecockneyan prison cell. She was not like the others, he felt, or maybe just wanted to believe. In truth, he found it hard to reconcile her actions with those of her draconic self. She had told him that there was a bond between them, and that, too, he wanted to believe – though at the moment he could feel no evidence of it. More's the pity, for he would have welcomed another rescue right about now.

The dragon facing him was but a fraction of Tiamat's size; nor did he sense, as he had with her, even before she had spoken to him from the other side of the screen, the presence of a formidable, if alien, intelligence. Yet that did not mean the creature posed no danger. Its malachite eyes were as comforting as a cobra's.

'Go away,' he said, gesturing with the adze.

The dragon darted at him more swiftly than he had dreamed possible. He did not have time to cut at it or to dodge. But it did not strike. Instead, it halted no more than a foot away, close enough that the breeze of its lashing tail and the heat that radiated from its supple body washed over his face. The odour of limes was so intense that it nearly choked him. The dragon hung there as if studying him, its tongue tasting the air. He was afraid to blink, to so much as breathe.

Then, as suddenly as it had approached, the creature arrowed off with a flick of its tail. It shot across the workroom, heading towards a ragged opening where a cannonball had breached the wall. Quare sighed in relief to see it go. Too soon, for the dragon – more of a dragonlet, he supposed – halted before the opening and turned back to regard him, wavering in mid-air.

'Oh no,' Quare whispered, afraid that it was going to come at him again. He brought up the adze, though he had no faith in his ability to defend himself.

But the dragonlet didn't move, only swayed in what seemed a beckoning fashion.

'Oh no,' Quare repeated, more softly. Did the damn thing want him to follow it? He raised his voice. 'I'm quite happy here, thank you very much. Go on, now. Shoo!'

At that the dragonlet did move, even faster than before. In fact, it seemed to wink out of existence, only to reappear behind him in the blink of an eye. Not that he saw it there, but he heard its angry hiss and felt a lash of heat across the nape of his neck.

Cursing, his prosthetic hand slapping at his neck, he spun about and would have swung the adze had a second fiery lash across the back of his flesh-and-blood hand not caused him to drop the weapon. Nursing his hand in the blessedly cool grip of its paler partner, the scent of limes overpowered by the stench of burned hair, Quare regarded the dragonlet, which regarded him in turn, its body rippling like that of an eel.

'Very well,' he said through clenched teeth. 'Lead on, damn you, if that's what you're about.'

The dragonlet swam off at a more leisurely pace, and Quare, with a low curse, picked up the adze and followed it across the workroom to the breach in the wall, a ragged gap through which he could step without stooping. Beyond, in the eternal dusk, snow was falling lightly over the ruins of the town. But the dragonlet did not lead him there; instead, once past the breach, it turned sharply to the right, disappearing from view. Quare poked his head into the colder air and saw a narrow staircase leading upward, nestled between an inner wall and outer façade. The dragonlet hovered, lashing its tail impatiently.

'Yes, yes, I'm coming.' Quare stepped over tumbled brickwork and passed through the breach, then slid into the space between the walls, which was wide enough to easily accommodate him. The dragonlet had already turned and was drifting upward with a slow, hypnotic squirm. Where was it taking him? What waited at the top of the stairs? He tightened his grip on the adze.

The stairs spiralled up, following the gentle curve of the walls, so that Quare had the curious sensation of navigating the interior of a nautilus shell, like Daedalus's famous ant. Here and there parts of the walls had been blown away, taking the stairs with them, and he had to either leap the gaps or, like a mountain climber, find hand- and footholds in the shattered brickwork that would support his weight. He used the adze to test these holds or to fashion new ones. It reminded him of his training as a regulator, during which he'd been tasked by Master Magnus with climbing the exterior of various build-ings in London – training that had culminated in a midnight climb to the roof of Lord Wichcote's town house, where he'd seen the legendary Grimalkin – or so he'd thought – fleeing the scene of a crime and had embarked on a wild chase across the rooftops of London, ultimately catching the thief . . . only to find himself caught. He was still caught, and all his efforts to free himself from the entanglements of that long-ago night had resulted in his being trapped here, at the very centre of the web.

It occurred to him after a while that the climb was taking longer than it should. He had stood outside the tower clock, or what was left of it, and knew its size. The climb from the ground to the campanile was a matter of moments. Even accounting for the damage and the delays that occasioned, it couldn't possibly take more than a quarter of an hour at the most to reach the top. Yet Quare's inner sense of time told him that he had been climbing for at least twice that long. And still the stairs curved relentlessly upward. Still the dragonlet led him on. There were no windows in the outer wall, but the shelling had knocked enough holes in the masonry to provide entry for a crepuscular light and a chill wind that whistled tunelessly. Through these holes could be glimpsed the war-torn wreckage of Märchen's snow-covered rooftops, always the same distance below, as if he were not ascending at all but merely climbing in circles.

Whenever he paused to catch his breath, the dragonlet gave a hiss whose warning was unmistakable. He cursed it roundly, but it did not let him rest for more than a moment before driving him on.

Little by little, the damage lessened and finally disappeared altogether. The walls on either side were solid; he could no longer see the rooftops of the town. Yet all was not dark, for the dragonlet had begun to shed a flickering light, so that it seemed less a creature of substance and more a kind of living flame, a will-o'-the-wisp drawing him on . . . to what?

Quare's leg muscles ached from the unaccustomed exercise, a nearer hurt than the duller throb in his bones. Dr Immelman had warned him that the pain would never fade entirely, that he would never know a moment without its steady companionship. It was as much a part of him, it seemed, as the scars covering his body.

A stiff, cold wind began to blow, its force increasing as he climbed, buffeting him and howling in his ears. The enclosed space had not bothered him, but now he became acutely aware of it, feeling constricted, hemmed in, as if the walls were narrowing to either side. But after the next bend, unexpectedly, the way straightened, the stairs rising to a rough-edged opening that shone against the surrounding dark like a scrap of cloud curtaining the moon. The dragonlet pushed undaunted into the gauzy glow and was gone.

This sight had a stimulating effect, sending an influx of energy to Quare's weary legs. Less concerned with what lay ahead than with leaving the stairs behind, he quickened his pace and soon found himself at the opening. It was not a doorway, as he had thought at first, but the mouth of a cave. Outside was a blur of grey and white, a snowy landscape joined to a snowy sky. The wind was a constant roar. But once again it seemed to him that there were words in it, whispers beneath the surface of things, beneath the skin of the world. Among them he thought to hear his own name.

He stumbled forward, one hand clapped to his tricorn, into the wind and the white. Where was he? This was not the tower clock; there was nothing manmade here. He looked around, and gradually, as his eyes adjusted to the light, and his mind to the scale of things, he realized that he was not in Märchen any more, for around him he could make out, through the driven snow, the vague but unmistakable bulk of mountains. Dead ahead a dagger of ice pierced the frozen sky, and suddenly it came to him that he stood atop the great glacier that overlooked the town: a climb of six thousand feet or more. He looked back in awe and disbelief at the cave mouth, and it seemed to him that it was in truth the mouth of a dragon, that the stairs he had climbed had taken him up the monster's gullet, and when he turned back to look once more at the tip of the glacier, he saw it afresh as an outstretched talon, as if the whole mountain were a dragon's body locked in ice.

He staggered then and would have fallen but for the reappearance of the dragonlet. The creature darted at him, spitting fire. He ran from it, slipping and sliding, the adze falling from his nerveless grasp, the tricorn snatched from his head by the gusting wind. The dragonlet harried him, driving him in the direction of the talon, and Quare wondered if it were going to force him to climb higher still. He would surely fall if he tried, and rather than go meekly to that certain death, he decided to fight. But just as he was steeling himself to turn, the wind shifted, parting the swirl of snow before him to reveal a small rise on which stood a circle of oddly shaped dark stones such as he had seen in the gargantuan underground vault of the Morecockneyans and through which the young woman calling herself Tiamat had carried him into the Otherwhere. He skidded to a halt.

Was this likewise a portal to that place between all places?

The dragonlet shot past him and stopped midway to the stones, hovering there just as it had in Dr Immelman's workshop, waiting for him to follow. Quare took a step forward, and as he did an invisible string seemed to spring into being between himself and the stones, taut and vibrating. The Otherwhere! He felt its presence, its promise, opening up before him and also inside him. Once again, as had occurred on the rooftop in London after Lord Wichcote had taken him on a stroll through the Otherwhere – intending, Quare recalled with a dizzying sense of déjà vu, to bring him here, to this very spot – he sensed innumerable pathways extending outward from the stones, or, rather, behind them, the strands of a web in which all that existed hung suspended like drops of dew. Only this time, he felt that knowledge make a connection to whatever had been inscribed in him by the book, and he realized that the lines of the book had also been in some way strands of the same web, written or spun in the same language. Lord Wichcote, like him, had opened the book and read of it, and it was that experience, Quare realized, as much as Dr Immelman's prosthetic, that had allowed Wichcote, like some fairy-tale hero with seven-league boots, to use the Otherwhere as a means of travelling instantaneously over vast distances. But while Lord Wichcote had only dipped into the book, Quare had read its entirety – read and quite literally absorbed it, taking its sense and substance into himself. Whether that had changed him, or merely awakened a potential latent within him, or built into him, he didn't know or, at the moment, care. What mattered was that he had found the means to leave this place.

He had been walking towards the stones all the while, and now, as he drew near to the dragonlet, it drifted out of his path, then fell in behind him. Uneasy as he was to have the creature at his back, Quare kept his gaze fixed on the stones ahead, which, with a low grinding noise, began to move, as though the hill on which they stood was a mechanical device that had not been used in some time, a rotating stage such as might carry a parade of automatons through their

331

paces. In some way, he realized, he stood upon the proscenium of Wachter's Folly after all.

As the stones moved, faster and faster, their shapes blurred and altered, until Quare was looking at just such a parade. He wondered if this was what Lord Wichcote had witnessed in Märchen, the display of townsfolk that had so captivated and then horrified him when he'd seen his own doppelgänger bringing up the rear. But if so, Quare was seeing that parade from a very different angle, for the figures that seemed to pass before his eyes were the size of giants, and they were not townsfolk going about their daily tasks but soldiers in heavy armour, an endless army marching past, their helmeted heads turning neither to the left nor the right, arms swinging in time, legs scissoring, boots crashing down in orderly avalanche.

Halted now, he watched in astonishment as the armoured figures began to fight. Suddenly he was witnessing a terrible battle, a brutal skirmish of all against all, and it came to him that this was the chaos depicted on the façade of the cuckoo clock, and, in more finished form, upon the tower clock as well. He felt the mountain on which he stood – the dragon, rather – shift beneath his feet and heard the crack of ice and stone giving way. Then, with a roar that snuffed out every other sound, the dragon was there, knifing through the midst of the soldiers, strewing them about like dolls. God, it was big! So huge that he could not see its entirety, but only bits and pieces of the whole. It was dark as earth, as stone, yet it poured itself through the air like water, a river with a bottomless mouth and an angry mind. Blood fountained and flowed in a torrent from the mass of broken soldiers, a flood that seemed sufficient to drown the world.

Quare cried out and threw his arm up as if to ward off that wine-dark tide. It crested over him, blotting out what little light there was, then crashed down.

And was gone. All was as it had been a moment before. The stones were stones again, and still. The wind whined. Snow swirled. Behind him, the dragonlet hissed.

Quare shook his head. What had he seen? A vision of the past, of the war that had set the Risen at each other's throats and left Märchen an abandoned ruin? Or had he been shown a future yet to unfold, in which the dragon gestating in the egg of the hunter had hatched at last and flung itself upon the armies of France and England with insatiable hate and hunger?

The dragonlet hissed again.

There were no answers here. Quare stepped between the two nearest stones and into the Otherwhere.

When last he had entered this place, it had been as a wounded man, limp and near death, caged in the talons of Tiamat. He recalled how they had flown for what might have been hours or entire years, passing through worlds as wondrous as any dream could conjure, and through other worlds more dreadful than any nightmare. It was then that the great black dragon called Hesta had dropped upon them from out of the sun and engaged Tiamat in an airborne battle that had knocked him from her grip and sent him plummeting like a meteor into the hard-packed snow of Märchen. But there was no sign of Hesta now, or indeed of any living creature at all besides himself and the dragonlet, which had entered behind him and now floated just to his left, at the height of his shoulder. The Otherwhere was as abandoned as Märchen had been. Quare felt the emptiness; it was as though a new sense had awakened in him. He was connected to this place, a part of it . . . and it was a part of him. He knew it like he knew his own body.

But where were the Risen? What had become of Doppler and the rest? Had they killed themselves off?

Pathways extended in all directions, branching and rebranching inexhaustibly, as in a hall of mirrors. He might follow any one of them . . . but which? And to where? Overwhelmed, Quare closed his eyes, blotting out the insane geometries by which his mind attempted and failed to impose order on the chaos of the Otherwhere. He stopped trying to make sense of it and instead simply let himself experience it, opened himself to it, let it echo inside him. And out of those echoes in the dark, like vibrations travelling down a wire, images arose in his mind.

A firelit drawing room, in which a drenched man lay unconscious if not drowned upon a soaked carpet, face sunk in shadow.

A rocky landscape crisscrossed with ropes, along which, like a sailor, or perhaps a spider, a man dragged himself hand over hand, his features obscured behind a wind-blown shock of red hair.

A woman in familiar grey garb stretched out on a narrow bed, long hair like a molten stream in the torchlight, one thin arm thrown over her face, one slim ankle chained to a stone wall.

Each called to him. But he could follow only one.

He made his choice in an instant, and in that instant was there.

10

The Portal

AFTER THE WELCOME HE HAD RECEIVED AT THE HANDS — THE FISTS, RATHER — of Cornelius, Lord Wichcote had imagined that worse awaited him. Thus it was a surprise when he'd been deposited in a room that, apart from the absence of windows and timepieces, would not have been out of place in his own London house. Indeed, there was nothing in this opulently furnished sitting room, lit by candles and a crackling fire, that testified to its underground location; had he lost consciousness after the beating and awakened here, he might have imagined himself spirited back to the surface somehow. But he had not lost consciousness, only feigned having done so, and as Cornelius's men had dragged him none too gently along, he'd marked their route through the maze of passages and caverns. It was a route already familiar to him, though he had not come this way in more than ten years — one leading to the palace of the King Beneath the Ground.

Once, he had been welcome here. Not as Wichcote but as Grimalkin, for King Jeremiah had found it expedient from time to time to employ the services of a master thief, and over the years that arrangement had matured into a friendship of sorts — to the extent that it was ever possible to be friends with a king.

Now Jeremiah was no more. Wichcote did not know how he had died, whether peacefully or by violence. He did not know whether the new king of the Morecockneyans was a descendant of Jeremiah, his heir, or a brash usurper with blood on his hands. But one thing seemed clear: whoever he was, the new king did not view Grimalkin in the same friendly light that his predecessor had.

Yet at the same time, Cornelius had brought him here, to this comfortably appointed room, rather than to a dungeon cell. The beating he'd received had been an impulsive act of revenge, for after all Cornelius had not expected Grimalkin to fall into his lap, and there had been a score to settle between them. Wichcote bore the man no grudge – it was simply how the game was played. But the fact that this room had evidently been set aside for Lord Wichcote implied that the new King Beneath the Ground, whoever he was, desired something from him: something better coaxed with kindness than compelled by torture or privation. It remained only to be patient and learn what that something was.

But patience came hard, because Wichcote did not know what had become of Cat. She had been taken elsewhere; no doubt they meant to use her as leverage against him. That, too, was how the game was played. Wichcote understood it. But he didn't like it. Though he knew that his daughter was more than she appeared to be, and was better able to defend herself than Cornelius or any human being could imagine . . . still, it distressed him to think of her at the mercy of these men. Cornelius had sworn that she would be safe, but Wichcote knew better. He had no illusions about what men were capable of: all too many of his sex wore their honour like a pair of expensive but ill-fitting breeches, exhibited with pride but divested with relief. And so he feared for her. It was not just that her honour was at risk; he could imagine only too well what would happen if her secret were discovered, as it must be should her captors decide to force themselves upon her. It galled him to be so helpless at the very moment she might need him most. But there was nothing he could do. There were guards posted outside the door, and the room, as best he could determine, had no other exit. He had, of course, tried again to enter the Otherwhere, but that route remained stubbornly closed.

So he waited. There was a mirror in the room, hanging from one wall, and in that glass Lord Wichcote examined his bruised and bloodied face. He was startled more by the gauntness of his visage than by anything else: the bruises would fade, the blood could be (and, with a handkerchief, was) wiped away, but what could not be erased was the toll of time. He was an old man. He felt it in his bones, and now he saw those bones so clearly beneath his skin that it was as if the skin had turned translucent and he was gazing at his own skull. But he was not dead yet. Not by a long shot. The sword thrust that had nearly killed him had taken something out of him, true enough, but finding his daughter had given him back even more. He grinned at his reflection as though it were the face of a stranger advancing upon him with sword in hand. How often he had grinned in just this way behind Grimalkin's grey mask! Perhaps age, too, was a kind of mask.

His hosts had provided food and drink, and Wichcote – certain they would not have brought him here only to poison him – did not hesitate to refresh himself. There was crisp, cool water, as fresh as he had tasted since his sojourn in Märchen so many years ago, along with a selection of cheeses the equal of anything to be found above ground. What there was not was anything that could be employed as a weapon.

He paced for a while like a restless animal in a cage, but at last, when he judged that half an hour or so had passed – his timepiece had been taken from him, along with his weapons and the pouches at his belt, with their clever little surprises – he stretched out upon a silk-upholstered divan, figuring that he might as well try to sleep if he could.

No sooner had he done so than, as if he had been under observation the whole time and his captors had only been waiting for him to let down his guard (which he suspected was in fact the case), the door opened. He did not rise or show any sign of interest, simply watched, with an air of languid boredom, as one of the guards entered. He, like his fellow outside the door, was smartly attired in the green and yellow uniform of the palace guard. He was a big man, more than six feet tall, and strongly built.

'On yer feet,' said the guard.

'I am quite comfortable where I am,' Lord Wichcote drawled in reply.

'Not fer long,' the guard said and advanced upon him.

'Hold!' rang out a woman's commanding voice. The guard stood sharply to attention as the owner of that voice swept into the room, closing the door behind her. She was lanky, evidently in her fifties or early sixties, and dressed as finely as any woman in the Court of St James. That did not surprise Lord Wichcote, who remembered very well, from previous visits to the palace, how the aristocracy below the ground dressed in emulation of that above. What surprised him was that he recognized the heavily powdered face of this woman, though he could not immediately place it. Even so, he rose to his feet at her entrance and bowed as courtesy demanded.

'Well, well,' the woman said, inclining her head in acknowledgement, a mischievous sparkle in her dark eyes, or so it seemed to Wichcote, 'two birds with one stone, indeed. Cornelius is apt to exaggerate, if not fabricate altogether, so I thought it best to come see for myself. But wonder of wonders, the man spoke truly for once. Lord Wichcote unmasked as the infamous Grimalkin!' Her laughter expressed pure delight. 'Why, you are a man after my own heart, sir – a man of many parts, so to speak. For I do perceive, now that I have clapped eyes upon you, a third persona in your repertoire: yes, unless I am much deceived, here, too, is the faithful – or perhaps not so faithful – Longinus, a fixture in the guild hall these many years!'

'You have the advantage of me, madam,' said Wichcote. 'Your face is familiar, but I cannot quite put a name to it.'

At which she laughed again. 'Can you not? You have seen me often enough, though in different dress and, indeed, different circumstances altogether.'

That was all the hint he required. 'Mrs Puddinge.'

'*Lady* Puddinge,' she corrected with a sniff.

'Your pardon, madam,' he said. 'I confess I did not expect to see you here. So you are a Morecockneyan, then. A spy in the world above.'

'One of many,' she said. 'And lately ennobled by the king for my services there.'

'You were Daniel Quare's landlady, as I recall.'

'He was one of my boys,' she admitted, not without a touch of pride.

'Yet you gave him up to Sir Thaddeus like a calf to the slaughter,' Lord Wichcote pointed out. 'Mr Quare told me of his encounter with Mr Aylesford in your rooming house. Why, if Aylesford was your ally, did you not simply capture Mr Quare and bring him here for questioning?'

'Indeed, I wish I had done so,' Lady Puddinge replied. 'For then you would not have been in a position to liberate him from his cell before Master Malrubius could put him to the question. But at that point, neither I nor Mr Aylesford knew that Sir Thaddeus already possessed the hunter. We believed that Mr Quare had the timepiece, or at any rate knew where to lay hands on it. I judged that he would be more likely to divulge that information above ground than below it. Our spies in the guild would report back to us quickly enough, and, if necessary, we could always steal into the guild hall from below and liberate him ourselves. Such, at any rate, was my thinking. I had not counted on your interference, sir.'

'If I have upset your plans in any way, I am glad of it,' Lord Wichcote said. 'Indeed, you may count on me to do everything in my power to thwart them.'

'Mayhap I can change your mind,' said Lady Puddinge.

'I don't see how. You have subjected me to a beating and brought me here against my will. In addition, you hold a young woman – my daughter, as it happens – and no doubt mean to threaten her with harm in order to compel me to some action I would otherwise be disinclined to take.'

'Why, you could not be more wrong, sir. Neither His Majesty nor I wish to see you or your daughter – a charming girl! – harmed. Quite the contrary. We have brought you here for your own good – or do you imagine that you would be welcomed with open arms by Sir Thaddeus and Mr Pitt? As for that regrettable beating, rest assured that Mr Cornelius will suffer for it. No, we did not bring you here to torture you into doing anything against your will but rather to place before you an opportunity I feel sure you will be quick to embrace, once you hear it and fully understand all that is involved in this matter of the hunter.'

'What is there to understand? The hunter constitutes a grave danger to this kingdom, and indeed to the world. Yet you have allowed Aylesford to deliver it to our enemies across the Channel. Thus armed, I do not reckon they will long delay their invasion of these shores. I can only imagine what you have been promised in return for this treachery. But whatever it may be, I do not think you will long enjoy it. The hunter is no mere weapon. It is, in a very real sense, alive, and it pursues its own wicked ends.'

'It is for that very reason we seek your help now.'

'My help?' Wichcote laughed. 'Madam, you are deceived if you imagine I will aid you in any plot against England. Even if I were of a mind to do so, that ship has sailed, as it were, with Mr Aylesford aboard.'

'Sailed, yes. But not landed.'

'What do you mean?'

'The ship carrying Mr Aylesford and the hunter to France was lost in a storm. All aboard were drowned . . . with the exception of your old friend Mr Starkey, our ambassador to the French court – or such, at least, are the reports from France.'

'The hunter is lost, then?'

'Just because we cannot find it does not mean that it is lost. As you have pointed out, the hunter is alive. It pursues its own ends.'

'Madam, you surprise me. If this was known to you, then why in the name of heaven did you entrust the hunter to Aylesford? Why did you not simply destroy it?'

'Such a thing is not so easily destroyed. Indeed, it cannot be destroyed here, in this world, but only in the place where it was made: the Otherwhere.'

'Now you truly surprise me,' said Lord Wichcote.

Lady Puddinge smiled. 'Let us have no secrets between us, sir. I know that you have been there. And what is more, that you have the ability to travel there whenever you like. I know of the creatures who dwell there – the Risen – and the war that has set them against each other.'

'How can you know these things? Have you been there?'

'No,' Lady Puddinge said with evident regret. 'But we Morecockneyans have dwelled in our subterranean realm for many thousands of years. Londinion, as we call it, has existed below the ground far longer than there has been a London above it. In the depths of these caverns is an ancient circle of standing stones: a portal between worlds. And through that portal, long ago, one of the Risen – the greatest of them – came to us and made us his chosen people. I speak of Doppler – that name, I see, is known to you.'

'Indeed,' Wichcote said with a grim nod. 'But if you serve Doppler, why did you not return the hunter to him instead of sending it to France with Aylesford?'

'I did not say we served him. Only that he chose us many thousands of years ago. But we did not ask to be chosen. We did not, ourselves, choose. The old king, your friend, was a faithful servant of Doppler. He would have returned the hunter to him. But not the new king. The new king serves no master: Doppler least of all. He has forged a fresh alliance – one that will bring the Morecockneyans, at long last, to our rightful place in the world. We shall be lords of London and Londinion – the King Beneath the Ground shall be king above it as well!'

'Who is this new king of yours?' asked Wichcote. 'And with whom has he forged this alliance?'

'Your questions will be answered,' said Lady Puddinge. 'But not by me.'

'By whom then?'

'Why, by the king himself. Kneel, sir,' she said, dropping to one knee.

'I beg your pardon?'

'Kneel in the presence of the King Beneath the Ground.'

'But there is no one here save ourselves and the guard . . .' Lord Wichcote glanced at this individual, who, until now, had stood as silently and stiffly as a pillar. But suddenly a smile cracked the man's frozen features, and his posture changed from one of blank servility to self-confident authority. So marked was the alteration that Wichcote was sinking to one knee almost before he was aware of it. 'Your Majesty,' he said.

'Rise, sir, rise,' said the man with an easy laugh. 'You, too, Lady P. We are all old friends here, are we not?'

Lord Wichcote stood, scrutinizing the man more closely. 'First Mrs – excuse me, *Lady* Puddinge, and now, unless my eyes deceive me, underneath that wig and powder is none other than Francis Farthingale, journeyman of the Worshipful Company – Prince Farthing, as the other lads called you.'

'King Francis I,' corrected Lady Puddinge.

'Forgive me, but I could not resist this little imposture,' said the king, smiling jovially. 'We are, after all, none of us what we seemed to be.'

'Your Majesty least of all,' said Lord Wichcote. 'I had thought you killed at the Pig and Rooster, along with your fellows – murdered by Thomas Aylesford. Indeed, I wonder now if any man died that night! Not you, not Daniel Quare, not even Gerald Pickens!'

'Mr Aylesford had his victims, but I was not among them. We were allies on that blood-drenched night. Prince Farthing had to die in order that King Francis might live.'

'And what of King Jeremiah? Did he, too, have to die?'

'Regrettably, yes. I know he was your friend. I mourn him, too, in my way. I was his son, you see, though he never publicly acknowledged me. His only child, even if a bastard born. I knew him, sir. And loved him. He was an easy man to love. An honourable man, a generous king. But trapped in the past. A slave to outmoded tradition and beliefs. He could not see that for the Morecockneyan race to survive in the modern world, we had to emerge from our bolt holes and take our rightful place above the ground as a sovereign nation.'

'So you murdered him. For all your grand vision of the future, you have come to the throne with blood on your hands.'

'What king has not?' inquired Francis with a shrug. 'If you seek to play on my conscience, my lord Wichcote, pray don't bother. What's past is past. My father's fate does not concern you – except insofar as you hope to avoid it.'

'We have come to threats much sooner than I had anticipated,' said Wichcote.

'That is no threat,' said the king, 'but a statement of fact. For we are all as good as dead unless you agree to help us.'

'As I told Lady Puddinge, I am not inclined to help anyone who

342

holds me against my will. I am even less inclined when an innocent girl is involved. I speak, of course, of my daughter. Produce her, sir, let me assure myself that she has come to no harm, and then perhaps we may talk.'

'You shall see her. I give you my word of honour on it. But we will talk first.'

'A king cannot afford a sense of honour. Your father told me that once, one thief to another, as he put it. So you will forgive me, Your Majesty, if I do not take you at your word.'

'Why, the impudence!' said Lady Puddinge. 'Sir, you forget yourself!'

'Peace, Lady P,' said King Francis with a negligent wave of one hand. 'Lord Wichcote is right, of course. A king cannot be bound by such petty constraints as honour. He must be free to act at all times in the best interests of the realm, as he perceives them. But right now, sir, those interests require your cooperation, and that cooperation will be best secured, or so I judge, by kindness rather than threats. Thus it is self-interest, not honour, that guarantees your daughter's safety. Besides, it is best that she does not hear what I have to tell you.'

'And why is that?'

'Because she is not human. She is one of the Risen – Doppler's granddaughter, in fact. You see, you have no secrets here, Lord Wichcote. I know all about your adventures in the Otherwhere.'

'Who told you – Doppler?'

'Hardly. Doppler takes us for granted. He explains nothing, simply issues orders from on high. He has not visited us in person for many hundreds of years. Indeed, there are those who believe him dead. I do not say I am one of them. But it is plain that his interests lie elsewhere now. He has forgotten us – though he still expects our obedience. That is why I have joined with his enemy, the one called Tiamat.'

'Doppler's wife.'

'The mother of your mistress, Corinna – which makes her grandmother to your daughter, Cat. She has offered us a brighter future in exchange for our help in her war against Doppler.'

'Then Cat must be your ally as well, for she, too, is on the side of Tiamat.'

'Is she? Did you know that she was raised by Doppler?'

'She has told me so. But only for half of each year. The rest of the time, she was raised by another man – a man she believed to be her father.'

'That I did not know,' said the king. 'Who is this man?'

'I have not met him,' said Wichcote. 'And Cat will not tell me his name.'

'Perhaps there is no such man,' mused the king. 'Perhaps there is only Doppler.'

'She would not lie to me.'

'She is your daughter, sir,' laughed Lady Puddinge. 'Of course she will lie to you.'

This left Lord Wichcote at a loss for words, for he suspected there was truth to it.

'Doppler seeks the hunter in order to use it as a weapon against his enemies among the Risen,' said King Francis. 'If that should mean the destruction of this world, so be it. He will simply create another. But I am rather attached to this world! Tiamat offers a different future – one in which the Risen can no longer meddle in our affairs from on high. She would use the hunter to pull down those false gods and usher in a world where there are no gods at all, but only human beings. In that world, we Morecockneyans will no longer have to hide beneath the ground but will take our rightful place above it, and Londinion will be numbered among the great nations of the Earth. That is why – to answer your earlier question – I allowed Mr Aylesford to take the hunter to France. He was to deliver it to Tiamat, who, under an alias, occupies a position of influence there. But as Lady P has told you, Mr Aylesford never arrived. His ship was lost, and the hunter along with it. I do not think that was simply bad luck. I believe the hunter itself caused the storm that sank the ship. It is out there now somewhere, intent upon its own designs.'

'No doubt you are correct. But what is that to me?'

'We must find it, sir. We must take it to Tiamat before Doppler can get his hands on it, or before the monstrosity it contains can hatch out into the world. There is not much to choose between those two outcomes. Only Tiamat can save us – only she has the knowledge and power to destroy the hunter.'

'Even assuming that to be true, I don't see how I can be of any help to you.'

'You have the ability to travel through the Otherwhere.'

'Perhaps I did, once,' said Lord Wichcote with a shrug; there seemed no use in denying it now. 'But the Otherwhere is closed; the way is barred. I cannot go there any more. If I could, I assure you that we would not be speaking now.'

The king frowned. 'That I did not know. But even Doppler cannot entirely bar the way into the Otherwhere. The portal that Lady P mentioned cannot be shut down. It remains open and always shall remain open as long as the world exists, for the terms of the ancient alliance between Doppler and the Morecockneyans stipulate as much, and Doppler, like all his kind, is bound by nothing save his own will. That is the sole constraint upon his power – but it is an absolute constraint. Thus you may enter the Otherwhere through that portal, sir, even if every other point of access is closed to you, and once there you may travel its highways and byways, such as they are.'

At this, Lord Wichcote could not forbear smiling – he was being offered the very thing that he and Cat had hoped to steal. But he was not inclined to accept so easily. 'And what shall I do there?' he asked. 'I am but one person, a human being. What can I do against the might of the Risen?'

'You can find the hunter,' said Lady Puddinge.

'How am I to do that, when Doppler himself has failed to find it?'

'It was you who brought the hunter into this world, all those years ago,' resumed the king. 'No human being has been as close to it as you have, for so long a time.'

'If you mean to suggest that I have some kind of connection to it, I'm afraid I must disappoint you. It's true that I possessed the hunter for many years, but not until it was stolen from me was it awakened from its sleep by the taste of human blood. Since then it has drunk the blood of many men – but not mine.'

'Can you be so certain that not a drop of your blood was spilled in proximity to it?'

345

Lord Wichcote hesitated, thinking back to that night in his attic workroom, when the faux Grimalkin – his daughter, had he but known it! – had pressed the tip of her blade to his neck and drawn a single red bead from his skin. 'Perhaps a drop, but—'

'That is sufficient,' interrupted the king. 'Indeed, even had there been no blood, the hunter will have fed upon your essence over the years – for it is not blood *per se* that nourishes it. No, nor any other vital fluid of the body. Such things are merely vehicles containing the concentrated essence of what it feeds on. I refer, of course, to time. You may have thought that the hunter was asleep for all the years you held it, and indeed, in a manner of speaking it was asleep, but it was not dead. It was alive all the while, and like all living things required sustenance. You have fed the hunter, sir. Do not doubt it. A connection exists between you.'

'If so, I am not aware of it. I have felt nothing. And in any case, its maker must be linked to it even more strongly than I. Why would Doppler not have used this connection to find the hunter?'

'Because the hunter is hiding from him. But I do not think it is hiding from you. I believe it has forgotten you. The fact that you are here now suggests as much, for if it remembered you, and took note of you, why, sir, it would have called to you by now and made some use of you. Perhaps it still may. But that is why we must act quickly. Once you have entered the Otherwhere, you will be able to sense it – so Tiamat has assured me. Then you will have only a brief window in which to act before it becomes aware of you in turn. In that time, you must take possession of it and bring it to Tiamat. She will know how to control it. How to bind it. How to destroy it.'

'It seems a slim chance.'

'It is our only chance.'

'And how am I to find Tiamat?'

'You will find her at Versailles,' said Lady Puddinge. 'Under the name of Madame de Pompadour.'

Lord Wichcote could not hide his surprise. 'The mistress of the king?'

'The same,' said King Francis. 'Well, you have heard everything. Will you do it?'

'You have overlooked one thing,' said Wichcote. 'The Otherwhere is closed. The only means of access to it is here, in the depths of Londinion. Let us say that I enter the Otherwhere through that portal, locate the hunter and acquire it, and bring it to Versailles. How, then, am I to return to the Otherwhere? For it is only there that the hunter can be destroyed.'

'The hunter itself is a portal,' said the king.

'Is it indeed? So, too, I suppose, are the jaws of a lion. One may pass through them – but at the cost of being devoured.'

'Tiamat will know the way,' King Francis insisted. 'You must bring the hunter to her and let her instruct you.'

'You ask much of me,' said Lord Wichcote.

'Much is at stake.'

'That is why, if I agree to help you, it must be on my terms or not at all.'

The king raised a hand to forestall an objection from Lady Puddinge. 'Very well. State them.'

'There is but one condition: my daughter. She will accompany me on this mad mission of yours.'

'Out of the question!' protested Lady Puddinge, able to hold her tongue no longer. She turned to the king. 'Your Majesty, it is plain that this man cannot be trusted. We must continue to hold his daughter as a guarantee of his cooperation. To do otherwise would be madness!'

'Do so, and there will be no cooperation,' stated Wichcote flatly.

'I am sorry, my lord Wichcote,' said the king. 'I find that Lady P has the right of it. I cannot bring myself to trust your daughter. She is a creature of the Otherwhere, one of the Risen. Once free, she may decide to make use of the hunter herself, or return it to Doppler. No, we shall hold her until you have successfully completed your task.'

'Completed it?' echoed Lord Wichcote. 'Why, I shall not so much as begin!'

'I'm afraid you have no choice in the matter.'

'So we are back to threats.'

'Not at all,' said the king. 'Your daughter will not be harmed, merely held in safekeeping, as it were. You, meanwhile, will be escorted to the portal and, if you do not enter willingly, thrown inside. In any case, you shall enter the Otherwhere. At that point, your interests and ours will be in alignment, for the sooner you complete your mission, the sooner your daughter will be freed.'

'King Jeremiah would never have behaved in such a fashion,' said Wichcote.

'That is precisely why he is no longer king.'

'And what of your promise that I should see Cat after we had spoken? Was that a lie?'

'Not at all,' said the king.

'Then take me to her.'

'I did not stipulate how soon after our discussion you would see her,' the king said with the grin of a chess player springing a long-prepared trap. He had wandered to the door while speaking, and now he rapped sharply upon it, his eyes never leaving Wichcote.

The door opened at once, and a bevy of guards in yellow and green uniforms pushed into the room.

'Take him,' said the king.

Lord Wichcote's hands were bound behind his back. He was then quick-marched down passages that led ever more deeply into the bowels of Londinion. In his career as Grimalkin, he'd made use of the spaces beneath London but had never cut loose entirely from the surface; the idea of it had never even occurred to him. Now he was seeing a world he had not encountered before, one that owed nothing to the world above.

The façades of civilization dropped away, leaving bare rock . . . or not bare, exactly, for the stone had been cut by human hands and was marked with carvings and a chiselled angular script he could not decipher, as well as colourful and energetic though technically crude paintings that depicted humanlike figures along with animals and creatures that until recently he would have thought could exist only in legend or nightmare but which he now suspected were all too real, denizens of the Otherwhere that had crossed for a time into this world, and for all he knew were here still. These adornments – visible in the greenish yellow glow of the luminous mushrooms cultivated as a light source by the Morecockneyans – grew more numerous the deeper they descended.

Both Lady Puddinge and King Francis had accompanied him. The king seemed inclined to serve as a sort of guide to this underworld, Beatrice to his Dante.

'Few topsiders have seen what you are seeing now,' said the king. 'Here is the history of the Morecockneyan race set forth in all its strangeness and glory. A pity we do not have time for a more leisurely tour. Later, when this is over, you must return as my guest, and I will show you such wonders as you have never imagined.'

'I do not think I shall ever be a willing guest of Your Majesty,' said Lord Wichcote.

'Bah, you take things too personally,' said the king as Lady Puddinge glowered at Wichcote in the light of the mushrooms, her pinched face rather like a mushroom itself.

The rest of the journey was conducted in an uncomfortable silence.

Lord Wichcote had never felt so helpless. For the first time, his title and position meant nothing, or very little. Nor did his talents as Grimalkin – there were too many men to fight, even had his hands been free and holding weapons, and his ability to enter the Otherwhere at will, which had got him out of many tight spots over the years, remained stubbornly denied. There was nothing to do but submit. Perhaps, once he passed through the portal, things would be different, and he would find himself able to rescue Cat somehow. It was a slim hope, more wishful thinking than anything else, but he clung to it in the absence of any other. That and the promise of revenge. One way or another, King Francis would pay for what he had done to Cat. And to King Jeremiah, a good man who had deserved better of his son. Just as, he could not help but feel, to his shame and frustration, his daughter had deserved better of him.

At last they came to a cavern that dwarfed any others he had seen. Floor, walls, and, presumably, ceiling were covered in glowing mushrooms of all shapes and sizes ('presumably' because he could not actually see the roof of the cavern, just a fine shining dust that sifted ceaselessly down from above like a luminous snowfall).

At the centre of the cavern, on a mound of packed earth, stood a circle of stones. There were twelve of them, each about five feet wide and taller than a tall man. They were shaped, he realized with a shock, like the figures he had seen on the face of the hunter. The stones were so black they seemed to shine, especially against the surrounding glow, which clung to everything else in the cavern except them. They looked like empty spaces, dark holes cut into the fabric of the world. He felt that if he could only look hard enough, he would see past or rather through them, right into the Otherwhere. But he couldn't fix the stones in place; his gaze slipped off them like water off an oiled surface. The air around them shimmered as if with heat. Or perhaps it was the stones themselves that were shimmering, moving in a kind of dance that pulled at some part of him even as it pushed his sight and his understanding away.

A crowd of monks awaited them. Or so Lord Wichcote judged them to be, for they were dressed in heavy brown cassocks and cavernous hoods that hid their features in shadow. But these monks wore swords at their sides. They wore, too, ropy cinctures that ended in thick metal nubs shaped like mushrooms. The loose strands of these belts were of variable length, some hanging to mid-thigh, some dangling to the knee, others brushing the ground. The cassocks, like the stones, were proof against the shining spores, which winked out as soon as they settled upon them. It was hard to judge the size of the gathering precisely, but Wichcote thought there must be at least a hundred monks arrayed before them. They did not move or make a sound. The stillness was eerie and oppressive.

'Here are the priests and guardians of the portal,' said King Francis in a hushed voice, 'the direct descendants of the first Morecockneyans. No one, not even I, may enter this holy place without their invitation. They will conduct you the rest of the way. I wish you luck, my lord.'

'If any harm should befall my daughter in my absence, I shall return and kill you,' Wichcote replied. 'Just so we understand each other.'

This threat seemed likely to earn him a beating, if not worse, from the guards, who did not look pleased to hear their king thus threatened, but King Francis was evidently in a forgiving mood. 'Let him be,' he said with airy benevolence. Then, addressing Wichcote: 'You yourself are the sole guarantor of your daughter's safety, my lord. To assure it, you need only succeed in your mission.'

'Then let us be about it,' he said grimly.

The king nodded, and two monks stepped up to take him into custody. Even this close, he could not make out more than the faintest suggestion of features beneath their overhanging cowls. Someone shoved him roughly from behind, and, as he stumbled, the monks took hold of him by his upper arms and propelled him forward, flanking him. Their grips were like iron.

The crowd parted to let them through. And then a curious thing happened – in some ways the strangest thing Wichcote had yet experienced in his time in Londinion. Certainly one of the most unexpected.

The monks began to sing.

There were no words that he could make out, just a collection of tones sustained over time. Individual voices joined in and dropped out, but the plainsong endured and grew louder, building upon itself. Into this vibrant thrumming came heavier tones, deep bass notes that made Wichcote's bones hum. These sounds arose from monks who, separated from their fellows, had begun to whirl the loose ends of their long belts through the air above them. Higher-pitched sounds were introduced by monks who spun their shorter belts before them on a vertical plane, like shields. The music thus produced was unsettling. It seemed to him that he was hearing only part of it, the smallest part. Yet he felt its whirring vibrations throughout his body – and nowhere more intensely than in his prosthetic foot, which tingled painfully, as if it had been frozen into numbness and was now thawing out, coming alive again in the heat of the music. But just as, when he tried to look squarely at the standing stones, his gaze slid away, unable to find purchase there, so too did the music relentlessly escape his grasp when he tried to fix it in his mind. Only, it seemed to him that the music and the stones were linked, each playing off and reinforcing the other, as though the stones were bells set ringing by the belts of the monks. And that ringing was echoing into the world and beyond it. He wondered if they were merely opening the portal or calling to something or someone behind it. He supposed he would find out soon enough.

Feeling very much like a prisoner being delivered to the gallows, Wichcote was marched up the mound of earth to the very threshold of the stone circle as, from all around him, the music reached an intensity he found difficult to endure. No more could he endure the sight of the stones; this close, their presence did not just repel his gaze but set up an unpleasant squirming in his mind, as if his thoughts were being bent out of true. He was reminded of how Wachter's Folly had affected him in Märchen. That, too, had been a portal. And was this, in the same way, a kind of clock? Recalling how Corinna had instructed him to keep his gaze fixed on the ground as they had approached the tower clock and the dragon that was its guardian, he forced himself to look down. But there was no reassurance there, for his prosthetic foot was glowing with a cold blue light that again called his experiences in Märchen to mind, as well as more recent encounters with the hunter. It was a light not of this world but of the Otherwhere.

The music stopped then, as suddenly as it had started, though its echoes lingered in the fraught air. A gasp went up from a hundred throats, and in response his eyes lifted; the same blue light was pouring from under the cowls of the two monks escorting him. Evidently this was no ordinary occurrence, for the voice of the king rang out: 'Stop them!'

Wichcote felt a tug at his bonds, and then his hands were free.

'Come, Father,' said the monk to his left. 'I fear we have outstayed our welcome.'

'Cat?'

A shining hand swept the cowl away to reveal his daughter's grinning face, transfigured into the face of an angel by the radiant blue glow emanating from her skin.

The other monk gave a chuckle, as if enjoying his surprise, and then added immeasurably to it by pulling his own cowl away.

Wichcote gaped. He was looking at the face of a monster. The flesh was a map of scars. But then he saw beyond or behind the scars, to the face shining through them.

The face of Daniel Quare.

Before he could say another word, or so much as gather his wits, Quare and Cat flung themselves between the nearest stones of the portal, pulling him along and into the Otherwhere.

Epilogue

STARKEY WAS IN GOOD SPIRITS UPON HIS RETURN TO HIS CHAMBERS. THE *MAÎTRE d'hôtel* lit him up the stairs, informing him as he did so that a visitor was waiting.

'A visitor?' he inquired in French, halting on the steps.

'A friend, monsieur,' said the *maître d'hôtel*, who also stopped, half turning to look down at Starkey. His long, solemn face, dusted with powder, gave him a ghostly aspect in the candlelight. 'Or so he said. He assured me that he meant your honour no harm and that you would be most pleased to see him.'

'Did he now?' said Starkey. No doubt the visitor, whoever he was, had slipped the *maître d'hôtel* a few livres to gain entrance. 'Do you make it a habit, monsieur, to give visitors easy access to the rooms of your guests?'

'I did not place him in your honour's rooms,' replied the *maître d'hôtel* frostily, with that superciliousness unique to the French servant class, which made even the haughtiest English servant seem a bumpkin by comparison. 'I can take you to him now, if you like. Or, if your honour prefers, I will bring him to you.'

'Describe this gentleman, if you please.'

'A Frenchman – or at any rate, a man fluent in French. He was hooded, your honour, and cloaked, so I could not make out his features.'

'And this did not strike you as strange?'

'This is Paris, monsieur.'

354

Starkey conceded the point. 'How long ago did he come?'

'An hour.'

'Did he say aught else?'

'Nothing, your honour. However, there was something strange about him, even for Paris.'

'Go on.'

'He was wet, monsieur.'

'Wet? What do you mean?'

'His clothes. They were dripping wet, as if he had been caught in a storm. But as your honour knows, there has been no storm. There has been no rain or snow this past week or more. And there was a smell to him, monsieur.'

Starkey felt a ripple of apprehension. 'Of the sewer?'

'No, your honour. Of the sea.'

At that, the ripple became a flood. But Starkey steeled himself against it. 'I am rather surprised that you admitted such a man,' he said.

'He is not an easy man to refuse,' said the *maître d'hôtel*.

'Why?'

'He has a certain presence, monsieur. I can say no more.'

'I suppose I must see him,' Starkey said. 'Give me ten minutes, then bring him to my rooms.'

'*D'accord, monsieur,*' said the *maître d'hôtel*, and resumed his climb.

Once in his rooms, Starkey primed and loaded his pistol, setting it on a low table where it would be close to hand. He then fortified himself with a glass of cognac, filled and lit his pipe – something of a trick, one-handed – and began to pace before the fire.

The knock announcing the return of the *maître d'hôtel* seemed to come far sooner than he had anticipated, or perhaps he had forgotten its imminence altogether, for he gave a start at the sound. Cursing under his breath, he set the pipe down upon the mantel and went to stand beside the table on which the pistol lay. After a brief hesitation, he picked up the weapon, then turned to face the door, with the pistol meanwhile concealed behind his back. '*Entrez,*' he called as the knock sounded again.

The door was opened by the *maître d'hôtel*. 'Your visitor, monsieur.'

A cloaked and hooded figure entered the room. Starkey had wondered if he might recognize the man, but there was not enough of him exposed to the light of candles and fire to recognize. He could have been anyone. He was shorter than Starkey, but the thick cloak concealed his build; it reached almost to the floor, and beneath it were visible only the toes of a pair of dark leather boots. That and a spreading stain of water, for, as the *maître d'hôtel* had said, water was dripping from the man's cloak, as if he had just stepped in from a downpour and had not spent the last hour waiting in a dry room before a fire. Except, as the *maître d'hôtel* had by some inexplicable omission neglected to say, the source of the water, at least as far as Starkey could tell, appeared to be somewhere *beneath* the cloak and the hood that so completely obscured the man's features.

These details by themselves would have been quite enough to account for the chill that ran down Starkey's spine. But there was in addition what the *maître d'hôtel* had nebulously but accurately referred to as 'a certain presence'. This Starkey experienced first as an odd and disquieting impression that there was something wrong about the way the man moved. He had not precisely walked into the room, for example; rather, he had seemed to glide. Or, no, that was not quite it, either. He'd floated. Yes, floated. He had seemed to drift along the floor, as if his legs were only mimicking the motions of walking, rising and falling like the legs of a marionette or a clockwork automaton, though not as stiffly as that, not so visibly counterfeit. But still false in some deeply disconcerting way. The second thing Starkey experienced along these lines was an unexpected difficulty in breathing. It was as though the air in the room had become thicker, less like air and more, well, like water. He was unpleasantly reminded of what it had felt like to drown. Such was the discomfort induced by this sensation that it was all he could do not to run to a window and throw it open to gulp the cold night air. But he held his ground.

'That will be all,' he said to the *maître d'hôtel* in French.

The man left with alacrity, closing the door behind him.

Starkey regarded his visitor with a mix of curiosity and creeping dread. 'Who are you?' he asked, again in French. 'What do you want here?'

The hooded man answered in heavily accented English. 'I 'ave been look for you, Monsieur Starkey.' He glided forward.

Starkey wasted no time in displaying his pistol. "Old up, mate. I don't know 'oo yer are, but if yer take one more bleedin' step, I'll blow yer brains out, see if I don't.'

The visitor stopped. He seemed to be swaying gently in place, as if buffeted by unseen and unfelt currents – unseen and unfelt by Starkey, at least.

'Show yer face,' Starkey said, or rather gasped. He was sweating profusely and felt as if invisible hands were at his throat.

Wordlessly, the man raised a leather-gloved hand and pulled back his hood.

Starkey groaned. He would have screamed, but suddenly there was not air enough for that. He staggered back sluggishly, the pistol dropping from his hand to clatter harmlessly on the floor. Shadows rushed in; the light of the candles and fire dimmed and wavered as if such things no longer had a place here. But there was still light enough for him to discern the bloated and ragged flesh of the man – or, to be more precise, corpse – that stood before him.

Starkey dropped to his knees.

Water was streaming from the pasty, ravaged face. It poured from the black holes that had once held eyes, emptied from out of the scalloped ears. It ran from the obscene slit of a nose and gushed from the open mouth whose lips had been chewed away. It fountained in such force and profusion that it seemed a whole ocean was spilling out of the dead man.

Starkey was struck numb with terror, but as the water rose swiftly on all sides, cold as ice and stinking of brine, something broke inside him. He surged to his feet and splashed his way towards the door, leaking fretful moans as he went. But the drowned man floated into his path, and he drew back from it as from death itself.

'Do you know me?' it demanded. It spoke clearly despite the water that continued to pour out of its mouth.

'No,' sobbed Starkey. "Ow could I?'

357

'I am Bagot,' said the thing. 'Captain of ze *Pierre*.'

'Bagot?' echoed Starkey. He wondered if he had gone mad.

'I 'ave bring you somezing,' said what had once been Bagot.

'No,' pleaded Starkey, for he knew what it must be. On some level, he had always known what this visitor portended. 'Please, no . . .'

The thing reached into the depths of its cloak, reached so far that it seemed to be groping within its own body – as if its flesh were as soft as the rice pudding it in fact resembled – and, with a horrible squishing sound, like that of a boot being pulled free of sucking mud, drew forth the relic that Starkey had last seen aboard the *Pierre* and had hoped, or rather prayed, never to see again. The severed hand of Daniel Quare, holding the hunter in its stony grasp.

The timepiece glowed a spectral blue.

'That ain't mine,' he said, shaking his head vigorously. 'That ain't got naught ter do with me. It's Aylesford's, I tell yer. 'E's the one yer want. Aylesford!'

'Thomas Aylesford 'as gone where I cannot follow,' the corpse of Bagot said. 'So I 'ave come to you, Richard Starkey. I 'ave drink your blood. I 'ave taste your zoughts. You will carry me now and in ze days to come. You will be my voice. And my sword.'

'No,' he whimpered. 'I won't . . .'

The thing extended the shining relic towards Starkey.

Weeping now, Starkey watched in horror as his left hand stretched towards it. He could not, for the life of him, pull it back. He could feel the ends of the broken bone shifting against each other, but still his arm extended, in the grip of a force greater than his will. Then came a blur of movement, a searing pain, and he gaped in disbelief as his hand dropped to the floor.

His hand.

Severed, as Quare's had been. The bloody knife was there in the corpse's gloved hand. He had not seen it drawn. He had not seen it move. Yet the thing had cut through flesh and bone with a stroke.

He fell to his knees again, gripping the stump of his wrist. Blood was flowing from the wound . . . but it did not fall. It snaked through the air and was sucked into the relic. Starkey had watched in horror as the same thing happened aboard the *Pierre*. But now he more than saw: he felt the tug of it. And then suddenly Bagot's corpse was no longer holding Quare's severed hand. Instead, that appendage had attached itself to Starkey's arm. The flesh melted into his flesh, the bone fused with his bone . . . and in the process his own broken bones mended. Sensation screamed along his nerves.

You are mine now.

This time the voice did not issue from the corpse, but instead rang out in his mind. It was no longer Bagot's voice. Nor was it Starkey's own inner voice, the comforting voice of his thoughts and prayers. That voice was drowned out in the thunder of this one. Everything that was Starkey quailed before it and bowed down. It was the voice of a god. But not his god. He knew that somehow. Not Doppler.

A greater god, thundered the voice.

But what, he wondered, could be greater than the god who had made all things?

The god who unmakes them, came the answer.

Starkey opened his eyes to find himself lying on the floor. The fire had burned out, and the room was so cold that he could see the fog of his breath in the grey morning light. There was no trace of water anywhere, or of his visitor. He jerked upright as the memory flooded back, and raised his left hand to the level of his eyes. Surely it had all been a dream.

But it had been no dream.

His broken arm was whole again. And the hand at the end of it was Quare's.

The wrongness of seeing it there, where his own hand should have been, sent a spasm of sickness surging through him, and he spewed onto the floor. But there was no purging himself of what he now carried inside. He knew that.

At last he was able to climb shakily to his feet.

His own lost hand, like the corpse of Bagot, was nowhere to be seen. He imagined the corpse picking up the hand, leaving the *hôtel*, walking through the empty midnight streets of Paris to the banks of the Seine, plunging over the quay and into the frigid waters, sinking to the muddy bottom, and then walking downstream towards the sea. Perhaps it was walking still, would walk until all the flesh had been stripped and nibbled from its bones. And even then it might go on walking, tirelessly circumnavigating the globe, a skeletal undersea Elcano, propelled by the will or caprice of a god, like the hand of a watch counting down to some fateful hour.

Starkey brought both hands up and flexed them, wriggled the fingers, examined them from all sides. There was no appreciable difference in motion or sensation between the two appendages. But they did not look exactly alike: there was a slight but noticeable discrepancy in size and colour, Quare's skin being somewhat darker in hue than his own, no doubt from greater exposure to the sun.

He thought of cutting the new hand off, but as soon as he did so was convulsed with pain such as he had never experienced or imagined possible, pain that knocked him back to the floor and had him, on hands and knees, heaving his guts out all over again, empty as they were. He did not think they would ever be full again. In this, he would soon be proved wrong.

Afterwards, standing even more shakily than before, he decided that perhaps gloves were a better solution. But before fetching a pair from his trunk, he reached into one of the pockets of his coat and pulled out the hunter, which his new hand had apparently expected to find there, had no doubt put there, though he had no memory of it. This object Starkey now raised smoothly to his mouth, inserted into that orifice, and, with some difficulty, swallowed. It sank to his belly and pulsed there as warmly as a foetus in the womb. Impotent tears ran down his cheeks.

Outside, a light snow began to fall over Paris as Starkey methodically packed his things. Within the hour, he was the sole passenger aboard a coach bound for Le Havre.

Acknowledgements

With deepest gratitude, the author acknowledges the support of the Hawthornden Castle Fellowship in the completion of this novel.

The Emperor of All Things
Paul Witcover

'Tempus Rerum Imperator.'

The year is 1758 and England is at war. In London, evidence has come to light of the existence of a singular device – a pocket watch – rumoured to possess seemingly impossible properties that are more to do with magic than any known science. Daniel Quare, Regulator with the secretive Worshipful Company of Clockmakers, is tasked with tracking down this sinister mechanism. But he is not alone – enemy agents are also on its trail . . .

And the path Quare must follow is a dangerous one. Full of intrigue, betrayal and murder, it will lead him from a world he knows and understands to another, where demigods and dragons dwell and in which nothing is as it seems.

Time least of all.

'Hugely entertaining . . . comparisons to Neal Stephenson and Susanna Clarke are only very slightly premature'
INDEPENDENT ON SUNDAY

'An Enlightenment-punk vision of England, before taking detours to the Alps, subterranean London and the utterly fantastic ****'
SFX

'Excitingly and brilliantly realised . . . full of atmosphere and vibrant imagery'
SFFWORLD.COM